A Well Dressed Corpse

Jo A. Hiestand

L & L Dreamspell
London, Texas

ISBN: 978-1-60318-396-3

Library of Congress Control Number: 2011924105

Visit us on the web at www.lldreamspell.com

Published by L & L Dreamspell
Printed in the United States of America

Acknowledgments

A book comes together through the work, talent and patience of many people. I thank those who have helped me:

Detective-Superintendent David Doxey (ret.), Derbyshire Constabulary, who helped me through a sub-plot and, as usual, cast his eye upon the entire manuscript; Detective-Sergeant Rob Church, Derbyshire Constabulary, who answered procedural questions and my many emails about DNA result time, electoral rolls, the police Golden Rule, and Derbyshire's abandoned coal mines; Dr. Ruth Anker, who supplied medical information on bones and bodies; and as always to Paul Hornung, for Scott's incredible chapter and for illuminating problems. I also want to thank Dr. Simon Sherwood, Senior Lecturer in Psychology at the University of Northampton, for his information on the black dog.

Thank you to Lisa of L&L Dreamspell, who accepted the series, seemingly without a moment's hesitation, keeping Taylor & Graham alive.

A heart-felt hug to everyone who has supported me through buying books or inquiring about my writing. Both mean a lot.

Errors, if any exist, are solely mine.

Jo A. Hiestand
St. Louis, March 2011

~

Dedication

For Esther, who cheered me on through her own ghostly events and who never gave up enthusiasm for our Spirited Mysteries.

Note:

The shuck, or spirit hound, is a large black dog, usually calf-size, that either brings ill fortune to those who see it, guards/protects someone (like the grave of its master), or else appears as a warning when danger threatens the town/family with which it is associated. The shuck may be headless, possess glowing eyes, have yellow teeth, float on a layer of mist, or be comprised of any other similar effects, but all dogs seem to have the capability of vanishing and passing through solid objects. Shucks are also known by the more generic term 'black dog' or 'phantom hound.' If there is 'good news' to seeing one of these large phantom dogs, it is that none of them have ever physically harmed the viewer.

Well dressing is a custom unique to Derbyshire. Ancient in origin, this annual event is a celebration and thanksgiving for the community's water. Small, natural items are pressed into wooden frames filled with wet clay to create colorful pictures that adorn each well or spring in the village or town. For readers in the States think of a Rose Parade float flattened into a postcard. The celebration usually lasts a week and marks the beginning of the community's fete.

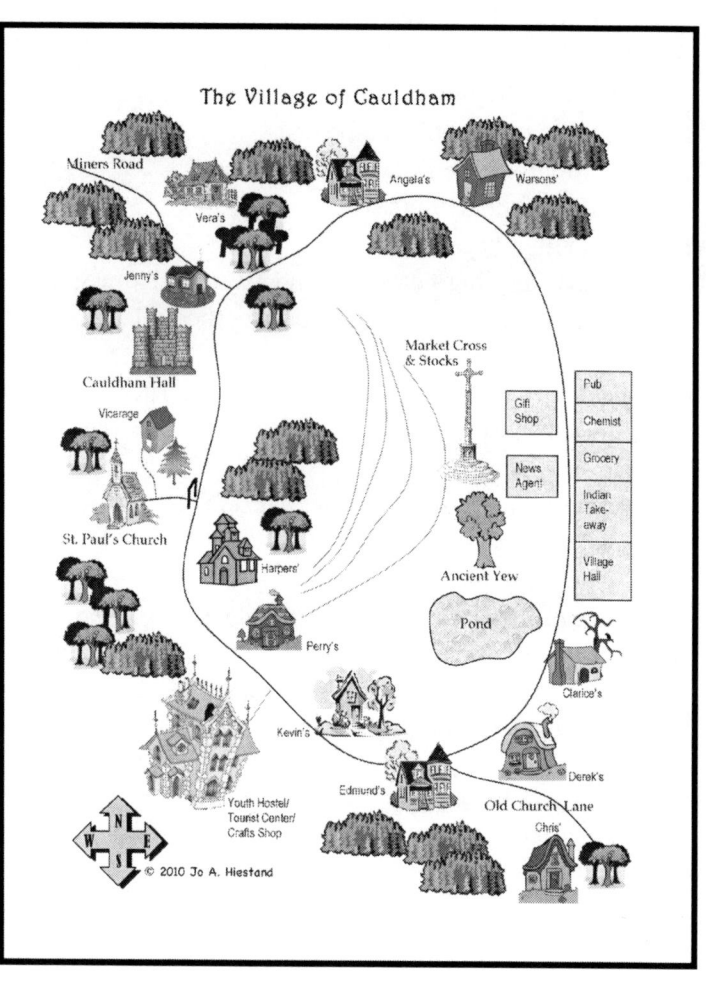

The Village of Cauldham

Miners Road

Vera's

Angela's

Warsons'

Jenny's

Cauldham Hall

Vicarage

Market Cross
& Stocks

Gift
Shop

News
Agent

Pub

Chemist

Grocery

Indian
Take-
away

Village
Hall

St. Paul's Church

Harpers'

Ancient Yew

Perry's

Pond

Clarice's

Kevin's

Derek's

Edmund's

Old Church Lane

Youth Hostel/
Tourist Center/
Crafts Shop

Chris'

N
W E
S

© 2010 Jo A. Hiestand

Cast of Characters

Locals:
Reed Harper: Coordinator/director of village well dressing
Marian Harper: Reed's wife
Ilsa Harper: Reed's and Marian's daughter
Kevin Harper: Reed's brother
Edmund Worrall: Reed's half brother
Jenny Millington: Reed's assistant
Clarice Millington: Jenny's sister
Harding Lyth: village vicar
Angela Ellis: Harding's daughter and MC of well dressing fete
Chad Styles: well dressing director in another village
Trevor Styles: Chad's son
Christine Stevenson: acquaintance of Reed Harper
Perry Bowcock: Chris' uncle
Vera Howarth: missing woman
PC Clayton Warson: Vera's former fiancé
Lynn Warson: Clayton's wife

The Police of the Derbyshire Constabulary:
Detective-Sergeant Brenna Taylor
Detective-Chief Inspector Geoffrey Graham
Detective-Sergeant Mark Salt
Detective-WPC Margo Lynch
Sergeant Adam Fitzgerald
PC Scott Coral
DC Byrd
DC Fordyce
DC Oglethorpe
WPC MacMillan
Jens Nielsen: Home Office forensic pathologist
Dean Hargreaves: civilian Scientific Officer employed as police photographer
Detective-Superintendent Simcock

One

Plunging Into Our Mystery: 1989-the present

Vera Howarth walked out of her house, into the bowels of the earth, and was never seen again.

At least that is how the Legend grew.

That had been twenty-two years ago. Despite the official missing person report, searches by villagers and police, and posted monetary rewards, Vera remained missing. Her clothes waited in the wardrobe; her family waited by the phone. Traces on her bank account, credit card statements, and mobile phone showed no activity. Psychics and sniffer dogs zeroed in on their targets, only to come up with nothing. No trail, no scent, no body. As though she had never been born. As though the earth swallowed her. As though she vanished into thin air.

With the seasonal changes, her story faded into the folklore of the village and surrounding countryside, told in the same breath one used to speak of lamenting brides, lost miners and glowing-eyed shucks. Whispered around wintry fires and on moonlit nights, with a hint of fear and a glance over a shoulder. If Vera Howarth, fiancée of a policeman, could vanish so completely, so could anyone.

Vera's legend had transformed with the telling and retelling, enlivened by snippets of other local tales until the arrival of the current variation. Even if most people didn't believe in ghost dogs or phantom horsemen, the area sported enough spooky spots to make the staunchest scoffer rethink his decision at night.

And wonder if the recently discovered bones were Vera's or somehow had nebulous ties to the other missing villager.

"I know two people have gone missing." Graham looked at me before returning his attention to the bones. "But the one's disappeared only a day ago, so this obviously can't be he. And as for Miss Vera Howarth..." His head tilted slightly to the right and his right eyebrow rose slowly.

I knew that gesture, seen it often enough over the past several months. I, Brenna Taylor, a detective-sergeant in the Derbyshire Constabulary, Graham's work partner, knew what was coming. The bones intrigued him, whispered to him. He was about to jump into the investigation with his entire energy and wouldn't let go until it was solved. I said, "The problem is the site, yes, sir."

"Correct. Not my idea of a choice location, Taylor. Have these bones been recently unearthed after lying buried for decades, or have they been constantly out in the open to be buffeted by the weather? Makes a difference."

Of course it did. But with the tales of people gone missing from the village—plus the local ghost story that still haunted me—immediately putting a name to the bones didn't seem that far fetched.

The bones had been found about a quarter of a mile into the forest that hugged the village. An ancient forest of conifer and deciduous trees—and ghosts. Fairy tale fiends were said to roam the valley's dark dells and disused coal mines, though flesh and blood murderers also imprinted its past. The bones merely confirmed the truth of the tales, though village speculation favored Death by Ghost for the unlucky victim. A logical choice, considering the abundance of local spirit dog sightings. But I had never known a ghost to bury anyone, so I favored the human hand in all this.

Which was why we were here—the CID Team of the Derbyshire Constabulary.

Though not originally to investigate the bones. We'd been

called out on the missing person. The bones kind of fell into our lap.

Walking over to an oak, I watched the Home Office pathologist slowly separate a long bone from a fragment of blue fabric before carefully sealing the bone in a transparent evidence bag. The site had been thoroughly photographed and a scale drawing made well before she had been allowed into the area—a procedure from which Graham never varied. Graham, a detective-chief inspector and my immediate boss, stood outside the cordoned off area, aware of the dangers of compromising the scene and the evidence. And the possible danger of bubonic plague spores nestled and still alive in the remains.

I shook the water from the hood of my mackintosh as I eased it off my head.

Rain, relentless and driving, threatened the integrity of the bones earlier this morning. Scattered along a haphazard trail several feet long, the skeletal remains now glistened under the brilliance of the police work lamps. Raindrops eased down sodden ferns, tufted hair-grass and tree branches to break on the forest cast-offs and rocks, throwing back the lamp light with the intensity of faceted gems. The light found a handful of bones and drew them from the muddled earthen browns harboring them. From beneath their woodsy covering, the bones—damp and white—peeked out at us. Bleached and broken ends hinted at years of arboreal rest. Graham conferred with the pathologist while I glanced at the sky. The dark clouds had rolled on to the west, leaving a sodden recovery site but drier working conditions. And the haunting question: Who Is It?

Two

Beginning of the Case Proper: 21 June, this year

"Any idea yet who it might be?"

I blinked, startled by the voice. Margo Lynch, a detective-constable and my best friend, stood beside me, nodding at the cordoned-off area. I shook my head. "Not really. Not officially."

"Sounds as though you have an idea, though." Her brown eyes held the silent challenge that I should confess what I suspected, even if this was premature and before the postmortem. When I remained silent, Margo said, "Come on, Bren. Who do you think it is?"

"You know a good detective shouldn't form any kind of opinion before the evidence is in. It's way too early for any supposition. Besides the postmortem, DNA testing may be in order. That takes time."

"I know that." She said it as though I had come right out and said she was an idiot. "But that woman's been missing for a long time."

"Twenty-two years," I said, getting exasperated at Margo's spin on this.

"And she was never found." She nodded at the crime scene, at the Home Office pathologist labeling the evidence bags. "As much as I'd like to see this be a happy ending, I have to admit this could be just about anyone. This area has an unusually large amount of missing people, what with the old mines and sink holes around. Even if you put the newspaper articles down to sensationalism to increase their sales, the police reports should convince you of the numbers we're dealing with. Look how often the Peak District Mountain Rescue group gets called out each year." Her eyes softened and she frowned. "I'm afraid it could be just about anyone."

I agreed. Though the findings could go either way, depending, as Graham had just said, how long the bones had been buried or exposed, if wild animals had been at them. "It's odd, though, isn't it? Two people disappear from the village. Granted, the stretch of time between them is a little over two decades, and this in no way could be the man reported as missing yesterday. But still, if you count the reports of the others missing from the area, as you said…" I twisted my engagement ring. It was still new enough to feel strange, and I was keenly aware of it at times. Especially when I felt uncomfortable or emotional.

"Do you know anything about either case, about either of them?"

"I don't know about the woman—that was before my time— and of course the man disappeared Tuesday."

Margo nodded. "While working on the village fete." She shivered, rubbing her arms and glancing around our immediate area. The wood seemed suddenly ominous, I thought. Margo's voice sank to a near whisper. "Talk about creepy. Who goes missing while working on well dressing preparations?"

"Someone who wanted to disappear?" I countered, the cases of spouses walking out on their marriage to start a new life with a lover too numerous to mention. "I don't know all the particulars," I said, aware that Margo had just arrived, not part of our team who had appeared two days ago to look for the recently missing villager, "but I do know he coordinates the whole thing."

"Panels and the fair?"

"Yes. Evidently they'd just finished some meeting having to do with the well dressing. They said their good nights, wandered off to their homes." I glanced at Graham as he lifted the blue-and-white police tape for the pathologist. "But Reed Harper never made it home." I tried not to superimpose the feeling I got from the thick, dark forest onto Reed's disappearance. I was already battling the local ghost story; I didn't need to impart elements of that into Reed's situation.

"Tuesday night. More than him having a row with his wife and needing time to cool down, then."

"They didn't have an argument. At least, the wife isn't admitting to one."

"Could have got into an argument with folks on the fete committee. Lot of feelings come to the surface when you're working on those well panels. You ever done any well dressing, Bren?"

"A few times. When I was a teenager."

"Yeah. Me, too. I thought it fun. When I retire, I'd like to do it again."

I echoed her decision. It had been fun, seeing what the year's theme was, if it was environmental, religious or historical; making the mosaic-like tableaux from natural materials, seeing the biblical Joseph or endangered tiger or VE Day symbol come to life in the village hall and then placed outside at the various parish wells, the week-long fete of carnival rides, booths, dances and contests. A lot of work went into the creation of the well dressing panels as well as into the planning and set-up of the fair. Feelings ran high not only from pressure of completing the panels on time but also from the pageant competition. I wondered if Reed Harper had simply walked out on that stress, planning on returning after the fete was over, or if something had actually happened to him—fete related or not.

"Sounds rather childish to stay away if you've had a tiff with someone over something as inconsequential as booth sizes or artwork for the program booklet," Margo said.

"Especially if he's been the chairman and done this before," I countered. "Anyway, it's too near to the fete to pull a stunt like this."

"Why? When is the well dressing festivity?"

"Begins twenty-ninth of June, I believe."

"Ten days. St. Peter's Day."

I shrugged, not knowing the saints' specific feast days.

"The village church is probably St. Peter's. See if I'm right."

Not really listening, I mumbled something I hoped would pass for interest.

"Wonder if he'll come back. You know," Margo added, a touch of dramatics in her voice. "He walks up as the vicar and choir are assembling next Friday. Makes some little speech and everyone smiles and claps him on the back." She suddenly stopped, and screwed up her face. "The fete *does* start late Friday afternoon, doesn't it? I just assumed it did 'cause all the others I know about start then. Right before dusk."

"I don't know, Margo. I've not got that far into the case," I reminded her again.

"Well, anyway, the fete is a little over one week away. Plenty of time for him to cool off and come back before the opening ceremony."

I was going to reply, but Graham drew my attention. He bent, pointing to something at the base of an oak, when a shout broke the relative quiet. He turned toward the voice, his head up. I took a step toward him as the words echoed, increasing in their unease and possible implications.

"Mr. Graham, sir! I've found what looks like another body here!"

Three

We Begin the Investigation: 22 June, this year

We sat in the basement of St. Paul's Church, our incident room created by moving the parishioners out and our police equipment in. We sat on metal folding chairs, hard and cold as the case facts we were hearing. We sat in a group, close together, like the friends we were—Mark, Margo and I. The others—press liaison officer, leaders of various teams, and specialized skills people—clustered around and near us, so that we were, in fact a Team, no matter each individual's skill. Graham leaned against the edge of a table, his long legs crossed at his ankles, his voice low yet holding the sharpness of urgency always brought on by a murder investigation.

So here we were again, Mark Salt, another detective-sergeant; Margo Lynch; a smattering of other constables, crime scene investigators, and of course Graham. Detective-Chief Inspector Geoffrey Graham. Tall, super-model handsome, intelligent. And my heart's desire a little less than a year ago...until I became engaged to Adam. All of us from the Derbyshire Constabulary and all of us still trying to grasp these case facts, meager as they were. The bones had been classified as human, and most likely had been scavenged by forest-dwelling animals and scattered from its shallow grave. And since the corpse had been intact, we were clearly dealing with two different people.

"The corpse has been identified as Reed Harper, the person

reported missing two days ago," Graham said, moving to the whiteboard behind the table. He wrote quickly, placing Reed's name at the top of the left hand column. Scribbling several question marks at the head of the other column, he turned back to us and said, "But let me talk about the bones, first. The bones are an unknown person. Female. The pathologist's report estimates her age between thirteen to twenty years old. DNA extracted from the bone marrow determined gender, much more accurately than can be determined by the pelvis size."

He tacked up color photos of the site where the bones were discovered. They were the first graphic job aids posted on the whiteboard and, as such, instantly brought the case to the reality of a murder investigation. Graham's gaze fell on me as he said, "To bring those who weren't there up to speed, the bones were recovered over a several-foot wide area. Weathering and animal foraging uncovered the bones. The small bones—hands, feet, vertebra—were the most widely scattered. Some were missing, either carried away and gnawed on, deteriorated, or washed downhill. The Crime Scene Investigator lads found some ribs, the skull, humerus, pelvis and a femur. The pathology report states that the bones are discolored from their contact with the soil and the elements, and sport a good deal of mold. Dr. Nielsen states also that there is a nick on one of the ribs, which points to a knife thrust. It passed just beneath that rib and probably killed her.

"Hair was found, but again, it is very sparse. No skin or sinew could be recovered, though bits of clothing adhered to a few of the bones and were located in the immediate area." He tapped on one of the photos that showed a close-up of a piece of blue print fabric. "She was probably wearing heavy, cotton trousers—this fabric was stuck to the recovered femur—and a woolen zip-up jumper. The zipper looks nearly as pristine as the day it was made. The clothing may help us identify her, for, to date, we have no one to ask for a DNA sample in order to positively name her.

"Both the bones and the body were discovered, as many of you know, well within the wood on the northwestern edge of the village. Miners Road cuts through a section of the wood but is well away from the area in which the body recovery sites lay. It's a steep, rugged area, strewn with boulders, knee-high ferns and sporadic open areas of heather. The site lies about a half mile north of Cauldham Hall, backs up to the Hall's north wing, actually. St Paul's Church is about a half mile south of the Hall. The Harper house is one quarter mile south of the church."

"Which makes the site where he was found slightly more than a mile from his house."

"Yes. The closest neighbors to him and to the body recovery site are two single people, plus a constable and his wife.

"As to the body…" He tacked another set of photos to the other side of the board. "The body is Reed Harper. Bits of mud and flower petals clung to his forehead and back of his right hand."

Startled, I looked up from my note taking to look at the photo. A close-up snap showed the flower petals stuck into the muddy clumps. Odd, I thought, for those were the only places on the body that held those traces. What had Reed Harper been doing prior to his death?

Graham pointed to the photo. "The mud is not necessarily odd, but the petals are. Some white flower—perhaps a daisy, chamomile or eyebright. Another of the same white flower was crammed into his mouth. This constituted part of the stem, leaves, and flower. The stem had been cut, not broken, which signifies that it was carefully planned. No wildflowers grow in that vicinity, so perhaps the body collected the petals and mud if it was dragged to the location. The lab will identify the flower and let us know—that will help us determine where the flower might be found. Postmortem examination reveals he died from exsanguination, having been stabbed in the heart but by way of the back."

"Which indicates a fairly long knife blade."

"Yes. The weapon was not recovered, but we'll put more personnel on that job of work. Dr. Nielsen says it is a straightedge knife, as compared to a serrated blade, approximately eight inches long. The body was discovered twenty yards from the bones."

"Coincidence or deliberate?" Mark asked, leaning forward in his chair.

"When we know that, we may have a better clue to his killer's identity."

"And he was found in a shallow grave, right?"

"Yes. A hastily-done affair, from the look of the soil, leaves and brush piled on top of the depression."

"So, what revealed the body, if it was buried?"

"A light-reflecting strip incorporated into the design of the trainers he was wearing. This particular shoe model had the reflective material on the heel and side of the shoes. The edge of his left shoe was exposed—probably rain washed away some of the soil. Luckily the rain from earlier that morning had quit and PC Byrd saw the glint from the shoe. Like any good copper, he investigated." Graham uncapped the dry marker and stood beside the board. "As long as we're talking about investigation, the lads on fingertip search came up with something that may or may not be interesting."

Again I paused, my gaze fastened on Graham's face. We'd all done our hours of fingertip searches as constables—pulling up plants, turning over rocks and tree twigs, bagging everything on the ground in case the beer can or cigarette or crumpled piece of paper should prove to be a clue later on in the case.

"While searching a bit farther from where Reed Harper's body was found, Constable Oglethorpe located a latch key." He waited while we twisted around in our chairs to look at Oglethorpe, then went on. "It has been exposed to the elements for quite a while. It's quite rusted. Perhaps lost years before Reed's murder." He tacked the photos of the key on the board. The tip of someone's pen holding back a leaf and flower head of a daylily was barely discernible in the first photo. The round, upper part of the key could just be seen among the leaves and branches littering the forest floor. "Dean photographed the site and Oglethorpe then bagged the key. It may be nothing, of course. Still, you never know. Further poking and prodding in the vicinity produced no other suspicious objects.

"Oglethorpe, I'd like you to look into the matter of tracing the key. You started us on that path so you may as well get all the glory of the Big Discovery. May not be an easy task," Graham told him, "but it looks like someone's latch key. If so, that person may have had to get a replacement made. Ask about in the village—try the hardware store first. They may have a record. Yes, I know it's a long shot, but we might only be talking several weeks. It's not like the clerk has to look through a year's worth of sales receipts. We'll at least get a lead that way, if we're lucky."

Oglethorpe nodded, took the key and wandered off.

"If the murderer did drop his latch key," Graham said, "he wouldn't have risked searching for it in the dark. A torch flashing about in the wood in the dead of night might attract attention, and that's one thing the killer doesn't want. So he'd curse his clumsiness and leave the key, hoping the police won't find it." He grinned, slapping his hands together. "We just may be on to something. At least we're not looking at more bodies. Not there, at any rate."

I hoped we had got a break. It would be a refreshing change to begin a murder investigation with a solid lead.

Graham leaned against the whiteboard. "So, what else do we know besides someone losing some type of key sometime?"

"He went missing three days ago, on Tuesday, nineteenth of June." Mark settled back into his chair. "He attended a meeting in the church hall. That lasted from seven to half past nine. The meeting, not the hall," he said, glancing at me.

"Thank you for being so precise," Graham said. "What else?"

"He apparently disappeared right then." Graham wrote the points on the board. "His wife didn't see or hear from him. None of his neighbors did, either. The last people were those who were at the meeting with him. He just seems to have walked into oblivion."

"Until Byrd found him yesterday."

"No one knew where he was, then, for the days he was missing." Margo looked up from her note taking, her pen still touching the paper.

"No. The usual appeals had been put out through the media, his mobile phone and credit card accounts monitored but there had been no use. His wife and family got no demands for ransom, so kidnapping seems to be ruled out."

"He was a candidate for that? I mean," Margo said when Mark and I stared at her, "he had the wealth that someone might target?"

"Yes. Old money, they call it. Besides having inherited a substantial sum, his wife brought her own money into their marriage."

"But neither she nor his relatives ever got a ransom demand," Margo suggested.

"No."

"At least no one admitted it if he had," I suggested. "Any other possible motive? We know he didn't kill himself and pull the leaves over himself."

"We may need another whiteboard to list *that*, Taylor."

Four

Diary Entry, 26 April 1981

Today is my tenth birthday! Gran made me a cream trifle and sausage rolls and pickled beets for my tea. It was ever so smashing and she set out her best china 'cause she said I was now a young lady and know how to behave and birthdays are for celebrating. Gran had out the silver candelabra and her cut glass trifle bowl and she put a vase of daisies and roses on the table. Daisies 'cause they're my birth month flower and roses 'cause she says they're the flower of love and she loves me.

Oh, it was all so lovely with the lace tablecloth on, too. My class had a party for me in school and everyone gave me candy or flowers or a card or little toy. I got a bracelet from my boyfriend. He gave it to me on the walk home. Didn't want to give it to me with everyone looking. It's silver colored and has a heart dangling from the chain. I love it and won't ever take it off, no matter if Gran says the bath water will ruin it.

After tea Gran showed me the photo album of our family. Gran was so beautiful when she was younger. She is beautiful now but she looks different so she is beautiful in a different way. I love her old-fashioned clothes and her house. I wonder how it was growing up as Gran in that long ago time but I never can think that way. I guess she liked it. She's never said otherwise. She seems happy in the snaps and she seems happy now living with me. There's a torn photo of Gramps but I don't remember him at all. He looks happy, too. He's hugging Gran and laughing. His hair looks white but Gran said it's just the bad color of the photo 'cause it was really light blond.

And there are a lot of snaps of mum and dad but none of anyone else. I made Gran tell me about them, how they were both only children and how they met and fell in love. I love hearing that story. I feel so close to Mum and Dad when I hear it. I can see them as Gran talks, but I can't see anyone else 'cause Gran said the other album of my great aunts and great uncles and Gran's parents are back at her other home. One day I'll get to see it. When we can go to that house.

I love seeing my mum and dad, how pretty she is and how handsome he is. Gran said the snap was taken right before they left on holiday. They are smiling and look excited. I wonder if they liked Australia. Gran says it took a day to get there! After the pages of snaps of mum and dad there was a half page of photos of me as a baby. There's another blank page after that. Gran says she'll fill it with more photos of me when she gets the time. We looked through the snaps she keeps in an old cardboard box. I remember some of them and remember when they were snapped. But I don't remember all of them. Gran looked on the backs to read where they were taken. There are a bunch taken at Castleton and Dove Dale, but I don't remember that. I like the tiny train and pools at Buxton. Gran said she'll take me back some time. Maybe I'll be too old. Maybe I'll be the right size for the boats at Matlock Bath. Maybe I'll be old enough to row this time! Aren't birthdays grand things?

Five

We adjourned after Graham created teams and handed out assignments. He reminded us, "It's easy to assume the bones are the remains of Vera Howarth. But don't assume anything. That's perhaps the most fatal mistake an investigating officer can make." And, after all, we didn't have anything to which we could match Vera's DNA, she being a single lady with no known living relatives. Even items from her residence were non-existent. Hardly anyone had been that far sighted twenty-two years ago to collect samples that could be used for DNA testing now.

Mark and I grabbed a quick cuppa before striking out to discover possible motives for Reed's disappearance and subsequent murder. He grabbed two chairs sitting in a patch of sunlight and I listened to the clank of his metal spoon hitting the side of his ceramic coffee mug while I studied his face. He didn't notice my perusal, for he was intent on reading his case notes. Rather than saddling society's slap of Age on Mark, the streaks of gray in his brown hair gave him a mature, wise look—completely opposite from the brash, conceited officer I'd known in police college. The gray hued strands did not lie, for Mark, now in his mid-thirties, had indeed mellowed and matured; he was an extremely competent detective and our acquaintance had mellowed into a firm friendship.

He scanned his notes, set his mug down with a thump, and stood up, asking if I were ready. Nodding, I abandoned my half-consumed drink and glanced out of the window as I grabbed my shoulder bag. The village of Cauldham was not particularly large, but Reed could have friends and relatives in other parts of the country, so we could be in for a very long task.

"So, who does Graham want us to talk to first?" Mark held the door of the church open so that I could precede him outside.

On first glance, the birds seemed to be the only things awake in the village, for rooks, sparrows and magpies sang into the morning stillness. A few rooks took flight as the door banged shut behind us, flapping across a smear of white clouds before banking and settling into the boughs of an oak. Starlings, screeching their squabbles, strutted and pecked at interesting-looking bits in the front lawn of the church. Frightened, they rose in a mass of black, vocalizing their alarm and annoyance.

Mark paused under the lych gate roof, eyeing the road as though mentally rolling dice to decide where to begin.

The village lay along a circular road, created by two roads converging and curving in opposite directions. Climbing the hill on the western portion of the circle, Old Church Lane did, indeed, hold the church. It also held the vicarage, Cauldham Hall, and the old C of E grammar school, now converted into a youth hostel, tourist information center and crafts shop. At the summit of this steep hill Miners Road bent to the north and east. Along its sides was the village proper with shops, pond and pub. Most of the more modest residences nestled among the trees on the northern and southern portions of this circular road, although some houses dribbled down Old Church Lane before the forest reclaimed the land.

Disused lead mines dotted the land north of the village, remnants of the mining glory days from centuries before. Sinkholes, too, pockmarked the region, and ramblers were warned to stay on the designated path through the wood that blanketed the region.

I glanced at my notes, seeing which of the pertinent people lived where. "Reed's widow."

"Marian Harper." Mark nodded and staring to our right. "Nice and convenient. Their house is down the road a bit, on the opposite side from the church."

"That's not why he suggested it," I said, wondering if Mark was joking. "Spouses are always questioned first."

"She was, Bren. This past Tuesday, down at the police station. I led the interview. You weren't part of that because—"

"I know why," I said, still slightly miffed that Graham had kept me here that first day, questioning the Harpers' daughter.

"So I don't know why we have to talk to Marian again. My interview went well. Graham even said so. What more can she tell us in two days' time?"

"I guess we're about to find out."

"I still say it's a waste of time. I talked to the woman already. Graham ought to have told us to question the vicar." He sounded hurt, as though his pride were wounded.

I glanced toward our left. The vicarage hugged the edge of the lane, perhaps built closer and more accessible to the villagers, mutely offering round-the-clock advice and a cuppa, should they be needed. The church, though approachable, huddled against the western face of the hill, protected by clumps of yew, spruce and pine. Though farther in distance from the lane, its steeple seemed to pull the building and surrounding churchyard nearer to heaven, the golden-hued spire nearly reaching the treetops and scraping the clouds.

"The vicar."

"Harding Lyth," Mark muttered, scowling as he eyed the vicarage. "Probably still home, seeing what an ungodly early hour it is."

I glanced at him, again unsure if it was a deliberate pun. Mark grinned down at me from his six-foot-two stature, the sparkle and hint of mischievousness glinting from his gray eyes. For an instant, the teasing look suggested the Mark of old, the Mark who had christened me The Cop during our schooling, belittling not only my resolve to be the best detective in the Derbyshire Constabulary but also hoping I'd quit the otherwise all-male class. Graham had taken the derogatory tag and turned it into TC, a nickname that now signified the esteem and friendship he held for me. But the sparkle in Mark's eyes vanished as he watched the house-to-house team set off down the road. He was ready to get to work.

"Come on, Mark," I said, somewhat emphatically, and turned right as I stepped onto the lane.

"Right. Marian Harper." Mark jogged up to me and settled in for the short stroll to the large, stone house. "Always question the spouse first. Why do so many marriages end in divorce, Brenna?"

"You'll have to ask a marriage counselor. Or a divorce lawyer. I haven't the faintest."

"You're sure about Adam, are you? I mean," he said as I stopped abruptly to stare at him. "You have no doubts that marrying him is right for you?"

"Honestly, Mark! This isn't the time or place for this discussion. Plus, it actually concerns only Adam and me."

"Just looking after your welfare, Brenna. I don't want to see you hurt."

"I thank you for your concern, but I really don't want to talk about it. We've got an investigation to get on with, anyway."

"Oh, sure. Right." He hurried after me, and minutes later we were seated in the Harper front room and talking to the teary-eyed widow.

Marian Harper personified the Grieving Widow...at least, the majority I had dealt with. A soft-spoken, thin woman in her forties, Marian handled her eye-dabbing and our questions with equal ease. She sat well back in her wing chair, her left leg crossed on top of her right, and absentmindedly petted the white Persian cat that sprawled across her lap. "You like cats," Marian said, noticing the direction of my gaze. When I nodded, she said, "She's feeling her age, poor dear. Twenty-four. Ancient, aren't you?" She stroked the cat and cooed to it. "She means more to me now, with Reed gone. Well, I don't know what I'd do without Marguerite." Marian clutched the facial tissue in her right hand. Her eyes, as well as her voice, were steady, looking at Mark and me without flinching as she talked about the evening of her husband's disappearance. "I've gone over this before," Marian said, the quiver of her voice held in check. "Two days ago, when Reed first went missing. I told all this to the people from the media. And to police officers. You," she added, recognizing Mark as her interviewer. "You have all the information." She raised her eyebrows slightly, no doubt hoping Mark would ferret out the report and leave her alone.

"We realize that, Mrs. Harper," Mark leaned forward, his forearms on his thighs, "but we'd like to hear it again, if you are able to tell us. You might have remembered something else by now, something you forgot to mention when we spoke." His face held the hint of a smile, one of his most beguiling expressions, and Marian nodded.

"Certainly. Anything to help with this. Well, it does make it somewhat different, doesn't it, now that he's been...found." She broke off and took a sip of tea before continuing. "Reed went missing Tuesday, nineteenth of June."

"What time was that?" I readied my pen, not wanting to miss anything so she'd have to repeat it yet again.

"Immediately after the meeting ended. Around half past nine, I'm told."

"You weren't at the meeting, then."

"No. Only members of the Fete committee attended. They met in the church hall. Six of them. Reed needed to see how everything was getting on. There are so many details in the fete and well dressing. Even though it's practically the same thing each year, still, you need to see about the booths and entertainment and food."

I believed it. Just seeing to the creation of those two-dimensional mosaic-like tableaux could take nearly a week. "And your well dressing celebration is...?"

"It begins Friday next and runs for ten days. Sunday, eighth of July is the last day."

"A week from today?" Mark murmured.

"Twenty-ninth of June, yes. Is that a problem? You won't shut down the well dressing."

"I'm just surprised. I haven't seen any preparations for it."

"They'll start tonight or tomorrow, no doubt. The booths can be erected early because the vendors like to get started on that. But the creation of the well dressing panels won't start until Sunday or Monday, I shouldn't think. The mud and flowers dry out so quickly if it's assembled too soon, don't they?"

"Who attended the meeting?" I asked, eager to get the questioning back on track.

Marian stirred in her chair, already tired of the retelling. "Besides Reed, there was the vicar."

"Harding Lyth. What is his role in the festival?"

"He chooses the hymns for the wells. And of course plans the service for Sunday morning."

"The hymns for the wells?" Mark looked at me for clarification.

"The vicar and choir lead a procession of villagers to start the well dressing festival," I explained. Mark may have been reared on a farm not far from here but he quickly made the transformation to city boy. "They stop at each well and sing a hymn. The vicar—and the minister, if there is a Chapel congregation in the village—give thanks for the water at each well. It's a custom unique to Derbyshire, do you know? Began in Ashbourne, I believe, as a thanks offering to God when the villagers were spared from the plague. Others have suggested that it's the remnant of an old custom the Romans brought with them. Giving thanks for water is neither new nor confined to the Romans; there are many cultures that do and have done that. But I have never heard of another culture doing it quite as we do in Derbyshire, with our flowered panels. Interesting, don't you think?"

Mark nodded, still looking confused, then bent over his notebook. His bluff didn't work on me. I prompted Marian again for the rest of the meeting attendees.

"The vicar's daughter, Angela Ellis."

"She married?" Mark asked, raising his head.

"No. That's her stage name."

"*Stage* name? She famous, then?"

"She wants to be. She's the emcee of the entire festival, so she needs to be at the meeting. Reed's assistant, Jenny, has charge of overseeing the various booths and games." She took another sip of tea, holding the warm cup in her hands.

"Who are the last two?" I asked, gently nudging her to talk.

"A police constable and his wife. They live in the village. It's nothing to do with Reed's disappearance. Though he did get involved quickly enough. The constable, I mean. Clayton Warson. His wife is Lynn. Clayton oversees security and needs to know about parking concerns, one-way traffic and such. Lynn takes charge of the food ordering for the tea tent, the various smaller booths that sell bottled beverages and snack foods."

"As you said, a lot of work."

"Not half. Still, it's tradition, isn't it? Well dressing is a Derbyshire custom."

"Where were you at that time?"

"Here. I can't prove it, if that's what you want to know."

"When did you realize he was late returning home?"

The question seemed to have no effect on Marian. She held her cup and gazed at something on the far side of the room—Reed's portrait, perhaps, hanging above a damask-covered settee. Was she remembering some happier time with him, or the discovery of his body in the forest? The chatter of the starlings stirred her from her reverie and she said rather slowly, "That evening. Around eleven o'clock. I knew how long the meetings usually lasted, so when it got to be so late I rang up Harding."

"The vicar."

"Yes. He sounded surprised that Reed hadn't come home. We live so close together, and the meeting was at the church."

"A few minutes' walk from your house."

"Did he usually walk or drive to these meetings?" Mark asked.

"Oh, walk, always. It's ridiculous to drive that short a distance."

"Anyone walk with him? Or see him leave the church that night?"

"Everyone else lives north of the church. The Warsons—Clayton and Lynn—of course the vicar and his daughter, and Jenny. Odd how that turned out..." Her voice trailed away and her attention returned again to her husband's portrait.

I consulted the map one of the constables had sketched of the village and wondered if it was significant that Reed had walked alone on the dark road. *If* he even got that far.

Mark asked if any of the others had actually seen Reed leave the church.

Marian shrugged, unable to verify that. Rearranging the neckline of her silk blouse, she said, "I just know what they told me. I-I had to talk to them, you know, to ease my mind. I was that frantic when Reed didn't come home. So I went to each person's house and asked if they knew where Reed was. I thought he may have said. You know." She stared unblinkingly at Mark. "Tossed off a casual remark as the meeting was breaking up."

"And did anyone know?"

"No. At least, no one recalled it. They may have told the police later." She broke her gaze and sniffed. "It's so unlike Reed to do this—go off without telling me—that I had to talk to everyone. Well, most people would, wouldn't they?"

"What did they say about him leaving after the meeting? Did you learn anything?" I knew all this from reading the case notes, but I wanted to see if Marian's recital changed for some reason.

"The vicar and his daughter were the last to actually leave the church since he had to lock up. Reed stood outside by the lych gate, talking to Clayton and Lynn. Angela, the vicar's daughter, walked up to them and chatted with them until her father joined them. Jenny had gone on before, a minute or two earlier, saying she had to get home. Clayton, Lynn and Angela then went on,

Clayton and Lynn living the farthest from the church and could escort Angela to her house."

"That leaves the vicar and your husband."

"Harding—the vicar—told the police that he left my husband still at the lych gate. Harding cut across the churchyard, the vicarage is just west of the church. He's always taking that short cut. There's a path between the tombstones and a large oak; it goes to the back door." She paused, as though picturing the tableau or the churchyard. "He said he didn't see when Reed left. It was so dark, you know, at that hour. And Reed had been standing on the side of the lych gate that is nearest the road."

"The eastern side."

"Yes. The path to the vicarage is on the west side of the gate, nearest to the church."

"And Harding didn't hear anything."

"*Hear* anything?" Marian's eyes grew larger, giving her the look of a child peeking out from beneath the bedclothes. "Like what?"

"Oh, your husband's footsteps on the gravel; him whistling, perhaps, talking to someone. I just thought Harding might have heard something and then mentioned it."

"I don't think anyone was there. All the others had gone by the time Harding walked home. I doubt if they gave any thought to Reed. It's not like this is a high crime neighborhood and they walk each other home." Her fingertips lightly touched her lips, as though she had let some taboo subject slip, or the tactile sensation anchored her to the real world in the midst of her nightmare.

"So, the road from the church to your home is dark." Mark watched Marian's fingers pull at the corner of her lips. "Your husband is the last to leave, and he's left standing at the lych gate. The church is just about a quarter of a mile from your house. Yet, his body is found over a mile away, in the wood. Can you explain that?"

Marian's eyes widened, giving her the look I'd seen so often in family members when they received bad news about a missing relative. She stumbled over her words, trying to make sense of Mark's inference. "No. I don't know how he got there. It's unthinkable that he should walk there, especially at that hour. And I don't know who would have driven him there." Her words trailed off. Perhaps the scenario played over in her mind.

"Had he any enemies? I ask that because he ended up there somehow, and the logical assumption is that his killer took him there."

"No! Of course not! Reed may not have been on everyone's 'favorites' list, but he certainly wasn't the kind of person who had enemies." She broke down for a moment, consumed in body-shaking sobs. I offered her a facial tissue and she sat holding it, her head bowed, the tears rolling off her cheeks onto her lap. When the worst of her grief had passed, she blotted her eyes, smiled weakly at me, and apologized.

"No need to," I replied. "Would you like to do this another time?"

She shook her head, the crumpled tissue in her hand. "No. Please. Let's finish this. I-I'd like to put it behind me." Running her hand over her arm, she looked at me, then at Mark, perhaps wondering to whom she should speak.

I said, "Not any enemies, then. Perhaps someone with whom he had an argument? A neighbor, or someone here in Cauldham? Even a colleague at work? What was his business, by the way? I know he was the director of the village fete, but surely that's not a year-round paying job. How did you get your income?"

She shifted her posture and the cat leapt from her lap and padded out of the room. Sweeping the stray cat hairs from her clothes, Marian said, "We own an ad agency. In Buxton. On the High Street. He'd taken it over from his father when he retired. His grandfather had it before that. It's been in the Harper family for several generations. They branched out in the 1950s to include marketing and promotional management. They've always been successful. To the point that his grandfather invested great sums in the mines in this area." She rubbed her lips again, glancing from me to Mark. "I know what you're going to say…that most of the mines have shut down in Derbyshire. That's true. The lead mines around Castleton are all played out now. Were long ago. But his grandfather mined for fluorspar, and that brought in a great deal of money. He invested that money in other things, so when the coal and lead mines did officially close, the family didn't suffer financially. I always feel sorry for the miners, you know." She eased back in her chair, the anonymity of nameless and faceless people a buffer to her grief. "So many men laid off, so many families fell on hard times. I don't know where they went, what they did to survive. And those mines…" She looked out of the window, as though she could see beyond the village, through the great mountain gorge known as The Winnats, into the deep, dark depths of the earth that hugged mines like Odin, Goyte, Thatchmarsh. Closer to Cauldham, perhaps, to envision Ladywash, Portway or Dirtlow Rake.

I found myself thinking about the men of those mines, especially the workers who mined coal on Derbyshire's eastern side. Those mines had closed in the late 1980s. Not so long ago that the bitterness over job losses would still be felt. Safer working conditions may have made the work less hazardous to health and physical labor in recent years, but did that compensate for the termination of a career, a way of life that might stretch back through generations, the cessation of a family's income?

Mark had been a miner. I had seen the coal dust ingrained into the skin at the bridge of his nose, ground in when he rubbed the corners of his eyes, a sort of tattoo he flaunted when we first met in police school. Coal mining had been the major industry around Bolsover, where Mark worked. But in the death rattle of its last lucrative days, Mark applied to the police force; his acceptance saved him from the fate that fell to so many thousands. I glanced at him to see if the talk about closed mines made him uncomfortable. He gazed at Marian, perhaps waiting for her to continue.

"Could it have been a kidnapping gone wrong?" Mark asked.

Marian blinked, her hands trembling slightly. "What do you mean by that?"

"Your husband was kidnapped and held for ransom, only it ended tragically with his death. Was anything like that suggested, or possible? Would someone—villager or agency client—assume you could come up with the money if your husband was kidnapped?"

"As I said, we had the agency business and my grandfather, and my cousin, invested the money elsewhere. We enjoy a high return on that. Plus, I think I mentioned, I have my own money. My family owned land around the village," she said, allowing herself a slight smile. "Quite an extensive tract. By careful investment, that continues to produce income. We're well off but can hardly afford a several-million-pound ransom, if that's the norm for kidnapping payoffs." She dabbed at her nose with her handkerchief.

"Do you know of anyone at your husband's ad agency who was angry with him? Something connected with his job? Or a client?" I said.

Marian shifted her eyes back to me. She shook her head slowly. "I'm sorry, miss. I don't know of anyone. Someone could have done, of course, but I wouldn't know. Reed didn't talk about business here at home."

"You or your daughter have a problem with anyone? I know Ilsa is seventeen—that's a difficult age. Perhaps someone at school, or a former boyfriend."

"Why do you ask that? You're thinking some sort of revenge, a retribution?" When I opened my mouth to reply, she rushed on. "That is absolutely absurd! This is the twenty-first century. We left honor killings and such far behind."

"Still," Mark said, "things like that do happen. Had anyone got mad at you or your daughter? Did you receive any ransom demands when Reed went missing?"

A wrinkle in her silk trousers occupied her attention for a moment. Her fingers pressed the fabric against her knee, as though the pressure could iron out the small crease. Giving it up, she said, "No. We never heard a word. The last anyone saw of him was at the meeting, nineteenth of June, until you discovered his body." She took a deep breath before rephrasing her response. "I'd been praying ardently ever since he went missing. Yes," she said rather hastily, as though to ward off our interjections, "I realize it's been just two days, but I've spent most of that time praying. Even driving to and from your police station I prayed. I went to church Wednesday and Thursday, lit candles, asked every saint I could think of for intersession. I even begged Harding to pray with me, thinking a man of the cloth would have a greater pull. All to no avail." She patted her cheeks with her fingertips. "I'm a regular churchgoer, so it's not like God didn't know who I was. I believed if I asked, he would help me. I don't know why this happened to me." She ended in a quivering of her lips and another sniff.

"No one contacted you during this time. I realize two or three days is not very long, but if your husband had been kidnapped, for instance, surely the kidnapper would have had his plans in place and would have contacted you the night Reed went missing. Or at the very latest the next day."

Marian shook her head and dabbed again at her eyes.

"No email, no phone call, no letter?" I said, nudging her for a response.

"No. We were frantic with worry. I had no idea what had happened to him. He didn't go on business trips and he had no outing planned with any of his friends. He would have told me."

"Where did he like to go on these outings? Did he have a specific group of people who usually went with him?"

"Reed liked to get away when his work got too demanding. He'd take off twice a year, usually, to do some hiking. He said it did him good, getting some vigorous exercise like that."

"Any particular spot he'd hike? Or regular people he'd walk with?"

"His brothers, nearly always. And my cousin."

"Their names, please?"

"Kevin Harper—he's fifty, ten years older than Reed, and his full brother. And Edmund Worrall, who's Reed's age. They have the same mother. And Perry Bowcock, my cousin. Also forty."

"And their occupations?"

She blinked several times, then said, "Perry is retired but has taken the role of photographer for village events. Kevin works and is a shop owner here in Cauldham. Edmund doesn't do much of anything but garden, wander about the village and sit in the pub—nosey parker things, if you want to call it that."

"Did they see a lot of each other throughout the year? The hiking jaunts weren't the only time they got together?"

"No, they were very close. We'd go to the opera in Buxton, gather for birthdays and dinners and the like. Reed just liked to get outdoors every so often. They had a great time together."

"Where did they like to hike?"

"Moorland walks, mainly. I don't think they had a favorite. You can ask Kevin and Edmund, of course." Her voice had dropped and taken on a hardness not evident at the beginning of our talk. I sensed it was something more than just talking about her husband. When I asked, her fingers toyed with the opal pendant, sliding it back and forth on its gold chain. "You mustn't think I begrudged Reed his time with his brothers, miss. I had my time with my girl friends, so why shouldn't he take a weekend with Kevin and Edmund?"

"But there's something more, I think."

She pulled in her bottom lip, flattening it against her lower teeth. I thought she had finished her talk but she said rather suddenly, "It's just that damned dog of Edmund's."

"What about it? Did your husband and Edmund quarrel about the dog?"

"I'm sorry. It's too silly. You'll think me a fool."

"If it's bothering you, Mrs. Harper, then it's not silly."

"And," Mark said, "if it's linked to your husband, it may be pertinent."

Marian sighed loudly, as though resigning herself to sounding like a berk, then said, "It's just that, well, Poe—that's the dog. A great bulk of a black lab, nearly as big as a calf but with a wolverine's disposition." She gave me an apologetic look and said, "I never could warm to that dog. There was something about him…"

"Did he frighten you? Or play too rough?"

"No, no. Nothing like that. Just that, well, every time I saw him I thought of a shuck. Now I feel even more strongly about it because Edmund brought the dog here, to the house, the day before Reed disappeared."

Six

Diary Entry, 26 April 1987

Today disappeared before I knew it. My birthday. Sweet sixteen. Isn't that what they call it? Glorious day, even if the weather didn't cooperate. Gray and rainy. How I wish mum had had me in the spring—how super it would be to walk barefoot on the lawn or walk through the wood to find wildflowers. But it can't be helped so I concentrate on Clayton to be happy. I'm over the moon! He came over for tea, then we drove to Glossop to the cinema. I chose the film, since it is my birthday. We saw *Lady Jane*. It's been out only a month or so and I've wanted to see it. Helena Bonham Carter and Cary Elwes (Lady Jane Grey and Guilford Dudley) seemed to have a special chemistry on film. I wonder if they do off the set? Their acting was simply superb but I thought Cary too handsome to take my eyes off even when Clayton gave me a kiss. I thought Guilford's line "Some of the greatest battles are fought with the heart" particularly significant. I mean, isn't that how I feel about Clayton?

He gave me a blue silk scarf and a silver locket. To keep a lock of his hair in, he joked. But I will. When I get up the nerve to ask him. I hope he didn't spend all his money on me. It's a super gift, and all, but we have to save for our future. Still, it'll be nice to have a part of him so close to my heart.

Got home late. I was in a muck sweat coming home, thinking I'd get the rocket from Gran. She was cool. Said I had only one 16th birthday. Glad she didn't explode. It would've ruined my day. Clayton and I parked in the wood behind the Hall, and all the time he was kissing me I imagined he was Cary Elwes. But I'll keep that a secret, take it with me to my grave.

Seven

"I admit I may take the subject too gravely," Marian said. A family photo album lay open on the table and she now picked it up. She slipped back a few pages, came to the section she wanted, and angled the book so Mark and I could see the photos. The time period looked to be Victorian, with women in long-skirted dresses, men with full beads or muttonchops, and horse-drawn carriages populating the streets and rural roads. Tapping her finger on a portrait of a middle-aged man in tweed knickers and vest, she said, "Reed's great grandfather. He was walking with friends near Dirtlow Rake and fell through a sinkhole. Despite his friends' frantic efforts, he died. A large black dog had been following them for a mile, despite the men's efforts to chase it off." She cradled the photo album against her chest, her arms wrapped around it. "Reed's great uncle fell off the grassy bank of a river. The water level was high and the current swift due to extensive spring rains. His heavy clothing took him under. They found his body some hours later, wedged inside one of the river's sluice gates. A dog had been seen prior to this, standing on the ridge of the hill next to the gate.

"We would write this off as accidents but several years ago Reed's aunt went on a walking tour with friends. They evidently were near Mam Tor. She broke through the top crust of a sinkhole and fell twenty meters to her death. Her friends saw a shuck—the ghost dog—for that's what we believe it is, near the lane when they walked back over the Tor." Carefully laying the album back on the table, she said, "You can laugh. There's nothing scientific about any of this. But every member of these three parties saw the spirit dog—and these incidents occurred decades apart."

"You believe the dog is linked to your family for some reason?" Mark asked, his eyes shifting from the album to Marian's face.

"I can't explain it any other way. Doesn't the black dog foretell misfortune or death? It seems to in Reed's family," she added, somewhat reluctantly.

"How did you meet Reed?" I wanted to know—it might be pertinent in the investigation, giving us a new lead—but it also might ease her discomfort if she talked about happier times.

"By accident."

"You mean, a random encounter, like at the green grocer's or somewhere."

"No. Literally by accident. My car hit the back of his. Sounds like something from a novel or a film, but that's how we met. Dusky, late autumn day, rain-slick road. Me, a new driver and not accustomed to driving in adverse weather." She allowed herself a faint smile, as though the years had been swept away by this simple recital and she was standing in the rain, talking to Reed. "He was such a gentleman about the whole thing, didn't get upset at all. He just laughed it off and we ended up in a little pub exchanging names and phone numbers, insurance contact information and the like. He rang me up a few days later, wanting to know if I had any problems with a stiff neck, if I were all right. He sent flowers, too." Taking a deep breath, she fixed her attention again on some place on the far side of the room. Did she see Reed standing there, smiling at her? I had nearly convinced myself to turn in my chair to look when Marian added, "We ended up going to a dance that next week. It wasn't long after that I knew I was in love with him."

"Was your husband as sure of his feelings then as you were?"

"Oh, yes. He always said it was love at first sight. Well, love at first crash, was actually his phrase. He joked about being struck with Cupid's sledgehammer and not a dart. An exaggeration, of course, for my car hardly did more than a small dent in his boot. But he liked to talk about our meeting and how he got knocked off his feet." Marian refocused on my face, her eyes steady and bright. "I guess it was one of those things that are meant to be. We were attracted to each other instantly. I like his family, too."

"That makes married life easier."

"It does. My folks liked Reed, too, so we had a lot of help and love at the start. And throughout our marriage," she added, nearly as an afterthought. "But it's the first year or two when a supportive family really help to ease you into married life. When you're just getting to really know your spouse."

My thumb and middle finger pressed against my engagement ring and I found myself wishing a prayer that Adam and I would settle into our shared life with minimum problems.

Mark added a few names to his list of family members, friends, acquaintances, and work colleagues—a list he created when he had first interviewed Marian at the police station. Now he got the name and address of Reed's garage—the people who serviced his car—and people who worked, however remotely, on the village fete. In total, she'd given him just a half dozen new names today but, as Mark reminded me on leaving her house, you never knew who had a reason for murder.

～

Mark and I left Marian's shortly after that, finding out that Reed had lived in the house since he was born—as had his father and grandfather. On marrying Reed, Marian had moved in, but they kept her family home outside Flash, in Staffordshire.

"Wild, rugged country," Mark said as we walked down the hill to Kevin Harper's house. "Nothing much in Flash but the pub, is there?"

"There's got to be something more."

"Something more than its connection with counterfeiting money, you mean." He shook his head and kicked a small stone out of his way. The stone skittered across the road and banged into a tree trunk.

"It's a nice area. Great for rambling. Lovely scenery."

"If the wind lets you breathe, I guess it's lovely. That bunch of rocks—Ramshaw? Yeah, that's them. Ever see that group called the Winking Man? Downright spooky, I call it."

"It's all right when the sun's not behind it," I countered.

"Yeah, well, I'll just stay in Derbyshire, thank you. That area gives me the creeps. Caves, sinkholes, rivers. You know about The Devil's Hole? You ever hear that thing?" He looked at me, silently challenging me to deny it held no mystery to it.

"It's just the wind, Mark," I said. "It's incredibly breezy on top of the Roaches, as you just said not a minute ago. I grant you it sounds like a ghost or something is lamenting, until the wind comes from another direction..."

"Fine. Okay. Nature at its strangest. What else would you expect from an area that has yak and wallaby wandering around?"

"I thought the wallabies were nearer to Mam Tor or Kinder Scout."

"They hop, don't they?" He looked at me, Superior Knowledge beaming from his expression. At least he'd forgotten his anxiety over the ghosts. "Anyway, that whole area wallows in unexplained phenomena. Farms up there didn't get an electric supply until the late 1960's."

"What does that mean?"

"Just that the region is remote. Wild, like I said. Anything could be living up there. Or going on up there."

"Oh, really, Mark! You're sounding like a fiction writer. Besides, Marian Harper was talking about a black dog in Derbyshire, not in the Roaches region of Staffordshire."

"Not that far away. They walk." He glanced around, perhaps expecting to see a wallaby or black dog. "I repeat—I'm staying right here. Preferably in a pub or other civilized place." He bent down, picked up a twig, and threw it across the road. "What have we stumbled into, Brenna? Black dogs, moaning rocks, sinkholes... I wish I knew a priest."

I patted his hand. "You'll be just fine. Concentrate on the case and the ghosts will disappear."

He would have said more, but we were at the front garden gate of Kevin Harper's house. Kevin said we'd caught him just before he left for work and that he could give Mark and me fifteen minutes.

"And what is your work?" Mark asked after we were seated in the lounge.

"I own the gift shop here in Cauldham."

Mark blinked and glanced at me. I hadn't expected that, either. Kevin's bulky build put me more in mind of a weightlifter than a jockey. Recovering his composure, Mark said, "You're not in the family business? We spoke with your sister-in-law and she told us that Reed headed the ad agency. I would have thought that you, as the older brother, would be doing that."

He flashed a quick smile before staring at Mark. "You'd be wrong."

"Why aren't you managing it?"

"No mystery, detective. I have no interest in it."

"Did you work there and then relinquish it to Reed?"

"No. Reed took over from our father. I realize the elder son usually controls the company, but I didn't want to. Reed was old enough to take over. He'd been working there since his teen years, during school holidays. He knew the business quite well. Dad handed over the reins and we've all been happy ever since."

"Your brother did quite well with the company, I understand. He has a large, beautifully furnished house, drives a vintage sports car—"

"Yeah, Reed's done okay by the business. But Marian's no hanger-on. She brought her own money to the marriage."

"Oh, yes?"

"Maiden name is Good. Her family owns Good Teapot Company."

I knew the business. Their slogan proclaimed, "Why settle

for an ordinary pot when you can have a Good one?" I always thought that clever. Maybe Reed's company had come up with it.

Kevin said, "Besides having shares in the company, she has an inheritance from her maternal grandmother. She's financially secure. And so is Ilsa, their daughter."

"When did you buy your gift shop?"

He glanced at his watch but made no move to get out of his chair. "Twenty-five years ago. The sale fell into my lap."

"Meaning?"

"Meaning I was old enough, was looking for a location, had the urge and the brains and the skill to do it, and liked that business. It also serves as an outlet for my paintings. I sell them in the shop. They sell quite well, too. I have a few in the arts and crafts shop in the old school, too. Do you know that? Just south of the church? Used to be the church school in the good old days when more people sent their kids to such places. But the desire or the population has dwindled, so the main section of the building's been converted into a youth hostel. The tourist information center shares the ground floor with that handicrafts shop."

"You said the sale fell into your lap. How?"

"Previous owner wanted to move to Canada. Some place in Saskatchewan, I believe. As I stated, the timing was right, so I grabbed it. I've not been sorry. I love my job and I meet interesting people. I always knew this area had a lot of tourists but I'd no idea how many, or the diverseness of places they came from, until I opened my shop."

"You don't share your brother's love of the family business. Do you help with the well dressing or the fete?"

"Only by submitting a design for one of the wells. All entries must be into the committee in September so that they can vote on the designs. The village has three wells, so three designs are chosen. I'm lucky enough that most years my entry is chosen for the church well."

"But the well dressing isn't until the twenty-ninth of June. Why are the designs submitted so early?"

Kevin looked slightly amused. "You've never done a well dressing, then. The designs have to be decided upon so that the villagers will know what sorts of things to save."

"What sort of things?"

"You've seen a well dressing panel before, haven't you, detective?"

Mark pressed his lips together, as though he'd been insulted. "Sure. Lots of times. In Buxton, for instance. They're mosaic-like pictures. Big things, six or seven feet tall, about three or four feet wide. Displayed vertically, like a painting, but at the well site."

"If you ever look closely, you'll see they're made entirely of natural things. Flower petals, moss, tree bark, bits of stone and eggshell, sheep wool… Nothing manmade is allowed. Although most folks save eggshells, for example, all year, sometimes the chosen well panel design designates something rather odd. So the villagers need to know the designs well ahead of time so they, in turn, have time to save up."

"Like, if one of the designs is about conserving the Lady's slipper orchid, people would have to come up with something reddish-pink for the flower."

"Precisely. We did a panel on the black grouse last year."

"Its numbers are severely down," I said. "In England and in Wales."

"That's right. The National Trust has been instrumental in reintroducing it into the Peak District's Derwent Valley. I mention the bird only by way of illustrating how difficult some of these well panel designs are to reproduce using natural materials only. The bird is black and white, with a vivid red topknot. The feathers had to be a shiny black. Where do you get that?"

"It can be a problem," I agreed.

"As I said, that's why we need to decide on next year's design rather quickly after the current year's well dressing is finished. It's not always easy to find enough items. Blue sky, for instance. Hydrangeas produce a nice blue, but as most gardeners of that bush can tell you, the blue isn't a guarantee. Pink and purple are notorious for popping out when you need a good blue. Consequently, we don't encourage designs that call for a vast expanse of blue sky."

"Reed never contributed any designs or ideas for the panels?" Mark asked.

"No. He could have done. I know he had deep feelings on topics he wanted done, but he felt that as coordinator of the whole thing it wouldn't be right. Besides, Reed knew his strengths, and drawing wasn't one of them. He had enough to do going around after people and fixing their sloppy work."

"What's that entail?"

"Re-working the writing for the program booklet, moving a well panel slightly so it sits at a bitter angle, maybe replacing the bunting on the stage with something else. He wanted everything perfect. You know…for the competition."

"Anyone get mad at him?"

"Why should they?"

"I can't think of many people who'd take kindly to being told that their efforts were unacceptable. Rather take it as an insult, I'd suspect."

"You've got it all wrong. Everyone wanted the Hope Valley Cup and the prize money. No one minded that Reed went about making things better. There was nothing egotistical in any of that. It was for the good of the village."

"Have you any idea why Reed was murdered, or who murdered him?"

"You're thinking it was one of us. One of the fete workers who became incensed over Reed's meddling, as you're implying."

"Not so difficult to imagine, or assume."

"Rubbish. We all loved Reed and were happy to have him manage the whole affair. Look at what it brought the village—the Cup, the prize money, and tourists with open wallets."

It also might have brought his death, I thought. I asked Kevin about his whereabouts the night of Reed's disappearance. "Starting around seven o'clock," I said, not wanting a recital of the entire time from tea onward.

"I'd been in my shop."

"You didn't go home for an evening meal? Were you open late for some reason?"

"I ordered a takeaway from the Indian restaurant. It's just down from my shop, on the opposite side of the street. You can ask them."

Mark made a notation in his pad of paper.

"You and your wife have a fight?" I asked. "Is that why you worked late and ate in your shop?"

"No, we didn't. We're happily married. I ate at the shop because I was working late. I was taking inventory. I do this twice a year. At the same time each year. There's nothing nefarious in it. Ask my shop clerks. Or my friends. Ask my wife," he offered as he stood up and grabbed his car key. "Please find the person who killed him. I-I miss him so much already. I loved my brother."

～

Mid-morning made its presence known by the familiar rumbling in my stomach. I wanted to stop in the incident room, grab a cuppa, and type up my notes. Mark wanted to check on Kevin Harper's alibi and told me he'd meet me in the incident room. I nodded to his back, walked up the hill, and was sipping hot tea when Margo walked in. She tossed her shoulder bag onto the table and sank into a chair.

"Honest, Bren, if I have to show these clothing photographs to one more person..." Her cheeks puffed out as she exhaled heavily.

"Not your idea of a good time, I take it," I said.

"Oh, it's all right. Better than digging into bank accounts. But when I get through explaining where the clothing was found and under what circumstances and I see the people's expressions..." She grimaced.

I leaned over to her and patted her hand. "A policeman's lot is not a happy one, Margo."

She glared at me but held out her hand.

"What?"

"Just a sip."

"You can get your own, you know. The kitchen is not twenty steps behind you." I nodded toward the serving window. Its counter held stacks of white ceramic mugs, saucers, small plates and large chrome urns of hot tea and coffee.

"Yours is closer. Just a sip, Bren."

I relinquished, handed her my mug, and after she'd taken a long gulp and handed it back, I said, "You and Byrd are making the rounds, right? Any headway on identifying the fabric remnant found with the bones?"

"Yeah. That is, yes, we're making the rounds. No to making headway."

"He still talking to folks?" I looked around the room but couldn't see him.

"He wanted to get one more finished before his elevenses. Honestly, I don't know how he gets the energy."

"You'd think someone would recognize the material."

"Twenty-two years is a long time."

"You can't assume it's Vera Howarth's clothing. It could have been in the ground longer than that."

"But it was found where the bones were, Bren. A piece had even adhered to a bone. If they're not Vera's bones, whose are they?"

"We don't know yet. Maybe it's someone else. But you can't assume she wore that."

"Someone else? How many murder victims are there in the wood?"

"Hopefully, no more." I took a sip of tea—opposite the spot Margo had sipped.

"Vera Howarth or not aside, the clothing faded in the soil. It won't look the same. I don't know if I'd recognize anything that old even if it were my mum's."

"You might if she went missing."

"I don't think I would. Not that I'm not observant, but you

don't memorize what your family or friends have on each time you part company. If mum's just going down to the newsagent's, I'm not going to look at her clothes in case she doesn't come back. It's not natural. Anyway, I bet you can't tell me what I wore yesterday."

"No," I admitted reluctantly.

"And we were together for hours. And remember, Bren, that Vera Howarth had no family in the village. Who would remember what she was wearing when she was last seen…twenty-two years ago?"

"Okay, you've got a point, Margo."

"I rest my case."

I set aside my tea and typed up my notes. PC Byrd entered the room, grabbed a mug and poured himself some coffee. I was about to talk to him when Mark came in, spotted me, and walked over.

Collapsing into one of the chairs, he said, "Check off Kevin Harper as having a solid alibi during the time of Reed's disappearance. He was working at his shop—two employees just confirmed they were with him, Ilsa Harper also helped out."

"Reed's daughter?"

"Happens to be Kevin's niece, too. Plus, the Indian takeaway sold four meals to Kevin and his energetic crew."

"At what time?"

"Seven o'clock."

"But Reed didn't go missing until the meeting ended at half past nine. That one's no alibi."

"I agree. But we have another witness who can place him there from nine forty-five till a bit past ten o'clock."

"Is he trustworthy?"

"You tell me, Bren. It's Clayton Warson, a fellow cop."

Eight

Clayton Warson showed no surprise when Mark and I showed up at his house. After all, the village grapevine spread the word about the discovery of the body faster than a bent lawyer learned of a potential client. So where was the surprise that we were investigating?

The time had just gone half past eleven, and I was surprised to find him at home. But Clayton was on a later shift, so he had time to talk. We sat in the home's front room, in a patch of warm sunshine, and declined the offer of tea.

The room's décor belied the impression I had on looking at the ancient home's exterior; it was done up in sleek, modern furnishings and hues of white, black and yellow. I tried not to stare at the cubist painting above the sofa, expecting to hear the arguing couple's tirade. At least, I think it was an arguing couple. It could have been a frog dealing a poker hand.

"I heard you lot were in the village," Clayton said, unconcerned about the game-playing amphibian. Dressed in his uniform—black trousers and tie, white shirt—Clayton looked ready for whatever the day would hand him. In the way of his job. He didn't look as confident when I took out my pen and notepad. "It's about Reed, then, that you've come."

"You've heard that his body was recovered," Mark said.

"I should think the entire village has done. It's not the sort of thing that can be kept quiet. Anyway, there's no need to. Everyone knew the minute they heard that it meant a police investigation.

Even if he eventually walked home of his own volition, the police needed to be brought in that night, and the media alerted." He jiggled his foot—his right leg lay horizontally across his left, the ankle resting on his left thigh. The faster he talked, the faster his foot shook. "It's fortunate for Reed, and Marian, despite its horrendous implication. It's a terrible thing to think about, what she must have felt not knowing where he was. At least now she can come to terms with it all, maybe get some peace, however cruel the outcome for them both."

"You knew Reed, I assume."

"Oh, yes. I should think everyone in the village did. If they didn't from the well dressing festival, they knew him as a neighbor."

"Was he well liked?"

"Well liked and well known. He's been the coordinator of the festival for probably fifteen years."

"As long as that?"

"Give or take a year. Reed's forty. I know because I'm two years older. He took over as director when he was twenty-five."

"You're certain."

"Certainly. He made a big thing of it all—twenty-fifth birthday, directing the fete… He had a bash at his house. His wife hired a band and had a catering company do the food. Quite nice do, actually."

"Is that usual in villages, to hold the managerial position for a fete for such a long time? Wouldn't there be others who would want to try their hand at it?"

"There may have been. I don't know specifically."

"You don't help make the well panels or do anything else?"

"I'll take my hour with the panel or puddling the mud, but it's sporadic help. Some people always work on the school panel, for example, or get the flowers from the florist, or design the program booklet. I never know when I'll be able to help, due to my work schedule, so I just fill in whenever and wherever I can. It works out all right."

"So there's no history of a villager wanting to be fete director—the publican, for example—but Reed never relinquished his position."

"Not that I've ever heard. And I think I would. Cauldham is a small village, detective, and ill feelings circle our community quicker than buzzards circle carrion. Everyone was content with whatever job of work he had. And to tell you the truth, I think most of us were glad Reed took on the managerial role."

"Why is that?"

"Too much work." He leaned forward, as though about to impart a secret. "Way too much time involved for most of us to take it on, as the greater percentage of residents work outside the home. Then there's also the pressure of making the festival better each year."

"Some sort of competition among other villages?"

"Yes. Especially between us and Upper Hogsley. Chad Styles manages their well dressing and fete—has done for donkey's years. It's a friendly rivalry but it does carry the prestige of the Hope Valley Cup with it. A trophy awarded yearly to the best overall well dressing display, as judged by a five-person committee. Along with the silver cup goes a monetary award. Quite nice, too, actually. Five hundred pounds that is to be used for the village. We fixed up the children's playground with last year's prize money."

"How long have Chad Styles and Reed been vying for the Cup?"

"I don't know an exact number, but at least as long as Reed's been directing our fete. Chad's a few years older than Reed, so maybe that's got something to do with the competition between them. Then, too, there's the practical end of it."

"What's that? The loser stands the winner a round in the pub?"

"Could do, I guess. But it's the practicality of the previous year's win. The Cup designates that the well dressing display as well as the fete in general are superior, so that brings in more visitors."

"And more visitors bring in more money for booth and food purchases."

"It all boils down to money, doesn't it?"

"Probably more times than we'd like to admit. Had you seen Reed the night of his disappearance?"

"We were at the meeting in the church hall."

"What time did that break up?"

"Near half past nine. Lynn—my wife—and our neighbor Angela, who's the vicar's daughter, walked home. I think Reed was the last to leave. I don't know why. He lives the closest—well, excluding the vicar, of course. But he lagged behind, seemed to be waiting for someone."

I asked if Reed had mentioned anything specific about having an appointment at that late hour.

"No. But he wouldn't tell me things about his personal life, would he? Not many people would. No, it's just a feeling I had, an impression of the way he paced a bit, rocked on his heels and smoked. He just stood by the gate and kind of looked off down the lane."

"Did you three go straight home?"

"I saw Angela to her door. We get to her house before ours. Then I dropped Lynn home and I walked into the village proper."

"May I ask why?"

"I fancied a pint at the pub. Vicar doesn't serve beer at the meeting." He smiled and laid his hand on his foot. It stopped bouncing.

"So, you walked into the village. How long does that take from your house?"

"Two, three minutes. The pub's at the bottom of the hill, closest building to my house, actually."

"And you saw nothing unusual all that time, heard nothing odd like a yell or a car's motor."

"You want to know if I heard Reed being abducted, clobbered on the head and driven away at a frantic pace. No. I didn't. But I did hear the burglar alarm sound at the gift shop. Kevin Harper's place—you know him?"

I nodded. "What happened with the alarm?"

"I ran over there. I was close by, wasn't I? The gift shop is directly across from the pub. No one was at the front door so I ran around to the back. I could see the lights on inside, so I thought maybe I had a real burglary in progress. But not ten seconds after I got to the back Kevin barged through the back door, swearing. The alarm stopped and Kevin called inside to someone, saying the alarm company must've turned it off."

"He has a contract with a professional company, then."

"Yes. Many of the shops in Cauldham do. It's sort of a necessity these days, isn't it?"

"Did you see the person Kevin spoke to?"

"Yes. It was his niece."

"Ilsa Harper."

"Right. She came out—the back light fell full on her face. She joked about next time they take inventory he should supply earmuffs. Someone laughed from inside the shop. I walked up to them to make sure everything was all right. Kevin apologized for his stupidity at setting off the alarm. I said it was fine and that I'd supply a report to the alarm company if it were needed. I walked around the shop, looked in all the storerooms and closets and the back room. Looked behind the checkout counter. No one other than Kevin, the two shop clerks and Ilsa were there. The windows and front door were secure; there were no signs of an attempted entry inside or out, so I proceeded to the pub for my pint."

"Nice that you were so close and could take care of that."

"Don't know that I particularly took care of anything, but I was glad to hear of the false alarm and that everyone was safe."

"When did you leave them and go to the pub?"

"Around ten minutes past ten. I looked at my watch, in case I'd need to testify to anything about the insurance or alarm."

"So when you left Reed, everything was quiet. No suspicious cars waiting beside the road, no one standing by a tree, for instance."

"No. All the excitement was in Kevin's shop. The rest of the village, including the church and churchyard, was quiet as the grave."

"Did you happen to see anyone walking up the hill, perhaps in the direction of the church?"

"No. I was nearly the last person to leave the pub, and the road was pretty well deserted by then. Besides, I just have a short walk to my house from the pub. The church is too far away for me to see."

"Have you ever heard of any ill feeling toward Reed? Perhaps connected with the well dressing?"

"If you're looking for motive, you'll have to look outside the village. Everyone liked the bloke. He helped a lot of folks, too. Why kill someone like that?"

"But someone did, didn't they?"

Clayton resumed his foot bouncing. "There's always accidental death."

"Then why was his body buried in the wood? Why not ring up the police right then and tell them what had happened?"

"Why do people run from the coppers when they have just a traffic offense? Why do folks make a lot of things tougher than they need be?"

I debated with myself for a second, then pulled the photos of the clothing remnants from my shoulder bag. I glanced at Mark as I handed them to Clayton. "Does the fabric look familiar?"

He stared at the photographs, his eyebrows lowered as he tried, perhaps, to remember where he might have seen them. Shaking his head, he returned the pictures. "Sorry. Nothing comes to mind. These from Reed?"

"They were found with the bones. You heard about their discovery yesterday?"

"Yes. Quite a shock. None of us was expecting another body—well, bones—to be found. Do you know who it is?"

"Not yet. Have you any ideas?"

He shrugged, his gaze on something outside the window. "I

would have thought them to be animal bones, of course. That's a common discovery. But if you say this fabric was found with the bones…" His eyes shifted to my face. "Was the clothing actually found *on* the bones or just nearby? It makes a difference, doesn't it, to the assumption."

"On the bones."

"Well, then, that changes the animal theory."

"You've no suggestion whose bones these are, or haven't seen this material before, then."

"Maybe if the fabric had been in its pristine condition, but it looks to be quite faded. Who knows what its original color had been?"

"Even if it was a navy blue as compared to this baby blue, it certainly should spark a remembrance if you knew anyone who wore something in this blue print. The zipper probably comes from a woolen jumper. Do anything for you?" I eyed him, trying to read his facial expression. He remained mystified.

"Sorry. Can't say I've ever seen it…or remember it. Perhaps an animal carried it to the bone recovery site. They do forage, you know. Walk away with large bones, take them to their dens." He glanced out of the window as a car drove past his house. "You found these near Reed's body, I heard. Which was how you discovered him."

"An unexpected find, yes. We were in the village investigating Reed's disappearance when the bones were discovered." I hesitated slightly before repeating the question. "And you've no suggestion as to the bones' identity."

"Wish I could."

"I understand a young woman also went missing from this village." Pausing, I glanced at Mark. He sat well back in his chair, staring at Clayton.

"I don't know about another missing person, other than Reed."

"I'm referring to Vera Howarth." I spoke the name slowly, wanting it and its implication to sink in.

This face remained unmovable. "I don't know if I'd classify her as missing, exactly."

Mark bent forward, his face darkening. "How would you classify it, then? She disappeared, as I understand it. Never seen again, leaving her friends worried sick that something unspeakable had happened to her."

"Something did happen, but not what you're thinking."

"Then *what*? Tell us."

Clayton uncrossed his legs and clasped his hands. In a slow, deliberate voice, he said, "She ran out on me. She sent me a goodbye note and then ran off like a ghost in the night."

Nine

Books from the Library: *Derbyshire's Tales of Ghostly Goings-on and Haunted Homes*

The night had been as dark as the inside of a cave when moonlight finally broke from the bank of clouds. Sam and Will had been playing cards that night in Bradwell, staying too late with friends, and now walked home in the dark. The moonlight helped them see their way but also showed something to Sam that made him clutch his brother's arm in fear.

Will asked what the problem was and Sam pointed to an approaching large dog, big as a calf and black as the night itself. Despite the moonlit landscape and Sam's persistent indication, Will could see nothing.

Thinking Will had either gone blind or was playing a trick on him, Sam nodded to the great beast, which by now walked up to them. Sam froze, his gazed fixed on the dog. It breathed heavily, its eyes seeming to glow in the darkness, and stopped in front of Sam—so close he could feel its hot breath on his face. An instant later, the dog vanished, leaving the wood quiet and Sam visibly shaken.

When he told Will what he had seen, Will laughed, insisting nothing had been there. "Yer't daft if yer thinkin' there wuz summut there." All the way home they argued, Will convinced that Sam had gone mad.

When Will dressed to go to work the next morning, Sam begged Will not to leave the house. "Yer that upset, still, 'bout that there dog," Will said, mocking his brother's continuing fear. "Stay to home, then, like the auld woman yer be," he said, and left for the mine.

Sam remained inside their cottage, his anxiety mounting hourly, convinced the huge dog's appearance forecast some terrible coming event. Later that day a group of miners slowly came up to the cottage door, their hats in their hands, their voices low. Will, along with several other men, had been killed that morning when a portion of the cave roof fell on them.

Ten

"Vera Howarth disappeared—if you want to classify it as that—from the village in April, twenty-two years ago." Clayton pulled in his bottom lip, as though debating with himself whether he should or should not expose the village's problems to us.

I glanced at Mark. He periodically looked up from his notebook, glanced around the room, then returned to his writing. I had no idea what he found so interesting or important and was trying to catch his attention when Clayton continued. Mark abandoned his notation and listened intently. "Even though I fell under suspicion and was questioned innumerable times, her departure was nothing to warrant a grand scale police search or news alerts in the media. She mailed me a note, saying she was going to London. I was devastated, of course, but by the time I received her message, it had been two days since I'd seen her and she was gone."

"Did you go to her home to see if she'd actually left? Talk to her parents?"

"Her parents were dead. They'd died in Australia when she was four years old. Her grandmother reared her. She's the only person I ever saw with Vera at home."

I asked again about relatives or friends who might lead us to Vera, or at least supply more information about her. Clayton shrugged, stating once more that the grandmother was the only person he knew. I asked Clayton to write down names of villagers who had moved since Vera went missing, giving addresses or phone numbers if he knew them. I also asked him to jot down a time table of the last day he spent with Vera, listing activity, approximate time it took place, and where they were.

If Clayton suspected the real reason for this, he didn't mention it. As a copper, he probably had an inkling, but he may have thought it best not to voice his suspicion in case it hadn't occurred to me.

"How did you meet Vera? Do odd jobs for the grandmother or something like that?"

"Not at first. I saw Vera one day in the village. She had a lot of groceries and I helped her carry them home. I'd do that periodically. Then I just fell into doing a few things for them, like weeding the garden. That's how Vera and I came to know each other. We were mates since she moved in with her gran. I don't know how old I was when I learned that she was living permanently with the older lady and not visiting her."

Trying to keep my voice nonchalant, I said, "Where did Vera and her grandmother live?"

"Pardon?"

"Just inquisitive. After all, Mark and I have been around the village, talking to people. I'd like to mentally put them in one of the houses. It gives me a sort of link to them. Doesn't it, Mark?" I glanced at him, hoping I looked convincing. "You know I work better if I can see where they lived."

Mark looked at me as if I had finally, irrevocably gone round the twist and he'd be bringing me fruit baskets on visitors' days. I smiled, let him imagine the worst, and looked expectantly at Clayton.

He, too, had not expected my request. He blinked, cleared his throat, and said, "Why, uh, on the north side of Old Mine Road, where it joins the village circle road. You know where Angela lives…" he said, nearly directing me to confirm that I did. "Well, Vera's house is at right angles to Angela's, farther down Old Mine Road, though. Nearer to the wood and the, uh…the recovery site."

"Is the grandmother still there?"

He shook his head.

"Anyone live there now?"

"Uh, no. After Vera left, we all assumed she'd be returning, no matter what her note said. You know…go to London, try out your dream for a bit, then realize you're not good enough or it's not really what you want, so you come back."

I realized I was nodding, remembering my own brief fling with professional singing. I'd been seventeen, not even seriously considering a career in the police yet. But I played guitar and sang. My friends encouraged me to become a singer. Since I was the best in our group, the suggestion didn't seem outlandish. I'd sung in folk clubs and had been well received; why not on a grander, more permanent scale as a career? I discovered 'why not' shortly into my Grand Launch; I hated the back stage life—who was sleeping with whom, the jealousies, the backstabbing. But obviously everyone is different. Vera may have overlooked that. Or thrived on it.

"I understand her grandmother left the house to her," Clayton said. "I didn't know what to do with it after it was evident she wasn't returning. She had no will that the police could find, and of course we couldn't find the grandmother in London, so the house sat until the grandmother or Vera showed up again or put the house on the market." He twisted his wedding ring on his finger, perhaps envisioning what his life would be like now if he and Vera had married. "It's a shame to see the house deteriorate, but I've no authority to fix it up or sell it. And I don't know anyone who has."

"Well," I said, as offhand as I could, "thanks. I'll drive by it, if that's all right."

"Sure. Fine. It's seen better days, but you'll get an idea." He sighed heavily and grimaced. "I feel so bad about it. The grandmother put so much work into the house and garden. It's a shame."

"Any idea the grandmother's age?"

"Her age?" He blinked, obviously confused in the change of topic.

"Yes. Approximately how old was she when she left? I know you were a teenager, and everyone over twenty-five seems ancient, but any idea now, looking back? If Vera was eighteen when her gran went to London…"

"Oh, Yeah. Well…" He scrunched up his eyes and thought for a few seconds before saying, "Probably in her sixties. She couldn't have been so very old or she wouldn't have moved, would she?"

"Anyone help her? Besides the removal van people."

"There weren't any."

"Sorry?" The answer surprised me.

"She didn't hire any removal firm. She left the furniture for Vera and I think she just took a carful of clothes and knick-knacks with her."

"Who drove her? A friend from London, someone in the village?"

"Vera."

My image of getting a name, address or phone number of the driver crumbled. There went that lead. "Well," I said, grabbing on to what we still had, "at least I can see her house. That'll be a big help to me, Clayton. I do so like to put people into their surroundings. You have no idea how better I work if I know that."

I took the paper from Clayton, thanked him, and said that we might get a break in the case this afternoon.

He merely nodded, his eyes speaking of the torment consuming him.

"Did you write to or ring up her grandmother to ask where Vera was?"

Clayton rubbed his forehead and avoided looking at us. When Mark repeated the question, Clayton raised his head. His eyes had a haunted look, the whites suddenly more intense and the dark irises bright with light. "Vera wrote that she was going to London. To follow her dream, was how she phrased it. Her granny had moved to London the previous year, before Vera left. I had no idea Vera had such plans—to move and leave me without letting me know. We had our own plans, you see. We were engaged.

She was eighteen and I was nineteen. I thought we had our future together sorted out. When I got her note, well, I still didn't really believe it. Didn't believe it was a permanent move. Not if we were engaged. I don't think she knew anyone in London, at least I had never heard her talk of any friends or family. That's partly why that damned note was such a shock. Going off to live on your own in London. Absurd! So I assumed she went to live with her gran while she sorted out her life."

"You couldn't contact the grandmother even if she had moved to London the previous year?"

He shook his head and the color drained from his face. "I didn't know her name—she was merely Vera's maternal grandmother. And I think Vera changed hers because, despite inquiries through the Metropolitan Police, they could never find a Vera Howarth residing in the area." He looked at me, perhaps needing a woman's understanding. "London houses around nine million people. Where would you begin to look?"

∽

Mark threw Clayton's question back to me as we sat in the pub. Since it was just going on toward noon, we had decided to have lunch, time the walk, and ask the publican what he remembered about Clayton's time there. "Even if he found out the grandmother's name," Mark noted the time on his watch, "somehow traced the parents' deaths through death certificates issued in Australia, he still has a trillion-to-one chance that he'd find Vera in London. It's a bloody big place."

I nodded, thinking both statements were correct. The waitress came with our lunch order but before I could take a first bite of my salad, my mobile rang. I glanced at the caller ID display and flipped open the phone. Turning slightly from Mark, I lowered my voice and said, "Hi, Adam."

Mark snorted and busied himself with texting a message on his mobile.

"Hi, sweets." Adam's voice lay warm inside my ear. "Are you able to talk for a minute?"

I glanced at Mark. His phone still occupied his attention. I brought the phone closer to my mouth. "Sure, Adam. We're just having lunch."

"We?"

"Mark and me. We're at the pub in Cauldham. Know it?"

"Neither the pub nor the village. You're on a case, then."

"Is there any doubt?" I refrained from saying I wouldn't be out socially with Mark since I was engaged to Adam. "Any particular reason you called?"

"We need to talk about the wedding, Bren."

"Now? This very minute?" Besides being an inappropriate time and place, the wedding was the first of December, six months away. I know most weddings are planed a year or so in advance, but Adam's and my wedding was going to be small. Simple. Handwritten invitations to a miniscule number of people. No church reservation, orchestra, or caterer required. Just standing outdoors in a breath-taking, soul-inspiring natural setting for the ceremony, then to a friend's house for a reception or meal or tea—whatever fit in with the time of the wedding. I wanted morning, as the sun rose; Adam wanted early evening with the glow of dozens of candles the main source of light. He also preferred it indoors with a band, afterwards, that we could dance to. Needless to say, there were a few differences we had to negotiate.

"No, not right now, but soon. If you're on a case, you won't be free tonight," he said, his voice trailing off in disappointment. "But do you think it'd be next week sometime?"

"I honestly don't know, Adam. I have no idea how long the case will last. I could phone you when I get a better sense of time. Would that do?"

"Sure, Bren. Fine. It's just that…" Again he sounded unhappy, or that he didn't want to impart bad news.

"Just that…what?"

"My parents would like to help."

"Your *parents*? Are you serious?"

"Mum knows a bit…" He coughed, I suspected to hide his

embarrassment, and exhaled loudly before continuing. "I told her something of your situation and she wants to help. Dad does, too."

"Generous, I'm sure, but what's my situation?"

"You know."

"No, I don't, or I wouldn't ask you. What did you tell them?"

"About your parents, your relationship with them."

The first trickle of irritation seeped into my bliss. Fighting to keep my voice level, I said, "Why did you mention that? It's really of no one's concern but me and my parents." I took a deep breath, feeling the heat flood my cheeks. "Honestly, Adam, I can't believe you mentioned this to your folks. That was completely unnecessary and out of bounds. I had more trust in you." When I had finished, Mark glanced at me—probably to see why my voice was rising—and then snapped his phone closed.

"Sorry if I overstepped your boundary, Bren, but I was just trying to help."

"I appreciate you wanting to help, but I don't know what this is in aid of."

"Oh. Didn't I say?"

"No."

"Oh. Well, I mentioned how you and your family were, uh, kind of at odds right now."

"Delicate way of saying they brushed me aside...probably forever. Go on, what else?"

"And that you really doubt if you would get any help from them for our wedding, either help with planning or finances or just plain moral support."

"Smashing. Anything else? I may as well know the other secrets you've revealed so I can be prepared when I meet them."

"Brenna, it's not like that. I know the bind you're in, with your parents more or less ignoring you. I just mentioned it to Mum that we wanted a simple wedding and somehow the history of you and your family came out."

"So, what do your parents want to help with? Must be urgent or big, or you wouldn't be calling me now."

"Well, they'd like to talk with us. They, uh, would like to help us through this."

I exhaled slowly, my mind already envisioning what lay ahead.

"They'd like to pay for part of the wedding. They'd also like to physically help. They've got some suggestions as to reception caterer, wedding ceremony location, honeymoon. That sort of thing."

I don't know when I finally got my voice back. Adam's news shocked and irritated me beyond any reply I could readily give. I know he meant well—assumed his parents meant well—but to reveal my miserable relationship with my parents, the problems I've had struggling for their acceptance, was near to betraying a secret I had no wish for anyone to know but my closest friends. Perhaps I would have mentioned part of my family life to Adam's mum and dad, but it wasn't a revelation I wanted even before I'd met them.

My reply took too long. Adam said, "Well, Bren?"

"What?"

"Can I let Mum know we'd like to talk with her?"

"Not just yet."

"Why not? You want to see how the case is going?"

"It's not that."

"What, then? You mad at me?"

I paused, wondering how to phrase this so he wouldn't be mad at *me*. Mark had nearly finished his sandwich and I had yet to start my salad. I said, "I've got to go, Adam. We'll talk about this later. Maybe tomorrow."

"You're angry."

"Adam."

"You are. I can tell by your voice. It goes all tight and cool when you're angry."

"Adam—"

"I'm sorry if I betrayed your trust, if I said something my parents had no need or right to know. I guess I blundered in my haste to get our wedding planned and us married. Mum and Dad have the best intentions, Brenna. They just want to make all this easier for you. For us. They don't mean to shame you. They already love you. Well, not to the degree that I do, but…"

"I'll call you tomorrow. I've got to get back." I rang off not knowing how I felt.

"Trouble in paradise?" Mark asked the question seriously, his lips not smiling in a mock of my situation, his eyes steady and hinting at offered help. When I took a forkful of salad, he said, "Everyone I ever knew who was about to take the plunge had pre-wedding jitters, Bren. Had to sort things out and learn what was acceptable and what wasn't. You've known Adam for years but you haven't been close for that long. It's new, this diary-like confiding in someone. Especially when you want two different types of weddings."

"I never said—"

"You don't have to. I know you. I know Adam. I can imagine your back-to-nature insistence and Adam's equally resolute insistence on a church wedding." He looked at me from over the rim of his coffee cup. "Well?"

The salad got the brunt of my anger. I stabbed a chunk of tomato, piece of hard-boiled egg, lettuce leaf and crouton. "Stay out of it, Mark. I know you mean well. *Everyone* means well. You, Adam, his parents…" I stuffed the salad into my mouth and wiped the bit of salad cream dribbling down my chin.

"Just as you say, Bren. But don't be too hard on the chap. He loves you; he's only trying to ease your burden. No matter if you're standing under a tree or in front of a church altar, the stress is similar. Just hang on to your love and nothing else will matter much."

We finished the rest of our meal in silence, letting the conversations from nearby tables grab our attention.

On the way out, Mark asked the publican if he remembered Clayton Warson being in the pub the night of Reed's disappearance. The publican said yes. He recalled it because Kevin's burglar alarm had sounded and he and most of the other pub patrons had gone to the windows to see what was happening. Clayton came over to the pub, had a beer and played a game of darts until closing time.

"That takes care of that little loose end," Mark said as we made our way back to the incident room.

"Handy, isn't it, to have such a memorable alibi?"

"You thinking Kevin set off the damned alarm to give himself an alibi?"

"Either that, or Clayton needed one."

"Why? You heard the publican. Clayton was there from just after the time that meeting at the church broke up and then stayed until much later."

"Ahh, but we don't know what time Reed really disappeared, Mark. Maybe Clayton met him somewhere after the pub closed."

"Then Clayton's pub stint doesn't mean a bloody thing."

⁓

Clayton's wife, Lynn, ushered us into her office at the tourist center, stating it was less disruptive. I thought, however, that she merely didn't want others overhearing us. She shut the door, leaning against it so it clicked firmly closed, and motioned us to the chairs by the window. We sat in the sunlight, warm and intense, asked her about the night of Reed's disappearance.

"I was at the meeting in the church," she said, leaning back in her desk chair. The blonde streaks in her dark hair shone like gold in the light, underscoring the yellow and tan in her print blouse. "I guess you know that." She paused, perhaps wondering what we wanted to hear.

Mark asked about the order in which people left the church.

"Yes, that is pertinent. Well, Jenny left first. Earlier than the rest of us, in fact."

"How much earlier?"

"Can't say precisely, but I would think by a few minutes. Not more than five. I doubt if it was five. Probably more like one or two minutes."

"Did she leave before the actual meeting had finished?"

"No. We were just talking. You know how you do when you're

winding down and the talk's turned to chitchat—and Jenny mentions she has to get home. So she left."

"Did she drive or walk?"

"Drive. She lives on the north side of Cauldham Hall, where Miners Road curves into the village proper. Her house is just a mile from the church, but she usually didn't like to walk that upper stretch of Old Church Lane after dark."

"Why is that? Nervous, is she?"

Lynn paused, perhaps wanting to phrase her response in a kind way. In the brief quit I glanced around the room. Nothing much cheered it or imprinted personality onto it—it wallowed in the nondescript tan, cream and white hues of an unimaginative worker. White Venetian blinds clanked at the open window; the desk and bookcases were painted tan; the area rugs by the desk and window held nothing more than a rectangle of tweed-flecked browns. In addition to the usual office furniture and supplies the room also served as a sort of closet, for stacks of brochures, books and picture postcards filled many bookshelves and the tops of a filing cabinet and small table near the door. The towers of literature and books all appeared to be on sites and history of the region. I noticed the book of Derbyshire customs I had first seen while on a case in December, and wondered how the book was selling. When Lynn cleared her throat, I glanced back at her.

"Not particularly. But she's young, about twenty-five, and she said she had to get home. Probably something she needed to attend to promptly, so she drove."

"How about the others who attended the meeting? Did everyone else drive? Did you and your husband?"

"Jenny was the exception. The rest of us walked. The vicar, of course, had only to walk across the churchyard. Reed is the next closest, a quarter of a mile from the church, so he walked."

"That leaves you, your husband, and Angela."

"Yes. Clayton and I walked Angela home. We're neighbors, on the eastern side of Miners Road. We all left the church at the same time, a few minutes behind Jenny. Harding and Reed were talking. I think by the lych gate. I'm not certain. I do recall Harding telling Reed that he must hurry to his home, so perhaps he left next. Does it matter that much if Reed or Harding was the last to walk home?"

"And the meeting broke up…when?"

"Half past nine, give or take a few minutes either way."

"After you and your husband got home, did you two go out again?"

"I was too tired to do much of anything but have a cuppa and read a bit. Clayton said he wanted to talk to Kevin Harper, so he walked down to Kevin's gift shop."

Mark and I exchanged glances. I said, "At that hour of the night? He couldn't talk to Kevin Harper the next morning?"

"I guess not. Clayton didn't come into our house, he just unlocked the front door and saw me safely inside, then he went to see Kevin."

"Why did he think Kevin would be at his gift shop? Quarter to ten is unusually late to be working."

"Kevin was doing shop inventory. He does it the same time each year. It's common village knowledge. I suppose Kevin needed to know something, so Clayton dropped in to talk to him. It's not that far of a walk, anyway."

"Had Reed mentioned anything, maybe offhand, about another meeting he might have that night?"

"Because he went missing, you mean."

"Yes. Since he was such a successful businessman, plus directed the well dressing and fete, perhaps he had an appointment with someone after your meeting broke up. Did he say anything?"

"That's why he may have been the last to leave."

"Doesn't seem unreasonable, does it?"

"He may have said something to Harding. I thought they were talking when Clayton, Angela and I left."

"But you didn't hear anything specific about him having something after your meeting had finished."

"No."

"You mentioned Jenny, Reed's assistant, driving home. Even if she wasn't particularly nervous after dark, that's a dark, deserted stretch of road near the church and Hall. Did anyone in the village—and I don't mean the fete committee—anyone at any time in the recent past have trouble at night?"

"You mean go missing?"

"That, certainly, but is there a history, however minor, of attacks or robberies in Cauldham?"

"You're thinking Reed's disappearance is linked to something else, then."

"Not necessarily," I said. "But if someone else had been attacked…"

Lynn shook her head, her mouth a thin, bloodless line in her ashen face. "I don't know your definition of 'recent past,' miss, but nothing like that's happened here."

"What about that woman who went missing twenty-two years ago?"

She sagged against the back of the chair, seeming to deflate like a witness who's lost her bluster. Giving a look at the closed door, she said in a faraway voice, "Vera Howarth has nothing to do with Reed. You can't possibly connect two incidents so distant in time."

"It's taken on a local mystic, though, hasn't it? Almost a ghost story."

"Don't make a common event into something it's not. She disappeared, yes, but after leaving a note."

Mark leaned forward in his chair, and I caught a whiff of his aftershave before he said, "What sort of note?"

"I don't know. I never saw it."

"But you know about it. You heard about it from someone. What kind of note was it?"

"A note of farewell."

"She left this person, walked out of his or her life?"

"Yes. She left the village to start a new life."

"Did she mail it or hand it to the person?"

"I believe she mailed it."

"How long before she went missing did she send it? Did she post it locally or somewhere on the road, perhaps?"

"Locally. Not from her new address. I suppose she didn't want to be found, and the postmark would give a clue as to her new residence. The recipient got the note two days after she left Cauldham."

"This recipient…who'd she send it to?"

Lynn stared at her hands, clasped and sitting in her lap.

Mark repeated the question and Lynn's eyes met mine in a look of pain. Her words came out slowly, as though each one tore out a piece of her heart. "Please don't get the wrong idea. It's not as damning as it might sound. She sent it to my husband, Clayton. But he never saw her again."

"When was this?"

"Years ago. Twenty-two years ago." Her eyes turned defiant and she said rather sharply, "If you think Clayton killed her because they had a falling out or she was pregnant, you're daft. Reed Harper's the only womanizer around here—is now and has been for *years*. More than twenty-two years."

Eleven

Marian Harper quickly "straightened us out," as she put it, about her husband's supposed indiscretions. Coming as no surprise to us, she denied the accusation. Being married for twenty-five years, she would know about any affairs Reed might have—and he hadn't. She also declared that Lynn Warson was a woman frustrated with her mid-life crisis, declining youth, and a husband who worked such erratic hours that she needed a hobby other than storytelling.

"She should keep her rocks to herself, instead of flinging them at others' houses," Marian said, then hinted that either Lynn or Clayton spent enough time alone that they could have affairs and the other spouse would be none the wiser.

"Sour grapes," Mark said as we stopped at the vicarage.

"She might be lashing out in her grief," I suggested, but I made a notation anyway.

Harding Lyth, the vicar of St Paul's Church, talked to us in the lounge of the vicarage, a squat, gray stone house roughened by weather and age. Yews and oaks, nearly as tall as the church steeple, hugged the house. A patch of yellow daylilies bracketed the front walk and spilled into the nearby churchyard. I wished some of that brightness were inside the vicarage walls, for the interior of the room was dark and somber with brown, black and purple.

We sat around a low coffee table, the top of which nearly drowned in books and albums. Harding grabbed a few of the heftier volumes, piled them on the floor, and set the tray of coffee things in the cleared space. I took a seat on the brown velvet sofa, next to Mark. A photograph of a woman in her thirties had a prominent place on the fireplace mantle. I commented on how beautiful she was.

"Th-thank you," Harding stammered.

"Your daughter?"

"No, my wife." My look of surprise no doubt prompted him into adding, "She died twenty years go."

Mark and I murmured our apologies.

Harding said it was quite all right. "To every thing there is a season. Some seasons don't last as long as others, unfortunately."

I glanced at Mark, wondering how to ease the situation, when he asked Harding about the fete meeting.

"Yes, I left Reed at the lych gate that night," Harding said, his coffee mug resting on his knee. He appeared to be nearly sixty, yet his tall frame still had the muscular tone of someone half his age. A thick head of grey-streaked hair contrasted dramatically with his piercing blue eyes. He took another sip of coffee before adding, "He didn't seem concerned being the last one. But I wouldn't expect him to be."

"Never known him to be frightened of anything, then," I said.

"No. But, then, there's no reason to be frightened in Cauldham. We've no problem with serious crime."

"Do you know if Reed planned to meet anyone after your fete meeting ended?"

"Because he seemed to linger behind, you mean?"

"Yes. Since he didn't walk home right away, leaving at the same time as everyone else."

"He didn't say anything about that to me. Perhaps he just wanted to smoke. I don't allow it in the church, you know."

"He smoked cigarettes?" Mark asked, interested in this new information.

"Yes. Marian, his wife, didn't allow smoking in their house. She said it damaged the furnishings and her fine paintings. She had too much money tied up in those things to see them ruined.

A lot of the better pieces were family heirlooms, so of course she'd be careful about them."

"Reed always smoked outdoors, then."

"Oh, yes. Winter or summer, day or night. He'd stand outside their home, by the edge of the garden to have a cigarette, or walk down the lane. Especially Old Church Lane, where the church and his house are located. He liked that better than Miners Road, which curves through the business section of the village. So you see, I didn't think a thing about his lingering by the lych gate after we'd all parted. He's stood there many times before, having his cigarette before going home."

"Is that the only place he smoked? I don't mean the lych gate—outside. Not even in pubs or restaurants that allowed smoking before the national ban was implemented?"

"Not to my knowledge. Marian is allergic to cigarette smoke. If he sat in the smoking sections of those establishments he would come home reeking of smoke, and that was about as bad as if he smoked in their home. No, he always had his cigarettes outdoors."

"He couldn't have been waiting for someone…a woman, perhaps?"

"Why would you think that?"

"Just asking. We have to eliminate scenarios and suspects."

Harding shook his head. "Nothing like that, sorry. Reed and Marian enjoyed a strong marriage. You'll have to search elsewhere for a mysterious woman…if there is one."

The clatter of the back door closing and an inquisitive "Dad? You got a minute?" barged into the room. Seconds later Harding's daughter, Angela Ellis, came in.

As tall as her dad but with the looks of her mother, Angela came across like the pop star she yearned to be. Long, dark hair fell freely down her back and her eyes shone with an exuberance for life. She'd look good on television, I thought, but also thought her far too thin. Still, she seemed the right age for pursuing the career, probably around twenty years old with a flawless complexion. I glanced at Mark, knowing his penchant for dark-haired women. He was looking out of the window.

"Sorry, Dad," Angela said, looking at Mark and me. "I didn't know you had a counseling session. Pardon me." She shot me a tentative smile. "You getting married?"

Observant. Sees no wedding ring on my finger.

"No, dear," Harding said, putting down his coffee mug. "These are the police. They're asking questions concerning Reed's…uh, disappearance."

Instead of leaving or stammering an embarrassed excuse, Angela settled on the arm of a chair. "Like when you saw him last, that sort of thing?"

"Yes," I said, standing up. "If you have a minute, would you mind talking to me? We'll leave the men and go outside, shall we?" I led the way outside and we strolled among the tombstones as we talked. "You were at the meeting that night, weren't you, Angela?"

"Since I'm the master of ceremonies for the fete, I had to be."

"And the well dressing and all that is a week from today, correct?"

"Next Friday, twenty-ninth of June, yes."

"St. Paul's Day."

"Unless we can't go on…" she said, hesitating. "I've heard where the police shut things down. Events and concerts and things. You know, to find the criminal."

"With Mr. Harper's disappearance and subsequent murder, I don't see what we could gain by shutting down the well dressing."

"Good. We've worked so hard on this, for one thing. And for another, all the food's been ordered; we'll start putting together the panels Sunday. And there's the disappointment to the kids and all. Though I doubt," she added, "all those things matter that greatly when the police are trying to solve a murder."

"Maybe not," I said, "but we don't like to disrupt community life if we can help it. Unless Detective-Chief Inspector Graham says otherwise, I don't see why we'd have to close the fete."

"I wouldn't be especially sad for myself, but the village could use the prize money. If we win it."

"Seems like a good possibility, doesn't it? The village has won the competition for quite a while, I understand."

"Of course we will win," she said emphatically, perhaps invoking whatever well dressing gods had rule over such things. "We've won it for ages. Have you seen the photos of past years' well panels? They're probably stuffed into a cupboard in the village hall or some unappreciative place. The snaps'll give you an idea of the quality of our work." She smiled, as though recalling one particularly nice panel. "Anyway, we've no doubt about the outcome. We're going to do over part of the youth hostel with the prize money." Angela perched on top of a weathered, round-topped tombstone and looked thoughtful. "That's part of what we were deciding at the meeting. It's important to have nice accommodation for our visitors. Just imagine if you were staying at a hostel that needed new paint and mattresses and such. You wouldn't come back. And you'd talk about the rotten lodgings to your friends. So you see why winning is so important this year. The tourist information center and the handicrafts section are fine, but we've got to bring the bedrooms and kitchen up to the same level. It's beneficial to the village in general if we can keep the tourist trade high."

"Did you see Reed Harper leave the meeting?"

"We all left the church together, chattering away—well, all of us except Jenny Millington, Reed's assistant. She'd gone on a few minutes before. But the rest of us walked outside together. I walked home with Clayton and Lynn Warson, since we all go the same way. I don't know about Reed. I expect he chatted a bit with Dad and then went home. But I don't know."

"How did Jenny and Reed get on together?"

"They worked together; of course they liked each other."

"Doesn't necessarily follow. I don't know statistics, but there are thousands, probably millions, of employees who can't stand their bosses. But they put up with the poor working conditions because it's a job and it's better than having no pay packet at all."

"Well, I don't think it was bad as all that. I never heard any specifics, but I never heard about any quarrels."

"Did they socialize?"

"Nothing outside work, no. And even then, it wasn't that often. I think Reed had house parties mainly for his agency group."

"Jenny didn't work there?"

Evidently we were straying into waters Angela didn't like. She glanced at a nearby tombstone. "Oh, no. Her work with the well dressing festival was strictly on a volunteer basis. Reed was the only person paid. And very little salary at that."

"Then what does Jenny do?"

"She's a writer. Quite good, frequently published. Makes a substantial living from what I understand. At least she has her own house and car. She works freelance, writing for magazines and newspapers. You'll have to find someone else to fit your jilted lover role—that *is* what you want to know, isn't it, with all these questions?"

Twelve

The Hope Observer, 14 April 2010

Young lovers might no longer run away to Peak Forest to be married, but Lovers Leap nearly saw its old function renewed recently.

Friday, 13 April, Jennifer Millington left a distraught message stating she was going to take her life by jumping from Lovers Leap Hill.

The note, handwritten and lying on her kitchen table, briefly stated she no longer wished to live since she could not be with the man she loved.

Millington's friend called police from the Derbyshire Constabulary to her home around half past six Friday night. "We were supposed to have tea together," the friend, who wishes to remain anonymous, said. "When it came on to five o'clock and she still didn't come, I started phoning her house and mobile phones. Toward six o'clock, I finally went to her home. She didn't answer the doorbell, so I got worried and phoned the police."

On entering and searching the home, officers discovered the apparent suicide note in the kitchen. The note stated that she would throw herself from Lovers Leap Hill.

Officers called for more support and quickly converged on the hilltop and base. They discovered Millington sitting on the cliff edge, a photo of the man in her hand. Although distraught, she allowed officers to escort her down the hill and into a waiting ambulance. She was taken to Devonshire Royal Hospital for observation and medical attention. She refuses to name the man connected to the case.

Lovers Leap Hill, one mile east of Buxton, is actually a large natural cleft in the region's limestone rock. It is connected in legend to a young 18th century couple, who leapt the chasm on horseback whilst escaping pursuers engaged by their distraught parents.

Millington, 24, lives in Cauldham and is a successful newspaper columnist and travel writer.

Thirteen

Jenny Millington was what Mark a year ago would have called a "looker." Tall, brunette and blue eyed, she had a model's figure and the beauty essential for the camera. But as she talked to us in her house I detected an underlying despondency. Her eyes held no sparkle; her lips did not curl readily or frequently into a smile. I settled into my chair, willing to let Mark do the questioning while I divined the cause of her sadness.

"How long have you worked with Reed Harper?" Mark asked. A trace of friendliness tinged his words and his eyebrows were raised in anticipation of establishing a rapport. He leaned forward, his forearms on his thighs, and smiled.

"Several years," Jenny replied, as though considering what we wanted to hear. "I thought it would be fun, so I volunteered. Since I'm a writer, I can use my skill in developing the releases for the newspapers and the opening speech. I've a bit of graphic art skill so I also design the posters we put up at the visitors center, the pub, and other places. Not that the villagers need reminding," she added, almost allowing herself to smile, "but we do get a lot of tourists, since we've won the Hope Valley cup so often. Lynn Warson wants the posters in the visitors center as a way of letting outsiders know about the fete. I suppose it helps bring in some money."

"You don't sound very certain about that. Or as though you're in favor of it."

"I'm not, actually."

"Oh? Why is that? Too many people attending?"

"Yes. But don't get me wrong—it's not tourists in general."

"What, then?"

"You'll think me awfully selfish." She had taken time to choose the correct word, and now that she had uttered it, she blushed.

"Why selfish?"

"Because I like our fete just as it is. The size is perfect. We're a small village. If we get too many visitors, the parking will become a major problem, the village will be littered, and folks will be poking into everything. We've enough people right now, with our winning the Hope Valley cup. I don't want us to overflow with people, like what's happened to some of the other villages in the area."

"That is a concern," Mark agreed. "I don't know where you put all those cars now, so I can't imagine what will happen if your popularity increases."

"And there's the gardens, too. Some tourists think nothing of walking through the plantings around the market cross and by the pond. I've even seen people pick a flower or two from private gardens. What's happened to respect for other people's things?"

"Did Reed Harper feel the same way? Want to keep it small?"

"Not at all. He thought the bigger the better. Each year he was quite keen on bettering the fete and the well designs. He said the more tourists we had, the more money we would have flowing into the village. He was like that—concerned about improving our life style, upgrading the village. Money gave us the means to fix up the youth hostel, fix up the children's playground...that sort of thing."

"He sounds as though he was a very caring person."

"He always thought of others. He hadn't a mean bone in his body."

"You just said you weren't that enthusiastic about the possibility of the village fete expanding in size. Do you know if anyone else was opposed to plans Reed may have had? Did he make anyone mad?"

"Mad enough to kill him, is what you want to know."

"Yes, since you said it."

Jenny's eyes widened slightly as she shook her head. A strand of her shoulder-length, curly hair slipped forward but she seemed not to notice. "I don't know."

"You don't know which—if someone was opposed to his plans or if someone was angry with him?"

"Both."

"You worked with him, Miss Millington. You never heard a conversation or took a phone call from someone who was upset with Reed Harper...for some reason?"

"No. I wasn't his secretary."

"You were his assistant. Isn't that nearly the same thing?"

"In some ways, yes. I typed letters and made phone calls, but I never heard that anyone was angry with him or with the fete plans. We've done this for decades, you know. The village, I mean. It doesn't vary much, so why would anyone get upset with Reed?"

"You just mentioned you'd be unhappy if the festival got too big," Mark countered, his stare becoming more intense.

"Of course. I won't deny that! But being concerned if the fete grows too large and killing someone...well, that's rather a stretch, isn't it?" The statement came out as a squawk protesting her innocence.

Ignoring her objection, Mark said, "If you feel that way about keeping the fete from growing too large, surely there are others with similar opinions. It's not absurd that someone might over react in the heat of the moment. It's happened before."

"This is a small village. I would have heard if someone was mad at Reed. If not directly, then by someone else."

"Gossip."

"If you want to call it that, yes. Nothing much stays secret in Cauldham. I would have heard." Her voice trailed off, simultaneously sounding sad and regretful.

"Did you know if Reed had an appointment with anyone the night he went missing?"

"I never heard, though he may have done."

"You were with him in the church that night."

"Yes. As were Clayton, Lynn and Harding," she added quickly, as though that supplied her alibi.

"What time did you leave the meeting?"

"When it had ended. Around half past nine, I believe. Maybe a few minutes before. I really didn't look at the clock."

"You were the first to leave."

Jenny shifted her gaze to her lap. Her hands were clenched and trembling, the knuckles blanched. Lifting her head to meet Mark's stare, she said, "I had things to do. I don't like to stand around chatting, wasting time."

"What was so urgent that you left before the others?"

"That doesn't concern you. Or Reed's death."

"How do I know that if you don't tell me what it is?"

"I don't lie."

"Perhaps not, but I don't really know you, do I?"

"Unless you arrest me, I'm afraid that has to remain one of those things you will have to accept as true." Her voice had strengthened somewhat during this short recital, and she looked at Mark as though challenging him to charge her with Reed's death.

We left it at that for the time being, thanked her, and walked out of her house, aware that she watched us from behind the drawn, twitching curtains.

⁓

Margo and I dawdled over a late dinner at the pub. I had talked with her and Mark for some time in the incident room, having a cuppa and theorizing "theory" and "alibi" in an offhand, informal way. Graham wanted an early morning meeting tomorrow to go over the facts of the case, but the questions already plagued me and I wanted to play "what if" *now*, with my colleagues. We quickly tired of it, though—perhaps too mentally dead from the long day—and Mark picked up an Indian takeaway to eat in his bedroom upstairs in the pub. Margo and I needed the mind-numbing chatter of the pub patrons, so we sat in the main room, our dinner over, and slowly sipped our beverages between bouts of conversation.

The pub had been modernized, but probably not in the manner that the average person would phrase it. Electricity had been added in the form of light fixtures, a television set, and a sound system for the weekend musicians. Gas radiators placed strategically along the walls chased the chill from the rooms. Other than an updated kitchen and the loos, the lounge and private bars hadn't changed much from their coaching inn days. The atmosphere and heavy oak beam interior also helped draw in the tourist crowd.

"Ready to call it a night?" Margo stood up, grabbing her shoulder bag, and turned slightly to the entryway.

"I should, I'm so tired, but I can't settle down yet. I'm restless."

"Too much to think about, Bren."

"You think?"

"Sure. The Reed Harper case, the bones identification, Scott's recovery—"

"I wish he were back on the job," I said.

"It's not even been a month since he was released from hospital, Bren. Give him some time to heal."

I nodded, knowing Margo's words to be true, yet I wished Scott were around to talk to. A response driver out of the same police station and Section as the rest of the CID Team, Scott Coral had been severely injured while trying to apprehend a criminal last month. He had done well under hospital care but he still had a long recovery time ahead of him. Even when he came back to work he could be placed on light duty. But he had become such an integral part of my personal life, had been the sane voice of reason for my work and social problems, handed out opinions and solutions, helped with our murder investigations, that I felt suddenly alone without him close by. Which was absurd. Not only did we have a crack team of detectives in Margo, Mark, Graham and the others, but also I had Adam to confide in. I better turn to him first, I thought, digging my room key out of my trousers pocket. Fine way to start off a marriage, yearning to talk to another man.

"Have you heard how Scott's doing?" I asked. If Graham didn't know, Detective-Superintendent Simcock might. I hated phoning Scott's home; I never knew if he'd be sleeping.

"No. But he ought to be doing well. He wouldn't have been released if the doctors weren't certain he's out of danger. You know how they are...careful. Don't want to get sued."

It all boils down to money. Hadn't someone just said that today?

"You coming, then?" Margo gave me her look that was halfway between a question and a demand for an answer.

"I'm too fidgety. I'm going to walk around the village before I turn in."

Margo glanced at the old clock above the bar counter. "Would you mind if I join you? It's not so awfully late."

"Afraid I'll go missing, too?" She fell in beside me as we walked outside.

"Don't be such an idiot. You look like you need to think aloud, that's all. I'm a good ear, or have you forgotten?"

"Come on, then. I can see it's useless to send you to bed."

We started up the hill, the lights and laughter of the pub falling behind us. For all of Margo's assumption that I needed to think aloud, and for my own admission that I had several issues to think about, we were amazingly quiet. Our footsteps echoed against the stone faces of the houses, then faded into the night as we left the residential tract and came to the northern branch of Miners Road. Margo and I stopped and stared at the black ribbon of road that twined through the wood. Even now, well into the dark hours, we made out the cut through the forest, the gapping chasm forever dividing the forest into Safe and Unsafe. Where a murderer disposed of a body and where nothing sinister spoiled the beauty.

Margo nodded at the treetops, just visible against the streak of lead gray clouds. "They look different from this angle, at this time of day."

A breeze tossed the uppermost boughs and the hint of ghostly arms stirred in my imagination. I shook it off as the clouds parted to reveal the silvery crescent moon. My voice sounded far away as I said, "What are we doing walking alone, Margo? We need two handsome men, a babbling brook and little light music."

"You can always ring up Adam, Bren, but don't pair me with Mark."

I laughed, remembering how Mark had tried to date Margo in the earlier months of our working together. To say it didn't work out is like saying Superman has a slight problem with Lex Luther.

"Incidentally, how are the wedding plans coming along? Decide on anything yet?"

We walked past the junction and Jenny Millington's house. Cauldham Hall seemed to loom out of the night, its black hulk giving it greater substance and more authority than it possessed in the daylight. Beyond the hall, I could vaguely see the whitish headstones in the churchyard. The church merged with the black mass of trees surrounding it; the vicarage peeped out of the obscurity by a light in a back room.

"Well?" Margo turned her head to look at me, though what she could discern of my facial expressions is debatable. I hesitated too long and she added, "The place, the reception hall? Surely you've settled on the date, Bren." Her voice raised a few pitches and she said, "Your dress?"

"The date is Saturday, first of December. You'll get an invitation, if that's worrying you."

"I would hope I'd get an invitation. Getting you married has been one long project."

I would have laughed, but her statement was too close to the truth.

"So, what else? Where, got your dress picked out? Give with the details, girl."

I stopped opposite the church lych gate, where the shadows lay thicker and darker. For some reason I needed the anonymity of a curtain before my face. Leaning against the nearest upright support, I said, "It's all a mess, Margo. I'm afraid we're finished."

Margo put her hands on my shoulders and turned me so that I faced her. "I don't believe a word of that. What happened between you two? Maybe I can help."

She released her grip and I felt suddenly alone. "We can't decide on anything. We're at complete opposites. He wants a church ceremony; I want to be outdoors. He wants a reception with a dance band, I just want friends to gather at home. He wants the tux and fancy white dress and aisle of candles, and I want us dressed as we really are—nice clothes, of course, but the *real* us. I want this to be a ceremony I can feel, Margo. I need to look at the space we're in and feel a part of it. 'Place' is very important to me. I have to have that link with God or Nature or people who have gone before us to feel truly alive and one with the world. A church wedding won't do that for me. I can't stand there in a dress I'll never wear again, have my friends sitting in rigid rows, seeing the back of me. Outdoors they can stand facing me, I can feel the nearness of heaven through the beauty of nature. Adam doesn't understand what a church ceremony will do to me." I looked at Margo, trying to see her reaction.

Her arm slipped around mine and we started walking again. "This is probably negotiable. Does Adam know how you feel about this?"

"Yes."

"And he won't let you have the wedding you want? I always thought him intelligent and head-over-heels crazy for you. What's wrong with the man?"

"His mother."

Her silence stated she understood.

"To be fair," I added, "it's his parents. They want to meet with us and talk."

"What's that mean?"

"Exactly my question. They want to help us pay for the wedding. His mother has suggestions about which caterer to use, what reception hall, what church. She even has ideas about our honeymoon."

"Just so it isn't her and Dad going along."

"This is serious. I haven't met them yet and already they're trying to take charge of the whole thing. This is Adam's and my wedding—his parents have had theirs. This is our turn to have what we want."

We came up to the Harper house. Rather than it being the blaze of lights I had assumed, only two lights burned—one in the front room and the other farther back, perhaps in the kitchen. It gave a vague impression of comfort and protection in the surrounding darkness.

"I think you need to sit down with Adam and tell him exactly how you feel, Bren. I mean *exactly*. This is no way to begin your marriage, hurt and angry and resenting his parents—and probably him. You'll never last a year; your love will never endure. Am I right?"

I felt her staring at me, even through the blackness. I nodded, wondering how I would find the courage to tell Adam. But I'd have to say something tomorrow, for I had told him I'd speak to him then.

We had nearly completed the circular route around the village and were just approaching the takeaway when Marian Harper and a man walked toward us. They strolled hand in hand, their faces turned toward each other, their voices low in conversation. As they passed, the man dropped Marian's hand and slid his hand around to her waist. He pulled her closer to his side and Marian clutched his near shoulder as they took the hill. I made some sound and Margo replied that they looked awfully cuddly.

"Maybe he's just comforting her," I said, feeling particularly vulnerable about relationships at the moment. "Who is that chap? Do you know?"

"Even if the streetlamp isn't a blaze of light, I'd know that physique anywhere. I talked to him today in conjunction with the fabric found with the bones."

"So, who is he? Her brother?"

"Close. Her brother-in-law. Well…by halves. Edmund Worrall. Reed's half brother."

"Looks as though he wants to become more closely related," I muttered.

For some reason, we watched until they disappeared. Either the night or a stand of massive oaks swallowed them.

"Going to her home," Margo said, her voice abruptly loud in my ear.

I nodded and murmured something about there being a lot of details to attend to for her husband's death and estate. "I can't imagine what she's feeling," I said, moments later when two dogs had quit barking. "Or how she'll carry on without Reed. I can't fathom what it must feel like to lose a spouse, or face the empty bed and house."

Margo stepped in front of me, laid her hands on my shoulders, and peered at me. I caught the look in her eyes, the streetlamp's light revealing her lowered brows. "Bren, something's wrong. What's the matter? And don't tell me again it's Adam or his parents or your ceremony plans. No one talks like you just did if everything's rosy. You sound like you've lost your best friend."

"I feel like I have."

"I thought you were about to marry him."

"Well, I am. At least…"

"What's going on?"

"Oh, Margo, I'm so muddled. It's not just the problems with the ceremony and reception and dress. It's Scott."

"You're joking. He's married!"

I shook my head. This wasn't what I had meant at all. I started walking toward the pub. Margo fell in beside me and asked me to explain myself.

"I know I'm over reactive, like I said earlier. But I haven't heard a word about Scott, and he's one of my closest friends." I stopped abruptly. Margo took a step backward and stood with me just beyond the pub's door. "I know Adam's supposed to be my best friend. Well, he is…in a way. But not like you are. We've not been close enough for that long."

"But you will."

"Oh, sure. Of course! But not like *us*. Not to share girl stuff with."

"That's natural, Bren. My married girl friends always tell me stuff they don't share with their husbands. Guys do that, too, with their wives. That's why they've got all that male bonding. You know—punch each other in the shoulders when they meet, call each other names like Old Soak and Son of a Bi—" She stopped and grinned. "Well, you know. They paint their faces to watch football matches, they prove they've still got it by being weekend warriors or playing sports till they can't move without groaning the next day. It's like a 'pack' thing and an alpha male syndrome rolled into one. I can't figure them out. They probably can't either. But the point is we're different creatures, Bren. I think you've got the wrong expectation about husband/best friend. You can still have me or anyone else as a best friend, but you relate to Adam in a different way." She stared at me, her eyes mere dark spaces in the shadow from the streetlamp.

"Yeah, I guess. I know that," I added. "Like I said, put it down to nerves or Scott's condition or worried about King Roper or something."

"Let's ring him up. That'll make you feel better if you talk to Scott."

I glanced at my watch. "Awfully late."

"Then, tomorrow. You'll look at this whole subject differently when you find out how he's doing. Now, off to sleep. For both of us."

Nodding, I followed her through the pub door. As I passed close to the end of the bar I saw the publican pick up the phone and nearly immediately heard his explosion of joy and banter. "Keeler, you old soak! Why you ringing me up during serving hours…or is this a subtle way of telling me business has fallen off at your ruddy gaff and you're finally on the teapot? Or is it that you want some advice about running a proper pub?" His voice died under the conversation of the room as I walked upstairs. I faltered on the first step, wanting to listen to the publican, needing to hang onto that little connection with Scott. I knew Keeler was the publican at Scott's favorite local and, as such, offered me a thread to him, a thread I wanted right now to keep hold of, for I fiercely missed Scott. But I climbed the steps, letting the link and the moment drop away, and half-listened to Margo's good-natured chatter.

We said goodnight where the hallway branched. Margo told me to go straight to bed, waved, and disappeared down the dimly lit corridor.

My room was several doors down but I don't recall walking to it, opening the door, or washing my face. I do remember debating briefly if I should brew a cup of tea or just fall into bed, but the ringing of my mobile ended that discussion. I glanced at the caller ID, curious about who would be phoning me. I flipped the phone open as Scott's name registered in the front display window.

"Not disturbing your sleep, am I?" he said.

"You couldn't disturb anything." I settled on the mattress. "You are not going to believe this, but I nearly rang you up a few minutes ago."

"That just proves that line about great minds. Why didn't you?"

"I didn't know if you would be sleeping."

"Well, we've got that question answered, then. How are you, Brenna? How are Mark and Graham and everyone?"

"More importantly, how are you, Scott?"

"I'm out of hospital, but I suppose you know that."

"Yes, but how are you feeling? Any update on your condition?"

"Oh, the usual medical jargon. Doesn't really mean anything. You know." I imagined his green eyes darkening in his frustration, the corners of his mouth screwing up in his lopsided grin.

He could be propped up in bed, pillows behind his back, or on the sofa—anything to accommodate comfort to his tall frame.

"Are you keeping something from me?" I almost couldn't form the words, for the image of tubes stuck into his hands and conferring doctors gripped my throat. "You'd tell me if anything was wrong, wouldn't you?" My heart rate soared at the thought of him permanently disabled. What would he do with his life, I wondered as the quiet welled between us. Scott was not the sort to sit behind a desk; what other career would suit his temperament if he had to leave the job?

"God, what a worrywart you are, Brenna." The humor in his voice was as good as cold water thrown on a sleeping person. "Of course I'd tell you anything. We're friends, aren't we? And second," he continued, without giving me time to respond, "there's honestly nothing to tell. Just lying about the house, getting in my wife's and kids' way, eating too much and watching too much telly. What a wasted life I lead. Pathetic."

"And playing poker."

"Okay. You know me too well for me to pretend to be the perfect patient."

"But the doctors have talked to you, right? They've told you what to expect about your recovery time and if you'll be back, good as new." The scene in the wood near Howden Reservoir flashed again in my mind, Scott's body lying beneath the massive trees and ferns, his blood staining the rocks and seeping into the ground. "I mean," I shook off the nightmarish picture, "you can return to active duty…soon."

"They told me—sorry?" A muffled voice floated over the phone line and then Scott replied to the speaker. He must have turned back to me, for he said rather too cheerily, "The wife's telling me I have to get some rest. As though I'm running a marathon or something." The sound of springs compressing and of heavy breathing seeped into my ear. "Never disobey the spouse, Brenna. Second rule of a good marriage. Sorry. Gotta go. Talk to you again." He rang off before I could even wish him good night.

I eased the phone closed, laid it on the bedside cabinet, and slid into bed. The curtains at the open window angled into the room, like pale arms rising to pronounce a blessing. I turned onto my right side and stared through the window, into the night. Scott's wife must have been frantic when Scott was in hospital. Had she nearly panicked, thinking him close to death? Or could she cling to her faith, receiving a calm hope that Scott would fully recover? After my marriage, what will I feel if that is Adam? Will I find a way to live with my fear every time he goes on a call at night? Millions of other police spouses could do it, so why not I? I punched the pillow up beneath my head, encircling it with my arms, pretending I could be strong—for Adam and Scott. But despite Scott's assurances, I remained uneasy about his recovery. The knife thrust had been deep, the blows to his body multiple and severe. He would need months of recovery. Maybe even physical therapy. Was I about to lose my best friend in the job, my best source of help and advice? The night closed around me, lulling me to sleep with the sounds of baying dogs and singing whippoorwills, mixing with the suspicion that Scott's wife had ended the phone call at an opportune time. He never did tell me when he would return to duty. Or if.

Fourteen

From the desk of Scott Coral

"Scott! Answer the phone, you lazy-ass man! How long does it have to ring! Ahhhhhh! I'll get it myself!"

Quiet small talk and murmuring in the background as I sat in my favorite recliner. I'd just returned to watching a replay of Chelsea/Arsenal from last week, after concluding the phone conversation with Brenna, when another vocal tirade cut through the air.

"Itttt'ss foorrrr youuuuu!"

Most men married for 15 years would cringe at that, but I was just happy to hear a voice. The only sounds, courtesy of murderer King Roper, I should have been hearing were the sounds of dirt hitting my coffin weeks earlier. It was good to be alive.

"Hello?" I said cautiously.

"Is it really you, Coral?"

"Good to hear your voice, too, Keeler." I grinned at the straight-to-the-point greeting. Even if I hadn't recognized the voice, the accompanying environmental noises swelling in the brief conversational quiet identified the place. I could almost smell the cigarette smoke and feel the dimples of the heavy glass mug beneath my fingertips. "Perfect timing. I could use some of that swipes you keep with my name on it."

"You're dreamin', man. You've *never* had anything bad at my pub. You must be thinkin' of that slop The Mottled Duck serves."

"I guess so. I think that's where they get their beer, actually."
Keeler's laugh roared over the phone line, drowning out the
shouts from a nearby darts game. I refrained from saying what
I thought of his miserable hospitality as he added, "The lovely
Alexa Coral says she has had about enough of you around the
house, Scotty. I believe she would be *more* than willing to get shut
of you and let you out for a few pints. Which, by the way, could
be on the house as long as you keep us well chuffed with stories
of how the nurses 'took care of you' in hospital."

I didn't need to see him to know he had emphasized that last
phrase in finger-wiggling quotation marks. Of all the times for
me to be out of arm's reach...

The laugh exploded in my ear, underscoring that he was having me on. "It'd be smashing to clap eyes on you, Scotty. Besides,
I'd like you to meet someone. What are the chances of havin' a
chinwag soon?"

"How about now? I'm actually on the mend and can use the
time away."

"Right, then. I'll be here, but I warn you—we're busy. Don't
go gettin' yourself in another dust-up. I wouldn't want to have to
save your sissy ass for the millionth time." Click.

~

I laughed for a good two minutes after I left home. As I drove
to the Black Eagle Pub, I recalled the first time I met Stanley Keeler,
the pub owner. I was a new copper on the beat when several units
responded to a massive brawl. The man, although in his late forties at the time, towered above all others, and displayed massive
strength in his broad shoulders and chest. Years in Her Majesty's
Navy had given him a weathered look, thinning gray hair, and a
fondness for the occasional scrap—of which I doubt he ever lost.
His common sense style of dealing with a variety of patrons, as
an owner and as a man, during day or night shifts earned him
my respect and praise. I thought he would have made the perfect
copper, but I was glad he owned a place I considered my refuge.

"Coral!"

Keeler's booming voice somehow echoed through the entire establishment upon my entry. This was quite the accomplishment, what with the music, the loud replays of the day's matches on the tellies, and the obligatory drunken debates on who was really to blame for last year's World Cup debacle.

The bear hug was as powerful as the voice still pounding in my head. I hadn't even had my first Bass yet and I was already squiffy from sensory overload. Intensive care and lying around the house really did take it out of me. "Easy, old timer! I have a scar as long as your wanker and it's not quite healed." As I said it, I pulled the top of my shirt down across my shoulder and back. Although it was mostly hidden from my view, it was in full clarity to the others by the looks on their faces. The scar was a full 11 inches from shoulder to lower back.

"My Lord, Scotty, he filleted you like the cod I got in fresh from O'Leary's market this morning." Keeler chewed on his lower lip as he exhaled heavily. I thought he was going to storm out of the pub, jump into his car, and drive off to find Roper. Shaking his head, he said, "Well, not to worry about your little souvenir. When you speak to my friend Hugh, here, I'm sure he'll brighten your day. Hugh Claxton, meet Scott Coral."

Claxton smiled, but looked a bit dubious as he inclined his head toward Keeler. "Are you a friend of this chap, Mr. Coral? He tells me you're one of the few who can get through a scrum under any condition. And by the looks of that scar, and the fact that you're here to speak of it, I believe his assessment of you is spot on."

I grinned and tried to yank my shirt back into place. "For that compliment, the first round's on me."

Keeler smoothed the shirt across my back and carefully laid his arm across my shoulder. "Bahhh! I told you I had you covered this evenin', boy." He paused as he looked around the packed room. On the fringe of the main area, three chairs had been tipped forward so that they leaned against a table, making it the only unpopulated spot in the entire place. A subtle space, perhaps truly distinguishable only to the regulars, had been created by shoving the nearest tables somewhat away from this table. *In the room, yet apart.* It had the feel of a moat isolating a fortress, a no man's land designating opposing forces. So anyone sitting there could talk without being overheard? I glanced at the window near the table. It was set high enough into the wall so that no one standing outside could see in. Plus, it was closed. Nothing was discernible beyond its white painted wooden frame but the blackness of the night. The whole thing reeked of Secrets and Riddles. Pressing slightly on my shoulder, he nudged me forward. "Now, let's grab you a table so we can chat. Hugh, here, can be trusted. He's worked at Wakefield Prison for seventeen years and is now a Principal Prison Officer. He has some power—make no mistake, Scotty—and he gets that power through information. You may be shocked to hear what he's discovered." My face whitened as Keeler revealed the real reason I was summoned to the Black Eagle. Pints of Bass with old friends discussing all things fun was no longer a possibility. This was all about King Roper.

We were seated near Keeler's private office, in a corner as far as possible from the main action. The dart players, football diehards, and young courting couples were for the most part in the main dining and bar area away from us. Privacy was ours. Except for the eleven or so rugby players who just made their grand entrance. From the looks of them, it seemed they were all around twenty-two, built for the sport, and not at all happy for taking what appeared to be a loss prior to making it to the Black Eagle. Keeler would have his hands full with them as the beer flowed. Nobody better to handle it, though, as he would be in the middle of them within minutes, talking of their game and making new friends.

"I wanted to sit with you two for a moment before I get back to the bar," he said, perching on the edge of his chair. "Scott, Hugh is in a position to help, and more than that, he wants to do what is right by the police. He can do his own talking in a minute, but what gets said here, stays here. Roper must be dealt with. No friend of mine gets gashed open by slime like him; no other coppers get murdered with no repercussions aside from a prison stay." Keeler's face was getting more and more red as he spoke; the reason for the meeting was now clarified. My weeks in intensive care and at home recovering—thinking about retribution for Roper—were now coming very much alive. I was more than a little interested in hearing from Claxton now.

As I stared at Keeler, my words came slowly. "You know what I am, Stanley. My badge hasn't been tarnished in many long years in the job. It's how I can go home and look at my wife and kids with no shame, no regret." My fingertips tapped on the side of the glass as I expressed my feelings. "Let's be clear here. Roper murdered several people in cold blood. And now...well, look at me. A graying old copper who never thought he could lose a scrap—just out of hospital, which is where I should have died if the statistics had gone the other way. All from one thing I can loosely call a human being. King Roper." As I spoke, Hugh Claxton very noticeably shifted uncomfortably in his seat. He was now leaning forward, keeping his mouth shut, but anxiously waiting for a pause to jump in.

With his wire-rimmed glasses, Claxton had the look of a professor. Yet, his build reminded me more of a runner. But perhaps more than that, he appeared more studious than a person who merely worked with the worst of the worst in a maximum-security facility such as Wakefield. Although I trusted Keeler with my life, the tone of this conversation made me wonder who Hugh Claxton really was, and if he fully realized who he was dealing with by being here.

As I was about to speak, Keeler's massive right paw grabbed me by the back of my head and pulled me to within inches of his face. His words were like ice water splashing on a sleeping giant. "Roper will suffer in Wakefield, Scott. It *will* happen."

The room sounds faded as Keeler's words echoed in my head, louder and louder until I thought everyone else in the pub must surely hear it. How did Keeler know that? What was going on?

Claxton spoke quickly, quietly, emphasizing Keeler's last statement. "As Stanley here is well aware, Mr. Coral, King Roper also killed a very close friend of mine. I will not go into further detail. I don't need to remind you, either, that he put a fellow copper in the morgue, put DCI Geoffrey Graham in a coma, assaulted WPC MacMillan, and put you, Mr. Coral, in intensive care. A person such as that should not be sitting in front of a telly for the next fifty-four years of his life, getting fed and taken care of. He belongs in a deep pit to rot. Or…possibly other alternatives would be fitting." Claxton continued inching closer as he spoke. I didn't know whose eyes were more strained, his or Keeler's, as both men seemed capable of staring holes into rocks as he held my gaze.

Claxton eventually nodded at Keeler and, as if on cue, Keeler excused himself from the table. "Trust him, Scotty," he grunted, patting me lightly on the shoulder. "You're like my son; I wouldn't steer you wrong. Hear him out." He wandered back to the bar, his broad shoulders perhaps straighter than I'd ever seen them before.

"I don't know how familiar you are with corrections intelligence at Wakefield and other facilities," Claxton continued, "but our units are quite spectacular on the whole, learning who is affiliated with whom inside the walls. I can tell you Roper thought he was a big fish until he landed inside. Make no mistake, Roper has influence both inside and out of Wakefield, but the larger, more established gang sets are not at all happy with his arrival. In fact, we have learned some would like to see him go away permanently."

My heart kicked into overdrive, as though I'd just completed a mile run after an escaping burglar. Sweat suddenly beaded on my forehead and my throat tightened. I gripped the glass, pushing the blood from my fingers until the flesh showed white, needing something to hold on to as the room tilted.

Claxton, evidently, didn't notice. He took a quick sip of beer before asking rather nonchalantly, "Let me ask you, have you ever heard the name Sam Taylor?'"

The room pulsed between dark and darker as I fought to

understand the significance of Claxton's question. What was coming? Something to do with Brenna? I replied, "He's the brother of an acquaintance. I'm quite certain you knew that prior to your asking."

"Indeed. And he was moved on my authority after our unit found his life was in danger from henchmen loyal to Roper, henchmen doing time at Strangeways prison."

"Where Sam Taylor is," I murmured.

"Right. But here's the part we did *not* expect. As soon as the plot to kill Sam Taylor was uncovered, we learned that those three having contact with Roper regarding the Taylor plot all had backgrounds as informants with the Greater Manchester Police Drugs Squad. In fact, all had a role in taking down a major trafficking operation that landed two of the highest ranking gang members in Wakefield."

My head felt like it was going to spin off my neck. What other bizarre turns was this case going to take?

"They're referred to as the Dodders," Claxton went on. "An offshoot of the old Doddington gang. To say they're big fish is an understatement. You, being in the job as long as you have, are well aware of the deadly path the Doddingtons have blazed throughout the country."

I nodded, hoping that would suffice. I was incapable of speech at the moment. Wasn't this the stuff of Hollywood films? But this was real life.

"Both men have forty-year sentences as a result," Claxton said. "We have nine intel specialists devoted strictly to that group."

He rushed on before I could completely appreciate the manpower involved in all this.

"But here is the beauty of it all. In return for helping turn evidence against the Dodders, the three loyal to Roper all had their sentences cut in half. In fact, with good behavior, all could be out within two years." Claxton looked around the room, as though he expected to see the three sitting at the next table. "We know for a fact that Roper would be dealt with quickly if the Dodder hierarchy learned of his control of those three informers, the three who put their gang leadership in Wakefield through their cooperation with the Drugs Squad. In fact, the mind wonders at the level of suffering Roper would go through."

Again I nodded, my mind quick to picture some of those methods.

"Of course, how that information would be leaked, if ever, would be unknown to anyone, here *or* elsewhere, Mr. Coral."

The groundwork being laid was quite brilliant, and I found myself whistling quietly under my breath. But this was a dangerous conversation and I knew it. Should it ever be leaked, my knowledge of it would destroy my life. Oddly, my internal turmoil was minor, at best. Actually, it was nonexistent. I wanted and needed to hear more, but why was Claxton risking everything to tell me? He assumed—correctly—I would not get on the phone at that moment and have our own intel unit, not to mention MI-5, outside the door waiting for him at the end of our talk. After all, this was a plot to kill a killer. To remove a man who had caused more death and destruction, who had ruined more good families, who had been the closest to pure evil, than I had ever seen.

Claxton took a sip of his Tanqueray Ten on the rocks. How can I not like this man, I wondered. He knew quality gin.

He sat back as he drank, looking quite informal, and glanced around the pub. I chuckled to myself and leaned forward. Keeler was behind the bar, speaking with one of his employees and pointing to the rugby group. As I looked at him, he briefly nodded at me, as if in assurance that all would be right in the world very soon. I turned back to Claxton, but while doing so scraped my back across the chair. I gritted my teeth as the wood pressed against my still-tender flesh and the scar tissue. Ah yes, another reminder of Roper that I would carry until my death.

My resolve was complete, and, frankly, never in question with this plan. I asked Claxton to give me an idea of Roper's life while I'd been in recovery. He nodded, yet waited as David Keane, a pub employee, came over to us with a fresh pint of Bass.

"Funny you should ask." Claxton smiled for the first time that evening. He took off his glasses, exhaled on the lenses and carefully wiped them clean with his handkerchief. Replacing them, he made certain David was well away from us before adding, "I want you to know that you did quite the number on him."

"I'm glad something good came out of our little duel," I said, sniffing.

"I'm not sure you're aware, though, that you're not the only one with a permanent reminder of your 'meeting' on that day."

I wondered if one of the constables or prison officers had been injured escorting Roper to his cell.

Claxton soon cleared up that point. "I hear per our medical staff that King Roper will only have partial usage of his right arm. More specifically, you really screwed up his elbow and wrist. Something about ligaments being 'snapped' and permanent damage... Well, his attempts to hide his deficiencies from other inmates inside the walls have been the source of great humor to our staff. On that we congratulate you." With that, Claxton held up his glass, to which I gladly—and proudly—clinked with my Bass.

I had heard Roper was hurting when they got him into custody. But nobody ever told me the specifics after I was released from hospital. Noting I was in deep thought, Claxton asked if I wanted him to continue with his information.

My mobile phone rang into the brief quiet, sounding like gunshots and startling us both. I looked at the called ID panel. A call from home.

"Hello?"

"Scott, I hate to do this to you but work called and they need me in now. Can you come home? I know you've needed to get out during your recovery, but this is important."

Alexa needing to go into work at this hour was unusual, maybe a once every six months occurrence. But when it happened, she had to go.

"I'll be there soon," I replied. "No worries. I love you."

"Me, too. See you soon. Bye."

Hugh Claxton watched as I flipped the phone closed. His voice seemed more at ease, more casual now that the discussion about Roper was over. Perhaps it had all been a strain on him, too. "I understand if you must leave. Family, I assume. So go, and maybe we'll meet again down the road."

"A meeting I'll look forward to with great anticipation. Shall I say you have my wholehearted support, or did you already assume it?" We stood and shook hands.

"Please understand that this meeting was just to have a drink, should anyone ever learn we met here. Just a couple of old mates of Stanley Keeler sharing war stories." Claxton did not appear nervous as he made the statement. This was one cool customer, as my American wife would say.

"Right. Just a drink. Nothing more. It's been…interesting. Night." Keeler was not to be found as I thanked Claxton. And with that, I left the Black Eagle a different man.

Fifteen

I wasn't the only person stumbling into the early morning meeting the next day. Mark looked as though he suffered from a hangover, though he was immaculately dressed in brown trousers and tie, and a green and tan striped shirt. PC Byrd hurried in at the last moment, still talking on his mobile. He glanced at Graham, had the grace to look embarrassed, and snapped his phone closed before taking a chair somewhere in the back of the seating area.

Margo nudged me, asked if I had talked to Adam yet this morning, when Graham walked up to the white board, leaned against the edge of the table, and bid us good morning. Looking as though he had been up for hours, he was dressed in black trousers, aqua-colored shirt and tie. He took a quick sip of hot tea before dropping his opening bombshell.

"We've just begun investigating Reed Harper's murder," he picked up a dry erase marker, "and you've already assembled some valuable and interesting information. I congratulate you on this. Hold that in your mind while you hear this next bit. As you know, in any case there is a degree of pressure." He paused, waiting for our apprehensive murmurs to subside. "This case, unfortunately, brings more pressure than any of us, including me, has probably previously experienced. To be specific, the victim. Reed Harper is the brother-in-law of Divisional Commander Dirk Tierney." In other words, Superintendent Simcock's boss… Graham's boss' boss.

He let us think through the implication, his gaze taking in our reactions. Margo muttered something about all hell to pay if we did a cock-up on this investigation, while Mark exhaled heavily. After giving us a minute to more-or-less silently vent, Graham apologized for the pressure we were now under. "But Superintendent Simcock's feeling it from Divisional Commander Tierney, and I, in turn…" He stood up, the sign he was ready to begin our session.

"As I've just stated, we've begun making headway on the Reed Harper investigation. Margo and Byrd have been showing photos of the cloth found with the bones to the village residents. Detective-Superintendent Simcock has given us both cases, which you may know why…or can at least conjecture upon, if you're new to this type of case." He took another sip of tea before continuing. "Both remains, body and bones, are treated under the same investigation due to the golden rule of investigation. Which is?" He waited for someone to show that such a basic bit of school hadn't been forgotten.

"We don't believe in coincidence," Margo said.

Graham smiled and set down his mug. "Thank you, Miss Lynch. Coincidence can prove fatal. For us, the location where the body and bones were found could have significance to the murderer or body disposer. So we inquire about both, believing there to be a link. If there is none, another DI takes over the bones case.

"With that in mind, have either of you anything to report on the fabric investigation?" Graham looked hopeful, gazing from Margo to Byrd. Margo shook her head and Byrd said that no one could confirm that the fabric looked familiar. "Perhaps they just didn't want to," Graham said. "Do you think it's another case of not wanting to get involved with a police inquiry?"

Both constables said they had the impression that no one remembered seeing the fabric.

"Well, keep trying, will you? I suppose there are no photographs in the pub or the church hall, showing village events through the ages?" He walked around the table, staring at the walls. Nothing more recent than the announcements of the well dressing work schedule and the fete activities were posted. "Still, that doesn't predispose there aren't photos. Maybe tucked away in the vicarage, or the pub's back room. And I don't need any volunteers to chat up the publican and workers, buying pint after pint to 'pay' for their information. There are other ways to gain information than by my team sacrificing themselves for the sake of hangovers."

The comment produced laughs and groans, with some of the men snapping their fingers in disappointment.

Graham thanked everyone for their dedication to duty and walked back to the board. "Now, the facts so far on the Harper case." He picked up the dry marker, not so much to jot down notes—for the information was outlined and tacked up there already—but to use as a pointer. Rolling the marker between his palms, he started at the beginning of our case, restating and refreshing our minds as to the pertinent facts. He talked about Reed Harper's personal history—the many women he had had affairs with, how he and Marian met and married, the ad agency, Reed's work with the village fete and dominance as its director. Graham took us through the timetable of Tuesday night—when Reed was last seen, the order in which people left the meeting and Marian's subsequent talk to each person as she tried to find out where Reed had gone. Graham then moved our thoughts to the crime scene: who found the body, the how/when/where and why of the discovery. He talked about the scene itself—did it have significance to the killer or was it just a handy, anonymous spot where he could dump the body with little threat of being seen? From the body, he directed us to the postmortem report and to the opinions by the forensic team, pathologist and Home Office biologist—the insect cycles testifying to Reed's body having laid there approximately thirty-three hours, which gave us the probable time of death as ten o'clock Tuesday night.

Slapping his palm on the covers of several large albums lying on top of the table, he said, "If anyone needs to refresh his or her mind as to body and bones condition, crime scene make-up and detailed plans drawn to scale, or the postmortem…" He paused, looking around the room at each of us, his gaze finally settling on me. An unspoken, shared in-joke about my inability to get through a PM without getting sick. The room fell silent as each person, perhaps, mentally focused on a particular part of Graham's talk. A car roared down the road outside the church, and for a moment I thought of the lyrics coming from the car's radio or CD player. "Leave him lying in the bracken, leave him lying where he fell, better bier ye cannot fashion, none becomes him half sae well…"

I knew that song. It lamented the 1692 massacre of the Scots in Glencoe. The lyrics quickly faded as the car presumably drove off, but the seed had been planted in those few seconds. Had Reed Harper's killer made a statement by dumping the body in the wood? If so, as Graham had just reminded us, was the significance linked to the killer…or to Reed? I had no time to consider each option, for the ringing of someone's mobile phone broke the quiet, and I was mentally back again in the incident room.

Graham remarked that the major players—those associated most closely with Reed—were still being questioned and their alibis tested and retested. "Which brings us up to this moment. What about alibis or, conversely, opportunity for those connected with our victim? Taylor?"

I glanced at the open page in my notebook, then said, "The spouse is usually the first suspect, but Marian Harper doesn't strike me as Reed's killer, no matter if she hasn't a watertight alibi. She hasn't the build to haul a body around, but I suppose she could have an accomplice to do the heavy work. She had opportunity, being home at night. She could have met him somewhere. We don't know. But the time element suggests she could have killed Reed, though I don't know why. They both have money—both from family wealth—and the ad agency is doing well. So unless it's some motive we haven't yet uncovered…" The image of her and Edmund Worrall walking all snuggly up the hill last night hovered in my mind. I said rather hesitantly, "There's always the possibility of an affair, but I haven't learned anything like that yet."

Graham nodded, wrote the names on the whiteboard, and asked for other likely suspects.

Mark gave a brief recital of Kevin Harper and Clayton Warson. "That burglar alarm mishap smells like three day-old fish, but I can't see a reason for pulling a stunt like that. Kevin didn't need it as an alibi because he had the other workers with him while he took shop inventory. And Clayton told his wife he was going to the pub, which he did."

"If he told her ahead of time," Graham said, playing devil's advocate, "it makes Kevin Harper's burglar alarm episode look like the real thing. Clayton came along at the right time, thought it was a real burglary and stopped to investigate. Simple and innocent."

"Unless *Clayton* set it up," I suggested, my mind on fire. "Maybe Clayton told some story to Kevin, made it sound innocent, but said he needed to involve Kevin, himself, or have a story of an investigation. So Kevin falls in with Clayton's joke or whatever it is, sets off the alarm, and Clayton comes along and 'investigates the burglary' and then trots off to the pub."

Graham frowned. "What's the reason for this charade?"

"I don't know, sir. I've just thought of it. But for whatever reason, Clayton sets it up for that night, when Kevin has additional witnesses at his shop."

Margo glanced from me to Graham and said, "Maybe he, or Kevin, set up the phony burglar alarm as a reference for the future."

Graham leaned against the corner of the whiteboard and told her to continue.

"Well, Kevin, or Clayton, set up this phony burglar alarm mishap. It's set up on this night due to the employees being in the shop, so, as you said, there would be witnesses. Then, some near date in the future, Kevin's shop is robbed. The burglar alarm doesn't sound because Kevin purposely didn't set it—and the shop is burgled. Kevin loses money, items, whatever. Maybe he does it, maybe he's got an acquaintance who does it. However he sets it up, his shop is wiped out. He collects the insurance money and gets the double bonus of the money from the sale of the items when they're fenced." She waited for an opinion, for someone to shoot holes in her suggestion or to jump up.

Graham drew question marks after Kevin's and Clayton's names on the board. "Interesting, Margo. We'll keep that as a possibility. Anyone else?"

Mark said, "I keep thinking about Reed's assistant, Jenny Millington."

"What about her, Salt?"

"She left the meeting at the church that night before anyone else."

"You think she lingered in the shadows, waiting for Reed to be alone?"

"Possible. We talked to her yesterday and she wouldn't give us a precise answer as to why she left earlier. I know it may not mean anything—some people are just reticent to reveal their private lives to the police—but it's something we have to consider for the moment, at least."

"How would she know he would be the last to leave, that he would be standing there alone?"

Mark frowned. "That I don't know, sir. But several people stated that Reed seemed as though he was waiting for someone. He smoked a cigarette, implying he might be waiting."

I reminded him that Marian wouldn't allow Reed to smoke at home.

"So? Why smoke at the church, in the thick of the dark forest? Why not walk home and stand on your doorstep to do it? No, I don't buy that. Reed gave all the signs of waiting for someone."

"For his killer."

"Right. But of course he didn't know the person would kill him."

"Who do you favor as the killer?" Graham asked, his hands on the tabletop and leaning forward slightly.

"Got to be Jenny, doesn't it?"

"Doesn't *got* to be anyone, Salt. There's no proof yet. What's her motive? Blackmail? Revenge? Love? Protecting someone? Ambition? Answer the basic questions: who, what, when, where, how and why. Then you may be able to answer *my* question about motive."

"That's the same for Marian, Kevin and Clayton," Mark said. "All had opportunity, so the 'when' is pretty much taken as after the meeting. 'How' could be luring him to a house or into a car. Probably a car, so they could actually kill him there and drive him to the forest."

"But you've got all that nasty blood to get rid of in a car," I said.

"So they got him into the car, knocked him unconscious so he wouldn't question the forest destination and put up a fight when he was knifed, and drove him to the wood. Which also takes care of 'where,' in my opinion."

"But," I said, "*how* could Jenny have abducted and killed him? We saw her yesterday. She's tall, but she's slim as a model. She hasn't the muscle to lug him about. He's awfully big, Mark. You can't just skim over that with a blanket statement. That's a major detail. How? Did she set him up so he comes to her house and someone kills him there? Then she and this other person drive him to the wood and dump his body there? Did she just act as lure, someone he knew and therefore felt comfortable with, but the other person killed him? If so, again we have the problem of how he got to the wood."

"I didn't say it was perfect," Mark muttered, settling back in his chair. "So there are a few loose ends."

"Unfortunately," Graham said, "we can't say for certain how long Reed remained at the lych gate, smoking or not smoking. No one has admitted passing him on the road, seeing him at ten o'clock, say, still standing by the gate. If we had a witness..." He snapped his fingers and smiled. "Or if we had Mr. Holmes' favorite clue, the cigarette dog-end..." He picked up one of the albums that housed the photographs of the churchyard, handed it to Mark, and told him to find the snaps of the lych gate. As he walked back to the whiteboard, he said, "Marian Harper told me when Reed went missing that Reed smoked Lambert & Butler king size cigarettes. Now, despite that being the most popular brand in the country, we have his DNA sample—taken from the cigarette dog-end on the ground and matched to Reed. The photo—" He broke off as Mark pulled several photographs from the album's plastic sleeve sheets. Graham collected them and waited while we looked at the photos, then handed them back to Mark, who returned them to the album.

"One dog-end," Mark said, rather wistfully. "Not there very long, then."

"It still doesn't answer the question," I added, "if Reed smoked before going home or if he waited for someone."

"Which still could be Jenny. She left a few minutes before everyone else. She could have waited for him in the churchyard and they walked to her house together."

"Having an affair, do you think?"

"Motive?" Mark shrugged. "Though that did come up. Who said that?" He flipped through the pages of his notebook. "Ah!" He looked up, his eyes on me. "The constable's wife. Lynn Warson. She said Reed was a womanizer."

I nodded, recalling the interview. "She gave the impression he's had affairs nearly forever. Said he's been like that for twenty-two years."

Graham screwed up his lips. "Really? She literally specified that exact length of time?"

Mark pointed to the entry in his notebook. "Yes, sir. I thought it was odd, too. Sort of brings something else to mind, doesn't it?"

"Our missing person, Vera Howarth."

Sixteen

Derbyshire Dispatch, June 2009

Ryan Jones walked away from his friend's house in Cauldham, walked into the foggy night and disappeared into history.

Jones' disappearance more than worried his family, friends and police. It unfolded like the retelling of the legend of the black dog haunting the Winnats Pass region.

According to Jones' friends, whom he spent the evening with, Jones left around midnight.

"We were having a super time," David Brown said. "We played video games for a bit and had a beer or two. We played a few hands of poker and then Ryan said he had to leave. He had to get up early for work the next morning and didn't want to be out too late. I asked if he was okay with walking home alone 'cause it was kinda late and the fog was settling in. He said he'd be fine and he left. I don't know what happened, where he is. It's scared the hell out of us."

Jones and his friends met at the home of Tyler Smith, just outside Cauldham, on the Miners Road into Chapel-en-le-Frith. Brown, who left several minutes after Jones and following the same route, states he never saw Jones on the road. "I was driving slow 'cause of the fog. I was kinda surprised 'cause he couldn't have got home that fast. But there's a path that cuts through the wood, not far down the road. I thought maybe he took that route, saving some time 'cause it was late."

Brown and Smith add that as they stood outside the house, bidding Jones good night, they heard a dog howling. "Deep-throated bays," Smith said. "Never heard anything like it before. I thought I saw a dog across the street. A big, dark thing like a lab or boxer, but the fog was thicker over there. I wasn't sure. 'Sides, my neighbors haven't a dog."

Police have made extensive searches of the wood, roadway and the area around Cauldham. Caves and old deserted lead mines are rife in the region. Speculation that Jones might have fallen into an uncharted mine opening prompted further searches. Nothing has come to light as of this writing.

Supposition about Jones' disappearance runs the gamut from willful disappearance to spirit abduction. Which pulled the whispers of the black dog legend into the light of day.

Anyone with information on Ryan Jones or who may have seen something in the vicinity of Cauldham that night are encouraged to contact the Derbyshire Constabulary in Buxton.

Seventeen

Chad Styles, the well dressing coordinator in Upper Hogsley, seemed to Graham and me to be the person who could supply many of the Five W's and One H answers to our killer's identity, so Mark and I drove to the village.

"Rivalry can run deep," Mark said as we approached the Winnats Pass. "You've seen enough of that as a copper, Brenna. I shouldn't have to remind you." He slowed the car as he glanced at me, not knowing how I'd react on driving through the mountain gorge.

I gripped the armrest on the door, knowing I was acting a fool, but I needed to hold on to something. February's escapade may have been four months ago, but it still seemed like last week to me. Plus, I associated it with Scott. Scott, who had saved my life. Scott, who might not return to police work.

"You okay?" Mark asked, glancing at me.

I nodded, not wanting him to hear the tremble in my voice, and watched the mountain face slip by my window.

Upper Hogsley, nestled just off the A625, between Cauldham and Chapel-en-le-Frith, claimed a greater physical area and population than Cauldham, but it couldn't seem to claim the coveted Hope Valley Cup. About its only real tourist attraction was its medieval hall, nearly surrounded by sycamore and lime trees. Within the hall's great room, carved oak paneling presented a fine backdrop to the magnificent tapestries and an extensive collection of early keyboard instruments. I thought briefly how much Graham would like to play those virginals and harpsichords, thought how much I'd like to hear him play, then focused on the case.

"I agree, Mark, that rivalry sometimes runs deep," I said, glancing at him, "but to kill someone over a trophy? That seems absurd!"

"To you and me, sure, but maybe this well dressing clash has been going on for years. Maybe Chad Styles reached his breaking point and decided to eliminate his main competition before the competition started. Maybe by killing Reed, he thought to throw the coppers off the track. 'What? Me involved with Reed's death?' It's hard to imagine, but look at some sports team rivalries. Look at anglers' competitions."

"That's a bit extreme, Mark. Not every football fan or fisherman kills his opponent."

"Of course not! Not every jealous spouse kills his rival, either, but it happens. That's all I'm saying."

We drove the remainder of the trip in silence, Mark thinking of God knows what, and me watching the Peak District rush past us. A lone hobby soared above the heathland, searching, perhaps, for a meal. Hogweed and black horehound shook in the car's passing breeze, the white and pinkish lilac flowers reeling and clashing against each other. Clumps of timothy waved their brownish seed heads at us, the rustling of their tall, thin stems barely discernable over the drone of the car tires. In not too many more minutes Mark turned the car down a small road and on emerging from a tunnel of trees the village of Upper Hogsley sprang up before us.

After inquiring and much searching, we found Chad Styles at St. Basildes Church. He was directing the setting up of worktables in the church hall. Buckets of all sorts of natural objects, large scrolls of waxy yellow paper, and a collection of dressmaker tracing wheels, ice picks, knives and skewers fanned across a small table. A woman pinned a small, full-colored drawing of that year's well dressing designs to a corkboard.

"Chad Styles?" Mark asked as we walked up to a tall, hefty man.

"No, no. Set those buckets near the rest of the material," the man said, rather exasperated with a worker placing tall, aluminum buckets at each worktable.

"You're not Chad Styles? The woman by the door said—"

"What?" The man blinked, staring from Mark to me. "Sorry. Yes, I'm Chad Styles. You from the *The Hope Observer*? I didn't expect any reporters so soon."

"No. Police." Mark showed his warrant card and Chad took a step backward.

"Really?"

"Really."

"Why? What's the trouble?" He stared at me, perhaps wondering why a woman was needed to break bad news. For that was the usual assumption when police officers appeared on your doorstep…even figurative doorsteps.

"I'm Detective-Sergeant Brenna Taylor," I said to allay his fear. "This is my colleague, Detective-Sergeant Mark Salt. Derbyshire Constabulary. We'd like to ask you some questions concerning the disappearance and subsequent murder of Reed Harper."

Chad peered at my warrant card, turned pale, and motioned us to a corner. Mark set up three folding chairs and waited until we were seated before stating that we understood there had been a degree of rivalry between the two villages. "Between you and Reed Harper, too," Mark added.

"Oh, that." Chad squeezed out a smile from his ashen face. "I—You're making too much of that. A friendly rivalry, that's all it was. Just private bets between us each year. Nothing more."

"The Hope Valley Cup didn't mean anything to you, then?" I asked.

Chad's head jerked toward me. "Oh, sure. But not in the way you think. Friendly, like I said. I'd never— Well, I wouldn't hurt Reed. God, what kind of person do you think I am?"

"Pretty nice purse that goes along with the trophy. I've known people who'd kill for a lot less than five hundred pounds."

"I wouldn't. What I mean is, I wouldn't kill for any amount of money." Chad looked around the room, perhaps hoping he could make an excuse to end this. "Anyway, the prize money goes to the village, not the event's director. You've got it all wrong." Having said that, he seemed to relax. His posture slumped a bit and his back actually touched the chair.

"If we're wrong, we'd appreciate you telling us the truth, Mr. Styles. When was the last time you saw Reed?"

"This past Monday. Eighteenth of June. The day before he went missing."

"Where was that?"

"At his home."

"What time? Was anyone else there, or see you and Reed when you left?"

"You're saying I need an alibi? He went missing on Tuesday. I saw him on Monday. Many people saw him on Monday. People saw him on Tuesday, too. Even you can't believe I killed him the day before he still was seen." His anger had wiped out the anxiety that a police questioning sometimes brought on. His right hand swept over his head, bald and throwing back the light from the overhead florescent fixtures.

"I understand that, Mr. Styles, but what time in the day were you at Reed's house?"

"Oh." His tone dropped slightly, more in the realm of normalcy, and he said, "Noon. I left at two o'clock. We had lunch there and talked about possibly having some sort of event with our two villages."

"During the well dressing fetes?"

"No. Later in the year. Harvest home or some time."

"Were you the only guest?"

"What? Oh, yes. We hadn't decided on anything definite, just in the talking stage. When the event took shape we would invite others to think through the details. But that was a long way off."

"Reed's wife and daughter?"

"Not there. His wife had fixed a nice cold chicken salad for us—left it in the fridge—and baked rolls that we just had to heat up. She was out shopping or visiting someone, I believe. Maybe

I never was told." His hand slid down to his lap. "Whichever it was, she wasn't there. The daughter, Ilsa, was at school—or I just assumed she was."

"How did Reed seem that day?"

"How did he *seem*? What's that mean?"

"Did he seem worried or anxious about anything? Did he keep checking the time on his watch? Did he jump at ordinary sounds?"

Chad's lips pressed together and he glanced towards his right. He frowned, as though recalling that day five weeks ago. Rubbing his chin, he said, "No, nothing like that. He cracked a lot of jokes about the rivalry being dead, and wondered if his half of the cup would stand upright without needing to be propped up. Stuff like that. No, he wasn't worried about anything. Just confident and smiling as usual. In fact, when I rose to leave, he asked if I didn't want to stay a bit longer."

Mark shook his head. "He asked you to stay longer? What for?"

"Damned if I know. I thought we'd concluded our talk. The discussion had lapsed into the subject of healing wounds, on the personal and communal level. He said our villages needed this common fete, that it would benefit people in ways they couldn't imagine, that his family needed it more than anyone he could think of."

"He *said* that? He said his family needed to heal?"

The corners of Chad's mouth scrunched up and he looked faintly ill. "Why? What's the matter?"

"I don't know," Mark said, his fingers digging into the back of his neck. "Didn't that strike you as an odd thing to say?"

"Yeah, but I thought maybe he was exaggerating. You know how people do…say stuff to drive home a point or sway an opinion, make it sound worse or more exciting or glamorous than it is."

"How long have you known Reed? Were peculiar statements normal with him?"

"We've been friends for about twenty-five years, I guess, give or take a year. I could figure it our precisely if you need that."

"That's fine. Where did you meet?"

"At the Cauldham fete, actually. I'd heard it was nice…well, especially nice for a small village. I had just taken on our village's well dressing event, so I made the rounds of other fetes in the district, hoped to get some ideas. Reed hadn't yet taken over the managerial duties of Cauldham's fete, but he was the mastermind behind the well dressing panels. I wanted to glean the best of all the surrounding villages, polish up the ideas and make them our own. We needed to have the best fete, create the best well tableaux. That's the only way you bring in the busloads of tourists and their money." He waited for Mark or me to say something, then plunged on when we didn't. "Please don't think me greedy or unfeeling, but competition for the Hope Valley Cup is fierce. A dozen villages vying for the prize money and the prestige of winning, the prestige that guarantees tourists by the hundreds. Everyone wants to see the best well dressing panels, don't they?" He looked hopeful, willing Mark and me to understand and not condemn him.

"Do you know of anyone who might have been angry with Reed? Not necessarily connected with the village fete, but perhaps some other reason?"

Chad exhaled slowly and glanced at the workers in the room. "Not a soul. That's what makes this such a nightmare. Reed was highly respected. He did wonders for his village, garnering the prize and the assurance of the tourist trade. Why would anyone want to kill the golden goose?"

That's what we're trying to discern, I thought, looking at the worktables and the villagers arriving with boxes and buckets of material to create the well panels. "Your well dressing must come before Cauldham's, Mr. Styles. They've not begun even setting up yet."

"Yes. We're the day before Cauldham's. Our dressing is this coming Thursday, the twenty-eighth. That's St. Basildes' day. Our church is St. Basildes."

"What's your theme this year?"

"Przewalski's wild horse. The wild horse of Mongolia," he

explained when I looked blank. "They're endangered. A beautiful creature. We hope that with our panels we can bring attention to their plight and do some good for them."

Mark and I thanked him for his time, gave him a business card, and got his assurance that he'd phone us if he thought of anything pertinent to the case.

We were just to the door in the church hall when a man of about nineteen came into the room. He nodded to the greeting thrown out by the woman at the front table and brushed past Mark's shoulders when I turned and called out his name.

"Trevor?"

He stopped mid-stride, spun around on his heel, and asked if I needed to speak to him.

"If you're Chad Styles' son, I do," I said as Mark came up behind me.

Trevor's eyebrows raised in curiosity when I introduced Mark and myself and explained that we'd like to ask him some questions about Reed Harper.

"Sure. Anything." We walked to a quiet corner of the room. "Not that I'll be much help. Dad knew Reed a lot better than I did."

"How long had they known each other?"

"Hard to say. Longer than I've been alive, I know that. Maybe two decades, maybe longer."

"Were your father and Reed merely business acquaintances or were they also friends? Business acquaintances as in they were both directors of their respective village's fetes."

"They talked occasionally about their festivals—you know, discussing the funding that was drying up from the councils and how to attract more people to their events. But it wasn't all business with them. They'd go fishing together, or go to a football game, but it wasn't what I'd call regular. Not like a pint at the pub every Friday night." He looked at us with wide, honest eyes. They were hazel, nearly matching his dark blond hair color. He hadn't his father's height, being approximately five foot eight, and he was thin—a contrast to Chad's bulky build. But where

Chad's strength may have been in his managerial prowess, Trevor's strength lay visibly in his biceps. Probably from shifting those heavy well dressing panels about, I thought, envisioning Trevor throwing the thick-beamed wooden frames over his shoulder.

"Did Reed irritate anyone?"

"What do you mean irritate? He came on a bit thick at times, all gung ho and my way or the highway attitude, but he got results, didn't he? Look how often Cauldham's won the Hope Valley Cup. You can't argue with success."

"Some might," Mark said, drawing Trevor's attention. "Is it the end justifying the means, or is it do unto others?"

"So he was a bit ruthless. No one got hurt from his bulldozing method. He's a ruddy good manager and his whole village probably thanks the day he took over that job."

"Did his job intrude upon his home life, do you know?"

"Can't say. I know he had his nine-to-five job at the ad agency. That must've taken a bunch of time in itself. Then he'd be working on the fete on his time off most of the year. People don't realize how much time and planning those things take. If you're going to bring in name talent, that takes time to negotiate. Then, there's also the judging of the well panel art submissions, the judging of the queen and princess contests, not to mention booklet design and printing and hunting down the info for those, the concessions and game booths and rides."

"I understood he had assistants and volunteers to help with that."

"Sure. Every village does. But he's got to meet regularly with the committees to see if there are problems. It takes a lot of time. Why, nearly as soon as this year's well dressing is over they'll start in on planning next year's."

"So, what you're alluding to is that Mrs. Harper might not necessarily see her husband all that much."

"I don't know, but I don't see how. Ilsa, their daughter, complains a lot that her dad was never around to do things with her or go to her recitals and stuff. It was hard for her."

I asked how he knew that.

He averted his gaze and fell silent for a moment. The hubbub of the room filled my ears—table legs scraping across the linoleum floor, metal buckets clanging together as someone carried them to another place, doors opening and the kitchen hatch rolling open, ceramic mugs clinking as they were stacked onto a plastic tray... Trevor looked at me, his eyes suddenly filled with pain. "Because she told me. Because we love each other and we're going to be married. Because she's ready to strike out on her own, away from her parents, and control her own life." He finished in a rush of words and feelings.

"What does she want to do? You mentioned her recitals. She performs, obviously, but what? Is she a pianist?"

"That, yes, but she's mainly a singer. She's star quality. Really." He smiled tentatively, willing us to believe him. "I'm not just saying that 'cause I love her. Ask anyone—here or in Cauldham. She's super."

"Does she perform at the fete?"

Trevor snorted, as though that was the stupidest thing he'd ever heard. "Not allowed to, is she?"

"Who won't allow her to sing? Some committee? Is there a talent committee?"

"Harding Lyth won't let her."

"The vicar?" I didn't believe Trevor but asked, "What right does he have to stop her?"

"His daughter, Angela, is the MC of the fete. She's also the main singer. Well, except for any name group they might have performing. Angela's using the fete as a springboard to fame and fortune. She figures if she can get noticed, she'll have no trouble landing a job in some musical. Or even get offered a solo contract. And Harding, being a supportive, doting father, does the fatherly thing by keeping all rivals from Angela's microphone."

"I can't believe the vicar can get away with that. Surely there are other artists besides Ilsa who want to perform."

"Probably, but until Angela has her hard won contract, the

good people of Cauldham will probably have to put up with her MCing for years to come."

"How do you feel about Ilsa's singing career?"

He glanced again across the room. A woman tidied a stack of brochures she'd just set on the information table. "That's the trouble with this whole thing," Trevor said slowly. His right hand fingers curled into a fist and he slammed it into his open left palm. "I love Ilsa, desperately and completely. I want her to follow her star, to become the person she needs to be. But I don't want to lose her."

"How would you lose her? If you two get married—"

"I'd lose her if she maybe becomes the village MC one year. I'd lose her if she gets too famous and doesn't want to marry or settle down 'cause she thinks it will hurt her image with her fans… or she won't be able to shoot off for some venue in the antipodes. I'd lose her if her dad succeeded in getting Harding to let Ilsa MC and sing one year. Reed's like that…bribery to Harding in some form, or to Angela by getting her an agency contract. Reed may be a busy man but he does love Ilsa, and if she finally talks him into twisting Harding's arm so she can sing at the fete…" He sniffed, as though he was about to cry. "I mean, Ilsa is seventeen. She should live her own life."

I thought Trevor had just provided someone with a great motive for getting rid of Reed.

Eighteen

Diary Entry, 26 February 1989

Another birthday is looming. Two months from today I'll be eighteen. It's time for serious planning. I mean, I've got the rest of my life ahead of me. Clayton is pressing me for an answer, but I'm not that sure yet. I mean, I love him, and I hate it when we're apart, but how would it feel to always be with him? *Always.* A date is one thing—you spend the evening or the day together, but then you part and you go back to doing your own thing and you live with Gran and stuff. But when you're married you're together all the time. You go shopping or spend the evening with friends, but you have to go home eventually and then you're together again and start the whole thing over again. Gol, I just re-read these previous lines—it sounds like I'm not keen on Clay, or I don't want to marry him. That's the problem! I *do* love Clay and I *do* want to marry him, but maybe not right now. Not until I've had a chance to taste life, really taste it and hold it and see if I want to be something that necessitates further schooling. Clay is the love of my life and I can't see myself with anyone else, but I don't know if I'm ready for such a serious, unchangeable step. What if I tell him yes and then decide later I made a mistake? I'll hurt him and I'll hurt myself. It'll be with both of us for the rest of our lives, scar any future relationships we may have. I love Clay too much to hurt him like that. But enough gloomy thoughts!

I've not even decided anything yet and I'm sounding like an old maid! Too many emotions running around. I can't decide one way or the other like this. Another few months and I may know better what I want to do about Clay and about the rest of my life.

Nineteen

Driving back in the car, I told Mark that it could be quite handy for Chad Styles that his village had a day's advantage on Reed Harper and Cauldham.

"What do you mean?"

"Are the year's well dressing designs a closely guarded secret?"

Mark shrugged. "Don't know. Why?"

"If they *are* kept secret, and if Chad knew what the villagers of Cauldham were going to do…" I looked at him, hoping he was following my reasoning.

"You think Chad broke into the place where Cauldham's well dressing designs are kept, or bribed someone to show them to him. Then, having got a gander at the theme and drawings, Chad slinks back to his village, whispers into the appropriate ear, and they come up with something they think will best Cauldham."

I nodded.

"Won't do, Brenna."

"Why not?"

"There's no history of them doing the same theme. Besides, that coincidence would be a real finger-pointer to someone in either village being a spy and a sneak. No one's ever done that. Secondly, what's Chad got to gain? Even if he saw the well dressing designs, it doesn't mean Upper Hogsley's rendition of them would be better than Cauldham's. That's where individual talent shines. Cauldham may be a smaller village than Upper Hogsley, but they just might have better artisans for panel making. Must have had them for years, or Chad and his village would have won the cup. Nope. Try again."

We tried again with Ilsa, Reed's daughter. Being Saturday, we found her with a small group of villagers in the churchyard. They were weeding the perennial border along the south side of the church. Getting ready for the well dressing and festival, I assumed.

Auburn-haired Ilsa Harper sat with Mark and me on a wooden bench beneath a large sycamore. We were some distance from the church, out of the earshot of the workers. Although a few of them had cast curious glances our way, they soon returned to their gardening and chatter. I noticed a clump of daisies that needed deadheading, but the workers would get to that.

Ilsa confirmed Trevor's statement: she wanted to be a singer. "I'm starting to panic," she said, her brown eyes darker in the shade of the tree. "I'm seventeen. I haven't really done anything toward my career except get a portfolio together of photos that Perry Bowcock took of me. If I don't get a break soon, I'll be too old."

Mark said Trevor seemed to be very supportive of her career choice.

"He is, and that's partly why I love him. I know he'll follow me to the ends of the earth, help me do whatever I need to do in order to get my career."

"It's wonderful to be so focused and to have someone who believes in you like that."

"I know I'm lucky having Trevor. He's even suggested to his dad that I sing at Upper Hogsley's fete next week."

"Nice for you."

"Isn't it? If I can't perform here." She pouted slightly as she glanced at Harding, who was raking up a bunch of dead leaves wedged between a tombstone and a tree trunk. "Well, it's just nice to have someone who thinks you're good enough so as not to embarrass the village."

"Too bad your father couldn't get you a spot here. I'm surprised, actually, since he's the festival director."

She glanced in Harding's direction, but he had worked around behind the church. Looking at Mark, Ilsa said, "It's not that easy. Dad may have been the overseer of the whole thing, but Angela is the MC. Has been for years."

"Kind of a tradition."

"Yes."

"Still, I'd think that the MC job could be traded off a bit. Like every other year Angela could do it, letting other people, such as you, a chance. Your dad couldn't help you with other venues, perhaps? Or talk to Harding about it?"

"My dad helped a lot of people. He had a lot of connections, developed through his ad agency and during his tenure as fete director. People were always asking him for help."

"Financial?" I asked.

"No. More like…" Ilsa took a deep breath and bowed her head slightly. When she looked at me, her eyes were moist. "Getting them interviews or auditions. He knew a lot of people in the entertainment world."

"Anyone angry at him, perhaps over a failed audition or not getting to speak to some music mogul?"

"Not that I know of. Maybe mum would know. But I think I would've heard if there had been. Dad usually kept business and home life separate, but occasionally he'd rant to someone over the phone. Usually it was Harding or his assistant, Jenny Millington."

"But no one specifically you know of who might have been extremely angry or upset by an unsuccessful media deal or canceled contract or the like."

"No. I never heard. But I suppose that doesn't discount there being someone." Her fingers toyed with the charm on the gold chain encircling her neck. "I'd understand if someone was that enraged, though. It hurts when your dreams don't come true."

"And he didn't help you that way."

"No. I used to ask him for years, beg him to give me just one introduction, but he never would do. He said it wouldn't look right, him handing out favors like that to family. He'd lose all credibility." She gave me a hint of a smile, but her eyes remained serious. "I never could understand that. I used to lie awake nights trying to figure out why I wasn't good enough, what had I done to make him so mad that he wouldn't even help his own daughter when he seemed to help everyone else, including those who were leeches and clung to him. I've come to accept it, albeit slowly and with great pain. I understand the code he had, but it still doesn't soften the hurt. Not when you want something so bad." She wiped away a tear with the back of her hand, sniffed, and gave a slight shrug. "But that was Dad. Ethical and professional. And no matter how disappointed I was, I have to admit that he didn't do things behind people's backs like Uncle Edmund does."

I sat up straighter, preparing myself for a bombshell. "What does your uncle Edmund do?"

The answer came quickly and with a burst of emotion that surprised me, considering her short stature. "He tried to talk Mum into leaving Dad. Dad hadn't a clue."

~

Edmund Worrall, Reed's half brother, also seemed to be spending his morning gardening. He was attacking a large hosta, breaking it into smaller pieces, when we called to him. A half-dozen holes, dug beneath a good-sized birch, already held what looked to be a mixture of peat moss and fertilizer. Edmund set the hosta pieces on the ground, brushed his soiled hands on his worn jeans, and eyed our warrant cards with some misgiving. He nodded when we said we'd like to talk to him about Reed's death, and I joined him on a white painted wrought iron loveseat. Mark stood on Edmund's opposite side and fired off the first question.

"I did not *try* to get Marian to leave Reed," Edmund said, challenging Ilsa's statement. "I suggested it. As a way out of her misery."

"Her marriage to Reed wasn't going well?"

Edmund snorted. "That's one way of stating it."

"And the other?"

"It was going to hell in a hand basket. Fast."

"Did she tell you that?"

"Yes. We talked several times a week, over morning coffee or after tea, when Reed worked late. Sometimes we'd walk in the wood—she loved the wood in any season, any weather. She still felt a link to it, having once been in her family. Our talks were important, if for no other reason than to think aloud. She'd ask for my opinion or advice, but not all the time. Mostly we'd just sit and talk. Late at night seemed an especially good time because no phone calls interrupted us. Oh, nothing inappropriate went on," Edmund added heatedly, his face reddening. "Just get that thought out of your mind. I loved Marian as a friend. I couldn't stand to see her hurt anymore."

"Nice that she has someone to confide in."

"Yes, well, she needed to think it over. Her marriage, I mean. I was a natural choice."

"Because you're Reed's brother and knew their history?"

"That, sure, but also because we were close. Best friends close. It'd take weeks to explain everything to a marriage counselor. But I knew her and Reed, knew what had happened during their marriage. She'd confided in me for the last few years when their problems worsened."

I asked, "Did you know Marian before she married your brother?"

"Sure. She'd come over to the house for family parties, she'd go on short trips with Reed."

"How old were they when they began dating?"

"They were both twenty."

"And how long have they been married?"

"Twenty-five years."

"When did the problems in their marriage start? When did Marian begin confiding in you?"

"I don't know exactly. Maybe five years ago. It's been a while." He ran his handkerchief around his neck, blotting up the perspiration.

"Is that when their marriage became shaky?"

"No. She said she'd had problems earlier than that, going

back many years before she broke the news to me, but she never quite believed it. You know how you can talk yourself into imagining things."

"What were these problems? Money? Workaholic husband? How to rear Ilsa?" I deliberately didn't propose infidelity. I wanted Edmund to tell me without suggesting it. I needn't have worried.

"Affairs."

Mark caught my eye, shaking his head slightly. He said, "More than one?"

Edmund turned to face Mark, not an easy job considering Edmund's bulk and the smallness of the loveseat. "Yes. Reed may be my brother, but that's no reason to whitewash the truth. He was a womanizer, cheated on Marian during their marriage. Since *before* their marriage, if I'm completely truthful."

"Did Marian know this when she married Reed?"

"No."

"Did you know how your brother was like that when they dated?"

"No. He had a bunch of girlfriends, of course. Well, at twenty, you'd expect him to have dated a lot. But I never knew he'd actually slept with anyone. I found that out later."

"In time to tell Marian before the wedding?"

"No. I wish I had. It would have saved her years of pain."

"When did Marian first discover Reed was cheating on her?"

"I'm not sure. Like I said, she first started talking to me five years ago. She suspected he was sneaking around on her before that, but she wouldn't admit it. If you deny the reality, however much you suspect it, it doesn't hurt as much. Denial sometimes is a wonderful thing."

"How did she finally find out?

Edmund leaned forward, his forearms on his thighs, and clasped his hands. "The usual thing. Several phone calls. The old 'If a woman answers' cliché. Except, it proved to be real enough. Marian would answer the phone and the minute she'd say something there'd be a click on the other end and the line would go dead. This happened several times and Marian started getting suspicious."

"More coincidental than a wrong number."

"Yes. Her doubt grew as Reed's phone calls would end abruptly whenever she'd enter the room, his weekend work trips—though verified by his secretary and other co-workers—seemed disproportionate to the clients' needs. She eventually caught him through a mobile phone number scribbled on a scrap of paper and a lie."

"What was the lie?"

"That he'd been on a fishing trip with a client, trying to convince him to sign up with Reed's agency."

Mark shrugged. "Normal enough. On a par with wining and dining prospective clients, taking them to concerts or treating them to golf games."

Edmund nodded. "But firstly, the client phoned Marian to ask a question. This was a Friday afternoon, when Reed supposedly had met the client for the fishing weekend."

"Bad."

"It gets worse. Marian, of course, was surprised and confused. She asked the client if he had an appointment with Reed, and the client said no. She asked if anything had been set up, for any time, at the Izaak Walton Hotel at Dovedale. He said no. By the way," Edmund added, his voice lightening a bit, "Marian did find out Reed had been at the hotel at that time. But with a woman."

"Nail in the coffin."

"So, that's bad enough. Then, when Reed returns home quite late Sunday night, he has a few trout with him. To lend credibility to his fishing weekend."

"I suspect something was wrong with that."

"This all happened on the nineteenth of October."

I made a face. "Fishing season ends in that area four days earlier."

"You have to give Reed points for trying, even if he is a bastard."

"Did Marian find out whose mobile phone number he had?"

"Oh, yes. She called it. A woman answered, of course, but wouldn't reply to Marian's question who she was speaking to. She thought the voice sounded familiar so she looked through Reed's phone index. Voila, as they say. Clarice Millington."

"Who's Clarice? A relation to Jenny, I assume." First time I'd heard the name.

"Clarice is Jenny's sister, younger by three years. Twenty-two years old and acting like she's sixteen. Clarice met Reed through Jenny, Jenny being Reed's assistant."

"When was this fishing trip/Clarice thing?"

"Four years ago. Marian thought Reed's sleeping around would end because she confronted him with Clarice's name."

"But it didn't."

"Not as long as the sun rises each day." Edmund sat up, his lips pressed together, his breathing loud and slow.

Mark said, "Did Marian know how many woman he'd slept with?"

"I doubt it. I doubt, too, that Reed knows. But it's been dozens. Marian realized that when she found unfamiliar things in a box in his office."

"What sort of things?"

"A few letters, a necklace, photographs. Souvenirs, if you want to call them that, of his conquests." Edmund crumpled the handkerchief in his sweaty hand. "None of the affairs seem to last very long. But they don't have to; the sheer number and the betrayal hurt."

"Knowing all this, then, about Reed's philandering, you didn't physically try to break up their marriage? If you cared for Marian—"

"What was I supposed to do? Drag her off to a nunnery? I talked to her till I was blue in the face. She kept saying she needed to work things out in her own mind before she did anything as drastic as divorce."

"Even with all these affairs thrown in her face, she felt like that."

"I know she'd have been better off if she married me. I felt something for her when we first met, but she had eyes only for Reed at that time. As I learned about his affairs, I felt even more strongly that she and I should be together. Reed didn't have enough time for Marian—work, sure, but how can you make time for your wife if you're running around on her with this many women? But I didn't actively try to destroy their marriage. She always knew that I'd be waiting for her should she decide to divorce Reed."

"Do you think she came to a breaking point, that she couldn't stand his cheating any longer, so she killed him?"

Edmund took a few seconds to answer, his gaze turning in the direction of Marian's house. He said slowly, "I don't know what people are capable of. I don't know what happens when someone is pushed beyond her capacity to emotionally handle something. I only know about myself, about how I'd react to certain things. Don't they say we all have the ability to kill if someone we love is in danger, if it's a crime of passion?" His dark, serious eyes challenged me to contradict him. He added, somewhat as an afterthought, "Wouldn't she have snapped before this, though? Why would she kill him now?"

Twenty

Jenny Millington's sister, Clarice, boarded with a family several houses down from Edmund, on the northern side of Old Church Lane. She reluctantly let us into her main room—a sitting room converted from a bedroom toward the back of the house—and sat on the edge of her chair. Her gaze shifted constantly from me to Mark, as if wondering who would actually speak to her.

After introducing us, I asked Clarice if she knew Reed Harper.

She cleared her throat, blinked, and clenched her hands together. When she spoke, her voice broke and she cleared her throat again. "Uh, sure. Yes. I know him. *Knew* him. He coordinated the well dressing fete. Why?"

"How else did you know him?"

"How else?" Her eyebrows raised and she glanced at the clock.

"Yes. In what other manner? Surely that's not such a difficult question."

"Oh, well, do you mean my sister, Jenny, worked for him? She was his assistant on a sort of part time basis for the fete." She looked at me again, hopeful that she had answered correctly.

"You knew him another way, didn't you?"

"Well, I knew he owned that ad agency in Buxton, but I never went there."

Mark leaned toward her, cutting the space between them in half. "Quit wasting our time. You know what we mean. You and Reed had an affair. What about that?"

Clarice's mouth dropped open but she produced only a faint squeak.

Mark gripped the edge of the coffee table with his left hand and pointed his right index finger at her. "Marian Harper found out about it, didn't she? She phoned you, wanting to discover who her husband was fooling around with. When you wouldn't tell her, she found out anyway, in another manner." His voice lowered, taking on a conspiratorial tone. "What happened, Clarice? Did you confront Reed some time later? Maybe demanded that he choose between you and Marian?"

Clarice sank back in her chair, her eyes shining with fright. "No. It wasn't like that! That's not how it happened. Believe me."

"We'd like to," I said. "Tell us."

She glanced at Mark, perhaps making sure he wasn't going to spring at her, then told me, "We went away for the weekend."

"When was that?"

"Four years ago. Seventeenth through the nineteenth of October. Friday through Sunday. Well, we left the hotel late Sunday. W-we stayed at the Izaak Walton Hotel."

"Did Reed make any promises to you—either in regards to a career or marriage?"

"No. He treated me wonderfully. I-I'd never been treated like that before, not from any of my boyfriends. He made me feel special, like I was the only person he had ever loved or would ever love."

"You knew he was married," I suggested.

"Yes. But I'd seen the friction between him and his wife. Jenny, my sister, was aware of it, too. I should think that most everyone in the village knew they weren't getting along. Marian—she tried to hide it, and she probably did fool some people. But those of us who worked with them or were really close to them knew they had problems."

"Did you know what those problems were?"

Clarice nodded and bowed her head slightly as she said, "Reed was unfaithful to her."

"You didn't consider that you were compounding their problem?"

Her head jerked up and she stared at me as though I'd just slapped her. "How could I be compounding the problem when he told me he loved me, that he was never happier than when he was with me?"

"He never offered you marriage?"

"No. We never talked about it. Well, I said something once, but he changed the subject. He never brought it up again."

Mark and I exchanged looks. Amazing how gullible some people were.

"When did Reed first approach you?" I asked. "How long had your affair been going on?"

"Oh, he didn't start it. I did."

Mark frowned. "Pardon? *You* started it?"

"I'd always been attracted to him—he was so dynamic, always knew how to get what he wanted in life, always took chances and won. I-I didn't want anything for myself. Well, not what people usually plague him for. You know…introductions to agents, a try-out in front of some London theatrical producer, a recording session to make a CD demo. None of that mattered to me. I like being a receptionist in a car dealership. I didn't care what I did as long as I could be with Reed."

"But wasn't that relationship rather tenuous? After all, you weren't the first woman he'd had an affair with. Witness your sister, who was infatuated with him."

"That had more to do with her job than with him."

"Oh yes?"

"Reed made noises about making the well dressing and the fete larger next year. He wanted to best every village and town in the county. Jenny thought if the festival got too large she'd be swamped with work and she wouldn't have enough time for her freelance writing. She got paid something, of course, for being Reed's assistant, but her real job was her writing. She didn't want that to suffer."

"So if the festival grew too much—"

"She'd see her writing career go down the tubes. Her feelings for Reed were mixed. She slipped into a depression when she found out he was seeing me."

"Did that alter your relationship with her? You weren't concerned you were hurting your sister?"

"No. She kind of shoved that behind her and concentrated on her job. Anyway, she probably knew she never really had a chance with him. I mean, he's fantastic in bed and fun to be with, but Jenny's not exactly the life of the party. Reed liked lively women. That's why I thought we were so good for each other. Why I knew we'd end up together."

"He never left his wife for anyone, though. And how long had he been having affairs?"

"But our love was different. He told me so. Besides," she said, rather hesitantly, "I figured if he and Marian broke up, I would move in with Reed...either as a companion or as his wife."

"But your affair was four years ago, by your own admission. Did you do anything to try to get him back, to leave Marian?"

"No," she said, her voice tinged with grief. "I just thought he'd get around to it one of these days."

~

Mark and I were steps from the pub, needing lunch and needing to discuss that day's developments. I had just commented on what would be the faster choice to appease my consuming hunger—salad and scone or ploughman's lunch—when Clayton Warson walked up to us, calling our names.

When a copper connected however thinly to a case calls your name, it usually doesn't fill you with all the fun of a fair. Mark and I waited near the door and greeted Clayton when he joined us. His face was flushed and he took several deep breaths before explaining that he had been on his way to see us at the incident room. "But then I saw you here."

"You look rattled. Anything the matter?"

"No. I mean...well, yes." He took a paper-wrapped package from his jeans pocket. The packet was perhaps an inch thick and about the size of a tea bag. Holding it tightly in his hand, he asked if we could go somewhere private. "I need to tell you something."

I looked across the street. The bench beneath the huge yew was vacant. It also angled away from the street, lending some privacy to any conversation there. "Is that private enough, or would you rather go to the incident room?"

"No. The yew is fine. Anyway, I don't know why I'm so worried about being overheard. This'll be all over the village before too long."

We followed him across the road and sat beside him under the tree. As with Edmund, Mark chose to stand. He rested his right foot on the bench seat and leaned forward with his arms folded on top of his thigh. I asked Clayton what we could do for him and he laid the package on his lap.

"I need to confess," he said simply, shifting his gaze from Mark to me.

"Why?" I asked, wondering if our murder inquiry was going to be wrapped up as easily as a confession. "What have you done?"

"It's not in the league of withholding evidence, but I did have a struggle with my conscience about it." He handed me the package. It was heavy, a bit less than the weight of a small digital camera. As I unwrapped it, he said, "There's a long story that goes with this. That's what I need to tell you."

I untied the string keeping the brown paper folded, laid it on the bench, and slid the paper off the object. A silver pocket watch, its case covered with an engraved monogram, rested in my palm. The watch looked to be very old.

"It was my grandfather's," Clayton said, by way of introducing the subject. "I got it on my sixteenth birthday."

"Nice," Mark said. "This connected to what you want to tell us, then?"

Clayton nodded, his face losing its color. "There's no easy way to say this, so I'll just start. You know when you showed me the photos of the bones and fabric found in the wood?"

I nodded and Mark muttered that he recalled something of that nature.

"Well, I could've identified the fabric right away, without even stopping to think. It was from a blouse my girl friend wore. She wore it the last time I saw her, the day she disappeared. You see," he said, his voice barely above a whisper, "my girl friend was Vera Howarth. The woman who's been missing for twenty-two years."

Twenty-One

"I didn't want to admit it, not right then. I-I was afraid my wife would find out, that you'd question her immediately."

"Just having a former girl friend is not a thing a spouse would get upset about," I said. "Nearly everybody has at least one old boy or girlfriend. It's natural. You date before you marry."

"Vera and I were engaged."

"I still don't see why that needs to be kept secret."

"You don't understand."

"No," Mark said, irritation creeping into his voice. "We don't. If you'd quit pussyfooting around and tell us."

"If you'd open the case of the watch."

I pressed the button on the crown. Front and back covers opened simultaneously, hinging out from the numeral six at the bottom of the clock face. It was a double hunter case, exquisite in its craftsmanship and fascinating in its working mechanism. A lock of wheat-hued hair, tied together with a bit of blue ribbon, had been coiled inside the bottom of the clock but fell onto my lap as the case opened.

Clayton leaned over, picked up the hair and laid it gingerly inside the open case. I curved my hand around the clock, protecting the hair from any gust of wind.

"This is Vera's hair. She gave it to me as a Valentine's Day love exchange. I gave her a lock of mine. She put mine in a heart-shaped locket I'd given her for her sixteenth birthday, and I put hers...well, here in my pocket watch."

"When was this?"

"Twenty-two years ago. 1989. I was nineteen and Vera was seventeen. Well, nearly eighteen. Her birthday was quite soon, nearly two months away, on the twenty-sixth of April."

"When did she actually go missing? Right after Valentine's Day?"

"Oh no! Not until the second of April. So, you see, we had over a month together after I asked her to marry me."

"You asked her on that Valentine's Day?" I didn't say so, but I thought it a romantic gesture.

"Yes. She was just about eighteen, as I said. Only lacked three weeks."

"Why have you brought this to us now? Why not when Vera first disappeared?"

"There was no need to do it then. She just vanished; no body was ever found so there was nothing we could match her hair to. There was a search of the area, of course, but nothing turned up. It hardly began before it was called off."

"Yes. I remember, you told us yesterday about the note stating she decided to go to London."

"Which was postmarked on the sixth of April."

"You're certain of the date." I assumed he would be; your fiancée disappears, you're frantic with grief—yes, you'd recall the date.

"Oh yes. The original file the police made when she disappeared contains the envelope and note. You've probably got it with you at the incident room."

We probably did. Anything connected with our case would have been brought in.

"It's been authenticated," Clayton went on. "When the officers took the note, they compared the handwriting with some items in her house. It matches. It's her writing. Same with the notepaper," he added almost too eagerly. "They compared that, too. The note she mailed me was written on the same notepad. It's probably all in the incident room if you want to see it."

"Perhaps later."

Mark said, "How long have you and your wife been married, Clayton?"

He lost what little tinge he had to his cheeks. "I know what you're thinking."

Mark's voice raised in surprise. "Really? What, then?"

"That Vera and I had a flaming row and I killed her. Well, I didn't. I loved her, I'd just proposed marriage to her."

"How long have you and Lynn been married?" Mark repeated, louder.

"Twenty years."

"You've kept Vera's hair all this time without Lynn knowing of it?"

"Yes. I didn't see any reason to tell her. She'd just be furious."

"So you married Lynn when you were how old?"

"Twenty-one. I waited for Vera to come back, you see. I thought she'd come back to me."

"You waited two years. What made you decide to marry Lynn if you were so set on waiting for Vera?"

"It just hit me, that's all. I realized after the first year that she wouldn't return. There'd been her note at the offset, telling me of her decision. I figured she'd know by two years if she wanted to marry me. But she never wrote. There were never any other letters. Just that first one bidding me goodbye. I just got to thinking, I guess. I mean, if someone really loves you, no matter if she's gone to another city for a job or something…well, she'd write to you, wouldn't she? She'd want to hear from you, want to tell you she loves you, want you to write back and say you love her."

"But that didn't happen." Mark's voice had a touch of sympathy in it.

"No. There was nothing. When she didn't return…" He glanced in the direction of the church. "She would've been forty years old this year. I'm forty-two, did you know? Where does our youth go?" He said it so faintly, so slowly, that I could feel his hurt.

"We'll need to ask Lynn about all this," I said as gently as I could.

Clayton nodded, his head lowered in shame. "I know. That's why I didn't tell you yesterday when you showed me the photo. I tried to figure a way around this, so she wouldn't find out, but I know nothing's sacred in a murder investigation. I've resigned myself to her finding out. Talk to her—it's okay."

Mark said rather sarcastically, "So you bring us this hair, having wrestled with your conscience."

"I know I should have said something yesterday, but I was so shocked to see that blouse fabric and the—" He swallowed, looking slightly ill. "Well, I believe you can run a test on those bones, now. You can get the DNA from her hair. Then we'd know for certain if it's Vera. I'd know what happened to her, then. I'd know that she didn't run from me."

Mark snapped the watch closed, wrapped it again in the brown paper, and slipped it into his trousers pocket. "You told us yesterday about her grandmother and her parents, so I assume there's no one to notify if we get a DNA match."

Clayton stood up, his eyes boring into Mark's. "No. Vera never spoke of anyone and I never saw anyone visit them. It's like they were the only two people left in their family." He ran the back of his hand beneath his nose and added, "It's this damned village, you know."

"Why do you say that?"

"There's some sort of curse on it." He rushed on as he saw a hint of skepticism on Mark's face. "It's easy to scoff, but you don't live here. You don't know its history. Vera went missing, Reed went missing, and they end up dead. Two teenagers disappeared at separate times two years ago but luckily the police found them. One was wandering incoherently in the wood; the other was found near the disused Odin Mine. She'd fallen into a sinkhole and broken her leg. And there's Jenny Millington, who tried to kill herself. Seems above the law of averages, to me."

I looked at Mark. His expression was blank.

"Not counting the others who have seen the black dog around here. You can search the newspaper files, if you care to. Only don't laugh it off. Something's going on here that's got Other World stamped all over it."

"I wouldn't know about that," Mark said, his voice expressionless and hard. He stood up, his hand on Clayton's upper arm, and pulled Clayton to his feet. Pulling his mobile from his pocket, he said, "Right now, what concerns me is This World."

Clayton glanced from Mark to me, confusion in his eyes and a quaver in his voice as he asked what Mark was doing.

"Calling a constable."

"A constable? Why?"

"To drive you into Buxton. More specifically, to Silverlands, Sectional headquarters."

"Police head..." His eyes widened as the realization of his situation became apparent.

Mark finished talking to Graham, flipped his phone closed and repocketed it, and said, "Clayton Warson, you do not have to say anything. But it may harm your defense if you do not mention when questioned something you later rely on in court. Anything you do say may be given in evidence."

"You've given me a caution!" Clayton's voice shot up an octave as the color drained from his face.

"If you recognize it, you know what it means."

"But a *caution*..." His eyes searched mine for some sympathy or explanation. Finding none, he turned back to Mark. "You give cautions when someone's suspected of an offense."

"You don't call what you just did an offense?"

"What are you on about? *What* offense?"

"Obstruction."

"*Obstruction!* What did I—"

"Attempting to pervert the course of justice."

"You're joking." Again his gaze returned to me, a wild, desperate look that silently pleaded for help in this fast-enveloping nightmare.

"It's beyond a joke, Warson." Mark faced the man toward the approaching police car.

"But *perverting the course of justice?* You're daft, mate! I told you about the fabric, that I believe it to be Vera's. I brought you the lock of hair. Think about *that*," he said loudly as the car stopped opposite us and the officer got out. "Her hair. You've got something to match the bones to, you've got her DNA, for God's sake. You'll know if those bones are her!"

"You left this a bit late, Warson."

"But I *brought* this to you! I freely surrendered the hair to help with your case! You can't be serious about all this... I've just *helped* you!"

Mark helped the officer get Clayton into the car. The door closed with an ominous, heavy thud and I watched Clayton's panic turn more physical as he leaned against the back seat window and yell something at Mark. The rolled-up window prevented his words from reaching us.

As the car headed up the hill, I exhaled deeply. Mark's hand slipped around my shoulder. "Not exactly what I was thinking when this started," he said.

I nodded, unsure of what to say. We stood on the grass near the road, talking in near whispers, trying to make sense of Clayton's actions. Mark finally stirred, directing us toward the path of the long-departed police car. "I know Clayton thought he was helping, but he should have shown us that yesterday. And answered our questions more truthfully yesterday." He patted his trousers pocket, perhaps making certain he still had the pocket watch. "He did pervert justice, Bren. His answers were a load of rubbish. He tried to throw us off course and not incriminate himself. He should have relinquished that bit of hair yesterday when the subject came up."

"Actually, when Vera first went missing," I said, my mind still whirling.

"Yeah. Anyway, he waited too long."

"He'll get the rocket now."

"From his wife *and* from his superior."

I sighed deeply. "I don't know which will be worse."

"It's his own fault. He shouldn't have kept that all these years."

"I feel sorry for him." I glanced in the direction of the incident room we had set up in the church basement—our own patch from which our interviews emanated. Clayton would soon be enduring his own interview. I said, somewhat slowly, "He'll probably be suspended from duty. Maybe even be divorced when his wife finds out."

"Either way," Mark added, "he's in deep shit."

~

We were about to walk up the hill to the youth hostel, when raised voices forced us to turn in the direction of the pub. Chad Styles, whom we had left just hours ago in Upper Hogsley, stood in the outdoor eating section of the pub, yelling at Kevin Harper. Not just yelling, I noticed as we hurried up to the two men. Shaking his finger in Kevin's face. Chad's anger was matched equally in the volume of his voice and the redness of his cheeks.

"What's the problem?" I asked as Mark walked between the men, forcing them apart.

"Ask him," Kevin said, his voice quivering, yet at a normal speaking level. "I was just coming out of the pub and Styles nearly jumps me."

"You're exaggerating, mate," Chad said, his face still fiery. "I called to you, you ignored me, started to walk across the street, so I grabbed your arm."

"You couldn't just follow him?" Mark stood like he was expecting the men to start swinging at each other.

"He seems to have grown deaf," Chad said. "Selectively."

Kevin rolled his eyes. "I didn't hear you. I told you that."

"Your heard your friend easily enough."

"He was walking next to me, for God's sake! Of course I heard him."

"What do you need to talk to Kevin about?" Mark asked, visibly growing tired of the bickering.

"I want to know if I can get something of mine from your brother's effects," Chad said rather testily, as though he had repeated it several dozen times.

"Something of yours?" Kevin said, his eyebrow raised. "What? Why does Reed have it?"

"I loaned it to him a month ago. It's a photograph. Of last year's well dressing in Upper Hogsley, if you must know. I need it for our closing ceremony."

Kevin shrugged, his eyes dull and devoid of interest. "First I've heard of any photograph, Styles. Ask Marian for it."

"I didn't want to bother her. You know…"

"Yeah. You're insinuating she is mourning for Reed and I'm not."

"Don't be stupid. That's not what I meant. I saw you, thought I'd ask you and see if you could get the photo. It's easier for you to ask Marian for it, you being family, than for me to barge in on her."

"Well, I don't know about the photo and I'm not going to look for it. She's upset enough without me poking about in Reed's things. Maybe it's at the church or the village hall, since it's about the well dressing festival. Did you ask Harding?"

"No. I thought I'd try you first."

"Which you did. And I'm telling you I don't know a thing about it, so ask Harding. Or pop into the hall when there are workers about. But don't bother Marian." He held up his right index finger, silently warning Chad, and strode across the road to his shop.

Mark said, "You all right with that, Mr. Styles? Can you ask others besides Mrs. Harper?"

"Looks like I'll have to, won't I?"

"The photo's that important, then," I said.

"Yes."

"It won't complicate things, though, if you can't find it."

"I hope I don't find out." He strode off toward the church, a look of determination on his face.

～

Lynn Warson was in the tourist information center, talking to a family. Mark picked up a pamphlet from a rack near a photo display of last year's well dressing event and I busied myself by looking at the wood carvings of birds and small mammals. Lynn circled something on a map, jotted a few words on the paper's margin, and pointed in a generally northern direction. Must be telling them about the old mines and caves, I thought. A bit further discussion and Lynn folded the map and handed it to the father. As they left the center, she saw us and came over. Mark stuffed the pamphlet into his pocket and asked if we could speak to her.

"We just spoke yesterday," she said, annoyance creeping into her voice.

"That's as may be, Mrs. Warson, but we've learned something that may or may not prove to be pertinent to the case, and we'd like to talk to you."

"I can see I won't get a moment's peace until you do." She led us into her office, shut the door and asked what we wanted. She also remained by the door, as though she didn't want to waste a second getting to the door and opening it when we were finished. Standing against the wooden rectangle, her back tilted back slightly and touching the polished oak surface, she looked defiant and aggravated.

"Did you know your husband had been previously engaged?" Mark asked.

I don't know what I expected, but it wasn't the reaction she had. She folded her arms across her chest and half laughed. "That puppy love thing? I heard something about it."

"From your remark, you're evidently not jealous to know you weren't his first choice."

"That was twenty-one years ago. Clay grew out of his infatuation with Vera."

"Did he tell you about his former engagement or did someone else tell you?"

"What difference does that make?"

"Please answer the question."

She exhaled, clearly annoyed with the topic and with us. "I heard it from Edmund Worrall. He was Vera's best friend."

"Reed's half brother."

"Don't know of any other."

I said, "How long did you know Clayton before he proposed to you?"

"Six months."

"How old were you?"

"Really. I don't see what this—"

Mark inclined his head and spoke slowly and precisely. "How old were you when Clayton proposed?"

"Nineteen. He was twenty-one. I'd moved into the village with my parents at that time. That's how I met him."

"When did you get married?"

"Two months later."

"Awfully soon after that, wasn't it? Especially since you hadn't grown up together, known each other through school."

She shrugged, losing some of her animosity. "Why should we have waited? We loved each other and wanted to get married."

"Did you know Vera?"

"No. As I said, my family and I had just moved here. That was after she left."

"And you've lived in Cauldham."

"Happily ever after. Moved out of my parents' home and into mine with Clayton. Twenty years ago. Can you do the math?"

Ignoring her remark, I said, "So Clayton's infatuation with Vera, as you put it, was over when you two married."

"Yes. Of course. If not, do you think he would have proposed to me?"

"You knew about the note she sent him. Do you know about anything else from that part of his life?"

Her eyes narrowed and she looked at me like an uncooperative witness glaring at the opposition counsel. "What's that mean?"

"Did you know your husband has kept a lock of Vera Howarth's hair, kept it ever since they were engaged?"

"You're lying."

"Ask Clayton if you don't believe me."

"I don't have to. I know Clay. He wouldn't keep a memento of another love."

"That's your decision, obviously, but it happens to be true."

"You'll say anything to get people to talk, to turn on one another." She turned toward the door, stepped to the side, grasped the doorknob and flung the door open. "Now, I think we've talked long enough. I have work to do. Like fumigating my office."

Walking back to the pub, I said, "A woman that mad could be mad enough to kill."

Mark snorted and ran his fingers through his hair. "If she knew about the hair, she might."

"A husband that doesn't tell his wife about a previous engagement. What do you make of that?"

"He had something more to hide than a lock of hair."

Twenty-Two

PC Byrd drove the pocket watch and Vera's hair to the lab in Birmingham to run a DNA test on it and the bones. Graham had requested a rush on it, needing to know if we had found Vera's remains and, if so, would this pertain to the Reed Harper case. But even with a rush order, it would be twenty-four hours before we'd know if we had a match or not.

Having missed our lunch, Mark and I next headed to the pub, intent that no one would stop us from our meal. We took our food outside, sitting at one of the small wooden tables in the front courtyard. The late afternoon sunlight illuminated the shop fronts on the western side of the street, leaving us in shadow, but it was still pleasant, with a warm wind rushing down the hill and the leaves of the trees rustling under the symphony of birdsong. I took a long drink of lemonade, then scowled as my mobile rang.

"What is it now?" I muttered before glancing at the caller ID display.

"Better not answer in that tone of voice." Mark picked up his crab and olive sandwich. "Probably is the Vic, wondering where we are."

I glared at Mark, hating the nickname that many of my colleagues had bestowed upon Graham. Being a vicar once upon a time was no reason to ridicule him behind his back, and I told Mark so.

He raised his arms in surrender. "No harm meant, Brenna. It just slipped out."

"Better not slip out when you're with him." Glancing at the

name displayed on my phone, I said, "It's Adam," and answered.
Mark murmured, "All is well" and took a bite of his sandwich.
"Adam," I said, leaning back in my chair. "I'm glad you called."

"I couldn't wait any longer, Bren. I realize you said you'd call
me today, but it's past tea time and I just thought, for one moment, that you forgot or got wrapped up in something."

"You're on my list, Adam. I didn't forget. Just haven't had a
minute to myself."

"Sorry. Didn't mean to rush you. Is this a bad time?"

I heard the anxiety in his voice, the hope that we could talk
and the apprehension that I'd have to hang up on him. "Now is
perfect. I'm having a late lunch with Mark."

"Just so I didn't interrupt something with the case."

"No. You're fine." We lapsed into an awkward silence, both
of us knowing we had to talk about the wedding and his parents' wishes, yet neither of us brave enough to speak first. I took
a deep breath as Adam said, "Have you had a chance to think it
over, Bren?"

I glanced at Mark, needing an emotional anchor. He was
getting up, mouthing he would be right back, and walked into
the pub. So much for the life buoy. "Yes, I've thought about what
you said."

"And?" The hope swelled in his voice.

"You know I love you, Adam. You know I don't want to intentionally hurt you—ever."

His voice lowered. "Bad news."

"Not necessarily. I haven't said anything yet."

"It will be bad news. Whenever people start out with 'You
know I love you' or something like that, it's always what you
don't want to hear."

"Adam."

"Don't sugarcoat it. I can tell from your tone, you're not
budging."

"It's not a question of budging, Adam."

"What do you call it, then? You know my parents and I want
a church wedding, but you're holding out for some outdoor gala.

It'll be *December*, Bren! Trees and birds and sunshine is nice, but have you considered how cold it will be?"

"So we bundle up in overcoats and mittens for ten minutes. We can wear our fancy dress inside at our party afterwards."

Adam exhaled deeply, venting his exasperation with me. "Have you given a thought to my older relatives? What do you think traipsing through the wood or moor or wherever will do to them? Besides unable to walk far enough or steady enough to tramp through heather and ferns, you've got them standing outside in the cold, Bren. And don't say it's just for ten minutes, just for a quick ceremony. You haven't considered the little jaunt to and from your piece of paradise."

His anger shone through his tone, never mind the last ridiculing words.

"It's not so much the ceremony, Adam, as it is your parents' involvement."

"What's wrong with that? They're trying to help us by throwing in a few quid to cover expenses. Mom has a friend who's a travel agent, so she can get us good deals on honeymoon destinations. And another friend has a friend who is manager of a bridal dress shop—"

I felt lost in the gush of words. "Adam, I appreciate all that, but I don't want a fancy dress. Even if we had the ceremony in a church I wouldn't want that kind of dress. I know your folks are offering us help and advice, but why can't we have the wedding *we* want? Why can't we save our money for our house and have a simpler ceremony? Will anyone really remember the elaborate wedding twenty years from now?"

"My folks will. We will."

Where was Margo when I needed her advice? I took a deep breath and said, "Why is a church wedding so important to your parents?"

It was Adam's turn to take a deep breath. "My folks never had one. They were hippies and shunned that type of wedding. They—they've regretted it. They wish they'd had proper photos and the traditional garter and bouquet throwing. All the customs that link you to your ancestors. They realize what a mistake they'd made and don't want us to regret our wedding."

I didn't know how to respond. He had linked our wedding to his parents' mistake and remorse. Whatever I said had to be carefully worded; I didn't want to drive a wedge between us. "I'm sorry they regret their ceremony. Maybe they could do a vow renewal ceremony for their sixtieth anniversary...in a church with all the flowers and candles and music they missed. That would still be lovely."

"There's something else, Bren."

"Yes? What?"

"You know I'm an only child."

What was coming? "Yes."

"Mother's always dreamed of a church wedding for me. I know how that sounds," he said hurriedly, giving me no time to reply. "Usually the daughter's mother is the one keen on that. But I think it all relates back to their own poor ceremony choice. Not too many years after mum had me she and dad started to be disappointed about the wedding. She doesn't say so, but I think she'd like to sort of erase their own mistake by participating in my church wedding." He fell silent, perhaps waiting for me to reply, perhaps thinking about his own emotional situation with his parents.

I told him I'd think about it some more, told him I loved him, and rang off as Mark returned to the table.

He angled his head, giving me a concerned look. "You okay?"

"Yeah." I nodded.

"You're not eating." He pointed to my untouched sandwich. "You can't work a case on your nerves, Bren, and you can't think properly about the case, or about Adam, without food in your stomach. It gives you energy and brain power, or hadn't you heard?"

I glared at him, my hand lightly touching the glass of lemonade. The warmth of my fingers puddled the chilled condensation beneath them and the water droplets zigzagged down the glass' exterior and collected beneath it on the tabletop.

"I don't know the problem, of course, but I think things will look much better on a full stomach."

"Or in the morning. Isn't that the cure-all for everything?"

"Don't knock it. It's amazing what the brain can sort out while you're sleeping."

I made no move to eat.

After a minute Mark said, "Make an effort, Brenna. For the sake of everyone who loves you." His eyes shone with concern.

I picked up my ham and pineapple sandwich, took a bite and chewed, and Mark smiled. After swallowing, I said, "I didn't mean to bother you with this, Mark."

"No bother, I assure you. Feeling better?"

I chewed another bite of sandwich, nodding.

"Just what the doctor ordered."

"Speaking of ordered..."

"You want something else to eat?" Mark half stood up, trying to see the menu chalked on the outdoor blackboard.

"No. But you said 'ordered.'"

"At least your hearing hasn't suffered from your lack of food."

"Do you want to hear this or just mouth off at me?"

"Go on, please."

"Since Clayton gave us Vera's hair to run a match against those bones that were found, doesn't it make you wonder why both bodies were discovered in the wood, close together? I do. It makes me think about the order we found them in."

"What? Like the body wasn't laid out in some ritualistic manner, or the exact placement of it, according to the compass cardinal points?"

"No."

"The order we found them in—chronologically? Like, if the body had been discovered first? Would those bones ever have been found? Is that what you mean?"

"No."

Mark ran his fingers through his hair, the silvery streaks looking almost whitish in the sunlight thrown back from the building across the road. "Sorry. I still don't understand where you're going with this."

"Well, how did the two bodies get to the woods? A dead body's awfully heavy to carry. I can't see anyone running the risk of transporting a body in his car, either. Telltale DNA is left behind."

Mark nodded, perhaps remembering the case in March with the body in the car boot. "So we need to look at how the bodies were transported."

"Not only that, but why there? Why the wood? We know killers tend to dump their victims in places where they feel safe, or that holds some meaning for them."

"So we look for someone with a link to the woods. Or with coal mines, since the site is close to the abandoned Odin Mine."

"Or Angela Ellis or Jenny Millington," I added, writing these items in my notebook.

"Or one of those caverns. Which one is the closest? Speedwell?"

"Peak Cavern, I think."

"So any of these could have a meaning for our killer."

We exchanged anxious looks. I took a sip of lemonade before saying, "Getting back to how the bodies got there. You said 'ordering.' That's what made me think of this again. It would've been easier for the murderer if he ordered his victims to the woods, or ordered them into his car. Then he wouldn't have to struggle with a dead body."

"Provided he could persuade his victims to do that. Wouldn't it be even simpler to lure them to the area? Make an appointment on some pretext?"

"That suggests they were friendly, trusted each other. Why else would anyone meet someone at night in the wood?"

Mark grabbed his drink and sat back in his chair. "We won't know that until we know who the killer is."

"Just don't try to tell me it's tied up with black dogs and ghosts," I shivered. "Flesh and blood killers are hard enough to track down."

Twenty-Three

Books from the Library: Derbyshire's Tales of Ghostly Goings-on and Haunted Homes

One late winter night in February 1789, Charles Bowcock sat up late, reading in front of a low-burning fire. His wife had retired to their bed several hours earlier. Their children, Emma, John, and James, had preceded their mother, sleeping in their separate bedrooms in the west wing of the hall. Charles had spent a long day dealing with tenants and planning with his estate manager. His reading candle had burnt out, but the fire still cast its golden glow onto his paper and across the floor nearest the fireplace. A taper burned in the sconce near the stairway.

He leaned closer to the fire to see the writing on the paper better. There were other candles in candlesticks throughout the room—the family was not niggardly nor poor—but Charles didn't plan to stay up much longer. So he huddled over the paper, near the fire, and read.

At some later hour he awoke to the long, high howling of a dog. The fire had burnt to little more than coals by now and the candle in the wall sconce flickered on threats to die out. Charles poked up the fire, threw another log onto the meager flames, and lit one of the spare candles. Despite the wintry weather, he yanked open the front door and peered outside.

Snow was falling, and had been for some time, for an inch or two covered the ground. The frigid air whistled through the stand of pines at the northern edge of the door but Charles remained planted on the spot. The howling continued, louder and urgent, chilling in its urgency.

Charles stepped outside, scuffing the snow as he hurried beyond the flagstone terrace. Holding his candle high and shielding it from his eyes, he peered into the blackness in the direction of the sound. He could see nothing but swirling snow.

Assuming he had been dreaming, he turned toward the hall when the howl sounded again.

Charles hesitated, wondering if he should call out the men or ignore it. What was more common than the baying of a hound, he thought. But the intensity and pitch of the cry told him he heard no ordinary hunting dog; it was the Gabriel Hound.

He rushed back inside, nearly falling on the snow-slick flagstones. He charged up the staircase, calling his wife's name. She sat up as he burst into their bedroom, drawing the bedclothes around her and inquiring what was amiss.

"'Tis the Gabriel Hound, Suzanne, as sure as I'm born," he said, and ran down the hallway to the children's rooms.

On entering their daughter's room, he saw that she was well, sleeping and breathing peacefully. He eased the door to as quickly as he could and rushed to his sons' room, the next door down.

The two boys were in their beds; John lay on his side, a faint blush upon his cheeks. Charles lowered the candle to within inches of John's nose. The candle flame flickered as the boy breathed.

Fearing the worse, Charles stepped over to James' bed. One look at the little boy's ashen face confirmed his worst fear. As Charles scooped the lifeless form into his arms, the howling of the hound ceased.

A search of the grounds later revealed only Charles' footsteps in the snow; no dog print marred the pristine snow anywhere near the hall. Not surprising, if one remembers the Hound can only be heard.

From that time to this, the baying of the Gabriel Hound announces death or danger to the family.

The Hound doesn't restrict itself to the family or the Cauldham area, however. Perhaps attached to others as well, residents in Edale, Castleton and Hathersage have also heard the Hound's howling. Though mostly associated with great danger or disaster in some form, the Hound does occasionally serve to protect an individual, as when a young woman narrowly missed stepping into a sinkhole in the 1980s. Whatever its role, it is best not to ignore the baying of the Gabriel Hound.

Twenty-Four

We had a couple of hours before turning in, so Mark and I returned to Edmund Worrall's house. Mark's and my conversation concerning killer and victim being friendly and trusting each other nagged me, shouted at me. My question about why anyone would meet someone at night in the wood had been tossed out in frustration, but the more I thought of it as I ate the rest of the meal, the more it made sense. We needed to talk to someone who was not connected too strongly to Reed, but someone who knew the undercurrents of the village. Edmund Worrall immediately came to mind.

"I'd think most anyone in a village knows each other well enough to go to the wood at night. Not my ideal for a meeting place, but I don't know the people or the history behind it." Edmund had finished his tea and washing up, and we sat around the dining room table, sipping coffee and watching the storm clouds rolling in from the west.

Mark had thought this a daft idea, for we didn't know if Edmund had murdered Reed or Vera, whom we assumed to be our bones. But I didn't see what harm it would do. If we discovered later that he had lied to us, we would deal with it.

"You had mentioned earlier today that Reed cheated on Marian during their marriage."

"Right. He had a history of love-'em-and-leave-'em even before their marriage, but Marian went ahead with the wedding. I hated to see her have anything to do with Reed 'cause I figured she'd end up the same way. You can't change a leopard's spots, can you?"

"These other women he had affairs with…was Vera Howarth one of them?"

"Vera?" He held his cup shoulder high, ready to take a sip. "Don't think so. 'Course, I don't make it my business to be a nosey parker."

"Do you know anyone specifically who was involved with Reed? You gave us Clarice Millington's name, but is there anyone else you know of?"

He eyed us, taking time to sip his coffee. When he set the mug back on the table, he said, "Well, since you ask, I do remember one other woman. It's been a while."

"Mind giving us her name?"

"This is important, isn't it?"

"Yes."

"To Reed Harper's case?"

"Maybe with something else, too."

"Those bones?"

"The name, if you please, Mr. Worrall."

"Christine Stevenson."

"Where will we find her?"

"In the graveyard. She died last year."

Edmund gave us the name of Christine's uncle. Perry Bowcock lived next door to the Harpers, so we walked up the hill to his house.

Slightly smaller than the Harpers' house, Edmund's residence mimicked the style and gray stone of the other homes in the village. Nothing much changed, I thought, except the colors of doors and window, and the flowers in the gardens.

Recovering from the surprise of opening his front door to two police detectives, Perry invited us inside. He turned off the television in the back lounge and joined us again in the living room.

"Sorry about that." He straightened his T-shirt as he sat in the rocker. "I didn't know who was at the door." He seemed to be all muscle, tall and chunky, with an energetic crop of auburn haircut into a close trim. His forearms obliterated the chair's arms; his large frame completely filled the chair. He settled into a smooth rocking rhythm, his gaze alternately on the darkening sky and us. "So you want to know about Christine," he said, his voice taking on a far-off quality.

"We'd appreciate it." Mark leaned forward, his notebook and pen ready. When he had introduced us, he mentioned our investigation into Reed Harper's death. Perry didn't appear to think this was outside the bounds of police investigation.

"Christine was my niece. A beautiful girl with fiery red hair and cornflower blue eyes. Intelligent, helpful, super sense of humor." He wiped his eyes with his handkerchief. "Sounds like a cliché, what every grieving parent says about a child they have to bury, but it's true of Christine. She got involved with Harper little over a year ago. That's what led to her death."

"Did he have a direct hand in it?" Mark asked, his voice sharp.

"No, but I wish he had. I'd have taken a huge amount of pleasure in strangling him. Don't look shocked, detective. I would've, but I didn't. Christine was sixteen years old when Reed began an affair with her. Three years ago. She became pregnant." He paused again, gazing at the tabletop. When he continued, his voice was steady. "She was humiliated, embarrassed beyond reason. I tried telling her that she could give the baby up for adoption, but she wouldn't listen. She said she'd always be reminded of her sin and short falling even if the baby went to another home. She left the village four months ago, in February. Went to a bed-and-breakfast in Scotland. In Inverness. Well, outside the city, actually. On the south side of Loch Ness. I got a letter from her, saying she wanted to get away from Harper and everything that reminded her of him and think things through. A month later, just this past March, she committed suicide."

He uttered the sentence so slowly, so even-toned, that it caught me by surprise. I glanced at Mark, wondering if I had heard Perry correctly. Mark stared at the man, but Perry kept looking at something outside the window.

I squeaked out my condolences and considered taking our leave.

Perry added, "She didn't have to do that. I would've helped her, done anything I could for her and the baby. But it was her upbringing, you see. She was a strong churchgoer and couldn't forgive herself."

As Mark and I stood up, Perry finally shifted his gaze to my face. He said, "I'm sorry. I don't mean to wallow in my self-pity. If you need any more information…" He let the sentence dangling, for I could read the message in his eyes.

I placed one of my business cards on the table. "If you think of anything else we might want to know, ring me any time, Mr. Bowcock. *Any* time."

He nodded and as Mark and I stepped outside I could hear the steady squeak squeak of his rocker and his low, unabashed crying.

"Well, what do you think?" Mark said as we walked back to the incident room.

"What do I think about what?"

"About Christine, the niece."

"I think it's tragic. No one should kill herself. No problem should warrant that solution—which really isn't one. A solution, I mean."

"No, Bren. About the fact that it's suicide or not."

I frowned, glaring at him. "Why shouldn't it be suicide? What difference does it make? Anyway, that was last year."

"It makes a difference if Christine was actually murdered. It makes a difference because if she was, then maybe that links up with Reed Harper or something else going on in this village."

"Oh, right." I slowed my gait.

"We have only Perry's word about his niece."

"You're suggesting—"

"I'm not suggesting anything right now. But he's our only source of information at the moment."

Nodding slowly, I said, "It wouldn't be the first time some-one tried to make us follow a drag to an erroneous conclusion."

"I'd hate to attempt to count them."

"We'll look at the case files, then."

Mark nodded and we walked briskly to the church and were soon reading the case notes pertaining to Christine Stevenson's death. I felt sicker with each page I read. Her death was a sad, miserable affair that never should have happened. The case notes confirmed the verdict of suicide. I stood up and grabbed my shoulder bag as Mark returned the file. We silently nodded good night to each other, mutely agreeing to let that line of inquiry go.

~

Needing to clear my mind of the day's stress, I wandered through the churchyard. I am not a great lover of poking about among the tombstones to read their inscriptions, but churchyards are usually restful, peaceful places in which to stroll. And they are havens for birds, too.

I had walked for a while, meandering through the stones, circling the church several times, taking the path to the vicarage and strolling in the direction of Cauldham Hall. When I came within sight of the massive wrought iron gates I turned back, keeping to the path, my eyes on the way through the wood. Dusk was falling rapidly, but I didn't quicken my stride or shorten my walk. The wood was refreshingly cool and tranquil, a symphony of birdsong and a scented spa to my overworked nerves.

As I approached the church I slowed my gait. The sound of voices floated through the open door. Jenny Millington and Harding Lyth. Ordinarily I wouldn't have eavesdropped, for I counted the conversation between vicar and parishioner as pri-vate as those between doctor and patient, or lawyer and client. But the urgency in Jenny's voice compelled me to hesitate just outside the door. The words forced me to linger.

"But should I have said anything?" Jenny paused and there was a strangled sob, as though she had clamped her hand over her mouth.

"I don't know what you could have said that would have changed anything," Harding said. The tone was low, and as smooth and unhurried as a languid brook.

"But I'm haunted by it! I can't sleep. I can't go anywhere or do anything without thinking of it or seeing him before me. I-I fear I'm going insane."

"I've seen no signs that you are, dear. You're just under a great deal of stress. Anyone would be if they had your history or had suffered what you have."

"That doesn't put an end to my misery, Harding. Empathy doesn't halt the dreams I have. A pat on the back doesn't stop me from thinking of him, thinking that I could have handled it better."

"We all have regrets, Jenny. None of us has lived a life free of 'if only,' so you shouldn't beat yourself up so hard."

"But I could have done something more. That's the problem!"

"You left the meeting to deal with him, you told me. I don't see what else you could have done."

"I would have stayed to talk to him in person. I wouldn't have used the coward's way and spoken to him over the phone." Her sobbing echoed against the stonewalls and Harding's soothing sounds floated over the sound of her pain.

When the crying had subsided, Jenny said, "Will I be punished?"

"*Punished*?"

"For what I did."

"The police."

"I don't care about the police right now, Harding. I'm worried about when I die. Will God punish me? Will I go to hell?"

"Jenny, if you are truly sorry you will be given redemption. That is God's saving grace for us all. Christ came into the world to teach us that forgiveness for our sins is possible if we truly believe and are penitent of our fault."

"But this isn't something like cheating on a school test."

"I know what it is, Jenny. Even something as grievous as being responsible for a man's death will be forgiven. You just have to ask in your heart and mean it with all of your might."

"Truly? Even something as terrible as what I did? I will be saved?"

"God is love, Jenny. It isn't just a slogan."

"But to have a hand in a man's death. To have the police here." The sole of a shoe scrapped across the flagstones and I stiffened, wondering if Jenny and Harding were coming outside. No further sound followed that until Jenny spoke again. "I don't know what to do."

"Leave it to me, Jenny. I'll put things right."

"Thank you, Harding. It means more to me than I can say. Thank you."

"Try to let go of it, dear. Take it to God in prayer, if that will ease your mind and heart. But leave the physical work to me."

I tiptoed away as their footsteps grew louder. Standing behind a massive juniper, I watched them come outside and pause on the path as Harding gave her a swift kiss on the cheek before bidding her good night.

～

The temptation of the pub whispered to me as I climbed the stairs to my room. The day had been horrifically long and stressful enough, with people's emotions and wounds exposed once again, but now I had the mysterious tête-à-tête between Jenny and Harding to mull over. I would have liked to relax with a glass of wine or a shandy, but I didn't want to rely on crutches. I wanted to think.

I had brewed myself a cuppa with the electric kettle and a tea bag from the collection of tea flavors on the little table in my room, and had just settled down in the window seat when there was a knock on my door. I set down the mug, got up and opened the door. Adam stood in the doorway, a red rose in his hand.

"Hello, sweets." He handed me the flower.

I took it and let him in. He walked over to the window seat as I closed the door. "It's lovely, Adam," I said. "Thank you."

"No more than you deserve." He noticed the cup of tea. "If

you're having a night cap, I'll join you."

"For tea?"

"Sure. Why not? You weren't going to go to sleep right this minute, were you?"

"No." I refilled the kettle, flipped on the switch and dumped a tea bag and two cubes of sugar into a mug. He took my vacated place on the window seat and stared at the night sky until I handed him his tea.

"Ta." He took a sip, then smiled at me. He seemed to have all the time in the world.

I leaned against the dresser. "I should be surprised you're here, say what an unexpected pleasure it is to see you, but I kind of expected it. You want to talk, don't you?"

"I think we need to, Bren. I think you also believe we need to."

Pressing my lips together, I nodded. The rose angled across the top of the dresser, where I had put it to fix Adam's tea. I let it lie there, needing to make this conversation as emotionless as possible.

A fork of lightning lit up the black sky, throwing the oak outside the window into relief. I ignored my tea. Best to get this over with. "I'm really not trying to be difficult. That's no way to plan a wedding or begin a marriage. But—and I mean this in the nicest way—this isn't your parents' ceremony. It's ours. We're creating our own life together, our own memories. I feel for your mother. I realize she wants to help us avoid a mistake and end up with the same regrets she has now, but she's not us. She's not me and she doesn't have my life history. I need to be outdoors, Adam. I'll suffocate inside a church. I need to feel the natural world around me. I feel closer to God that way. Nature is something he created; man created religion. Don't you get a thrill out of listening to bird song in the morning, or feel the wind in your face, or the smell of a pine forest?"

"Sure, but that wind's awful cold in December."

"You know what I mean. It's just an example."

"But a church wedding is also beautiful, Bren. The church

at dusk, the aisles of lit candles throwing a golden glow over everything, the stained glass alive in a dozen dazzling colors, the bells tolling out our happiness."

The word nudged something in my mind. Usually scent did that, evoking strong associations and memories. But the remembrance of tower bells brought the sensation of church back to me with the vividness of yesterday. I associated tower bells with tragedy. We were teenagers—Frank, Glenda, Cheryl, Todd and I—learning how to ring the bells. Not only the physical control of the large bells, but also the basic patterns that we would play. We'd been warned about the bells, told about the dangers of practicing with the ropes without a qualified ringer present. But, as happens occasionally with teenagers, Todd sneaked into the church one night, climbed up to the ringing chamber, and uncoiled a rope, thinking to practice the hand stroke part of the pull. Because Todd still was a learner, he didn't have the skill to control the sway of the continually rising and falling rope. Nooselike, the rope looped around Todd's neck and pulled him twenty feet to the ceiling as the great bell swung through its arc. He died from strangulation. I saw him dangling in the dusky half-light, the rope slightly swaying, the silence overwhelming in fright.

I tried to convey this to Adam, tried to explain that the scene still haunted me. "I know I'm not rational, Adam. I know that happened twenty years ago, but I can't seem to shake it. It was an appalling sight. Besides, we were friends."

He set his tea down and came over to me. Wrapping his arms around me, he laid his chin on the top of my head and whispered, "My poor angel. I had no idea. You never said."

I lifted my face and he kissed me. "It's not the sort of thing I generally blab about. Big, brave copper still haunted by nightmares of decades-old accident."

"You don't think being with me, being in church for a completely different reason, would still that ghost?"

I murmured "I don't know" into his chest.

"You're afraid to find out, aren't you?"

"Not the best time or place to discover I still see Todd hanging there." I angled my head toward him and smiled. "I'll spoil the ceremony when I run screaming from the sanctuary."

Adam hugged me again and I broke from him. He said, "I'm willing to bet you any amount of money—well, nearly any amount—that you'll do fine. There'll be too many people there; we'll fill up the space so there's no room for Todd."

I should have laughed; I should have taken a breath and agreed to it, but Adam hadn't lived through my nightmares. I still had them occasionally, when I couldn't sleep or something, like Adam's remark, touched off a memory. I said rather hesitantly, still debating with myself, "I can't, Adam. You know I'd do anything I can to please you—will do throughout our marriage—but I can't do this. I hope you understand."

He glanced at the rose, forgotten on top of the dresser. "Anything to please me but grant me this." He exhaled heavily. "Fine. Maybe we can have a wedding by proxy."

"Adam..."

"We'll meet up later, at the reception. Oh, sorry. You don't want that either."

"Adam, we can figure this out. It's not insurmountable. I just have to think about this."

"Well, don't take too long."

"What's that mean?" I stared at him, afraid of an ultimatum.

"December isn't that far off. We need to make a decision soon if we're to schedule the ch—" He stopped, realizing what he had nearly said. Thunder growled overhead, as if it were in the room with us. "If we're to get the best patch of ice and nettles."

He strode from the room, leaving me thinking about give and take, parents-in-laws, and what I was really scared of.

~

My night was filled with exhausting dreams—when I did sleep—and what seemed to be hours of staring out of the window at the lightning-slashed sky and listening to Adam's voice whispering beneath the whine of the wind.

After showering and dressing, I somehow got downstairs and to the section of the bar that was open for breakfast. I took a table in the far corner, ordered egg, tomato juice and toast, and suddenly found Mark, decked out in light tan trousers, blue shirt and tie, standing at my side. He eyed me with that look of concern that was becoming all too familiar.

"Mind if I join you?" He pulled out a chair before I could answer and sat down. "I'll have whatever she's having," he said to the waitress, nodding at me. "Now," he said after the waitress had gone, "what's the problem?"

"Why do you think there's a problem?"

"I can read you like a copper reads a suspect," he said, letting the joke pass without comment. "You were fine when we parted last night, so I deduce whatever has upset you occurred between then and now. And I don't believe it's due to this fine establishment running out of tea...or whatever."

"Brilliant detective work, Mark. But I'm in no mood for this."

"Then I'll get you out of that mood. Anyway, it's for my best interest. I'll end up killing you if I have to endure your grouchiness all day."

"Then ask Graham for a reassignment. Byrd or Margo is probably still waving those photos around the village. Maybe you could switch jobs with Margo."

"I've felt the effects of her sharp tongue before, thank you. I'll chance it with you, no matter how detrimental it might prove to each of us. Now, tell me what's wrong."

"You can't fix it."

"Maybe not, but maybe I could. We'll never know if you don't spill the beans. What's wrong?"

The waitress came with our orders. When she wandered back to the kitchen I said, "It's between Adam and me. I appreciate your good intentions, Mark, but we have to figure this out ourselves. God knows we'll have other issues that need sorting out during our marriage."

The tower bells from St Paul's Church struck the hour and

my face crumpled. Before I could stop it, tears were silently flowing down my cheeks.

Mark leaned across the table and stuffed his handkerchief into my hand. "Normally I'd suggest a good, stiff drink, but seeing as how it's only gone eight o'clock…"

I blotted my tears, wiped my nose and managed to squeak out my thanks before my voice cracked.

"It can't be as horrendous as you think, Bren. Anything can be fixed. What's the matter? The church issue?"

Raising my head, I looked at him and nodded. "How'd you know?"

"Are my detective skills so poor that you forget this is how I make my living?" He flashed a smile and moved his chair next to me.

"Adam and his parents are set on him having a church wedding."

"And you don't want one. Why not?"

"It's a long, painful story, Mark. You probably wouldn't understand. And even if you did, I'd wind up sounding absolutely barmy and certified."

"Give me a chance. I'm smarter than you give me credit for. And sensitive."

Sniffing, I flattened out his handkerchief on the tabletop and smoothed out the wrinkles. He reached across the table, slid his coffee and plate of eggs and toast over in front of him, and waited for me to begin.

I told him about Adam's and my different wishes for our wedding, knowing I'd already told him this yesterday, but needing a basis for what was to come. After I'd recounted the story of Todd's accident and my finding him, Mark handed me my tea. "I understand your pain and your reluctance to have the church ceremony. I also understand Adam's side of this. Can't you reach some compromise so that you're both happy with your big day?"

"Like what?"

"Well, could you get through a church wedding if you had

moral and physical support? It's really not so much the formality of the church ceremony, is it, as it is the building, right?"

"I guess. I never really thought about it."

"So, if you got a lot of support, could you get through the ceremony…if it were fairly short, not one of those long affairs?"

"How?"

"Well, just thinking off the top of my head." He took a sip of coffee, letting the idea take shape in my mind. Setting the mug back on the table, he said, "Have Margo standing beside you. And anyone else you feel close to and who will support you. Graham, if you want. Scott, if he's better by then. Me, if you want to bend that low. To hell with politically correct and the rest of it. A friend of mine had a woman as his best man—they were best friends since primary school. Have a crowd of people around you. We'll build a barricade, keep Todd out, and hustle you out of the church and to the party before you can feel anything." He looked at me, his eyebrows raised, his smile beaming.

"Well, it might work." My thumb stroked the back of my engagement ring and I stared at the diamond. It seemed to wink at me in agreement.

"Super. You can compromise on the reception/party thing. Not a full-blown reception, but something nice, anyway. At a friend's maybe, with a small band to dance to. No fancy cake, if that's not your style, but something nice, maybe a potluck thing where everyone brings something and you have a cake from a bakery. Maybe a room in a pub." He glanced around. "Hire a publican and have all sorts of drinks. It would still be a nice party and there'd still be a cake to cut. That's not bad, is it?"

"No. That would be fine."

"For the honeymoon…" He paused, as thought the word was difficult to say. "You give Adam and his parents the wedding they want, you compromise on the reception, so you should have the honeymoon you want, right?"

I nodded, waiting to hear Mark's idea.

"You have your time with nature and Adam by going

someplace wild, like the Outer Hebrides, or backwoods Maine in America, or a quiet B-and-B in Cumbria or Yorkshire and you spend the days walking the countryside. Look something up on the Internet—there are dozens of those adventurous getaways." A ray of lemon-hued sunlight fell across Mark's hair, accenting the streaks of gray among the brunet strands. He looked wise and caring, as though he had struggled with this type of conflict before.

My emotions spilled out and I hugged Mark in a flood of grateful tears. Of course, Adam chose that moment to walk up to our table. His angry voice tore my arms from Mark faster than a yell of 'Fire!' would have done.

Adam hovered behind Mark's chair, eyes flashing fire, his breath short and shallow. His legs were apart, the left in front of the right, and his arms bent slightly, as though he were ready for a fight. He barked his question again, like a drill sergeant or a referee, expecting to be obeyed without hesitation or question. "What the bloody hell is going on?"

I pushed up from the table, my legs wobbly, my arms not too much sturdier. "Adam, darling, it's not what you think. Mark was only—"

"Mark was only trying to win your love, take you away from me. What else should I think?"

"It's not like that. I was upset about last night, and Mark—"

"How convenient you are still upset. And how convenient Mark just happened to be here to lend his shoulder. Who did the asking?"

Mark stood up, pushing back his chair. The wooden legs screeched against the stone floor. "Good manners dictates I will not make a scene in public. Especially when a lady is concerned. You need to cool down, Fitzgerald. You're so wrapped up in this wedding you can't see straight. Brenna, if you weren't such an idiot that you can't sense it, is extremely upset." He glanced at me as I pressed the sodden handkerchief to my eyes. "She loves you, though I don't know why, if you act like such an unfeeling berk. She's trying to deal with her fear and her desire to please you. We discussed it over breakfast and came up with a solution I hope will please everyone." He took a step sideways, allowing Adam to come up to me, if he wished. Mark's right hand had curled into a fist during his talk, and with obvious great effort slowly relaxed his fingers. He grabbed his coffee mug and walked to the far side of the table, putting a barrier between himself and Adam.

I waited for Adam to speak, to reach out for me or move closer. Some sign that he understood my dilemma and wanted to soothe away the pain. His breathing had become somewhat deeper and slower, but anger and betrayal filled his eyes, revealing his own bewilderment and confusion. He shot another smoldering look at Mark, then stared back at me. "You're right, Salt, I am an unfeeling berk. Better that, though, than a bloody cuckold. At least I found that out before it was too late." He turned swiftly on his heel and strode across the room. The pub door banged closed after him, announcing his rage and his opinion.

Twenty-Five

As was the usual start of our days, Graham had called a short meeting in the incident room. Mark and I were the last to arrive, which elicited curious glances from Margo and an annoyed frown from Graham. I had returned to my room, washed my face, powdered my nose, and put on a dab of lipstick and some eye mascara in an attempt to camouflage my crying jag. Mark looked me over when I came back to the dining area, pronounced my secret unguessable, and we walked up the hill to the church.

We were between services, though that hardly mattered, as we were in the church basement and the services were upstairs in the sanctuary. Still, it made it less awkward, eliminating answered questions on how the case progressed, if we could slip into the basement without confronting worshippers. Many of them would help with the well dressing work today, for I knew they would puddle the mud, pack it into the wood frames and then transfer the designs onto the mud. That would take place in the village hall, so I didn't feel guilty about us taking over the church hall.

Still upset over the recent confrontation with Adam, and embarrassed that Mark and I were the last arrivals, I stumbled as we came into the room and dropped my shoulder bag. Mark muttered I should go on and get a seat, picked up my bag for me, and apologized to Graham, who wished us good morning. Louder than need be, but I put it down to the stress he felt coming down from the Divisional Commander. Welcome to the club, I thought. I've got my own minor upheaval in my life, too. Graham waited until we sat—in the front row, unfortunately—and restated the purpose of the meeting.

"We can't rule out the deliberate dumping of both victims, and the conclusion that the killer knew the area," he said, the volume of his voice returning to normal.

I opened my notebook. The remark echoed the discussion Mark and I had last night. I settled into my chair, glad of the cold metal that kept me alert and thinking of the case, and listened to Graham.

"Since the bones have not yet been identified, we can't work from that angle yet. However, we can augment our suspect list, given that we've had another twenty-four hours to talk to people." He rolled the whiteboard marker between his palms. "Anyone with any astonishing information? Taylor, perhaps you'd like to start us off. I'd like to pretend your tardiness this morning is due to your feverish work on the case." He took the marker in his right hand, simultaneously implying his confidence that I'd learned something pertinent and putting me on the spot.

Flipping through the notebook pages I stammered, "Well, uh, there are several people who had a motive to kill Reed Harper. His wife, first off. He had affairs with women for at least two decades. And Reed's brother, Edmund. Perry Bowcock, Clarice Millington, Jenny Millington, Chad Styles and, oddly enough, his son Trevor."

Graham jotted the names and motives on the board as I related why I also included Trevor on the list. "He loves Reed's daughter, Ilsa. She has the show biz bug and he wants to marry her. There's talk that Trevor's father may feature her in Upper Hogsley's village fete. Trevor fears that if Ilsa gets famous, she'll move away or won't marry him."

"Not an absurd assumption. Fame and fortune have destroyed many marriages, so why not engagements? Or even love?"

WPC MacMillan gave us a rundown of the Harpers' financial situation. Their bank accounts, snug and happy in three banks, bulged like rising bread dough. Stocks returned healthy dividends and channeled their surplus cash into a trust fund 'Payable to Marian, passed on to Ilsa in the event of Reed's death,' MacMillan explained; and the Old Family Money percolated in various legitimate ventures, birthing offspring that galloped into the three banks' accounts.

"Could suggest an overture to death," Graham said. "I don't suppose anyone has uncovered an affair Marian might be having." He looked around the group, waiting for a new revelation. He got none. He suggested PC Oglethorpe make inquiries. "You never know. What's sauce for the goose…"

Mark glanced up from his notes and said, "I don't think we should focus on Reed's affairs as the sole motive, sir."

"Why not, Salt?"

"Well, as many as he's had, and as many people he's hurt through them, he also owned an ad agency and directed the well dressing fete. We mustn't forget those pieces of his life."

"You're suggesting that there could be a disgruntled client out there, or someone, such as his own daughter, who got upset over some aspect of the fete."

"Why not? He's bound to have made a client or villager angry at some time. We've got two examples right here of the frustration he caused by the village festival. Why couldn't Ilsa have topped him—not premeditated, but in an argument over her singing career? Or Harding Lyth, the vicar, even? Maybe Reed finally saw his fatherly duty and made noises of replacing Harding's daughter, Angela, as the singing master of ceremonies. Harding, in the bubbling emotion of the moment, stabs Reed. It's not so farfetched, sir."

"The killing, or having a vicar as the killer?" A slight smile played around the corners of his mouth and he gave three constables the job of talking to Reed's recent clientele. He tapped the marker beneath Clarice's name on the board. "She's a new addition. Why did you add her, Taylor?"

I told him she knew of the friction between Reed and Marian and appeared to live in hope that if they divorced she would become the next Mrs. Reed Harper. "She had an affair with him, so I don't know if they shared any valid pillow talk or not."

"But hope springs eternal," Graham said. "Well, we've got suspects and motives coming out our ears. I don't know if it's more of a help or a hindrance to have this large number to sift through. No one other than Kevin Harper looks to have an alibi for the time of the murder, so that's not much help in whittling down our list. How's the fabric identification coming along, Lynch?"

Margo said they had talked to dozens of people and no one admitted to recognizing the fabric found with the bones.

"We've got Clayton's admission that he recognized the clothing as belonging to Vera Howarth. We're waiting for DNA test results to confirm the bones are hers. Divisional Commander Tierney has authorized a 'rush job' on the samples, so the report should be back later this morning." He paused to let the significance sink in. "So that's all we can do right now in that quarter. Let's meet back here at one o'clock so I can advise you of the test findings and we can discuss where the case will go from there, if we have a match. Other than that…anyone have anything to add?" He waited like a lawyer, hoping to hear a confession from his client. When no one offered further comments, he said, "Despite comments from Certain People, I realize you're all working like Trojans. Please know that I appreciate your application and devotion to duty, and that I understand we all can move only so quickly through an investigation. You've produced outstanding results in the past; don't let your usual high standards slip due to unrealistic demands." He had been leaning forward, his hands on the table, speaking low, yet emphatically. As though he meant the sentiment with every ounce of his being, willing us to absorb his will and belief.

The room had become silent—no phones or faxes beeping, no coughs or murmurs from us; no birds chattering or car doors slamming. I knew Simcock could be relentless in his demand to wrap up a case; I knew he, in turn, felt the pressure from the Divisional Commander. Hearing Graham's even-toned comments and seeing his placid expression, I could merely guess at what stress he dealt with.

Straightening up, he said, "Right. You've got your assignments. If there are no further questions, let's get on with our day." He laid the marker on the tray affixed to the bottom of the whiteboard and walked over to his computer.

Mark got up and stretched. "What do you think, Brenna? Will the hair DNA match the bones, or not?"

"It would be simpler for us if it did, and probably better for Clayton if it did."

"Yeah. All those years of wondering what happened to her, thinking she just walked out on an engagement." He glanced at me before averting his gaze to Margo. At least he had the grace to not say anything. Picking up his notebook and stuffing it into his trousers pocket, he said, "That must be hell, not knowing. Has Vera any siblings?"

"No one but her grandmother. And we don't even know if she's still alive. That was nearly a quarter of a century ago."

"Sounds worse like that than saying twenty-two years. God, I'm getting too old for this, Brenna."

Getting my shoulder bag from the back of my chair, I said, "You've got another fifteen years to go in the job, Mark. Don't even think you're getting old."

He snorted. "You're only as old as you feel. And after yesterday, I feel at least one hundred."

"Couldn't sleep last night?"

"No. The storm kept me up. You?" He eyed me, perhaps trying to discern if I were going to lie about my fight with Adam.

"Yeah. Me, too."

"Next time let's go downstairs for a drink. Might as well do something worthwhile if we're awake."

"Bar's closed at that time, Mark."

"Oh, yeah. I forgot." Several months ago, when we first began working with each other, he might have suggested we get together in his room. Extra curricular activities were never far from his thoughts. But he'd ditched his smart mouth, maturing into a compassionate person. I rather liked the new Mark Salt.

"Well," I said, noting Graham talking on the phone, "we're not doing much good like this. What do you suggest we tackle first on our assignment list?"

Mark consulted his watch. "Nine o'clock. We've four hours. Damn. I'm itching to know if we've got a lead on Vera Howarth or not."

"We'll know soon enough."

"But it's important, Brenna. If it is Vera who we found, this means the two cases are most likely linked. It's against the law of probability that two murderers would pick the same dump site for bodies."

"And if it is Vera, we treat her and Reed's cases as one."

"This village is so intertwined with personal relationships and anger, we could catch a break on solving the case if it does turn out to be Vera."

Nodding, I thought of the pain, too. Pain Reed Harper had inflicted—not just on the women he abandoned after the affairs were over, but also on the family and friends of these women. How deep did this pain go? How extensive was it felt—just immediate family, or were friends and colleagues of the women and Reed hurting, too?

We were walking toward the door when Mark said, "You know, we're taking Clayton's word that it happened this way." I stopped abruptly, my hand on his arm. "I thought his wife mentioned she saw the note."

Mark shook his head and flipped through his notebook. Finding the interview with Lynn, he let me read his notes.

My eyes widened and I looked up at Mark. "She says she *heard* about the note. She claims she never saw it."

"*Clayton* is our source of everything we know about Vera's letter of farewell. *Clayton* says it was mailed; he claims he got it two days after Vera went missing."

"We can check that easily enough." I walked over to the stash of photo albums and case notes. I pulled Vera's original missing person file from the pile and leafed through it until I came to the letter. Mark bent over my shoulder and we read the note. "It must be legitimate," I said, straightening up. "The original investigating team didn't label it as forged. And that postmark looks authentic enough."

Mark shrugged. "What's good enough for our lads twenty-two years ago is good enough for me."

I agreed. I am no handwriting expert, but even I could mentally compare Vera's round, upright penmanship and small circles that passed for dots over the letter i to the sample we had of Clayton's bold, slanted scrawl, the list he had given us of Vera's friends. The possibility that Clayton had concocted the note whispered to me, but as Mark said, if the original team hadn't declared it a forgery, I was content to accept that the note was authentic.

"So, let's go with the assumption Clayton wasn't making that part up. Vera did write the farewell note and she did post it."

"Our helpful bobby. Well, I suppose we better get on with our assignment."

Mark put the case file away, muttering that it was too bad Clayton hadn't been that open and helpful with the lock of hair.

"Well, he'll have a bit of time to reflect on that," I said as I consulted our list. "You ready?"

"Rarin' to go, Bren. Where are we off to first?"

Graham evidently finished his phone call, spotted me, and motioned me to join him. I indicated Mark, wondering if Graham wanted both of us, but Graham shook his head.

"I can take a hint," Mark said, half joking, and said he'd wait for me by the front door.

"I can't think what I've done," I whispered as Mark squeezed my hand.

"Maybe he wants to commend you for something."

"That won't take long. Nothing much I've done lately would warrant that."

"You never know, Bren." He muttered "good luck" and headed for the door.

As I walked up to Graham I noticed the dullness of his eyes. He waited until I seated myself before speaking. Even then, it took him several seconds to begin. "I can't sugarcoat this, Brenna," he began, kicking my heart rate into overtime, "and even if I could, I don't think you'd want me to."

The same sensation I felt last month, on hearing on my brother Sam's involvement in illegal activities, washed over me. As I stared at Graham's face the room around him seemed to alternately pulse in vivid colors and then recede. Finding my fingers gripping the edge of the table, I barely breathed, afraid I'd miss his words.

"It's Sam."

Nodding, though not comprehending the significance of that simple sentence, I waited for an explanation. Why had Graham's voice grown so faint and my pulsing blood so loud? I managed to ask if something had happened, if Sam wanted to see me, if he was still in Strangeways.

"I don't know if Sam asked for you, Brenna," Graham said, his voice low and gentle. "That's not why I wanted to speak to you."

"But he'll be there just for the first three or four months, won't he? He's not going to Wakefield, or somewhere…" I couldn't believe that would happen, for Wakefield was a maximum-security prison—which Sam's sentence hadn't warranted. I looked at Graham, wanting to shout that he tell me and put me out of my anguish. "It's not…not Roper, is it?"

Graham shook his head. "No. He's sitting in Wakefield."

"Then what?"

"Sam's already received threats."

"Threats!"

"Nothing definite, nothing we can prove or discover where, when or by whom. They never are."

"But…but is he safe? Who's threatened him? What's happening? Can't we do anything about this?" I didn't ask who stood behind the threats. The answer was obviously King Roper, retaliating because Sam had fingered Roper and helped the prosecution. Even if Roper and Sam were in different prisons, Roper had long arms.

"The prison governor moved Sam today. This morning. Quite early. He's being transferred to Full Sutton."

"Yorkshire," I mumbled. "Wakefield's in Yorkshire, too."

"Different prisons, Brenna."

"Yes, sir." My hand dropped into my lap and I glanced at the wall clock. It had begun marking off Sam's time the minute the judge pronounced the sentence. Each day I mentally checked off another eight, twelve or twenty-four hours until Sam would be with his girlfriend and me again. "You said Sam was threatened. What was it? How was it delivered? When did Sam get it—just recently? Did the governor act quickly?" I took a breath, my heart threatening to burst from fear.

"Easy enough to threaten Sam. You know without me telling you, Brenna. Roper's cronies creep around in the shadows, ready to do his bidding."

Graham didn't have to define what that bidding would be. With Roper doing four life sentences, and a minimum of thirty years before parole would even be considered, he wouldn't be happy with Sam. He wouldn't lounge around in his jail cell, letting Sam pass time. Roper would immediately contact his men to see what prison Sam was in. The gang members would then make their own inquiries and it wouldn't be long until one of them located Sam. And to make the search a bit easier, all prisons seemed to harbor rumors of a few screws who were bent and quite willing to pass on information or leak sensitive details, provided the money was quick and plentiful. After Sam was located, Roper would be told and the method of retaliation set in motion. I closed my eyes momentarily, feeling sick. This wasn't just the stuff of films and novels; it actually happened. Several inmates would push Sam's arm into a vat of boiling porridge and hold it there until his arm was burnt. Or his fingers would be badly broken in a door or gate during a sham fight between inmates. Anything to look like an accident. They always looked like accidents. And the scary thing was that Sam's broken fingers would end his concert pianist career. Sam sat naïvely within reach of their dirty hands. I looked at Graham, afraid to hear any more, yet needing to know.

"Sam was threatened this morning at breakfast. A shove, not too subtle, while they were in line, pushed Sam against the hot, metal pot of porridge. The inmate whispered something like "Careful, careful. Little Sammy could get burned real bad if he's so clumsy, and then what would he do?" I'm sure Sam was stunned; he probably thought he was free of Roper and just has to behave himself in order to effect an early release."

"He *is* a babe in the woods in prison, yes, sir. He has no idea what can happen."

"Sam got word to the prison governor. I'm glad to say he acted quickly, for his own sake."

"So Roper won't know where he is…for a while, at least." I tried to make my voice hopeful, but I knew Roper's network would work quickly to find Sam. No gang member kept Roper waiting for long if he valued his life. As last month's case underscored.

"If you're thinking Roper's going to escape and personally go after your brother, don't. You know about Wakefield, Brenna."

"Yes, sir." Wakefield Prison is a high-security facility, holding approximately six hundred adult males—many in category A, meaning they were Britain's most dangerous offenders. As a high-security prison, no one ever escaped. Besides, Roper wouldn't do the deed himself. He'd have the alibi of his incarceration when something happened to Sam. The broken fingers would be just an unfortunate accident; Roper would be innocently in his cell at the time.

As I stood up, Graham said, "I don't mean to frightened you, Brenna. I just wanted you to know what is happening with Sam."

"Yes, sir. I appreciate you telling me. Thank you."

"I'll keep you informed, but hopefully nothing will come of this. Sam might be out within a year and Roper might never find him."

"Yes, sir." That's all I seemed capable of saying. I thanked him again and slowly walked to the kitchen.

Before I joined Mark, I took several deep breaths and vowed that he would not know what had just transpired. It was enough that Mark was involved in my disagreement with Adam; I didn't want Mark to become engaged in Sam's problem. So I downed a quick gulp of water, reapplied another coat of lipstick to make myself look cheery, and smiled hopefully as I walked up to him.

Eyeing me, he asked if all was well.

For a second I wondered if he could see through my act. I asked what he meant.

"Did Graham hand you a laurel wreath or a dressing down?"

"Oh." I forced a smile and opened the door. "He just had a question about our assignment." I turned from him, not wanting him to see my face. I never had been a good liar.

"It's good we found out about Clayton, isn't it?"

"Found out?"

"The note. That it's real."

"Oh. Right."

"It'd really finish me off to know that a police officer attacked a woman like that, but I suppose we're all just human."

Like Roper fixing an attack on Sam, I thought suddenly. Most anyone could arrange an assault if provoked.

"But Graham never mentioned that," Mark continued, "and there's no mention of that in any of the case reports."

I merely nodded and walked outside.

Twenty-Six

The Hope Observer, October 2010

Derbyshire police received an incident report yesterday afternoon of a big cat sighting. The caller stated that she had been walking along the disused trail around Mam Tor when she saw a blur of black among the clumps of fern and boulders. She stood still, fearful and unsure what to do, when the animal bolted. It was then she realized it was a black leopard.

Black leopards have been reported for decades in the Derbyshire Peak District, beginning in the 1960s. The sightings comprise an on-going group that also includes pumas, lions and panthers.

Big Cats, as they are collectively called throughout the area, have slipped into the shady realms of black dogs, hobs and phantom horses. Though not considered an actual black dog, the big cats are, nevertheless, an oddity, swelling the ranks of Derbyshire folklore.

Wallabies, released from a private zoon in the 1930s, are the other major animals that garner frequent sightings. In 2009, six sightings in the Peak District alone were reported to police.

The big cats may be pumas and black leopards illegally imported into Britain and then dumped as they grew too large for their irresponsible owners to handle. The fact that no one has ever reported being attacked by a big cat does little to calm the nerves of this most recent cat viewer. Prior to this report, a large black leopard was seen and photographed walking along the top of a dry stone wall.

"I just got lucky," Perry Bowcock said, referring to the photograph. "I'm out quite a bit, wandering around my village and the immediate area. I usually have my camera with me, but I just happened to be at the right spot at the right time to catch that leopard. I'm also a pretty quiet person when I do walk around. You have to be if you're going to photograph wildlife, and you hear a lot that way, too—the location of birds, the rustle of leaves that might harbor a pheasant or weasel. I've got some smashing shots that way, so it pays to be stealthy and listen. I guess the leopard just plain out didn't hear me. I surprised it as much as it surprised me."

Bowcock, an amateur photographer, lives in Cauldham, about a mile east of Mam Tor, where this most recent big cat sighting occurred.

Will this walker's experience put a halt to her weekend rambles over the moors? "I'll keep hiking but I doubt if I'll ever look at my little Sooty the same way again."

Twenty-Seven

Mark and I walked the long way to Vera's grandmother's house because, as I phrased it, I wanted to see all the steps of the well dressing creation. We walked down the hill, followed the road to the village pond. It was located on the south side of the giant yew, across from the village hall where the villagers would work on the three panels. As Upper Hogsley had done yesterday, the villagers of Cauldham would do today: set up the work tables, put out the buckets and boxes that held pinecones, moss, sheep wool, tree bark, dried beans, flaked coconut, rice, and other natural objects. Tomorrow, perhaps the workers would bring their individual lots of dried eggshells and seed heads, orange peel, fur, parsley, flowers and anything else they had saved. They would work in shifts over the next four days, for the panels would be erected on Friday. I remember from my own childhood stint in the village hall that timing was crucial—start the panels too early and the flower petals would dry out; start too late and time ran out. I promised myself I'd look in daily to see the panels take shape, for I did miss the fun of well dressing.

This was tomorrow, however. Right now, while Mark and I walked past, several men were submerging the wooden panel frames in the pond. The frames, with chicken-wire backs and usually seven to ten feet tall and several feet wide, needed to soak for twenty-four hours so the wood would be thoroughly wet when the workers packed the frames with the moist clay. The clay is actually a mixture of clay, salt and water. This mixture is 'puddled,' much like a traditional grape pressing, but the workers stamping through this muddy mess sport rubber boots on their feet. When the heavy panels are clay-covered, the villagers haul them to the village hall for decorating.

Each panel's design would be drawn on a panel-size piece of yellow waxy paper and laid on top of the smoothed wet clay. The design would then be transferred to the clay through a series of indentations made by pricking through the drawing with sharp implements such as ice picks, metal nail files, skewers, or seamstress' pattern wheels. The paper then would be removed as each section is ready to be decorated, leaving the outline of the design, much like the lead veins in a stained glass window. Working in sections like this keeps the clay moist until it is covered with the natural materials, which is the next step in the process.

So, I cast an envious eye on the men who were Wellington-deep in the pond, listened to the directives and chatter coming from the village hall's open windows, and left the villagers to their fun. Mark and I stopped in the grocery shop so I could buy a small packet of oatcakes—not the best breakfast, but tears had dampened my earlier appetite—and then walked up the hill to Gran's house.

"Which reminds me," Mark said as we were nearing the house. "What was that all about when you asked Clayton where Vera lived?"

"Sorry?"

"You know. That bizarre 'You know I work better if I can see where they lived' bit. I didn't know whether to play along with you or take you round to Bedlam."

"I want to look around Vera's house." I kicked a stone out of my way.

"Why? There won't be anything there after twenty-two years. That's what you're after, isn't it? Find some clue that solves the case. You won't. It's been too long. If the place isn't falling apart, weather or animals or vandals will have ruined or disposed of anything that might be significant. We can't even come up with her name. No one's said a thing about her working—and she might not have done, if she's that old. She could have been a housewife. We've no employer so we've no national insurance number to locate. It's a dead end. A waste of time." He jogged to keep up with me. "You're daft, Brenna. Besides, isn't that breaking and entering?"

"So, go back to the incident room and type up your notes. You'll impress Graham and you can claim you don't know anything about my illegal activities when you're called on to testify at my trial."

He groaned but kept pace with me. "If you're going to get into trouble, you may as well have company. We can talk to each other in our cells."

Of course he was joking, but it was comforting that he wouldn't let me fly solo.

"And what's with the age of the grandmother bit? So she's a grandmotherly age. What difference does it make if she's in her sixties or eighties?"

"A lot," I said while we walked up the road. "I wonder if grandmother had anything to do with Vera's disappearance. Even though she left for London the year prior to Vera going missing, Gran could have come back."

"And done what?"

"Been responsible for Vera's disappearance…or death," I added when Mark stared at me wild-eyed.

"You're totally round the twist, Bren. Why move all that distance—or make a pretext of doing so—and come back a year later? If anyone in the village saw her, they'd remember doing so. Anyone can easily confuse remembering what day he saw the vicar or the publican, for example, because they're seen daily. But someone who's moved out and returned a year later?" His head shaking said it all. "Gran would be taking a hell of a risk being seen. They'd call out to her, rush up to her, wanting to know how London life is, how she is, what she's doing back in Cauldham. No, Bren. You're barking up the wrong tree with this one. The grandmother's a non-starter."

"Just keeping an open mind, Mark."

About a half-mile down Old Mine Road we found Vera's house. Comprised of the same gray stone and dark slate roof as the other buildings in the village, the dwelling did indeed look deserted. Dirt splayed across the windowpanes, fallen branches littered the ground, and the front garden had grown wild years ago. Exuberant Virginia Creeper clung to and in the gutters, nearly smothered the southern face of the house. What may have begun as a modest clump of daylilies had now multiplied into a colorful ground cover. I paused at the front gate, my hand on its curved top, and wondered where the front path was.

"And me without my Boy Scout pocketknife," Mark said, his breathing in my ear. "Should have brought a machete, but who knew?"

"At least it will be easy to trail someone." I pushed the gate open, then leaned against it, mashing down weeds and flowers in an effort to make room for us. Flecks of paint came off on my hand and I wiped them against my trousers.

"That works both ways. We'll leave our calling card when we battle our way to the front door. The coppers won't have to look too far to find the burglars; all they'll have to do is look for clothes shredded by thorns and covered in white shit." He shook his leg free of a creeping thistle. A handful of white, down-like fibers sailed into the air as Mark brushed past a clump of cotton-grass, swirling into his eyes and against his nose.

"We have a legitimate excuse to be here," I said, gingerly pushing aside a thistle and holding it until Mark passed.

"Without the owner's permission? I'd hardly call that legitimate. Try convincing the magistrate."

"We'll be in and out before anyone spots us."

"That's if no one's camped out in the back garden or inside the house." He would have said more, I'm sure, but he sneezed and I walked ahead.

We came to the front door, a weathered plank of wood with

more bare areas than painted ones. I turned to Mark, asking what he thought would be the best way to enter, when he turned the doorknob and the door opened.

"Simple ways are always the best, Bren." He walked inside.

I refrained from saying simple methods fitted his mentality and followed.

If this were what the front room looked like in daylight, I'd hate to be here at night. Despite the sunny day, light barely penetrated the perpetual dusk of the interior. The dirty windows accounted for some of that, but half of the curtains were drawn and dust-covered. In fact, dust and cobwebs coated nearly everything. I tried not to breathe deeply, afraid of mold and bacteria from mouse droppings, and walked slowly around the room.

"Doesn't look as thought she left in any particular hurry," Mark said, shifting the magazines on the table. "Looks normal to me."

"What do you want, chairs knocked over and a lipstick scrawled message on the wall?"

He snorted and poked through the contents of the desk drawers. I leafed through the address book and a fabric-covered stationery folder. An envelope addressed to Harding Lyth was stuffed into the front sleeve. I took it out and pulled the contents from the envelope. It was a greeting card proclaiming thanks, signed by a capital V and underlined. I showed the card and envelope to Mark. "What do you think?"

"From Vera."

"We don't know; we assume it is."

"Who the hell else around here has a name starting with V?"

"Maybe that's what the sender wants Harding to believe."

"So someone was going to send some thank you card indicating it was from Vera? Stop reaching, Bren."

"I guess she might sign her name like that, among friends," I admitted. "Looks like it's been here a while."

"Wonder when this dates from."

"Wonder why she never gave it to him."

"A falling out?"

"Could do. There's no mention of what she thanked him for."

"Maybe she didn't get that far. You know," he said, shutting the desk drawer, "she was going to add it but changed her mind about the card."

"She'd have written a message before she signed her name. Most people do. The name's like the last thing before they address the envelope and post it."

"I'm not a mind reader, Brenna. Maybe Vera was going to add a personal message later, only she didn't get around to it. It's stuffed into the sleeve of a stationery folder. Doesn't that give you a hint?"

"Hint?"

"Stationery, Bren. I'd assume she was going to write something on a piece of stationery and inset it inside the card."

"Well…"

"It's logical."

I mumbled that it was very inconsiderate of Vera not to have at least started writing the note, and returned the card and envelope to the stationary folder.

"Lets check the upstairs," Mark said, and I slowly followed after him.

Three bedrooms, the bath room, and the separate toilet occupied most of the upper level, with a small room hardly larger than a wardrobe—this served as a storage room for old luggage, a dressmaker's mannequin, several cardboard boxes and an old wooden barrel. Mark stood in the half-light from the dirty window, scratching his head. "Wonder how they got that up here."

"Maybe it was here when they moved in." I opened the boxes and looked at the contents. "It's certainly dusty enough."

Mark shrugged and brushed his hands on his trousers. "If I spent all the time it would take to lug that thing up the stairs, I wouldn't want to abandon it when I moved out. It'd be like leaving an old friend behind."

I snorted and walked over to the luggage. Opening the first

one, I said, "If I spent all the time it would take to lug that thing up the stairs, I'd never want to see it again."

"It'd remind you of your aching muscles."

"Very funny. Well, nothing in this room," I said, straightening up from the luggage. "Let's look in the bedrooms."

The rooms held nothing suspicious, either in what items still remained there or were absent. "Anything speak to you?" Mark leaned against the doorjamb of one of the rooms.

"No. There are some items a woman would never leave behind, if she's leaving under her own volition."

"And?"

"Everything I'd expect to see gone is gone. No jewelry lying in the drawers, no family photos, no old letters." I shook my head. "I don't think Vera was dragged kicking and screaming from here, at any rate. She took everything that meant something to her when she left."

"Unless her killer is a woman and *she* went through Vera's things, taking just those items to throw off suspicion."

"But we've got Vera's farewell note," I reminded him.

"Sure, we do. But did she write it willingly, or did someone force her to do it?"

I stared at Mark, this new theory chilling me. "Let's do the rest of the house," I said, trying to sound braver than I was. The trapped summer heat of the house no longer held its warmth. I rubbed my forearms and hurried down the stairs.

The other rooms held no clues, either, to Vera's sudden departure. No half-eaten meal or unwashed pots littered the kitchen. I knew after all this time there would be no food remains, but plates and utensils might still be on the table. The tool shed was straight, and the gardening tools were hanging neatly in the garage. "No car," I said, unnecessarily, to which Mark replied that if Vera left for London, she might have driven, or sold her car for the extra money.

"Did the original investigating team follow that lead?" I asked as we returned to the kitchen.

"Yes. I remember reading that in the report." Mark leaned against the edge of the worktop, shaking his head. "This looks like a blind alley, Brenna. Nothing indicates she didn't leave of her own accord. Her grandmother's things are cleared out, so she evidently left the previous year, as Clayton mentioned. Some of Vera's clothes are in the wardrobe, but that doesn't mean someone abducted her. She could have taken a few things with her, not knowing exactly where she'd be staying in London. She could have thought she'd be back to close down the house. Trouble is, we don't know."

"Still, it looks odd that she'd leave the house furnished."

"Maybe better than having to deal with selling everything. That's a huge job. It could have taken months to find a buyer. If Vera were in a hurry to leave, for whatever reason, she'd not want to stick around to sell the house. She might have thought she'd be back to do that."

"Only, she hit the big time in London, decided to make a fresh start with new clothes and a palatial residence, and figures she can't be bothered with the ratty cottage anymore and abandons it." I eyed him, mutely daring him to dispute the scenario.

"Not what you or I would necessarily do, but she could have done."

"So, if she's so rich and famous and has a yacht in every cove, where is she?"

"If you're going to be facetious about this, when I'm trying to help—"

I threw up my hands. "Fine. She changed her name, she's living in Outer Mongolia; she has amnesia. Whatever fits your conditions. I still say something happened to her and those are her bones we found in the wood."

"Conveniently close to her house," Mark suggested as we walked outside and closed the door behind us.

"Meaning?"

"It's close to her house. If she was killed here, or in her garden, the killer didn't have far to move her body."

"He'd still have to move it, Mark. Doesn't make much differ-ence if it was one mile or a hundred. He's still got to transport it somehow—in his car, in a bag slung over his shoulder, on horse-back…" I turned to stare at the house and garden.

"What?" He bent over, trying to brush flower pollen from his trousers.

"Just thinking. I hope that missing person report will tell us the investigating team checked the house, garage and grounds for blood traces."

"If they're anything like Graham, they will have done. Come on. This is a waste of time." He tugged at the gate, pulling it closed. It hung at a crazy angle, not quite shut, its upright post sagging inwardly. A strip of trampled and broken plants marked our trip to the house. Several leaves and snapped stems littered the front porch and a clod of mud clung to the lowest step where Mark had scraped his shoe. Other than that, no one would know we'd been there.

~

We stopped at the vicarage to ask Harding about the greet-ing card. He looked as astonished as anyone I'd ever seen, shak-ing his head in puzzlement.

"I have no idea why Vera, or her grandmother, if it's from her, would send me a card," Harding said, the fingers of his right hand scratching his chin. "Trying to recall something that may have happened twenty three years ago is rather difficult. I have no idea," he repeated, blinking rapidly.

"No big birthday, then," Mark suggested. "You didn't give Vera something particularly nice."

"I don't think so. I don't believe I did. I certainly never made a habit of doing so. Once started, it's expected the next year, isn't it, and I didn't want that to start." He grimaced, evidently embar-rassed at the lack of money or emotional detachment this sug-gested. "Oh, I liked Vera, don't misunderstand. I don't think there was a soul in the village who didn't like Vera. But as to why she'd be writing to me, especially when we lived so close…" He rubbed his lips and shrugged. "Haven't the foggiest. Sorry."

"Nothing like first communion or joining the church, then."

"No. Now *that* I can definitely rule out. Vera never joined the church."

"Do you know why? Did you ever talk to her about it?"

"I tried to get her into the confirmation class when the others of her age group were taking their lessons—"

"What age is that?"

"Pardon? Oh," he added, his eyes widening as he thought. "Twelve, thirteen. Around there. But she didn't want to. I didn't push her. It takes some people a little longer to decide on things. I assumed she would join when she felt the spirit to do so."

"So you didn't try to talk her into it, or meet with her privately. That wouldn't account for the greeting card."

"I don't see that it would. No. As I said, I can't think of any instance that would call for such a card. Sorry I can't help."

We were too.

~

We returned to the incident room. Mark and I read the missing person report again, hoping for a new angle to follow, but the report confirmed what we had just concluded—the investigating officers had questioned everyone connected with Vera and corroborated that no one had seen her after Clayton Warson stated she left the village. No blood, skin tissue or unaccountable prints were found in the house or garage. No signs of soil disturbance marred the garden or adjoining land. Neither had the Secretary of State received the registration document indicating a sale of Vera's car.

"So that ends that," Mark said, tossing the report onto the table.

"You look displeased about the note Vera sent Clayton," I said. "Don't you want to clear a fellow cop?"

"Sure I do. It's the principle of the thing, Brenna."

"You want a thread to chase."

"Don't you?"

I agreed. "Maybe we'll get one at one o'clock."

We used up the remainder of the morning by typing up our case notes and tracing the few villagers that had moved. Luckily, there weren't many, and the phone numbers were still valid. No one contradicted Clayton's or the police reports. Vera Howarth's case still seemed on track, wherever that led.

Lunch was a quick affair at the pub. When we returned to the incident room for the afternoon meeting I crossed my fingers that we were about to get a break in the case.

Graham wasted no time in putting us out of our misery. "Thanks to Divisional Commander Tierney's rush order, we have the DNA test results on the bones and the hair sample we received from PC Warson." He paused, holding up the report and looking at each of us. "The DNA matches. The bones are that of Vera Howarth."

I think a cannon could have been fired and I wouldn't have heard it. All I could take in were Graham's eyes as he looked at me, and my images of the bones in the wood. A dark, eerie place that seemed to be haunted.

"Now that we can move ahead on this aspect of the case," he said, "we need to find out more about her. Not only why and when she disappeared—whether of her own volition or not—but also of her childhood. If her grandmother and she both went to London, perhaps there's a tie there...other family, close friends, a family home. Margo, I'd like you to research the house Vera and her grandmother owned. There's got to be a deed of sale on the grandmother's house—either she bought it or her parents bought it. Eventually, *someone* bought it and she came into possession of it. I understand we have no name for the grandmother, but if you can locate anything for Vera, that might give us a lead."

"Yes, sir."

"Byrd, if you could ask Clayton about the car color, make and model she drove, that might prove to be a lead. Maybe he'll remember the year model. Teenaged boys...you know." He gave us a quick grin. "That will be a big help. In the course of your research, you may come upon some item that will produce more information. You know what to do. Sorry if I'm preaching. Put it down to…well, this case."

He didn't have to mention the Divisional Commander's name. We knew he felt the pressure to come up with Reed Harper's killer.

Graham assigned other jobs of work to the rest of the team, giving Mark and me the first task of locating Vera's birth certificate. "Her parents will be listed. Then, look up each parent's certificate. Follow me?"

We nodded.

"Because we have Vera's bones buried so close to Reed Harper's, this may give us another break. As I mentioned before, the body disposal site has got to mean something to someone. Taylor, you and Mark tackle that after you come up with the birth certificate information and follow that as far as you can. A person doesn't just bury two bodies in the same place for no reason. We need to know why he chose that spot, which helps us identify our killer. Now, does anyone have any questions?"

I was going to tell him of the greeting card addressed to Harding, but Mark jabbed his elbow into my side and glared at me.

"Any problem, Taylor?" Graham asked, perceptive as always. "You wanted to say something?" He stood in front of the table, leaning against its edge. Behind him, tacked to the whiteboard, were photos of Vera's bones and Reed's body, plus the handwritten lists of Suspect, Motive and Opportunity.

"No, sir. Sorry."

"We've still got a good chunk of the day left, so let's see what we can come up with. I'll be digging into Reed's background, so if you need me, I'll be here. All right? Thanks." He dismissed us with a nod of his head and a hopeful smile.

"Research." Mark grumbled the word, barely audible as we walked to a table. He moved the computer's mouse, disrupting the screensaver undersea scene, and sat down. "Let's hope this isn't prophetic," he added as the fish and the sunken chest of treasure vanished.

"We're not sunk yet, Mark. We haven't even started."

"Yeah, well, this isn't my idea of a good time. Research. If I wanted to devote half my working life to research I'd have become a librarian."

I sat beside him, pouring out my sympathy and opening my notebook.

It took a while—dead end website trails, frustrating waste of time, and several cups of coffee—before we found the birth certificate for Vera Howarth. Date of birth suggested strongly she was the Vera we sought: 4 March 1971. The dates matched Clayton's remark that Vera would have been forty years old this year. Names of her parents were listed as Jane and John Smith. Not exactly suspicious, but beginning to smell. When Mark and I researched the Smith parents, typing in the given ages on Vera's birth certificate, we discovered through death certificate listings that both parents had been lost at sea, not dying in a road accident in Australia. We could accept that, putting it down to garbled family history or deliberate withholding of the truth to ease Vera's trauma. But Vera's grandmothers both had died young— the paternal grandmother in 1970 and the maternal grandmother in 1975. So who was this grandmother?

Twenty-Eight

Who had Vera been living with? Had Vera known she wasn't related to the woman? If so, why the deception? What difference would it make to Clayton or anyone if Vera roomed with an elder woman?

Mark and I spent another hour trying to answer the questions, entering dates and names in various data banks. We reached the same dead end and the same conclusion: no blood ties between Vera and the grandmother.

"Why pretend to be a family?" I asked Mark as we took another tea break. My head swam with data and questions, and I rubbed my eyes, trying to lessen the strain from staring at the computer monitor. "Who cares if they're not related?"

Mark dropped a second lump of sugar into his tea and stirred it absentmindedly. The metal spoon clinking against the sides of the ceramic mug threatened to break my eardrums. "Do you suppose it's some financial scam?"

I massaged my forehead. "Like what? Who benefits from that? Vera had no folks, no other relatives. She wasn't even married."

"How the hell do I know who benefited? Vera. The grandmother. Both. I don't know. What other reason would they pass themselves off as family if there's not some kind of pay-off?"

"But we discovered they're not related. It doesn't make sense if Vera or the woman were trying to avoid an inheritance tax or an estate tax. Either way, the beneficiary of the estate or the personal representatives of the deceased get slapped with a tax. Vera would end up paying the inheritance tax if she was willed the estate, relative or not."

"And why make yourself a relative when you're not? You'd have to pay the estate tax of the person who has died. As you say, Brenna, it doesn't make sense."

We drank our tea, chewed on our pencils, doodled on scratch paper—anything to stimulate our brains. I was drawing stick figures of Vera and her pseudo grandmother when I grabbed Mark's arm.

"What?" he grunted, startled. "Need a biscuit?"

"No. I think I'm about to be brilliant."

"I'm all for that if it shines a light in this mess. What?"

I pointed my pencil at the stick figures as I explained. "Why do they pretend to be a family?"

"That's the question we're trying to answer." He took a sip of tea, frowning at me from over the edge of his mug.

"We're trying to find a financial reason, but there are other motives to assume relationships." I waited for him to make the mental jump. When nothing came, I said, "Because Vera is illegitimate."

Mark shook his head. "She's got a birth certificate. We just saw it…how many days ago?"

I ignored his remark about the hours at the computer. "Yeah. Jane and John Smith. I will bet you that Margo, or whoever, finds no school records for Vera Smith—and how'd she get the last name Howarth, anyway? No," I said before Mark could speak. "It's a phony name. Either the false name was chosen for her by her mother so that the father wouldn't find Vera, or the woman paid to be her grandmother/care giver gave it to her." I fell silent, waiting for Mark to declare I was a genius.

He nodded slowly. "Sounds plausible to me, Bren."

That was good enough. I gave him a swift peck on his cheek. "I can't think of any other good reason. Why else assume a false name? Clayton says he knew her since they were children. She was Vera Howarth as long as he could remember. Why else change your birth name and hide in a tiny village, for that's what I think she was doing."

The silence fell between us as we considered the premise. Mark took small sips of his tea and stared into space. I sat back in my chair, watching Graham at his computer and wondering if I should say anything to him yet.

I was about to get up and walk over to him when he answered his ringing mobile. Standing at my chair, I tried to get a clue from his facial expressions and body language if Simcock passed the pressure from the Divisional Commander on to Graham, or if one of the team members had something to report. The call could also be private, I acknowledged. A girlfriend or family member. Graham had a sister, I remembered. Simcock had tried to contact her when Graham had been in hospital this past March. But Graham's demeanor held no suggestion of friend of family conversation. He remained upright, his back poker stiff, his face impassive but for his lips occasionally flattening against his teeth. Superintendent Simcock. Or Divisional Commander Tierney. Both would pressure Graham into getting a quick conclusion to the case. Simcock was Graham's boss and, as such, wielded a lot of authority to get the job done—it looked super on his record that his team had solved such a high percentage of cases. Technically, he was in charge of the actual case. But D.C. Tierney was Simcock's boss. He was head of the entire Division. B Division, our Division, based in Buxton. How much better it would look on his record if it showed that he could manage the six Sections of his Division and maintain not only solved, closed cases but also swift completion to those cases. I sat down, overwhelmed by the stress these two men could produce for Graham. Would he be in the pub tonight?

Graham closed his phone and returned to his computer when Mark nearly banged his mug down as he turned toward me, his eyes dark and staring. "Do you think Vera could have killed herself in shame, like Chris did? Or the grandmother killed her, having found out Vera was pregnant by Clayton?"

"We can't know that, Mark. All we found were her bones."

"Yeah. Right. I forgot."

"Besides, it has to be murder, whether she was pregnant or not. The postmortem report stated that the nick on her ribs was caused by a knife blade."

"Murder, most likely."

"Even if she killed herself she couldn't have buried herself. And someone killed her, or the original search team twenty-two years ago would have found her in the wood." I stared at my stick figure drawings again. Grandmother and young teen. Two women, related or not, comprising a family. "If she was pregnant, it's a good bet the father of her child didn't want to accept responsibility."

"She could have given him an ultimatum of marriage."

"Even if she wasn't pregnant, she could have had an affair with a married man. Maybe he got scared that he'd get caught."

"So he rubs out his mistake and kills her so she can't make waves. Who would murder her?"

Mark and I simultaneously said the same name. "Reed Harper."

Mark pushed his mug away and propped his elbow on the tabletop. "Do we know if there are other bodies in the wood?"

I felt my blood drain from my face and I stared at Mark in fright. "Have there been other people reported missing from the village?"

"That would look awfully suspicious. What about the general area? Did our Casanova wander about?"

I turned back to the computer monitor and brought up the police report of missing people over the last three decades. Finding a substantial amount of names, I said, "I think it's time to tell Graham."

Twenty-Nine

Derbyshire Dispatch, December 2010

Big cats, ghosts or hidden mine sink holes must be behind the large number of people reported missing in the High Peak region of Derbyshire this year. The suggestion, half made in jest by a spokesperson for the Dale Area Rescue Team, follows a rescue this week of a hiker lost on the moor at Kinder Scout.

"It's our seventeenth callout of the kind this year," the spokesperson says. "That's just for lost hikers, and that's double what we usually have."

The D.A.R.T. crew responds to emergency calls from the Derbyshire Constabulary to help locate missing or injured walkers and climbers. But they are also equipped to attend other incidents such as mountain rescue, stretcher carry-out and general missing person searches.

The search for the moorland hiker began when Caleb James was late returning home last Tuesday night. Family members became anxious at the lateness of the hour and the predicted weather conditions, as James is diabetic and must take his insulin regularly. Temperatures Tuesday night were forecast to dip to 1° Celsius. "We couldn't take a chance he would wander home on his own," the D.A.R.T. spokesperson said, "so the police asked us to search for him."

Despite the use of thermal imaging equipment during police helicopter fly-overs, James still remained missing. Rescue dogs were finally called out and, after a three-hour search of the moor on the western side of the Kinder downfall section, located the man an hour later near a steep crag. The team was able to carry him down the steep terrain with the aid of a litter, it being too dark and the area too dangerous for the helicopter to land.

Safe at home, James and his wife thanked the D.A.R.T. crew for their quick response and expert service. "I'd always heard what a fine group they were," James' wife said, "but now I know firsthand. And, no offense to any team member, but I hope this is the first and only time I'll have to meet them."

D.A.R.T. crew captain Tom Smith responds to the tales of permanently missing people as a case of inadequate information. "Many times a person will disappear on purpose to start a new life. There's not too much we can do in that instance. But if we have a good lead on a person's whereabouts, such as walking to and from specific points, we can usually find him. It might take a while, but we rarely fail."

What of those people gone missing that D.A.R.T. fails to find? Smith chalks that up to incorrect communication on the missing person/family member's part. Also on the large number of disused mines and caves in the area. "People might be surprised to learn that areas of the Peak District are as holey as Swiss cheese with covered-over sink holes and mine shafts. It just takes stepping on the right spot when the earthen covering has been exposed by weather to fall into an old mine. Those people are probably the most difficult to find."

Still, D.A.R.T. personnel have an impressive record. The team works nearly 400 square miles across Derbyshire, Staffordshire and South Yorkshire. Four search dogs, two all-terrain vehicles and two support units supplement the 50-person crew. In 2009 the unit received Tetra radios to help in their work. The radios link directly to a police force's control room, police officers, and other police vehicles such as helicopter and ambulance. "This gives us instant communication with law enforcement personnel and provides pinpoint accuracy to direct police to the exact area."

The team is one of seven civilian-staffed mountain rescue teams that, together, make up the Peak District Mountain Rescue Organization. Due to the nature of search and rescue missions, the team never sees a holiday or closed time, always on stand-by and available every hour of the day, every day of the year.

D.A.R.T. will see its busiest year yet at the end of this month, having responded to 75 search or rescue requests and nearly two-dozen dog searches.

In operation since 1964, D.A.R.T. doesn't see its job just as a search and rescue unit, though. "We are keen on teaching the public about safety on the mountains. Saving lives is important, of course, but if we can prevent accidents in the first place, all the better."

"Our success rate is high," Smith said, "but unfortunately not one hundred percent. There is still the lone person who goes missing and stays missing. That's usually the result of falling through old mining shafts or exploring caverns alone. It's a pity. We don't encourage anyone to go spelunking or hiking without a companion, or at least letting someone know where you're going and when you expect to return."

That sort of thinking counts largely in the successful rescue of lost hiker Caleb James this week.

And what of those tales of big cats, black dogs and ghosts that haunt the region? Let's just remember what Hamlet said. "There are more things in heaven and earth, Horatio, than are dreamt of in your philosophy."

Thirty

Graham brought me down to earth by reminding me that the specialist search team had done a fingertip search of the area on Thursday when the body and bones were found. "They found that key," he said. "If there had been anything else, they would have found it. And I'm not going to dig up the whole bloody forest. Nor am I going to arm you with a metal detector. There comes a point when you have to say you've done a good job and leave it at that."

I mumbled that I understood and went back to talk to Mark.

"He's right," Mark leaned back in his chair and eyeing me rather suspiciously. "But you don't really believe him."

"Yes, I do," I said, half-heartedly. "I know we can't turn the whole wood upside down, and the team probably found everything there was to find…"

"But you want to probe, poke, pick over, and peek into, behind and under every crevice, fallen log, bush, boulder, plant and inch of ground. Where, for God's sake? The village may be small population-wise, but if you're going to tackle all that terrain—"

"I just don't want this murderer to get away with Vera's death. I want to find something that will tell us who it is."

"You think I don't?" Mark asked, incredulous. "You think Graham doesn't? Or Simcock? Or Tierney? Or anyone one of us on the team?"

I leaned forward, feeling the edge of the table bite into my rib cage. "Look, Mark, how often have we found something incriminating at a crime scene?"

"I assume this is a rhetorical question."

"More often than we can count, right?"

"I'll give you that. A button falls or is torn off a shirt as they killer disposes of the body, he drops his wallet or sunglasses, he tosses a cigarette without thinking because it's a natural habit. Why? The team went over that area Thursday."

"I know. But look at it from another angle. Maybe the killer disposed of something on purpose, something incriminating that he couldn't afford to have found."

Mark sat up, interest showing in his eyes. "Very possible, Bren. Yes, that's logical. Where are you thinking of looking?"

I glanced at Graham. A phone conversation occupied his attention. Leaning closer to Mark, I said, "The grandmother's house."

"We just looked through it. There was nothing."

"We looked through the obvious places like the cupboards and desk drawers. But if you had killed Vera and you wanted to get rid of the murder weapon, for example…"

"I wouldn't put it back in the kitchen drawer or under my bed mattress." He stood up, staring at me. "So, where do you want to start? Back or front garden?"

∼

We found a woman's shirt buried in the front garden. Beneath a clump of hostas that was dramatically smaller than the others in the yard. "Probably broke off or divided the plant to make it easier to dig up," Mark said as he carefully lifted the garment from the soil.

"I should have noticed that earlier," I said.

"You were bent on looking for lipstick messages on the living room walls."

I peered at the shirt, now lying in the plastic evidence bag. It was a small sized, tailed shirt and it appeared to have been in the ground for some time, for parts of it were bleached out from the soil. What looked like white hairs or plant fibers clung to one section of the fabric. Dark brown spots dotted the shirt-front, sleeves, and one cuff.

"Blood?" I asked, to which Mark shrugged.

"Early days yet, Brenna. Graham'll get this to the lab before we can scream that we've got a bloody garment."

Which proved to be correct. "I congratulate Miss Taylor on her tenacity, if not her reasoning skill," Graham said when we assembled in the incident room hours later. The shirt had been sent to the lab in Birmingham and we were promised the test finding in twenty-four hours.

Since we had missed our evening meal, Margo and Mark volunteered to assemble a supper of sorts. When Margo set a trayful of mugs, hot tea, cheese, grapes and packaged biscuits on the table, I realized how hungry I was. We sipped and munched as we discussed the case.

The main problem as I saw it, was that even with the vague name for the grandmotherly woman, we had no London address, so she was untraceable. Jane Smith was about as helpful as looking for a Mary Jones. When I had asked residents in the village about her, I got a shrug or various names such as Vera's gran, or Mrs. Smith, or Jane. None of which brought us any closer to identifying the woman or told us where she now lived.

The card also niggled at me. Why did Vera, if she was the V of the signature, need to thank Harding Lyth? Why had she not posted the card? Better yet, why not simply give it to him? Or thank him to his face?

Too many questions stared at me from the page of my notebook. I watched Graham write 'Reed' on the whiteboard and draw lines radiating out from the name. We would add possible killers' names to those lines and discuss motive and opportunity.

Graham sat on the table, his legs swinging slightly as he talked about the names we had already listed as suspects. He announced that he would give a short press conference tomorrow morning. "Now that we know the first victim is Vera Howarth, we can make an appeal for information and show her photo. We'll do the same with the woman calling herself Vera's grandmother. Hopefully someone will know what happened and we could get a lead on the grandmotherly woman. I know the original team of officers inquired twenty-two years ago, but possibly the person who knows the elderly woman didn't see all of the press and publicity at that time. Also, at that time the plea was for information on their disappearance. Now that it's a murder case, perhaps someone might be brave enough to come forward." He gave a sort of seated hop off the table and walked over to the whiteboard. "A long shot, I know, but we'll try. Now. We have Vera's birth certificate, as you know. I'm going to the church office after we finish here tonight and look through the registry of baptisms. I can guess within a few years of her birth date. It might give me another lead. If this grandmother person reared Vera, perhaps the woman's name is in the registry.

"The lab identified the white flower petals found on Reed Harper's body. They are *Leucanthemum vulgare*, or the oxeye daisy. Common throughout the country, it grows in dry, grassy meadows as well as in ground that's been disturbed. A perennial flower, blooming from May through September.

"The mud..." He paused dramatically. I gripped my pen, wondering what was coming. "The mud isn't your ordinary garden variety soil. Or even the soil common in that section of wood. It's what well dressing workers refer to as 'clay.' The mud on Reed Harper's body is a mixture of clay, salt and water." His gaze traveled around the group, finally resting on me. His eyes were bright with excitement and he leaned forward as he asked, "What does all this tell us?"

I stared back at Graham, my mind racing. "Someone deliberately dressed his body with the well dressing clay and the flower petals. Someone made a statement."

"Someone connected to the well dressing or fete, or a disgruntled gardener?"

"If flowers were exclusive to the body, I'd say a gardener or florist. But since the clay for the well dressing panels is also present,

I'd say a participant in the well dressing or fete."

Mark sighed heavily. "That gives us just about half the village, I'd say."

Graham said, "Taylor, you mentioned the killer making a statement. Any ideas about that?"

"Well, sir, I don't know that we can go with the meaning of the specific flower. Oxeye daisies grow wild but they can also be cultivated. I have some in my garden. Plus, it might be as simple as that was the only flower accessible to the murderer."

"Either growing wild or in someone's garden."

"Yes, sir. We also can't assume the killer has the daisy growing in his own garden. That might be too much of a giveaway to the police. So he cuts two or three from some accommodating garden here in the village. What gardener will miss two flower heads if there are dozens blooming?"

"Provided no one sees the theft," Mark said.

"The daisy is the birth month flower of April," I said. "That could signify something to the killer or pertain in some manner to Reed Harper. The daisy has a certain significance, too. Like all flowers, it stands for a particular human quality or emotion. Color factors into a flower's meaning as much as the type of flower itself." I paused, looking at Graham, wondering if he wanted all this information. But he appeared interested, so I continued. Besides, the more information we had, the better our chance to identify the killer. He might have used the daisy for a particular reason instead of it just being available in his neighbor's garden. "For example," I said, rushing on, "the rose. Many people think of the rose as a symbol of love. But that's the *red* rose. A dark pink-colored rose means thank you, and a white rose signifies silence, secrecy or charm. It depends on the flower and its color as to what it means."

"Are you serious?" Mark shook his head. "If it had been a white rose instead of a white daisy plastered on Reed Harper's body, for instance, how would we know if we're looking for a killer who gave a message of silence, secrecy or charm? They're different."

"All I'm saying, Mark, is that the daisy might mean something. It might direct us to the killer. It could be nothing more than a flower. Not everyone knows the meanings of flowers."

"Well, when you figure it out, let me know. I'll be concentrating on something solid."

Graham asked what the daisy implied.

"Several things. Innocence, faith, cheer, friendship and loyal love. There are different colors of daisies, but white symbolizes purity or perfection. I think an old Celtic legend tells of infants who die in childbirth. Their spirits choose daisies to drop over the ground as a way of cheering their grieving parents."

"Reed's daughter is seventeen," Mark said.

"But he had affairs with other women," Graham reminded him. "Besides Clarice, were any of them pregnant?"

"Stuffing a daisy into his mouth doesn't exactly symbolize that legend to me," I said. "It seems more like a comment on the well dressing or fete, anger on the part of the killer."

"It would be completely different if a bouquet of daisies lay beside him," Mark agreed.

"Maybe it means something totally different," I said when we had discussed white flowers and brides wearing white.

"Like what, Taylor?" Graham leaned back in his chair, ready for a new discussion.

"We're forgetting the petals, sir."

"They're not signifying the well dressing?"

"Could do, of course, but there's the other meaning of the flower. Daisies don't tell."

"Maybe that's why it was crammed into his mouth."

We talked another half hour, then Graham told us to get some sleep. I wasn't sorry to trudge back to my room. It was just after ten o'clock and I was tired.

I returned to the pub by way of the village pond. I couldn't face walking past the southern fringe of the wood—not at this hour, not after poking about in the grandmother's house and finding it waiting for Vera's return. The whole setup had the whiff of the fishmonger, as Margo would say, and I was suddenly nervous for the entire CID team—that we were being watched and manipulated like a giant game of cat-and-mouse.

The last of the workers in the village hall turned out the light and locked the door as I strolled up. The man looked up quickly, startled at the sound of my footsteps on the road. I called out, asking how the well dressing was coming. He met me on the pavement, relaxing now that he knew who was out at this time of night, and said they would be puddling the mud and filling the frames tomorrow.

"We do all that on the green." He gestured toward the space south of the pond. "That way we keep all the excess mud outside, there's not as much cleanup inside the hall, and we don't have to carry it halfway across the village."

"Sounds like someone was thinking," I said, walking with him toward the pub.

"Oh, aye. It takes but a time or two to come up with the best way to do all this. We learn quick by our mistakes." His face wrinkled up in a grin.

"Did you live here when Vera Howarth and her…" I paused, then decided to continue with the elder woman's relationship. "…when Vera and her grandmother lived here?"

"You coppers are investigating Vera's death. I know. It's common knowledge all over the village."

"Yes. I'm curious if Vera or her grandmother ever participated in the festival."

"In dressing the wells?"

"That, yes, or volunteering with the fete set-up. Or perhaps donated a cake to the cake booth. Anything like that."

The man thought for a moment, scratching the rim of his ear. "I'm fifty. Vera went missing when I was twenty-seven. I remember 'cause it was such a big thing. Horrible, too. Shocked me to hear of Reed's disappearance, too," he added, rather reluctantly. "Can't help thinking the same person's involved. Responsible."

"Who do you mean?"

"Our bobby. Clayton. Nothing was ever proved that he had anything to do with Vera's disappearance—they said he got a letter from her, but I don't believe it. Not for a second. No offense, but coppers know how to manufacture evidence. How to cover up things, too. Now, I'm not saying Clayton did that, and I don't honestly believe he did—we've known each other forever, it seems, and I count myself a friend. But he could have had the knowledge how to do it, couldn't he? Like a doctor who's a murder suspect. I always think they're the perfect murderer 'cause they know how to muddy the medical waters."

I said rather slowly that anyone with skill or information like that could probably manufacture or destroy evidence.

"There was a lot of finger pointing at Clayton at the time, and a lot of whispered accusations, but that was all. And now Reed…" He wiped the back of his hand against his chin.

"How long did all those whispered allegations last? Clayton still lives here, I see."

"Not long. Things die down quick in a village. Nothing was ever proved against him, and Vera was never found. I think Clayton took it well, those few months. Some folks said they'd seen the note Vera sent him, but I never did. Wasn't really my business. I think Clayton showed how tough and innocent he was, withstanding all that gossip. But living with the suspicion, seeing the look in people's eyes, knowing they believe you guilty…of something—" He broke off and sighed deeply. "But that was then and this is now. History repeating itself, in a ghastly kind of way, with the police here again. Anyway, you asked about the well dressing. Vera may have put in an hour or so helping in some way. I can't recall. Can't recall about her granny, either. You know how it is," he said, sighing as though he were apologizing. "Things happen the same way, year in and year out. Same people involved, same jobs of work to get done. Angela with her master of ceremonies job, Perry Bowcock snapping photos, Jenny Millington writing up the speeches, the same lads each year soaking the panels and setting them up. Everyone knowing and doing his job so long that's it's become automatic. So you don't necessarily keep score of who shows up what year and who does what." He shrugged and apologized.

"If you do remember, would you ring me?" I fumbled in my trousers pockets for one of my business cards.

"It's important, then."

"Yes." I handed him a card. "If you'd feel easier about talking to me in person, I'm staying at the pub. Room 11."

"Well, I'll cast my mind back, but don't hold your breath. I wasn't involved in the decorating of the panels proper, you know. I soaked the frames in the pond and stirred up the clay. Did that then and I'm still doing it. It's my job of work."

"So you don't recall that Vera worked on the panels."

"No. But there's others that might. We've got photos of the workers for most years, too, if you want to look through those."

"Where would I find them?"

"In one of the cupboards in the village hall. They're probably put into scrapbooks or something. You can ask anybody who's working on the panels tomorrow. We all know where they are. Years ago the snaps would be displayed in a kind of Village Fete Volunteers spread, but we don't do that anymore. Too many years we had to scramble to cover up the display when it rained."

"And where is the fete proper to be held?"

"On the east side of the old school."

"The building that's converted into the youth hostel?"

"That's she. Good, big area for the rides and booths and such. 'Course, we don't have many of the bigger rides that the large villages have, but we have a nice selection. Anyroad, the favorite events tend to be the cake booth, big wheel, fortune teller and the flea market."

"The vicar allows a fortune teller?"

"We all know she's not one of them professionals. Just a woman from Upper Hogsley who dresses the part. It's more for amusement than anything else. We return the favor and give

Upper Hogsley a fortuneteller for their fete. Kind of a harmless competition."

"Do these two women just say general things?"

"Oh, aye, but they also get a bit of village gossip to slip in."

"Gossip? Like what?"

"Nothing malicious, mind you. So-and-so's going to be married this year; someone else will retire. You know."

"The fortune tellers must know the people well, then, in order to pull that off."

"Aye, they do. Been doing it so long that they know people by sight. Anyway, we're not that big a village so it's not a sea of faces. Besides, many villagers don't go to the well dressing or the fete. You can count on the same folks showing up year after year. Not hard."

"I suppose the fortune teller can always state some generality if she's unsure who she's speaking to, like a tourist."

"She can that. Got rather good at it, too, from what I hear. A real talent, that. Well," he waved to me as I opened the pub door. "Stop in the hall and see how we're doing. We've got the three panels to decorate by Friday."

I promised him I would and bade him good night.

~

I did try to sleep when I got to my room, but Sam's predicament, the flower significance and the possibility of Vera's connection to the well dressing kept me awake. I thought of seeing if Margo were awake, wanting to talk over this information, but decided to let her sleep. So I did what I usually did when I was restless: take a walk.

It had just gone half past eleven when I climbed the hill and came up to the church. A black silhouette against a dark backdrop of darker trees and hills, the church sat silent, as though brooding with me. The tombstones appeared to hover above the ground, pale gray forms dotting the inky ground. I paused at the lych gate, solid enough in this moody landscape. One of the picket gates stood open. Surely Graham was not still in the church office. I pulled the gate closed and was momentarily startled by the squeal of its rusty hinges. The sound flushed a tawny owl from its perch somewhere overhead. It flew silently to another tree bough and settled into the darkness, perhaps peering down at me, wondering who had disturbed him. I was grateful I hadn't heard its call, for the wavering whoo at end of its song would have been enough to unnerve me.

As I stepped from beneath the lych gate, footsteps crunched on the gravel path in the churchyard. I called into the blackness, in the direction of the sound. A cheery, puzzled voice floated back to me.

"Taylor?"

"Yes, sir, Mr. Graham." I hugged the edge of the gate, making certain it was he before I stepped into the open. The cloud slid off the face of the moon and white light filtered through the tree boughs. Graham walked across a patch of dappled earth, sidestepped around a tombstone, and pulled the gate open. The hinge again complained and the owl flapped quietly through the shaft of moonlight to disappear into a dark expanse of trees.

Graham closed the gate and walked up to me. The scent of his aftershave mixed with the aromas of crushed pine needles and damp moss, bringing police work and the outdoors together in one strange fragrance. Standing next to me in the shadow of a juniper, he spoke barely above a whisper, yet his voice sang in my ear and I could hear every breath he took.

"Out awfully late, Taylor."

I nodded, not caring if the gloom might have made my movement imperceptible.

"We've got an early day tomorrow," he added, as though intimating I should trot back to my room.

"Yes, sir."

We both stood by the gate, not moving, letting the night sounds wash over us. Finally, Graham took a step from me, in the direction of the Harper house. Dry chert crunched beneath his shoe and he turned toward me. "You coming?"

"I'm not really sleepy, sir. That's why I took a walk."

"Pre-wedding jitters, or is the case bothering you?"

"Little of both, I'm afraid."

"Maybe you need to sleep on it."

I wasn't awfully good at figuring out when Graham joked some times, but I was certain this was one of them. I smiled and replied that I should have thought of that.

"Have you tried warm milk or listening to music? The mind has an amazing ability to sort through things while we sleep. Or isn't it that simple?"

"It should be, shouldn't it? You want to get married; you're in love. Why shouldn't it be as simple as standing up and exchanging vows? Why does everything have to be so complicated for just a quarter hour service?"

Silence fell between us as I tried to think of some noncommittal subject to talk about, but I blurted out the question before I realized it. "You've heard nothing more about Sam, have you? I mean, he's still all right…" I tried to see Graham's eyes, to read the unspoken message that he might lie about or try to diminish its severity, but the shadows concealed his features and any hint of his response. I added when Graham didn't reply, "Roper hasn't done—"

"No, Brenna. Roper hasn't done anything. Nor has anyone else. I'm sorry now that I told you."

"Oh, no, sir, that's quite all right. I-I need to know about Sam. It's such a horrible situation he's in…sister of a cop, a police informer." I took a breath, not trusting my voice. "You don't think that will get around the prison, do you? About Sam's relationship to me, I mean. I—it's hard enough for him in prison without…" Again I couldn't finish my sentence. I guess my imagination worked too well. Or I knew first hand of too many 'accidents' that happened to inmates such as Sam.

Graham's voice floated over to me. "Sam's no fool, no matter if he was fool enough to get into that business with Roper. Sam will be on his guard. And even if Roper does have mates in Full

Sutton, your brother can be moved again. It will take Roper a while to find him right now, anyhow, never mind another move in the future, if that's warranted. There are a lot of prisons in England and Wales."

"Yes, sir." I was back to automatically answering just as I had when Graham previously brought up the subject. I tried not to think of the things that could happen to Sam, tried not to envision Roper giving the job of settling of scores to one of his mates. I had to stay strong for Sam, had to stay focused on our case.

As if searching for some safer topic, Graham cleared his throat and said, "By the way, congratulations again for finding that shirt. And, if I might add, those were excellent points you brought up about the flowers, Brenna."

"Pardon?" I blinked, uncertain as to where I was at the moment. Sam's face seemed so real, grinning at me from a shaft of moonlight. "Oh. Yes. The flowers. Thank you, sir. It—that just struck me odd, you know, that the killer took precious time and the effort to apply flower petals and clay to Reed Harper's body. You don't do that without a reason."

"What do you think that reason is?"

"That's part of my insomnia problem."

He laughed, a light, gentle touch of friendliness. "So, what have you decided on while tramping over hill and dale tonight?"

"The killer knows Reed through the well dressing festival. If it were anything else, there would be a totally different object buried with Reed. The killer needs this link to the well dressing. It's very important to him...or her. If it weren't, he would have just dumped Reed's unadorned body in the wood."

"So, it's not really the daisy itself that you think is the key."

"Well, sir, I don't know yet, of course. We just started exploring this angle. But that's what I think right now, and I'm certainly losing sleep over it."

He laughed again, not unkindly, and I said, "I wish the killer had chosen a flower that doesn't have so many connotations associated with it, if that is the way we're supposed to think.

Innocence, purity, faith, cheer, friendship, loyal love." I exhaled deeply, feeling the frustration mounting within me again. "It would be simpler if someone named Daisy is part of this case." I leaned against the gatepost, aware he was walking away, but not ready to go back to my room.

Graham's voice floated back to me as he strolled down the road. "Remember, Brenna, that daisy petals also count for 'He loves me, he loves me not.' Think about it. Night."

~

I had time to think about the daisy petals an hour later when I was called to Jenny Millington's house. If I had continued my walk around the village I might have seen something, prevented it. But that was daft, and deep within me I knew it. I sounded like Jenny talking to Harding, blaming myself for something that evidently I could not control.

Harding had found her. He stood on the front porch of the house, talking with Graham and me while the medical people examined her and bandaged her wrists. Harding's face looked ghostly white in the light of the porch fixture. His eyes seemed to be no more than cavernous sockets, devoid of expression, and he turned those dark hollows toward Graham and me as he tried to talk. "I-I was worried about her, you see. That's why I came over."

"What caused your concern?" Graham asked, the tone of his voice hardened by the tragedy. "Has Jenny tried suicide before? Or did she hint she would attempt it?"

Harding nodded, looking miserable. "She tried to kill herself before, yes."

"When?"

"I can't remember. A year ago, perhaps? Two?"

"Recently, then."

"Yes. She was distraught over her boyfriend…she said."

"She *said*? You didn't believe her, evidently."

"I believe that she is broken hearted, that she thinks she will never find happiness again. But I don't believe her about the boyfriend."

"Do you have a suspicion as to the real reason?"

"No. But I think it might involve Reed Harper."

Graham shook his head and I wondered what person Reed had not been involved with one way or the other in this village. Graham asked, "Did he and Jenny have an affair, do you know?"

"I don't think so. Nothing physical. If there was anything it would be an emotional affair on Jenny's part. She was in love with someone, and I just assumed it to be Reed."

"Why? Because she worked with him?"

"That might have fanned the flames. I think it was a complicated mix of father figure, yearning for a sweetheart, and best friend."

"She not have a father, then?"

"Yes, she had one, but only until she was six or seven, I believe. Then he abandoned Jenny and her mother, so she never had a father's love growing up." He rubbed the back of his neck, looking remarkably tired. "It's one of the necessities of life, isn't it? If you don't get a parent's love during the developmental stage, you continue to seek it in other relationships. How many of us marry someone because she reminds us of our mother, or father?"

"Same holds true for the best friend and sweetheart, I take it."

"Yes, poor girl. Jenny is pathetically shy. Oh, she has friends, but never anyone she can talk to. She chats with me at times, but it's not the same, is it? She never really confides in me."

I felt sorry for Jenny, never having a relationship like Margo and I shared. A great friend was more than an agony aunt to help solve life's problems; she was a conscience and a mirror.

"Has Jenny seemed unduly depressed recently? Is that why you came over tonight?"

"We'd had a talk…recently. She was distraught. I kept calling her house tonight to check up on her, but when she didn't answer her phone, I had the most awful feeling something had happened, so I rushed over."

"And that's when you saw her and rang up the police."

"Yes. Luckily I saw her on the floor, where the ambulance

attendants found her. She, uh, blamed herself for a recent event. I told her it had not been her fault, that she should forgive herself, but obviously she didn't heed my advice."

"And this event?"

"Again, I think it was a mixture of Reed's death and breaking off with her boyfriend. Not that he was a steady companion, or even a close one."

"Not what we usually associate a boyfriend to be," Graham added.

"No. Just a chap she knew…and liked rather well. And perhaps had hopes that it could become more. Become a future."

"Do you know his name?"

"No. I'm afraid I don't. She never confided in me."

"But you know she went out with this person on a fairly steady basis."

"Yes. I saw them several times through the year."

"You were never introduced, though."

"'Fraid not. Jenny's sister may know, however."

"Clarice."

Harding nodded, sighing heavily. "Yes. But I think most of Jenny's depression in the last few weeks, stemmed from Reed's disappearance, and now from his death. She left a suicide note when she jumped from Lovers Leap last year or whenever it was, and even though she didn't name a specific person, the police seemed content at that time to link it to Reed and the fact that he was…out of bounds, shall we phrase it?"

"Did Reed or this pseudo boyfriend show any concern at that time over Jenny's attempt?"

"I'm not aware of it, if either did. Maybe Reed expressed his concern at work. You know." Harding glanced at me before returning his attention to Graham. "Privately, in the office, where Marian couldn't overhear. Not that I am implying there was a physical affair—no! But if there's anything personal to say, it's safer and easier to say it when no one is around."

"Did Jenny recover quickly from that suicide attempt?"

"Outwardly, yes. I don't think most people remembered it after a while. She went about her work as a writer and volunteering for the village fete with her usual dedication to her job. But work is a balm many times and masks a multitude of problems."

"So she never said anything more about this to you, other than just recently, when she was concerned about something."

"Not a word. I didn't know she was depressed until our chat yesterday. If I had known how deeply she was bothered—"

Harding stepped aside as Graham held the door open for the ambulance attendants. Jenny lay on the stretcher, the bandages of her wrists startlingly white even in the light from the porch light. She raised her hand and called out to me as the attendants carried her toward the ambulance. I moved toward her, asking if she wanted to say something. She nodded and I asked the attendants to wait for a moment.

"I-I need to tell you something, miss," Jenny said, each word seeming to be a struggle.

"Can't it wait until you've recovered?" I asked, glancing at Graham to see if it was acceptable to talk briefly with Jenny. He didn't object, perhaps feeling it helped Jenny's emotional healing if she could tell me whatever she had to.

"Please, miss, I want to tell you." She reached for my hand and I grasped hers in a warm embrace.

"Tell me what?"

"Don't go looking for anyone."

I frowned and looked at Harding for interpretation. He looked as confused as I did, so I asked Jenny what she meant.

"No one did this to me," she said, moving her wrist slightly. "No one attacked me or coerced me to do this. I-I'm ashamed to say I did it myself; I tried to kill myself. No one else is to blame. Just me. I swear." Her gaze shifted to Harding, as though she conveyed a mute message to him.

Harding stepped forward slightly and murmured that he was deeply sorry he had failed to help her.

"No need to do," Jenny said. "You couldn't have known."

"I should have. A true friend should have."

"I know I've done wrong in God's eyes. But I'm a changed person." She glanced at her wrist and then at me. "You don't have to worry about me; no one has to worry. I'll be fine, I'll be stronger now that I realize my mistake."

The attendants made noises of wanting to get her into the ambulance and I told Jenny she needed to go to hospital, that we could continue our talk later.

She nodded, dropping my hand. As she headed toward the ambulance, she called, "It was me. Only me. You'll find my note." Her voice dwindled into silence as the men placed her into the ambulance and closed the back doors.

As though cued by Jenny's statement, a constable came out of the house and handed Graham a piece of paper that was encased in a plastic evidence bag. Graham read it, thanked the officer, and returned it.

"Her note?" Harding asked. "I wondered…" He paused and we watched the ambulance drive off, its blue lights flashing into the dark night and illuminating the underneath sides of the tree boughs and leaves overhead. We watched until the blue light became a speck traveling north on Minders Road, watched until the light vanished in the distance. The mesmerizing object gone and the spell broken, Harding appeared to regain consciousness. He blinked, concentrated on Graham's face, and said, "I hope there is never another instance of her writing another one."

We talked a minute more with Harding before he bid us good night and we entered Jenny's house. On looking around we found no signs of forced entry, no signs of a struggle with a possible attacker. Everything was neat, clean, and apparently in their usual places: books in the bookcase, cushions on the sofa, contents in desk drawers. Except for the pillow on the living room floor and the photo of she and Reed Harper propped up beside the pillow. And, of course, the small kitchen knife on the coffee table, and the bloodstained towel and carpet. It looked to be a classic scene of a suicide. I had no doubt Jenny had tried to kill herself and voiced my opinion to Graham.

"In case you're wondering," he said as we walked into the kitchen, "she stated in her note that last year's attempt and to-night's act are due to her boyfriend leaving her. Of course, see-ing Reed's photo by her pillow, I don't believe that bit of her note. Anyway, she wrote the word 'boyfriend' evidently as a late addi-tion, after scratching out the capital letter R. Sad, isn't it, Taylor?"

It was more than sad. Was that the sin she and Harding had been discussing…the sin of suicide? Or had she meant her sin of desiring a married man? That was no sin as I understood it; we all have people and objects and ambitions we long to acquire but can't. Obviously I was no theologian, but I thought Jenny's misery resulted from her love of a man she could not be with. And it didn't matter whether that man was Reed Harper or the sporadic boyfriend. It mattered that Jenny could not emotion-ally leave that man to find love and happiness with someone else.

Graham and I were there for a while longer, going over the scene and satisfying ourselves that no one else had been involved in Jenny's suicide attempt. He finally bid me good night and left, leaving me with a handful of constables in the house. I rang up Harding and Mark to ask if they would notify Clarice of her sis-ter's admittance to the hospital. Of course both men said they'd go to Clarice's immediately. Before ringing off, I asked Mark if he'd tell Clarice we'd make a family liaison officer available to her if she wanted.

"Sure, Bren," Mark's sleep-tinged voice came back. "Attempted suicide's horribly stressful for the family members. Don't worry. I'll let her know."

I rang off and walked outside. There would be no big inves-tigation here—we just look for a note, search the house, make sure it really was Jenny who attempted suicide by looking at the wound or the method, and write a report. This was not a crime; nothing illegal had happened. No case would develop from this.

It was just a sorry affair that should never have happened.

The constables left and I secured the front door. I walked halfway down the front path before turning slightly to gaze at the house. Maybe the village *was* hexed—someone had suggested that. Clayton had, when he handed in the lock of Vera's hair. I was beginning to believe it, for Jenny had been Vera's closest neighbor. Though in the village proper, sitting at the junction of Miners Road and Old Church Lane, Jenny's house backed up to the wood where the bones and body had been found. The structure didn't differ much from the other homes in Cauldham—stone façade, brightly painted wooden door and window frames, flowers in the front garden. Some of them daisies, I realized, watching their white petals bob in the breeze. Did someone—even Jenny, perhaps—pick them to dress Reed's body, or was it merely another common variety of flower that grew well?

I shuddered as one of the flower heads bent beneath the buffeting, brushing against my arm as though urging me to stay with them, or take a silent clue from them. Wiping the sensation of the contact from my arm, I concentrated on the front of the house. Poor, pathetic Jenny, nearly killing herself for the love of a man who, in all probability, might have used her and thrown her away as he had all the others. A near case of Jenny wanting to die for love...or lack of it. Daisy petals...daisy, tell me true. I walked back to my room at the pub, thinking maybe everything in the village boiled down to the daisy petals after all. 'He loves me, he loves me not' was, in my opinion, the real crime.

Thirty-One

I wish I had had a full night's sleep last night—I might have been able to help the team figure out what had happened.

Between the time Graham finished with his research project and left the church around half past eleven, and the time he unlocked the door to our work area this morning, someone broke into the church basement and rifled through our case notes. It was an unsettling sensation, a police room being burgled. I had more empathy than usual for the violated homeowner.

Graham asked one of the computer gurus if anything had been compromised. After clicking and mousing and logging into and out of, she pronounced our security unbreeched and nothing read or emailed.

"That's one good thing," Graham said as I rearranged the stack of computer paper. "Though it still disturbs me. What was the person looking for?"

"Something we mentioned when we talked to people yesterday?" Margo ventured.

"That narrows it down." Graham exhaled heavily. "The church break-in and the timing of it are not the super hero feats you might first assume, either," he added. "Jenny Millington's house is a mile from the church. All our focus and activity was there as we concentrated on her, leaving the church sitting in the dark. So, the field is fairly wide open for our culprit."

"'Course, it could be anyone connected with the case, but if we frightened someone earlier on, I would think that person would make a move before this. Why wait until we've had a chance to consider guilt?"

"Thanks, Lynch. I was afraid we'd have to consider the entire village population." He picked up a pile of photos and set them on the table. "Anyone you favor as getting his feathers ruffled beyond comfort?"

"Not really, sir. Mark and I walked to—" I stopped abruptly. Graham didn't know that Mark and I had entered Vera's house, that we had trespassed. This wasn't the time to tell him; he was upset already with the incident room event. He waited, perhaps not so patiently, for me to continue, so I pretended to have a small coughing spell, then said, "I mean Mark and I *talked* to Chad Styles and Kevin Harper, stopped them from laying into each other with their fists. But I don't think that was connected with this."

"Oh? Why not?"

I told him about Chad wanting to locate a photograph. "But all he had to do was ask the vicar or Marian Harper or someone working on the well panels. He wouldn't have had to resort to all this rummaging about."

"Does sound logical. I hope Chad thought as logically. Anything else?"

"We did some research on the computer—Mark and I. We thought we could find a relative of Vera or her grandmother that we'd get someone else to talk to. But we came up with that information about them not being related. The rest of the day we worked at the computer and you held the briefing."

"Anyone you talked to last night? I'm not accusing you of deliberately telling a villager something about the case, Taylor. But sometimes in idle conversation…" His gaze was steady, unblinking, quietly insisting I give him an answer.

"No, sir. I talked to one of the workers on the well dressing panels."

"When was this?"

"After we left here for the night."

"Meet him up here?"

"No, sir. I had walked down the hill and he was just locking up the village hall. We just chatted about the dressing process and I asked if he lived here when Vera or the grandmother had. I also asked if they had ever helped with the work."

"Why?"

"I thought he might have a photograph of them. Well, you do have that sort of thing in smaller villages. From morris dances, well dressing festivals, Christmas dances in the village hall, Harvest Home dinner. You know."

"Good thinking. And did he have a photograph?"

"He suggested there might be some in the village hall. Snaps from previous years' workers and the festival. You know."

He nodded without smiling. I realized he might be thinking back to his own career as a Methodist minister, to the village events he had attended. Photos of him probably adorned many scrapbook pages in the villages where he had served.

Continuing, I said, "I didn't say anything about our inquiry line, though, sir. I just asked about the two women and the possibility of existing photographs."

"If he was suspicious," Graham said, breaking his reverie, "I'd have thought the village hall would be ransacked."

We stared at each other at the same instant.

"No one's reported anything untoward," I said slowly.

"It's just gone eight o'clock." He consulted his watch. "I doubt if anyone's there yet. Would you mind…"

"I'll just go down and see, sir." I left the church nearly before Graham had finished thanking me.

I walked down the hill, past the youth hostel and the village pond. The house Jenny's sister lived in was opposite the pond and next door to the village hall. I had not taken this route to check out the woman's emotional state or to ascertain that the family liaison officers were providing comfort to Clarice; the route was the logical way to the village hall, being closer to the church than the northern path. However, I did glance at the front garden. A female constable sat with Clarice on a small bench. A goldcrest pecked at the earth beneath her birdbath, giving its high-pitched 'see-see-see' call. Clarice and the WPC seemed not to notice the bird, for the constable matched Clarice's bowed posture, intent on their conversation. I walked on, feeling incredibly despondent that Clarice had no family or boyfriend to help her through her pain.

A woman in her sixties was unlocking the door to the hall. I walked up to her. She turned, perhaps expecting to see another villager who was slated to work with her. On seeing me, she smiled hesitantly and remained with her hand on the doorknob.

I introduced myself, showed her my warrant card, and asked if I could accompany her inside.

Her eyes widened for a moment and she stuttered that of course I might enter. She unlocked the door, pushed it open and let me go in first. I don't know what she was expecting from my odd request, but evidently it wasn't what greeted us.

The buckets, boxes and bags of materials for the panel dressing were intact and undisturbed, but the cupboard doors stood open and the cupboard contents tipped out and strewn across the floor. I stopped the woman at the door and asked her to remain outside. She appeared to be only too glad to comply, and wandered across the road to sit on the bench beneath the yew.

I phoned Graham, told him our burglar had struck the village hall, and said I'd wait for some constables to process the scene. "I don't think anything was taken," I said as I stood in the doorway, viewing the open cupboards. "All the well dressing items are undisturbed—including the tables, supplies, paper designs and tools." I looked at the tables on which the mentioned items lay. "I'll talk to the woman who opened up, but I doubt if the thief took anything but a scrapbook or photographs. If that's what led to all this."

"Ask her if they kept money in the hall," Graham suggested. "Maybe it's a case of someone going after the cash box."

"Could be," I said, none too convinced. Especially after last night's conversation with the villager. "I'll find out."

"The lads will be down in a minute, Taylor." He thanked me before ringing off.

While I waited for the constables to arrive, I went to talk to the woman. She sat in a patch of sunlight, her eyes worried and watching me cross the road. As I approached her, she sat up straight and grabbed her carrier bag. I called to her, asking her to remain seated for a moment, and jogged up to her. At this nearer distance she appeared more curious than worried, and I asked what normally was kept in the cupboards.

"Nothing of any value," she said, clearly confused with the event.

"Like what, exactly?"

"Oh, just common supplies that anyone might need. The village hall is used for other things besides dressing the well panels," she said, needlessly.

I smiled and asked again what items were housed in the cupboards.

"Well, things like drawing paper, scissors and paste, crayons—art supplies, you know. And some hand tools like screwdrivers, hammers, pliers, boxes of nails. A small tape player and cassette tapes—blank and recorded."

"Recorded? Like what, meetings or concerts?"

"No. Professional tapes, like you'd buy in a store or off the Internet. Music for exercise classes. That sort of thing."

"But no one's conversations, nothing someone might tape at a meeting."

"I don't see why. Someone always took notes at meetings."

"Anything else?"

"Sometimes paper plates and cups, and plastic utensils, although we tried to keep those in the kitchen. But if something big was coming up, like the fete this weekend, they'd run out of space to store that so they'd use a shelf or two in the cupboards in the main room."

"Anything else pertaining to the festivals?"

"Well, there are some history books."

"Like notes or private recollections of the village that were typed up and bound?"

"No. Nothing so professional. Just some 3-ring binders or scrapbooks that you can buy in hobby shops or stationer's shops. We kept photographs of all the village festivals. You know, well dressing, Harvest Home, Christmas pageants in the church, Bonfire Night." She broke off, sounding wistful. "Of course, in the days when children participated more in village activities, we had troops of Boy Scouts and Girl Guides. The drum and bugle corps would parade through the village. That was always a treat. Also Mothering Sunday events and Armistice Day remembrances, but those have fallen by the wayside. I suppose people are too busy these days, or they don't care."

"I assume someone penned commentary beneath the photographs. What, when, people involved…"

She looked startled, as though it were the daftest suggestion she'd heard. "Certainly! Not much point in keeping up those books if we don't know who the people were or the date or anything."

"Did Chad Styles stop by here yesterday? Talk to you or anyone?"

"Not to me, dearie. I haven't heard from anyone that he did. He's the fete coordinator in Upper Hogsley, isn't he? Why would he need to talk to me?"

"I saw him in the village yesterday. He mentioned he might pop in here. Would you know if anything in those cupboards is missing? Like one of the scrapbooks, for instance? Do they have dates on them?"

"Of course they are dated. Makes it easier to find something if you're hunting for it, doesn't it?"

"When the constables are finished in the hall, would you mind having a look to see if anything has been taken?"

She promised most solemnly that she would have a look. I thanked her and joined my colleagues in the hall.

PC Byrd took photographs, and Oglethorpe and MacMillan

measured every possible to-and-from point. Two more constables dusted for fingerprints on the cupboard knobs and door edges, but I thought that a useless task. Besides the hundreds of prints left by people having a right to be there, the burglar no doubt wore gloves. Television shows and movies had ground that bit of procedure into most every viewer's brains.

I watched the work for a minute, looking around the room. One point more than any other bothered me: how did the burglar gain access?

The door lock was intact—the villager had unlocked it to let me inside the hall. Walking around the room, I checked the windows and their latches. Each one was closed and locked. I went outside and walked the perimeter of the building. None of the window locks or frames showed any signs of attempted forced entry. But a few scratches near the back door lock spoke of some attempt to enter the building. I bent down, looking closely at the marks. They seemed to have been done with a crowbar or screwdriver. Even the claw end of a hammer. The edge of the lock was slightly bent but hadn't been pried enough to break the lock. I stood up. A half-hearted attempt to get inside? Or a red herring, when the burglar had a key the whole time?

Byrd was outside by this time and photographed the back door lock. Before summoning a constable to take prints of the door's exterior surface, he commented that it looked like some teenager's first attempt.

When the hall had been photographed and measured and dusted to the constables' desires, they drove back to the church and I asked the woman to look at the items on the floor.

The crayons, colored pencils and paint brushes had fanned across several square yards in front of the cupboards, making it look messier than it was. The paper was easily picked up and restacked on the bottom shelves. So were the reference books of British customs and wildlife, regional history and local legends. It would take but a few seconds to shelve the bags of paper products and tins of tea bags. The only things broken—and even those weren't many or even a tragic loss—were the handle of a battered teakettle, a small ceramic candy dish, and a wooden picture frame.

I asked the woman if the picture had been stolen, but she assured me it was a superfluous frame and she really didn't know why they kept it.

As we put the scrapbooks back onto the shelves, we made note of the dates. The book for the years 1985-1995 was missing. 1989—the year Vera Howarth went missing.

Giving one last look at the room, I thought it obvious that the burglar had been after one of the scrapbooks. He had not bothered with the tape player, computer and printer, microphone and portable speaker—items that might have brought a nice chunk of change.

I thanked the woman, assured her we'd look into the incident, and walked back to the church.

When I told Graham about the break-in, he said we'd keep it on the back burner. "There are no such things as coincidences, Taylor. It's beyond my level of acceptance that the night I do some poking about in the church records the incident room and the village hall are searched. What did the burglar want? Did you determine how he gained entry into the hall, by the way?"

"Must have been with a key, sir. No windows were broken, the locks are all intact."

"Seems to rule out Mr. Chad Styles, then, for I can't believe he'd have a key to any place in this village. So why would our burglar mess about with the back door?"

"Maybe he left it, remembered the key, went home for it, and came back. Maybe an extra key is kept hidden under a flower pot." I shrugged. "Same with the church hall. All the windows are bolted shut, and you unlocked the door to enter this morning."

"A fair number of people must have keys to both places—vicar, Reed Harper...well, Marian Harper, now. Village council members. Who else?"

"The Harpers may keep their key in a drawer or key rack, where anyone can grab it. Ilsa, for example."

"Same for anyone who has a key. This isn't getting us anywhere."

But he did ask me to visit Marian and Kevin and any of the more prominent villagers, including the publican, and ask about the keys. "I'll have a quick word with Harding, since he let me into the church office last night. He probably has sets of keys to the village hall. He might know of others. Meet me back here when you're finished."

Marian admitted they had keys to the church and the village hall. "Reed sometimes worked late on the fete and needed to get into these places." Reed's brother Kevin had a key to the hall but not to the church. Edmund, the half-brother, had no key to either place...or so he said. I stopped in most of the shops and found out that both sets of keys were secreted in the village hall—they were still there, for I checked—and the publican had another set, also still in the back room. I didn't bother with the newsagent's, grocery, chemist or other shops, for those proprietors weren't involved with the case.

I met Graham back in the incident room and learned that Jenny Millington had a key only to the hall—but she couldn't be our culprit, since she was still recovering in hospital. Angela, the vicar's daughter, had no keys but knew where her father kept his set. Clayton wouldn't have keys to any premises in the village for precisely this reason—no police officer could then become embroiled in this sort of situation. Besides, Clayton was sitting in jail. "Anyone having these keys could have used them in the burglary and returned them when the job was over," Graham said, sighing. "Doesn't get us much further. Well, as I said, we'll keep this in the back of our minds and see if it pertains to something."

I nodded. The burglaries looked to be little more than serving as nuisance value. Nothing had been taken from the incident room—we checked all our records and photos. The notes on the whiteboard, although not top secret, shouldn't alarm anyone, for we hadn't named a killer yet. Still, perhaps we had unnerved someone, made him frightened to the point that he had to know what we had found out, so he broke into the church basement. As to the missing village scrapbook...

I hadn't talked to that many people yesterday. And even then, I hadn't named names or stated that we were about to make an arrest. The burglar had to be linked to my activities yesterday. Which meant looking about in Vera's house and garden and talking to the well dressing worker. Which also meant, I realized, that to know my movements was to spy on me.

That bit of reasoning didn't do much for my confidence. I sank down into a chair, determined to work out how this could have happened. Vera's house, though not in the wood proper, was situated in a lonely spot. No neighbors were near enough to see any stalking eavesdropper. The potential burglar could have seen Mark and me enter the house, sneaked up the garden path and listened at the door. I hadn't been obsessed with keeping a low profile or looking for snoops when we left. As for that evening, I had chatted with the well dressing volunteer. I suppose someone could have been listening across the street, by the big yew. It was dark and I hadn't been secretive about the conversation. Nor had I been considering that anyone would be skulking around in the shadows. But that certainly was possible. Were either of these two activities the incentive for our burglar to ransack the places he did?

Thirty-Two

The Hope Observer, 15 March 1989

A spate of burglaries has Derbyshire police, as well as residents and shop owners in the Hope Valley, deeply concerned.

Yesterday, at approximately 10:00 p.m., the residence of Vera Howarth was broken into. Howarth, 17 years old, was away from home at the time of the burglary but returned to discover a back window broken and personal items tossed about.

"I don't know who would do this," Howarth said. "I've lived in Cauldham all my life and am friendly with all my neighbors. It's unimaginable someone would have a grudge against me."

Books, knickknacks, and photographs had been swept from bookshelves and dumped onto the floor. Clothes in the bedroom littered the carpet and the bedding was pulled off the mattress. In the kitchen, pots, pans and lids had been yanked from the base unit and left in a heap on the floor. A cupboard door was open but none of the crockery disturbed. Items in the attached garage and garden shed also were untouched, prompting police to speculate that the burglar had been interrupted by Howarth returning home.

"I've never had any threats, nor argued with anyone. I can't explain it." The wooden frame holding a photograph of Howarth's grandmother was broken, the sheet of glass shattered. "It's like the intruder stepped on the photo on purpose. It's the only frame of my gran that I have. Maybe it can be flattened out and saved. I hope so. I love Gran." The photograph was creased and there was a large rip where the elder woman's right eye should be.

A police officer went over the house with Howarth, making notes on what she thought might be missing. "Though right now, with the condition the house is in, I'm not certain."

"Many times the homeowner will believe a particular item is stolen," PC Brown said. "But on straightening up and putting things to right, the item is discovered. I sincerely hope it is this way with Miss Howarth."

"I don't keep any money at home," Howarth said, "so I really don't know why the bloke was here."

PC Brown speculated that the intruder was after money. "So many of these dwelling house burglaries are committed by teenagers desperate for drug money. It's a sad statement on our society right now, but that's usually the situation when we apprehend these thieves."

The officer added that the Howarth burglary was one of several dozen that have occurred in the district, beginning last summer and still on the rise. Village shops have also been hit, though the criminals have had little success with large takes from the tills. "We are urging all shop owners to install alarms. That will dramatically reduce the incidents of burglaries."

PC Brown added that the smaller businesses and residences were usually targeted over stores because stores employed video surveillance cameras and burglar alarms as part of their security systems.

"We hope that if more shop owners and homeowners employ these alarms as part of their overall protection plan, we'll see a decrease in crime."

Howarth agrees. "I should have done this before, but I'll get an alarm tomorrow. There won't be a 'next time' for me."

Thirty-Three

I discussed the idea with Mark that someone had spied on our house visit, or had heard my chat by the village hall. Dressed in brown trousers and a turquoise-and-blue striped shirt, he looked up from the computer, mildly distracted, and nodded as I sat down.

"There's no other explanation," I said as Mark turned slightly to face me. "Whom else did we talk to besides Clayton? No one," I answered, leaving Mark with his mouth open. "Someone had to have listened to us."

"But even then, what did we do to prompt the two break-ins?"

I scratched my head. "I don't remember what we talked about."

"You wanted to see if Vera left in a hurry or there were signs of someone abducting her. There weren't. All was tidy. Except the garden," he added, his mouth curling in frustration. "I'm still picking that white stuff off my trousers. Who'd have thought it would cling like this?"

"We found that card," I reminded him.

"The greeting card signed with the V? I forgot."

"Do you think the burglar assumed we found it and took it with us?"

"Could do, which would explain this place being searched. But why the village hall? You didn't go into it last night, did you?"

"No. I just talked to that man as we walked to the pub."

"Then it doesn't make sense."

Sighing, I nodded and glanced at the wall clock. Mid-morning and nothing to show for my hours on the job.

"Did you talk to anyone else?"

"I don't know, Mark. It's all so routine. You don't really make a note of people you talk to. Outside of you and Margo and Graham…" I trailed off, suddenly recalling my moonlit stroll. "I talked to Graham."

"When?"

"After hours. After we all went to bed." I related my short ramble and meeting Graham outside the church.

"I don't suppose," Mark suggested thoughtfully, his eyes on the computer screen, "your mysterious spy might have thought he saw you give something to Graham or the well worker. You know, if you fumbled for Graham's arm if you tripped, or handed the worker something as innocent as your business card—"

I grabbed Mark's arm, squeezing it in my excitement. "I did! I gave the man one of my business cards. I told him to phone if he remembered Vera or her grandmother working on the well panels."

"So, if someone were watching you from the shadows, he might have thought you handed the man that V-signed greeting card."

"But why? We didn't take the card with us. All the watcher had to do, Mark, was go back to Vera's house and get it."

Mark stared at me, a slow smile consuming his face. His right eyebrow crept upward and he said, "Want to go now or later?"

~

This time I was aware of my surroundings. Unless someone had sat in the wood all night, wore a papier-mâché tree trunk or lay on the roof behind the chimney, I don't see how we could have been overheard.

The front path looked the same as I remembered it. No secondary path led from ours, indicating an intruder had walked around the house to gain entry elsewhere. Although I couldn't swear to it, the house interior seemed as we had left it. No wild searches through cupboards or bookcases, no carpets yanked up, no desk drawers open. More importantly, the greeting card was gone.

"What do you think?" I asked Mark on the walk back to the church. The sun was nearly overhead, casting thick, black shadows that hugged the base of every object. A slight breeze played with the longer strands of Mark's hair, lifting them from his collar.

"I think," he said, his voice strained with frustration and anxiety, "someone's just remembered that card and it's a hell of a clue to something. I think someone was in the right place at the right time and saw us enter the house, and that person searched the church and village halls in a muck sweat, trying to find that card because he assumed we took it. When he didn't find it, he went back to the house to get it. I think we're all being watched— maybe you in particular because you've been talking to more people—and our mystery burglar is trying his damnedest to keep us from finding out some vital piece of this whole thing." He stopped mid-stride and pulled me around to face him. We were opposite the lych gate and a shaft of sunlight slid through a tangle of juniper branches to fall on the steeply pitched roof.

"I just remembered something, Mark."

"What?"

"I told that well worker my room number at the pub."

"You *what?*" Mark's anxiety exploded into a string of curse words and didn't lessen as I said, "I forgot until just now. I thought the man might feel more comfortable in a non-police atmosphere. You know many people do."

"You gave him your mobile number. Wasn't that enough?"

"I wasn't thinking of anyone being out to get me."

"No. You never do. There's a killer loose in the village, Brenna. Or have you forgotten that's why we're here and not on the Riviera?"

"I'm sorry. I didn't mean to make a problem. He's just a bloke in his fifties, just an ordinary looking guy. He lives here in the village, Mark. He's not going to whack me on the head some night and drag me—"

Mark's fingers dug into my upper arms and his voice was low and sharp in his urgency. "I suppose Norman Thorne looked like an ordinary bloke, but 1925's a bit before your time. He murdered his fiancée, who should have every reason to think he was an ordinary bloke. How about Dennis Nilsen, who dismembered fifteen men in London? He looked normal, whatever that is. Or John Duffy, the Railway Rapist, convicted of twenty-four cases of sexual assault and murder."

"All right, all right. You've made your point. I was stupid."

"You were a flaming berk." He held me at arm's length, his fingers still tightly clenched around my arms. "You're sleeping in my room tonight."

I probably didn't have my mouth open for more than a minute.

"I'm sleeping there, too. Oh, don't worry," he said quickly. "You'll be safe enough," he added, his voice laced with reluctance. "I'll take the couch. Or the floor. Unless you are feeling magnanimous and agree to sharing the bed— No, I guess not. We tried that before and you never succumbed to my charms."

"Mark…"

"My room, then. I won't hear anything more on the subject. Until we wrap up this segment of the case, I don't want you on your own after dark. Even if your well worker is as innocent as a daisy, anyone could have heard you talking last night. I don't want to find you in that alley. Now. No more arguing. Subject closed. Back to work."

He remained silent as we entered the incident room and grabbed two cups of tea. We had just brought the computer screen to life when Margo came over.

"You had a phone call while you were out." She handed me a handwritten message.

"A man?" I said.

"No. Some woman. She said you two talked this morning at the village hall."

"Oh, right. She find something else missing?" I tried scanning the note but Margo interrupted my reading.

"I wouldn't know. She said only that she wants you to call her. ASAP," she added, smiling as she turned.

"You can't take care of it?"

"That's the price of popularity, Bren. She wants to talk to you."

I punched the phone number into my mobile and moments later listened to the well panel worker. "I'm sorry to disturb you," the woman said, "but you did say to ring if anything occurred."

"Quite right. Did you find something missing?"

"No. Just the opposite."

"Pardon?"

"I discovered a scrapbook of newspaper articles."

"Newspaper articles."

"I don't know if they'd be anything of interest for your investigation," she said, sounding vaguely flustered, "for I forgot they existed, to tell you the truth. I just leafed through the scrapbook before I rang you up, to make certain what I thought I remembered was true. About the types of articles, I mean. I haven't looked at them in years, haven't remembered they existed, but I thought you should know about them, now that I found them."

"What type of articles?" I crossed my fingers, hoping they would give more information on the grandmother.

"Oh, just clippings from several newspapers. Local ones. Articles pertaining to our villagers or our local Peak legends. That sort of thing. When I was putting away the other, I saw it. Haven't had the scrapbook out in years." She paused for breath and I could hear the quiet hum of conversation behind her as the volunteers began work on the panel decorating. "I doubt if the clippings would be helpful, and I'm rather embarrassed now that I rang you up, but if they do mention something that you need to know, well, I'd feel awful if I didn't say."

I thanked her and told her I'd be right down to get the scrapbook.

～

Mark insisted on getting the book, telling me I should research further into Vera's birth certificate. I knew it was busy work he handed me, but I couldn't get too angry with him; he was fearful about my welfare. I went back to my notes, refreshed my memory on birth date and parents' names, and then looked up the baptismal record in the church office.

Forty minutes later, he returned, a large book tucked under his arm and a smile on his face. I wondered if some of the older articles had photos of old cars, but I quickly saw what made him so happy. Our helpful volunteer had given us a treasure trove of information on the village history—crimes, missing persons and ghost stories. Mark plopped the book onto the table, grabbed a cup of coffee, and sat down. Opening the front cover, he said, "Whether or not this proves useful." He grinned, so I knew he had stopped to flip through it at the village hall. He liked to be certain of things.

We had barely got into reading the articles when Graham called us together for a short meeting. Mark closed the scrapbook and scooted our chairs over to the whiteboard. I knew he was loath to abandon our study, but we'd get back to it.

"Sorry to drag you all away from your jobs of work," Graham said, "but I thought we needed to discuss where we are with the case."

Mark relayed the information about finding the greeting card at Vera's house and our suspicions that it could be behind the two burglaries this morning.

I indicated the scrapbook and said we'd just begun scanning the articles. "They may mean nothing, but if something goes back twenty-two years and seems linked with Vera's disappearance and death—"

"Right," Graham said. "Someone's nose is out of joint, or that card wouldn't have gone missing. Well, what else do we have… or can we construe?" He stood by the whiteboard, ready to write down our brilliance. When no one spoke, he said, "We've got a greeting card, presumably from Vera Howarth to Harding Lyth, the vicar. Taylor and Salt found it yesterday in Vera's house and now it's gone. It's obviously important to someone. Who might that be? I'll give you a hint: Vera's not around, so you can count her out. And her grandmother isn't here, either. Who might look upon that card as having some significance?"

"Harding Lyth." Mark wrestled to find a comfortable position in the chair. "Despite his protestations of ignorance."

"Then why didn't he get it before now? He's had years to grab it. Why risk rousing the collective suspicion of the investigating officers and steal it now?"

"Because he saw Brenna and me go into Vera's house. When we asked him point blank about the card, he stole it."

"Wasn't he calling attention to himself by doing that? Why not just wait? The investigating team from twenty-two years ago saw no value to the card when they went over her house. They left it. You and Taylor also left it. Why would Harding point to its worth by stealing it? And, what's even more obvious, he steals it after he burgles two places to find it. He's got the keys to both places, on top of that."

I suggested it wasn't Harding who stole the card.

Graham cocked his head slightly to one side and asked whom I favored.

"Well, sir, I'm not certain, but I think it depends on who killed Vera."

"Go ahead."

"Well, when Mark and I were searching for Vera's birth certificate, we discovered her parents were listed as Jane and John Smith. While I was waiting for Mark this morning, I went into the little alcove where the books are kept. I found her baptism listed in the book of baptismal records. Besides the person baptized, it listed their age, gender, parents' names, place of birth, and the officiating clergy. It also listed witnesses. The only person mentioned in attendance was the grandmother. The year is 1971, the same as the birth year. According to Vera and the grandmother, the parents were killed in Australia five years later. Doesn't that seem rather odd?"

"Did you follow that up?"

"Yes, sir. I couldn't find any record of any Smiths' death in the intervening years. I can draw only one conclusion."

"She's illegitimate."

I nodded. "Harding Lyth is listed as the participating vicar." I let Graham and the team come to their own conclusions.

Margo said, "Harding is the father."

Graham asked if we knew Harding's age.

Mark went over to the computer and returned a few minutes later, announcing "He's fifty-seven."

"In 1971 he was eighteen."

Graham walked over to the edge of the table. "Not that it cancels out extramarital affairs, but when was he married?"

Mark again went to the computer and after summoning up several websites and jotting down some information, walked over to Graham and showed him the note he'd made. "Married when he was twenty-one."

"His daughter, Angela, is nineteen."

"Yes, sir." Mark took his seat. "Neither Brenna nor I could find anything, in any records, about Vera's parents. No driving license, no home ownership, no taxes paid."

I shivered, visions of March's case whispering in my mind. I said softly, "No one leaves a paperless trail."

"Unless they don't exist," Graham said. He sat down on the table, his left leg swinging. "I do believe we have a case of Ghosts. Someone conveniently creates two people for a birth certificate, then hands the child to a caretaker. But he doesn't quite abandon his daughter; he sets her up in the same village in which he lives, so he can watch her grow up and look after her morals. He can't acknowledge her because there's the little problem of his vocation. Yet, he does what he can, probably hiring the woman to play the part of the grandmother. He invents a plausible story, brings the child in to live with the grandmother when the child is five years old. That seems perfectly legitimate to the villagers, especially since the story gets around that the poor child's parents are killed in Australia. Who's going to track them down? Why would anyone care? The little girl's living happily ever after with her grandmother in a quaint cottage."

"How does Clayton Warson figure into this?" Margo asked.

"Oh, I think Vera and Clayton fell in love. There's nothing phony about that."

"But someone got rid of Vera. Not just drove her off, but murdered her."

"We can eliminate the fake Smiths. Harding probably invented the name of Vera Howarth to throw anyone off the track, should someone start snooping around." He clasped his hands and rested them on his thighs. "What do you think? Will it hold water?"

"If Harding kept Vera's birth and past a secret," I said, "do you think someone from Vera's past killed Reed Harper?"

"Why?"

"Well, sir, with Reed's history of extramarital affairs, someone could easily assume he fathered Vera. Maybe the killer got rid of Reed in a sort of revenge."

"That would mean the killer knew of Vera's past and parentage—if I'm correct about Harding setting her up with this phony grandmother."

"Marian seems a likely candidate to kill Reed."

"But we're up against the same old problem of moving the body," Graham said. "Marian is very petite. Can you really see her stabbing Reed and carting him into the wood?"

I shook my head at the improbable scenario. "Did she have help, like maybe Edmund?"

"Because he wanted her to leave Reed?"

I muttered I didn't know. "It's all tangled together. Vera, the grandmother, Harding, Reed. Too many affairs and children—if Vera was the product of an affair." I slumped against my chair, trying to think through the relationships.

Graham eased off the table. "There's a way to prove paternity, you know." He smiled as I said, "Nuclear DNA."

"The most common DNA used in forensic examinations. Yes."

Graham reminded us that DNA profiling had been developed in 1984. "But most people probably didn't give it much thought at the time. Who would have dreamt in 1989, when Vera went missing, that we could use nuclear DNA to pinpoint paternity?"

Silently, I agreed. A nuclear DNA test determines the biological paternity of a child. Since we inherit our DNA on conception, the test can compare the child's DNA pattern to the alleged father's. It is the most authoritative verification of a birth relationship.

Graham said, "Not meaning to insult anyone's intelligence, but you may be a bit rusty on your DNA facts. As you recall, the nuclear DNA test produces a simple positive or negative result: the male is or is not the biological father. There is no shade of gray. Tests are 99.99% accurate on this and, as I said, are most commonly used in forensic cases."

Margo said, "If this woman played the part of the grandmother, surely she took it on as a job."

Graham smiled. "I should hope so. How many years did she play that role?"

"What I mean, sir," Margo continued as Graham walked to the whiteboard, "is that I can't believe she did it out of the goodness of her heart. She'd have bills to pay, if nothing else. And food to buy, clothes for Vera, council tax…" She frowned, her pen tapping on her notebook page. "How'd she pay for all that? And if Harding—or whoever hired her to care for Vera—paid her, where'd he get his money? Can a vicar earn that much money that he'd have enough not only to keep an extra household going but to also give a woman a salary?"

We fell silent, astonished we hadn't thought of that. Mark went to the computer. It took a good hour and several websites, but Mark came up with a printout of Harding's financial history. Although he made an adequate salary as a vicar, we doubted he could afford to keep the second household. Mark could find no additional income from stocks, gambling or inheritance. So we were back to Margo's question: where did Harding get the money to pay the woman to pose as the grandmother?

Mark remained at the computer, looking up some additional information that Graham wanted. Or, as he phrased it, "Making sure we have the correct subject in our sites." The rest of us took our seats again and Graham drew columns on the whiteboard. He headed them 'Harding' and "Vera.' Below them, he wrote what we knew about each person.

Harding	Vera
Born 1953	Born 1971
Age now: 58	Age would have been now: 40
Old enough to father child	Young enough to be his child

He turned from the board and said, "*Reed Harper* is very unlikely to be Vera's father, as Reed is forty-five. You can do the math. Also," he said, letting a few chuckles pass, "even if he could somehow lie about Vera's age at the time of the baptism, I don't think the birth certificate would be incorrect. So we've still got Vera's birth certificate as our lodestar."

Mark walked over to the printer, gathered up the newly printed pages and handed them to Graham. As Mark sat down, Graham glanced at the sheets. I leaned toward Mark, my lips inches from his ear, and in a whisper asked what he had just given Graham.

"I'll tell you, Taylor," Graham said, seemingly amused that my cheeks inflamed. "And everyone else. At my request, Salt looked up something for me, something pertaining to Harding Lyth. Anyone want to guess what he found that I think is so interesting?"

Answers as varying as "Won the pools," "crack dealer," and "blackmailing Chad Styles" were offered.

Graham smiled, shaking his head. "I commend you all for thinking outside the box, but unfortunately you're wrong. Or, at least, as far as we now know. Salt dug into Harding's family tree. Does that give you a better idea?"

"Something to do with Vera," I said, rather hesitantly.

"Right. Keep going, Taylor."

"Something about their kinship…" I doubted if Vera's name would be so blatantly obvious as Harding's relation. I glanced at the board, then at my notes. What else had we talked about in conjunction with Vera? I said, "Vera's birth certificate. It listed her parents."

"And what have they to do with Harding?" He appeared to be amused and serious at the same time, looking at me, waiting for it to connect in my brain.

I leaned forward, my heart suddenly beating faster. "Jane and John Smith are related to Harding."

"Bingo."

Margo ran her index finger over her lips, frowning. "But, sir, that sounds like incest! If Jane and John Smith are Vera's parents—"

"Don't get upset. Jane and John Smith—well, let me put this on the board. It's easier to understand if you see it." He quickly sketched a section of Harding's family tree on the board.

Floyd Lyth — Jane S. Mills   Trevor John Smith — Rosemary St. John

David Lyth — Eva Moore   Giles Ryder Smith — Sondra Jones

Stephen Lyth — Margaret Ryder

Harding Lyth

When he finished, he turned back to us, the smile gone from his face. He tapped the marker on the board and said, "I believe Harding took the names Jane S. Mills and Trevor John Smith—leaving off Trevor, as it was a more unusual name and thereby more likely to induce remembrance—for the parents' names of his illegitimate daughter. And don't let Margaret Ryder's name fool you. Yes, by law, she should be a Smith, but she was adopted and kept her real last name. But that makes no difference to our investigation. Who would be likely to delve back three generations to verify that Vera, supposedly a total stranger to him, carried his family names?" He laid the marker on the table and said, "I can't prove it, but I believe Harding's grandmother—either Eva Moore or Sondra Jones—posed as Vera's grandmother. I believe this because I can't find evidence that Harding could pay her or did pay her. Eighteen years of giving up your own life and looking after a child should constitute some sort of payment."

"What do you think Harding did, then?" Margo asked. "She wouldn't have looked after Vera for free. Nobody does that."

"I think the woman consented to care for Vera until Vera reached the age of majority. If you remember, the grandmother left for—or returned to—London right before Vera turned eighteen. I think the woman consented to care for Vera because she was Harding's grandmother, or some kin to him." Picking up one of the sheets of paper Mark had handed him, Graham said, "Yesterday when Salt and Taylor searched for death dates of John and Jane Smith, they searched through the records that would correspond to Vera's parents' ages. I don't fault them for not going back two more generations. Hell, how many people, to satisfy idle curiosity, would look for death dates of great grandparents? Pretty brilliant of Harding, I'd say." He let the silence grow, waiting for us to consider what he had outlined.

I said, "Do you think Harding nicked the scrapbook out of the village hall, then? If the photographs and names of volunteers go back for decades, he would have wanted to cover his and his grandmother's trails."

"You can ask Harding, but I believe he did. I can't think of another reason why the scrapbook would be taken if not for the purpose of concealing an identity—and I'm thinking of the name, here. If the name Eva Moore or Sondra Jones is in that scrap book…"

"If the grandmother lived in the village for that length of time, wouldn't there be other records of her name? Maybe not the council tax. If Harding paid that, his name would be down as owner."

Graham looked at Mark, who returned to the computer. While he searched tax records, I said, "I know the house is north of the village proper, which might be why Harding chose it, but I can't see the grandmother living here all that time without her name being mentioned *someplace*. So she didn't join the Women's Royal

Volunteer Service or the church choir. There are other sources of noted documentation."

This time I grinned as Graham said, "The national census." He called to Mark, who said he'd print out that information. Shoving his hands into his pockets, Graham said, "To bring our younger colleagues up to speed, the national census began in 1801 and is conducted every ten years. I believe there's a fine—I don't recall the amount."

"One thousand pounds," Mark said from the other table. "I'm just at that site. One thousand quid levied against anyone not completing it."

"With that stiff of a penalty, I doubt if the grandmother or Harding would risk ignoring it. The census fell due in 1971 and 1981. In '71 the census date was 25 April. Before Vera was born."

"But they were living in the house for the following census," I said, getting excited.

"Yes. If Vera and the grandmother were in the village when Vera was five years old…" He wrote 1976 and 5 years old on the white board, then turned back to us. "…then the 1981 census should include the grandmother. Vera went missing in 1989. The grandmother moved the previous year, in 1988."

"This is our only chance to get the name, then." My heart jumped into my throat.

Graham said something about usually pulling up the name from the employee's national insurance number or the electoral poll, but since we hadn't had the elder woman's name…

Again we fell silent, considering the growing scheme and the complications the players created. Mark made a phone call, nodded vigorously, and wrote something in his notebook. On hanging up, he went back to his computer search and stayed with that for several minutes. When Mark finished he handed Graham the sheets of paper but remained standing by the side of the table. Graham slowly read through the new information, thanked Mark, and announced that the grandmother was Eva Moore. "Harding's paternal grandmother. Mark also crosschecked that

with the village chemist and the pension office. The pension because Eva Moore was the correct age to receive benefits—more
than sixty years old and having worked for more than thirty-
nine years as a nurse. The village chemist because, being that Eva
Moore was the correct age to receive benefits, Mark guessed she
might need some type of medicine. The chemist confirmed that
an Eva Moore regularly renewed a prescription for high blood
pressure." He laid the papers on top of the small stack on the table, smiling. "What do you think?"

"I think," Mark said, "we need to confront Harding with this."

Grabbing the printout of Harding's family tree, Graham said,
"Will someone bring along a cotton bud?"

Thirty-Four

"The paternity test requires a DNA sample," Graham said.

He, Mark and I stood in the front room of the vicarage. Harding sat on the edge of the sofa, his face as white as the paper Graham held in his fingers. Fanned out in a small half circle, we could easily grab him should he decide to bolt, but I doubted if he would. We had surprised him. Plus, in addition to believing he had outfoxed us, he probably hadn't thought he would need a place to hide.

Graham went over the data we had collected, recounting how we had arrived at the decision that Harding had fathered Vera.

Harding remained seated through the recital, mute and staring ahead of him. He seemed not to hear Graham say "We can collect one now, if you have a cotton bud, or we can go to the station to do it. It's painless—we swab the inside of your cheek. Of course," he lowered his voice, "you have the other option of refusing to give a DNA sample since no one is bringing a paternity suit against you. I just thought you might want to end this forty year charade and take the weight from your soul."

There are times, like this, that Graham spoke more like the former minister instead of the current detective. I doubted it would work with the majority of police officers, but Graham's voice retained what I called a pulpit-like quality, and Margo phrased cleric sparkle. That smooth speaking voice, steady and clear, that held a suggestion of authority or prod to the conscience to do the right thing. I had practiced many times in front of my mirror, striving to attain that manner and sound, but I never could do it. Perhaps a person was born with it; perhaps it developed from self-confidence. However it was attained, I doubted I would ever achieve it. But I was glad Graham had it—it brought many suspects into custody more easily.

Harding finally stirred and looked at Graham. His face had lost all its hue; his eyes were dull, without sparkle. Shaking his head, he said that wouldn't be necessary. "You're right. I'm Vera's father."

Graham seemed to relax. The muscle on the side of his jaw twitched, as it did when he was upset or anxious, and he asked Harding quite gently if he had killed Vera.

"God, no!" Harding's denial shot into the air. "Why would I keep her near me so that I could see her daily, see to her welfare, only to kill her, like she was some mistake I had to erase from my life?" His right palm kneaded his forehead and he sighed. "I was eighteen. Had just turned eighteen when it happened—I had an affair with a married woman." He had spoken this in a barely audible voice, the words coming in broken phrases. Now that he had begun, the avalanche of admission poured forth. Graham made no move to question him, rather letting Harding speak as he wished. "She was estranged from her husband at the time, so she didn't fear he'd find out about the pregnancy. However, since she was married and separated, she couldn't keep the baby." He glanced at Mark, exhaling in a near laugh at his predicament. "Think how that would have helped the husband if the marriage came to a divorce. Anyway, after near panic, we came up with the idea of letting my grandmother pose as Vera's grandmother."

"We found death certificates for your grandmothers," Mark reminded him.

"A clerical error," Harding said, looking ill. "We tried to get it corrected when we found out, but we never could. We had no way of knowing it would come in handy…years later."

Mark mumbled something about bureaucracy and computers before Harding continued.

"You might think Gran couldn't get away with it, that there'd be too great an age difference and people would think something was peculiar. But, fortunately or unfortunately, early families seem to run in my family. Grandmother Eva was sixty-five but most people thought her to be ten years younger. Gramps died a year prior to my asking Gran to rear Vera, so she gave up her London residence and moved here. I set her up with the house and she and Vera moved in when Vera was five. They'd stayed in London until then because we thought it would seem more logical if Vera was a bit older."

"You invented the story of Vera's folks in Australia," Mark said.

"Yes. Vera's mother gave her name as Jane Smith in the hospital, and I posed as the father. We got the names, as you suspected, from my relatives. I didn't think they'd ever be traceable. Or that anyone would need to."

"Just to satisfy my curiosity…did you pay your grandmother to take care of Vera?"

"Yes. Oh, it wasn't much. I don't make that much. But added to the money she got from Gramp's insurance and the sale of the house… Well, Gran was satisfied with the arrangement. She wasn't alone and she had a child to care for, someone to love. Someone to focus her affection on now that gramps was gone. It worked out well for everyone. Especially Vera."

"You say you didn't kill Vera," Graham said.

"No!"

"Did you kill Reed Harper?" He took a step forward and looked down on Harding. "Perhaps Reed learned your secret, threatened to tell everyone. You fought and killed him unintentionally. Is that what happened?"

Harding shook his head, his eyes shining with fear. "No. I swear to you none of that happened. I took the scrapbook from the village hall because I didn't want you to find a photo and the name of Grandma Eva, but that's all I did. I never broke into your work area. That was someone else. I took that greeting card,

though. The one left in Gran's cottage. I-I'd forgotten about it
until I you reminded me of it. I don't know why, but I got worried about the card. I had heard from Gran that Vera was going
to send it, thanking me for taking care of her."

"She found out you were her father?"

"Not found out. Gran told her. She thought it was time, that
Vera was old enough. Vera deserved to know. She was right. Vera
and I had a long talk one afternoon and I told her everything.
I'd been afraid she would be angry, but she was very loving and
understanding. I think Gran helped prepare Vera for the shock
of my statement, you see. Anyway, Gran told me later that Vera
was sending me the card, expressing her love and hoping to
make up for all the years of missed birthdays and Father's Days.
I-I took it because I didn't know if she'd written any note in the
card that would expose everything. I…well, I couldn't take that
chance of you finding out. Not after all these years and the work
Gran and I did." His gaze left Mark and settled on me. "I admit
I made a terrible mistake with this whole thing—the affair, the
false names on the birth certificate, passing my grandmother off
as Vera's—but I didn't kill my daughter. And I didn't kill Reed."

We left him repeating his innocence and begging God and
us to forgive him.

~

The test results had been faxed to us and were lying beside
Graham's computer when we got back to the church. We had
lunched quickly in the pub, putting our discussion of the case
on hold in case pub customers might overhear us. The brown
stains on the shirt were blood—Reed's and a second person's—
and only waited another sample to match them to that unidenti-
fied someone. Several human hairs, not Reed's, were found on the
shirt; they were stored, pending the arrival of a DNA swab from
our suspect. Several other hairs—cat, to be precise—were also
found, as were two types of flower pollen. The grains were so few
and tiny that we hadn't seen them when Mark and I had looked
at the shirt. We determined they were from a hosta and daylily.

Graham informed us that PC Oglethorpe had talked to the clerk at the hardware store, showed him the latch key, but could not come up with a person who bought that style of key lately. "I even phoned around, thinking someone had the cylinder of their door lock changed. Nothing.

"That key's probably been in the ground for decades," Mark said.

I snapped my fingers. "That key wasn't really found that close to Reed's body, was it?"

Graham asked what I meant.

"I'm not sure, sir, but it was farther from the body, right? If I had killed Reed and dumped him in the wood, and my shirt was bloodied from knifing him, I wouldn't bury the shirt next to the body."

"Go on, Taylor."

"Reed's body seemed to be a hastily buried affair, more of a shallow depression in the earth than a proper burial. The shirt was buried fairly deeply and buried at the grandmother's house. Mark and I only just found it because we were deliberately looking for it. The shirt, however, was buried at the grandmother's house. And the shirt was buried there so it wouldn't be found if the bones were found—the bones, not Reed's body, because the bones were obviously well buried, like the shirt, to avoid detection. Also, the shirt was buried at a different location either to throw suspicion on Vera or her grandmother, or to avoid detection, as I said. Why look in the grandmother's garden if the forest is the burial site for the bones or body?"

"The shirt's been there for much longer than the body," Graham said. "We commented that it looked as though it had been there for decades."

"Yes, sir. The shirt belongs to the person who killed *Vera* and disposed of her body. Her killer didn't have to worry about the grandmother witnessing the burying of the shirt because—"

"The grandmother had moved to London a year earlier," Mark finished, his voice barely audible.

"Yes." I sank back in my chair, aware of my racing heart and the cold metal of the chair frame. It all seemed logical but I couldn't prove it.

Graham drew our attention back to the columns written on the whiteboard. "We have Vera killed and buried. She lies there for twenty-two years, undiscovered. Who had motive twenty-two years ago to kill her? Consider any motive that could be connected with Vera and the people living here in 1989. Harding was here. Angela wasn't born yet. Reed and Marian were about to get married in June, I looked it up." He allowed himself a quick grin before adding, "But his affairs hadn't stopped with the wedding ceremony, might have been going on before the wedding." He rolled the marker between his palms, eager for someone's theory.

The columns of Suspect/Motive/Opportunity stared at me from the whiteboard. I glanced at the two lists comparing Harding and Vera, then at the photographs of Reed's body and Vera's bones. Pointing to the 'motive' column, I said, "I think it does boil down to the motive of affairs, but not Harding's."

"Whose, then, Taylor?"

"Reed's. His wife admits he's been having extramarital affairs throughout their marriage. Even before they were married. Marian probably should get the gold star for Patience—or Stupidity, depending on your outlook. She doesn't even know how many women he's slept with."

Margo agreed. "Her patience may have finally ran out and she killed him. Maybe not intentionally, but during an argument, perhaps."

"The proverbial straw."

"Yes, sir. Every person has her breaking point, and whatever Reed finally did, maybe even with whom, became too much for Marian to bear. They may have discussed it before this; she may have given him an ultimatum or got him to agree to go to a counselor."

I said rather slowly, thinking it through, "I don't know about that. I can't imagine how any wife would stand the years of affairs Reed evidently had."

"Would a stream of valuable jewelry or lavish vacations or expensive cars have been enough to keep her married to him?"

I shrugged. "Up to the individual, I would think. It wouldn't me." I felt my cheeks grow warm, so I hurriedly added, "If he did heap on the incentives it may have worked for a while, but I still believe it comes down to how seriously you take your weddings vows."

"Even if you didn't take them all that seriously," Margo said, "I think after twenty-two years of marriage, with your husband fooling around constantly, you'd reach your limit."

"We could probably make a case for most anyone in Cauldham," I said. "But it doesn't make sense to wait so long, Margo. If she was jealous or angry with Reed, she wouldn't wait nearly a quarter of a century to top him."

"Who else do you want?"

"I don't want more suspects, Margo. But I did just think of something."

Graham leaned against the edge of the table, crossed his long legs, and asked what it was.

"Well, sir, Mark and I spoke to Marian the first day of the investigation."

"Yeah," Mark said. "She was the first person on our list."

"Recall what she said?"

"If you want something specific." He began leafing through his notebook but I cut him off.

"Thanks, but I remember. Which is why I think it's significant. She told us that when Reed first went missing, she went to church every day."

"Right." Mark snapped his fingers and angled in his chair to face me. "She was trying not to cry when she said it, but her eyes were moist. She said she lit candles and prayed to every saint she could think of for help in finding Reed."

"Yes. She said she was a regular churchgoer, and I inferred from another statement that she was bewildered when God didn't help her."

"You're suggesting...what?" Graham asked.

"If she's that religious, has that much faith in God, she must take her wedding vows seriously."

"And in so doing, she had had it with Reed's continual affairs."

"Yes, sir. It's conjecture, of course." I settled back in my chair, unhappy that we couldn't prove Marian had killed Reed.

Graham pushed away from the table edge and came over to me. He picked up a vacant chair, turned it so the back faced me and sat down, his arms resting across the top of the chair back. "I think you're just one step away from solving it, Taylor. Look at it from the opposite angle."

I looked at him, trying to understand how I could be so close to solving it when it seemed like a dead end. We couldn't put anyone in the forest with Reed's body or Vera's bones. Graham, for all his calm demeanor, was trying to close the case and lift the pressure off the divisional commander. "I'm sorry, sir, but I can't—"

"You mentioned it yourself, Brenna, but I think you got sidetracked. What did you begin talking about?"

"Affairs."

"Reed, of course, springs to mind. But what if Marian, being the preserver of their marriage, didn't kill Reed over an affair?"

He grinned as I whispered, "What if she killed Vera to protect her marriage?"

"I believe she did. It was early into their marriage. 1989."

"The year Vera went missing." A chill grabbed me and I trembled. Mark threw his arm around my shoulders but I kept thinking out loud. "She and Reed were months away from getting married. Marian knew of Reed's amorous past; maybe Reed tried flirting with Vera. Whatever happened, Marian got jealous, maybe even frightened, believing Reed was about to have an affair with Vera or had already commenced one. So she kills Vera, thinking she's just put a halt to his transgressions."

"But killing Vera didn't stop Reed's affairs," Margo said. "It's twenty-two years later and he's still sleeping around."

"You're looking at this from the viewpoint of our present knowledge," Graham reminded her. "How was Marian to know

Reed would continue having affairs? For all she knew, and hoped, their marriage would be the stabling influence he needed to settle down."

The room grew silent as each of us reasoned through the new information. A flock of rooks landed on the ground outside the window, cawing noisily to each other.

Mark, his attention still on the birds, asked, "Where does that take us?"

"I can't answer that. I'm all in a muddle."

"We need Marian's DNA if we want to run a test to the blood found on that shirt." Mark shifted his attention back to us.

"That's fine." Margo grabbed a ginger snap. "How? Where are you going to get it? She's not going to give it to you, Mark, even with all your pretty ways."

Mark scratched the rim of his ear and said that was a slight problem.

"So we're back where we started from. No proof."

"We're a bit further along than *supposition*." Mark scowled. "We've *all* done our share, Margo. Every person on this team. Brenna and I have done a hell of a lot of computer work. Oglethorpe found the shirt and key, and Mr. Graham—"

Graham tossed the capped marker onto the table, watching it roll a foot or so before bumping into a stack of papers. "Mr. Graham," he said, getting up, "needs to see a man about a cat."

Thirty-Five

Graham walked into the pub several hours later, smiling like the Cheshire Cat. He abandoned his usual practice of letting us decompress alone after our day, and joined us at our table. Ordinarily this would put a strain on us, for we couldn't vent or talk freely, but tonight it felt quite relaxing to me—firmly establishing us as a team.

We had finished with our meal and had changed clothes, needing to shed even the impression of still being on the clock. Margo and I opted for jeans and cotton blouses; Mark wore the same tan trousers from this weekend but had changed into a polo shirt. We sat at a corner table, where it was less noisy, and had been talking about the case and our lives when Graham came up to us.

He obviously had something say; what other reason would produce the grin and the unusual chat over beers? Clearly agitated, Mark eyed Graham with all the disquiet of a prisoner awaiting his sentence. Margo sipped her wine, relaxed in her chair, and tolerantly waited. I pushed my glass of shandy around on the beer mat, curious nearly beyond patience.

When Graham had taken several swallows of beer, he deliberately set the glass down, leaned back in his chair and eyed each of us in turn. Then, leaning forward again, he said in a low, quiet voice, "Ever hear of cat DNA testing?"

Mark blinked, Margo coughed on her sip of wine, and I muttered 'Pardon?' Slapping Margo on the back, I asked what it was.

"Fairly new technology," Graham said after Margo's face had

subsided to its normal hue. "Giving you just the basics, cat fur found on a person or at a crime scene can be compared to *any* cat. A victim or suspect—or innocent person—can be linked to the scene or crime using mitochondrial and nuclear DNA testing. Cat's hair is as individual as a person's and therefore is as valuable and reliable a resource for identifying a specific person."

I had stopping playing with the glass and now merely stared at Graham. "You're talking about those white bits of fur on that bloodied shirt Mark and I found in the grandmother's garden."

Graham nodded, still smiling. "Mitochondrial DNA testing tends to be the most used because, due to its high mutation rate, it can be identified more readily between different individual cats. The genes also are quite plentiful.

"Nuclear DNA exists on fur that has root bulbs intact. When a cat grooms itself, sometimes particles of its skin adheres to the oil of its fur. Another source of DNA samples and another source of evidence in a criminal trial."

"You're not joking, sir." Mark looked like he wanted to stand up and cheer, but he wasn't quite certain if the cat hair scenario was real.

"Cross my heart, Salt," Graham said. "Hand on the bible. It's been used in cases around the world, probably the first in Canada when Douglas Beamish was convicted of murder."

"You're *not* joking," Mark repeated, staring at Graham.

"Do I need a bible?" He pretended to look around the room before saying that the conviction had been attained due to cat fur found on the suspect's jacket pocket. "Genetically connecting the victim's cat to Beamish. Sweet, isn't it?" He took another swallow of beer.

"You want to compare the cat fur on the shirt to Marian Harper's cat, don't you, sir?" I asked, hardly daring to hope that we were about to nab Vera's murderer. Marian was the only person who had a longhaired white cat.

"She'll scream, of course, but we've got probable cause to bring her in. We've built a case and we'll find DNA through her skin cells, hair and sweat on that bloodied shirt. I've no doubt hers is the other type of blood on the shirt, along with Reed's. That, along with the cat fur…" He raised his beer and saluted us.

It seemed like we had our killer. If the blood and skin cells on the shirt were Marian's, she couldn't plead that someone had worn the shirt to kill Reed and planted it at the scene. The third person's DNA would then be on the shirt. Graham was still talking about the cat fur DNA when I snapped back to the conversation.

"It's brilliant work, this cat hair DNA. Any person in a room automatically attracts cat hair to themselves. It's a natural occurrence. The oil in fur combines with static electricity and clings to people, clothing, footwear, furniture…anything. The mass volume of the hair also dictates that no one and nothing escapes the hair."

Mark nodded, glancing at me before replying, "I know. Every time I leave Brenna's house I've got cat hair sticking to my clothes. And I'm never there that long."

"Not only might a suspect transport a victim's cat hairs from the scene, but it also works the other way."

"Hairs from the suspect's cat could be shed at the crime scene."

"As I said," Graham smiled. "Brilliant."

Mark muttered something like "What won't they think of next" and slumped against the back of his chair. He set down his glass before wriggling against the wooden slats. Evidently uncomfortable, he finally stood up, reached into his back trouser pocket, and withdrew a folded piece of paper. Sitting down, he flattened the paper on the tabletop.

"What's that?" I asked, staring at the paper.

"Oh. That brochure I picked up in the tourist center Saturday when we stopped to talk to Lynn Warson."

"Right. I didn't know you'd taken one."

"I didn't think I did, but I guess it was a reflex. You know," he said, skimming the small article inside the brochure. "Surprised when she came up to us and I just jammed it into my pocket." He read for several seconds more, than said, "Listen to this." He angled the paper so I could also see it. The article seemed to nail the lid on our case.

Cauldham is a quiet village now, but its history winds back

centuries and is intertwined to the battles for royal thrones and mere survival. Situated in the heart of the Peak District, the village has seen demographic and physical change throughout its existence. The section of wood encompassing many of the mines and Cauldham Hall once belonged to the Good family, an ancient lineage stretching back to Plantagenet times. But, as many others have done before and since, the family steadily and gradually sold parcels of land as financially hard times gripped them. During the 1970s the family sold that section of wood to the Hall and the mining concerns. A sad commentary on family fortunes but a blessing to the village in general. The land is now…

I looked at Graham as Mark finished reading the piece. "Good is Marian's maiden name. I remember her speaking of her family the first day Mark and I interviewed her. She was proud of the fact that her family was so old and had such a long history." I pulled in the corners of my mouth, almost afraid to say the next thing. Taking a deep breath, I crossed my fingers and said, "You said something early on in the case about the scene where the body and bones were discovered. Something about the killer felt comfortable there, that there's a reason a certain site is chosen."

"I remember."

"Either the site is someplace where the killer worked or played. Or once lived," I added, feeling my breathing quicken. "Marian loved her family estate. Despite her tearful discourse of Reed's disappearance, she smiled when she mentioned the vast tract of land they had owned." I paused, trying to form the rushing thoughts into words. "Would someone who had grown up with tales of the ancestral estate and the expanse of once-owned land relinquish all that so easily if it had been sold only years before she was born?"

"The section of the wood was sold in the 1970s," Mark said, referring to the passage he had just read aloud.

"Marian was born in 1967."

"Which made her a teenager in the 1980s," Graham added.

"She could have grown up hearing about the wood. Maybe

she played in that section as a child or teenager. Maybe she continued to walk through that area later."

"And needing a place to dispose of Vera's body..." Graham's eyebrow rose. "Vera's house is also in that patch of former-family forest."

I stared at him, my excitement suddenly turning to fear at my envisioned scene.

"There is daylily and hosta pollen on her shirt," Graham added. "I recall pushing aside a daylily when I looked at the key that Oglethorpe found."

"Hostas also grow in the front garden of the grandmother's house," Mark reminded us. "It didn't register with me Sunday when we were there for the search, but why would hostas and daylilies be growing in a wood unless the land had once been cultivated?"

"Part of the Good family estate," Margo said.

"The plants have also run riot at the grandmother's place, too. And I got some of that lily pollen on my trousers. I can't get it off."

Graham thudded back into his chair, his eyes dark. "Just about puts the handcuffs on her wrists, I'd say."

~

We pointed all that out to Marian when we reassembled in her front room. She tried bluffing her way out of the charge, even ignored Graham's statement of caution. But at the mention of the cat hair and the fact that we would have a comparison test run on the hairs from her cat and the hairs found on the shirt in the wood, she paled and grew quiet.

As a WPC led her from her house, Marian turned to Graham. Her eyes, so full of anger moments before, now brimmed with tears. Her voice quivered as she said, "I thought Reed and Vera Howarth were lovers. It was a natural assumption on my part— that's all Reed ever did. It was his hobby. Collecting women instead of collecting stamps or rare books. It was easy to kill her, you know. Vera knew me. We'd never had words about Reed, so she wasn't suspicious when I asked her to drive with me."

"Where did you take her?" Graham's voice had turned cold and hard as the stones in the forest. I knew the case bothered him. From both sides. He hated the fact that Vera, a young woman, had been killed. He hated—perhaps more—that the murderer was a woman. He was old fashioned enough to want them to remain innocent and to need protection. Because the case involved women as suspect and victim, he felt the pain more intensely.

Marian spoke in a monotone, her gazed fixed in the direction of the wood. "To the forest. To the area where I killed her and buried her. I drove to her cottage. It was getting late, just going on to ten. In April, when I killed her, it's quite dark by then."

"What did you tell her to get her to ride with you?"

"I knew Vera was interested in the well dressing decoration. That's how I think she met Reed," she added. "I said I had an idea about that year's well dressing festival. I wanted to use a spring in the wood as a fourth site for a well dressing panel. I wanted to ask what she thought of it, if it would be too difficult for people to get to."

"Vera didn't think it odd that you would look at this site at night? Why not in the daylight, when you could see properly?"

"I told her it was secret, that I wanted to surprise Reed with the idea, if it was feasible. I wanted to go to the spot at night so that no one from the village would see us walking around in the wood and learn about the fourth well dressing site before we had worked out the details and surprised Reed. It may sound daft now, but Vera was excited. She wanted to be part of village history, when we created a new, fourth well dressing panel. If she was suspicious, she didn't show it. She didn't say anything to me when I picked her up. I drove to the spot, we got out of the car and walked into the wood. Then I killed her. Just plunged the knife into her. It was easy, you know. It usually is when people trust you."

The statement came so quickly, so unemotionally, that I gasped.

Graham asked Marian how she had killed Vera.

Marian shrugged. "Easy, as I said. We got out of the car and I led the way to the spot where I buried her. Vera kept talking, asking questions about the spring—how big was it, could some of this vegetation be cleared so people could more easily get to the brook, was there an easier route to get here. Quite annoying. I had my torch and shone the beam low toward the ground to eliminate it being seen by anyone in the vicinity. That was my only real worry, you know." She flashed a smile, as though it were a joke or she was proud she had circumnavigated that problem. "But Vera had no suspicions. She was concentrating on the new well dressing panel and the work that went with it. She didn't even think it odd when I walked around in front of her. I think she smiled just before I stabbed her."

Neither Graham nor I said a word. The silence grew thick in the room and I tried not to imagine the scene and Marian's knife flashing in the light from the torch. Finally, Graham asked what Marian had done with the knife.

"You can find it quite easily enough. I buried it near my shirt. There is a plant in the front garden—I don't know its name—that sheds white, downy fibers. Some kind of creeping thistle, I think. It may have died; it may have multiplied. I buried the knife there, separate from the shirt. I thought that if one was found the other item might not necessarily be found."

I refrained from saying that had proved true.

"Even if that plant's no longer there, you can dig about and find it. It's about five feet away from where you found the shirt, on the opposite side of the front walk. You'll know it's the murder weapon, Mr. Graham—the knife has a mother of pearl handle and the blade is engraved with some sort of twining vine and hearts."

Graham looked relieved. Those details helped with our case... details of the murder and murder weapon known only to the killer or the victim.

"I needed to eliminate her," Marian continued, her voice taking the tone she might use to tell her best friend about her day. "I needed to protect my marriage. Reed loved her type—late teens, early twenties. Not a dazzling beauty, but cute. Intelligent. Nice figure." She drew a deep breath, searching Graham's face, perhaps wanting to find understanding and sympathy in his eyes.

"Are you married, Mr. Graham?"

"No." His voice held no emotion—no regret, no relief, no desire.

Marian nodded, her gaze steady. "Cheating spouses cause more damage than they think. They believe the problems occur just between the persons in the triangle." She glanced at the waiting police car, perhaps envisioning the upcoming trial and the years she would have to endure in prison. "But it's a ripple effect, Mr. Graham. Affairs color other lives as well, even unto other generations."

~

Graham had gone off with the police car to see to the booking in process. Margo sat at a table in the pub's outdoor seating section, wanting to drown her emotions in a glass of wine. Mark and I wandered into his room upstairs at the pub. Without giving it any thought, I collapsed onto his bed and he put the electric kettle on for tea. I couldn't have moved if the call of 'Fire' rang out. I was suddenly exhausted, the result of the day and the arrest.

"You don't have to worry, Bren," Mark said as he poured the boiling water into the mugs. He glanced at his watch, timing the tea brewing. "I've got it all thought out. You'll take the bed, of course. Never mind my, uh…other idea," he added as thunder rumbled in the west.

I made no comment, suddenly feeling quite uncomfortable.

"I'll stretch out in the chair, here."

Glancing across the room, I was aware of the upholstered chair nearly buried under the gym bag, pair of jeans, sweaty tee shirt, assorted shirt ties and bathrobe. His used socks, I noticed, were wadded into two balls beside the chair.

"You'll never fit," I said, aware my voice was strained.

"Sure I will. I can stretch my legs out and rest my heels on the floor. Or on the gym bag," he added quickly, as though he had already felt the strain from the unusual sleeping position.

"It'll work. I'll be fine."

I looked at the bag, envisioning it as a footstool. It wasn't even a foot tall. "You won't be fit for anything tomorrow if you sleep like that, Mark. You need as much sleep as I do." I sat up, determined to bring a semblance of sense to this craziness. "I think I better sleep in my bed and you sleep in yours. Graham will have your guts for garters tomorrow if you can't keep awake."

"You're staying here, Bren. I'm not going to be kept awake all night, worried some git's trying to find you. We've not solved Reed's murder yet, and there's also the bloke who broke into the incident room to worry about. If someone was following you Sunday night and is eager to find out something about this case, I don't want you found. I also don't want to lose you." He face flushed slightly and he turned, busying himself with preparing the tea.

When I got over the shock of his declaration, I said, "How about I stay here and you sleep in my bed? We'll both get some sleep and you won't have to worry that the killer is sneaking into my room. He won't know where to find me."

Perhaps to hide the embarrassment caused by his last statement, he laughed. "Oh, super. You're here nice and safe, dreaming fine dreams, and I'm being mistaken for you in your bed, hit on the head and tied up. Thanks so much." He handed me my tea and swept the clothes and gym bag from the chair. Picking up his tea, he said, "Do me a favor—no, do *us* a favor. Just stay here tonight and let me worry about my bad back in the morning. I'll deal with Graham if I have to."

"Why don't I sleep in Margo's room?" I countered, the idea appearing to be a perfect solution. "She and I can share a bed, you'll be spared a bad back for the morning, and I'll be hidden away."

Mark looked as though he'd missed winning the pools by one number. "Nothing against you or Margo, but are you both up to snuff on defensive tactics? What if this bloke sneaks up on you, grabs you by the throat—"

"You're watching too much tellie, Mark. I'll be fine. I'll stay with Margo."

"I don't think that's a good idea. Why risk your safety? You need a strong, muscular bloke to look after you. Two women won't."

"I appreciate the offer, but Margo and I will survive. I'll just go get my things."

He exhaled heavily, perhaps knowing he had lost. "All right. You can stay with Margo. But we'll go together to get your clothes. I'm not letting you out of my sight. No telling where that bloke— Yeah? Just a minute." This he yelled to the door, as someone pounded insistently. He put his mug on the floor, went over to the door, and cracked it open. On seeing who stood in the hallway, he eased it open. "Fitzgerald! Uh, well, come in." Mark remained with his hand on the edge of the open door, his body blocking Adam's entry. He glanced at me, probably wondering what I wanted to do.

I still debated between diving beneath the bed and jumping out the window. It didn't matter that the window was closed or that we were on the second story of the building. Either alternative seemed better than being discovered in Mark's room after hours.

Adam pushed the door open and strode into the room. His gaze shifted from Mark to me as he took in my position on the bed and what appeared to be Mark's castoff clothing on the chair.

My face reddened as I slowly rose from the bed. A flash of lightning lit up the room, throwing our faces into startlingly bright relief.

Adam stood between the door and the bed, his face no doubt matching mine in hue. But where I'm certain I looked surprised, Adam looked angry. His hands doubled into fists but he fought to keep his voice even. "What the bloody hell are you doing here, Brenna?" He ignored Mark as he moved to the chair. "I stopped by your room. I knocked. Several times. When I didn't get an answer I walked down the hall. Margo was coming up the stairs from the bar area. She figured I had been looking for you and, being a friendly, helpful person, she volunteered that you were in Mark's room. Spending the night." This last bit was barely audible, nearly bitten off between his clenched teeth.

"I can explain, Adam," I started when Mark placed his hand on Adam's shoulder.

"It's really not what you think, Fitzgerald."

"Yeah?" Adam shrugged off Mark's touch but kept focused on me. "I came over to apologize. I realized I had overreacted at breakfast and I wanted to tell you I was sorry. Well, maybe I didn't overreact. Maybe what I thought was real."

"*Really*, it's nothing like that." Mark moved around so he faced Adam. "You see, I think there's some berk around here who might be watching Brenna. At night, I mean. We've had a spot of trouble here and I'm afraid this bloke is after her. He knows her room number here at the pub, and—"

"How convenient for you, Salt." Adam uttered it in a mixture of boredom and disbelief. "How long did it take to convince Brenna of your story? I assume you practiced it in front of your mirror, working out the weak spots."

Mark grabbed Adam's upper arms and spun him around so they stood face to face. Keeping a hand on Adam, Mark fairly yelled, "You bloody bastard. It's the truth. If you have no more faith in your fiancée than this, if you don't care about her safety—"

Adam took a swing at Mark and landed a punch on Mark's jaw as thunder cracked overhead. Mark staggered back and slammed into the wall. Adam faced me. "That's another fantasy element of your story, Salt. *If* she still is my fiancée." He turned on his heel and strode from the room. The door slammed into the quiet.

My tears started immediately. I was too stunned to feel anything, too bewildered to react. My fingers slid over the diamond of my engagement ring, my thumb rubbed the back of the gold band. Much as worry beads or rubbing Aladdin's lamp…anything to ward off this unbearable event. Mark's left hand went to his jaw, massaging the pain that must have been magnifying with every second. He pushed himself up with his right hand, shook his head as though clearing the stars from his vision, and shuffled over to me. By this time I had thrown my head back, stared at the ceiling and sobbed. He gingerly sat on the edge of the bed and placed his right arm around my shoulders.

"Bren, it's okay. Really. We'll let Adam cool down. I'll phone him tomorrow. I'll explain the whole thing. He'll understand the situation. I'll make him." He let me cry and cradled my head on his chest.

I half heard his words. I ached for myself, for my dashed dreams; I ached for Adam, for his fragile faith in me and for his own pain; I cried for Mark, that he had become an accessory to this; I cried for the apparent long years waiting for me that would be filled with loneliness and thoughts of 'what if.' And I cried for Sam, shifted to another prison because Roper was threatening his life.

As Mark lifted my face and dabbed my cheeks with his handkerchief, I pushed against him and struggled to my feet.

"Bren…"

"I've got to find Adam." I sniffed back another sob. "I can't wait until tomorrow or let you explain this to him. It'll only get worse if he has hours to stew over it. He'll concoct any and every situation he can and it'll be more difficult to convince him of the truth in the morning. He has to know right now that it's not what it looked like, Mark. He'll never sleep tonight if he thinks I've betrayed him. He needs to know I'd never do that, that I love him, that I want him…if he'll still have me."

I had yanked open the door by the time Mark got to his feet. "Bren, wait! I'll go with you."

"It'll take too long. You don't even have your shoes on." I was out of the room and had slammed the door before he could reply.

Rushing down the steps, I tried to think where Adam might go. Would he stop at the bar for a drink, trying to calm down? Would he stamp off to his car and roar away, driving recklessly? Would he sit in his car and mope, perhaps phone a mate and ask to meet somewhere for a beer? I had no idea. Not only was I fearful about Adam's state of mind and what he might do, but also I was desperate to explain the situation with Mark. The fright that he might actually call off the wedding drove me to near panic.

I paused just long enough to weave through the crowd in the bar area. Adam wasn't there.

I dashed outside, the heavy door thudding behind me. The cooler air of night might have startled me if I had really been aware of anything else but locating Adam, but I didn't feel it. Nor did I feel the sprinkle of rain that had already dampened the outdoor tables and chairs. A handful of young people stood hear a large container of annuals, bottles and glasses in their hands. I rushed up to them and asked if they had seen a tall blond man leave.

"Yeah," One of the drinkers nodded and pointed with his beer bottle toward the road. "About maybe a minute ago."

One of the group shook his head and said it was more like two minutes ago.

"Can't be," the first man said. "I just started talking to Cindy about—"

"Please," I interrupted. "It doesn't have to be that precise. He was here quite recently, then. Where did he go? Did he get into a car, walk somewhere?"

"Didn't get into a car, I shouldn't think. I wasn't particularly looking. He just kinda walked into the night, like. Across the road, here. Did you hear a car motor start, Dan?"

I thanked them and sprinted across the road.

The night seemed to grab me here. The light from the pub fell off close to the curb, leaving the road and the stretch of shops opposite the pub in darkness. I had no plan in mind—fright and near hysteria had made logical thinking impossible. My only conscious thought was to find Adam, so I ran down the road, toward the village pond, glancing at the cars as I passed and calling his name.

The rain fell heavier by the time I had reached the pond. I had heard no answer to my frantic call, no roar of a car motor, no footsteps approaching me. I was hardly aware of the rain soaking my clothes and hair, and my shoes stepping into puddles. The tunnel-vision that claims many police officers when in dire situations seemed to envelope me; I saw only the road curving ahead and the line of cars. The night closed in, leaving only a channel that I ran through.

Having reached the pond and finding nothing, I ran back to the pub on the other side of the road. The group of drinkers was no longer outside, the rain having driven them indoors. If I had been thinking, or smart, I would have ducked inside and tried getting Adam on his mobile. But I was neither thinking nor smart. I raced up the hill, still calling for him, still ignoring the rain that streamed down my hair and plastered my shirt to my back.

I must have passed the wood and Cauldham Hall because I suddenly saw the church. Maybe the black night and rain and mass of trees combined to mask the bulk of the building. I just remember the steeple and bell tower abruptly illuminated by a flash of lightning and my startled yelp echoing off the church's stones.

I paused at the lych gate, certain someone moved just within the churchyard. But who would be outside, standing around on such a night? Me, I thought, keenly aware of my stupidity and the situation and my sodden clothing. And Adam. Was it he I saw? I called his name, cupping my hands around my mouth so the sound would carry. But I heard no response. Adam did not rush up to me. Several more seconds ticked past as I waited and watched, wishing he would materialize out of the waving tree branches. But he didn't. And I knew he wouldn't. I hurriedly claimed the shelter of the roofed gate and drew my mobile from my pocket. Punching in Adam's phone number, I hopped to keep warm, much as a jogger keeps in motion when waiting for the signal to turn at a zebra crossing. The call went unanswered. Ignoring me, I thought as I repocketed the phone.

Thunder rumbled overhead, pulling a blink of lightning from the western clouds. The growl rolled across the sky and faded somewhere on the other side of the village. In the following stillness the steady plop of raindrops hit the lych gate's slate roof and the soaked earth. Copper downspouts gurgled as they discharged their channels of water. A tree bough thudded against something solid, the damp, baritone thuds underlining the sharp, soprano pings of water falling on stone. And something more…

A movement beyond the juniper.

Heavier, more carefully laid thumps than the drop of water onto wet ground resonated through the air. Like a heartbeat or a swinging pendulum, the dull clump measured the distance between the blackness behind the tree and the gate. I strained to identify it, tried to single it out from the other sounds of the storm.

The rain lessened for several seconds, perhaps gathering its strength for a new onslaught. In that transitory respite another sound floated over the precise thuds. A rasp, like an emphatic breath. Like something living that stalked in the dark and panted in its eagerness over sought-after prey.

My hand slid down the wet wood of the gatepost. In the sky-splitting flash of lightning the diamond of my engagement ring blinked at me. Was I so desperate to find Adam that I jumped and started at every sound? Was I going to pieces, losing my sanity?

I slowly got to my feet, alarmed at my reaction and at the unknown sound. My fingers wrapped around the post, pulling me up, keeping me from sinking back to the bench, for my knees threatened to buckle. I stared again into that shrouding blackness near the corner of the church, trying to discern a movement or an explanation for the deep breathing. All I could see was the jet-black bulk of the building, the sheet of rain and the faint impressions of gray tombstones.

Taking a deep breath, I relinquished my vise-like grip on the post and stepped onto the road. The coldness of the night air and my wet clothes made my movement sluggish. The road circled to the left and downhill to the southern end of the pond. I suppose I followed the route—I wasn't aware of much but the gust of wind through the trees and the vision of Adam speeding along the A625 to his home. Or to a pub.

I tried phoning him again, my fear growing to near panic. The ring went unanswered and I flipped my mobile closed, feeling—rather than seeing—my way along the road, for I was again sobbing.

It seemed safer in the middle of the road. I could see my

surroundings; there was space between them and anyone following me. I considered stopping at the Harper or Bowcock houses, but what would I tell them—that I was starting at shadows?

Another grumble of thunder rolled overhead. Above, the black bulk of treetops, like some angry thunderhead, bent in the storm. Mark's words about my possible stalker came back to me as a bough cracked from a tree and crashed to earth. Another noise, less sharp but closer, jolted me into running.

Trying to recall the sequence later, I'm still not certain where it happened. But it was somewhere between Perry Bowcock's place and the pond. That nearly deserted fragment of forest that surrounded the youth hostel and eased up to the homes of Kevin and Edmund. I could not have mistaken it, as I might have imagined the thumps and raspy breathing in the churchyard. I was on the road, in the open, running toward the pond and the village and people. But I know something was following me, and it ran at me with the long, undulating determination of a hound.

That I couldn't see it increased my terror. Mark's lecture about my hypothetical stalker paled as the legends of the shuck, the black dog forecasting dire events, burst from the recesses of my mind. Sobbing that something had happened to Adam, I ran down the hill. I slid on a patch of slick tarmac but immediately got to my feet, frantic that I would see the hound. That would bring on new terrors.

As I rounded the corner, coming into the row of shops, the grandfather yew emerged from the inky backdrop of night. A blink of lightning threw its shadow across the ground. The pond, its water ruffled and murky, lay dark at the tree's base. It was there that Mark found me sometime later.

Thirty-Six

Books from the Library: Derbyshire's Tales of Ghostly Goings-on and Haunted Homes

Few men in the land of the High Peak could match Innis Vance for strength. He had broken a man's nose, another man's wrist, two men's legs, and one man's neck. And those were during games. What he did to his enemies kept the gravediggers turning over sod.

His boast that he could lift a boulder, no matter its size, and heave it into the River Noe was challenged periodically, but the challenger never won. Consequently, Innis became head of a group of misfits and bullies who lived in caves and huts in the wild area around Kinder Scout.

The band lived rough and outside the law, laughing at any attempt by the residents of the scattered, small hamlets in the district to protect their property and bring Innis Vance to justice.

Efforts continued sporadically despite the difficulty in finding the outlaw group and in capturing Innis. The lawful citizens bent on apprehending Innis and ending his reign of terror had difficulty keeping him in custody, for shackles and chains seemed to break magically. If there was no Innis to try, there would be no peace in the region.

So vain and egotistical did Innis become that he soon believed he could take anything he wanted. After all, his strength was greater than anyone's—who would stop him?

One day, Innis saw Fiona, a lovely shepherdess who tended

her father's flock of sheep. Desire welled within Innis like a hawk shooting toward the heavens. That night, around the band's campfire, Innis told of his lust for the young girl. Though Innis was the undisputed leader of the ragtag band, several of the men spoke out, warning Innis that if he pursued the girl against her will, he would come to know the great shuck. For, as one of the group said, the black dog protected those whom it loved and hunted those it didn't—with disastrous results.

The man's warning had no effect. No one had been born who could successfully stand in Innis's way when he wanted something.

A week later, Innis lay in waiting at a small moorland pool where Fiona frequently came with her sheep. Dusk had fallen and the air held the scent of rain. As he waited, he failed to notice the sky growing dark or the drops of rain that began falling, so intent was he on watching Fiona walking toward him.

He also did not hear the baying of a large hound.

When she had stopped by the pool, Innis burst from his hiding place in the heather, grabbed her and forced her to the ground. As a roll of thunder covered her screams the howls of the dog grew louder.

Innis turned, his heart beating faster, knowing fear for the first time in years. The yapping grew louder, as though the dog were yards from Innis. He stood up, determined to chase off the animal, and grabbed a stone that lay beside the water's edge.

In one ear-deafening blast of rage, the hound rushed at Innis, visible at last. Innis screamed as he now saw the creature that before he had only heard. The dog leapt at the man, clamping its yellow fangs around Innis' throat and throwing him into the water of the deep pool. As the bodies thrashed, Fiona stood up, gathered her crook, and walked away. The hound vanished, leaving a boulder where Innis had fallen.

The pond dried up long ago, but the depression remains to this day. To this day, the giant black dog still warns villagers of certain peak villages of disasters and threats. To this day, too, you can see the petrified form of Innis Vance, known locally as part of the Wet Withens stone circle on Eyam Moor.

Thirty-Seven

I came to in Margo's lap. Mark was talking to someone, his mobile to his ear as he paced in front of us. As he closed his phone, I struggled to a sitting position, Margo's sharp commands for me to lie still ignored.

The rain had stopped, leaving a clean, fresh scent to the air. The sky over the western mountain rim was clearing, the clouds drifting off and revealing the crescent moon. A jacket or bathrobe had been draped over me and slipped from me when I sat up. Margo scooped it from the ground and hung it around my shoulders. Mark, I couldn't help but notice, stood sopping wet before me.

The cliché question slipped from my mouth before I was aware I had even spoken. "Where am I?" I shifted my gaze from Mark to Margo as she patted my shoulder.

"By the pond. Mark found you not ten minutes ago. He phoned me and I rushed down here." She pulled the jacket up higher on my shoulders. "We don't know, of course, but we think you've been here for several minutes. Mark's been out looking for you."

I stared at his tall form, trying to see his face, but the night obscured his expression.

"I don't know how I missed you," he said, his voice low but tinged with relief. "I guess I went the other way 'round the village."

"I went up the hill by Clayton's house," I said.

"Must've passed you in the dark."

"I zigged when you zagged, then." I tried to make light of the situation, feeling a total fool.

"Can you stand up?" Margo asked.

Nodding, I bent my knees, got my feet beneath me, and struggled to a standing position with Margo's and Mark's help.

"Anything hurt?"

"Besides my pride?"

"No headache, fractured wrist bone, bruised knee cap? Soreness from where you fell? Are you chilly?" She sounded like a nurse going down a checklist in an infirmary.

I shook off their hands and handed Margo's jacket back to her. "I'm fine. Honest."

"Yeah, you sound fine. Your teeth are chattering."

"I've been rained on, Margo. My clothes are wet."

"Back to my room, then. A hot shower, a cuppa, and a good night's sleep." She turned toward Mark. I could imagine her glaring at him, daring him to challenge her directive.

"Fine," I said, too exhausted to complain. "Wherever. Nothing much matters anymore." We walked to the pub, their hands still supporting me and guiding me around the puddles on the pavement. Mark picked leaves or twigs from my hair and Margo chattered like a cooperative witness, telling me that Graham had called for an early meeting tomorrow.

I nodded, not trusting my voice, not much caring about the case. Adam was my immediate priority, but I had no idea how I would ever heal the wound. I also had no idea if I had dreamt the black dog's pursuit or if it had been real. I would not ask Mark to search for paw prints in the muddy ground—he would certify me as mad and cart me off to the asylum.

It couldn't have been too dreadfully late, for the publican called for last drinks as we came into the pub. Happily, no one seemed to notice my unkempt state. I got to Margo's room and showered, sank into an upholstered chair and fortified myself with a hot cup of tea before Mark returned.

"Do you think that bloke hit you with something, Bren?" He had taken the other chair in the room. He balanced a cup of coffee on his thigh but seemed more focused on me at the moment.

"If so, we need to get you checked out at a hospital. You might have a concussion."

"Don't be absurd. I fainted. Nothing more. I didn't hear anyone or notice anyone. It's a combination of the weather and my, uh…"

"I still think we need to be certain you're fine."

"I am. I just need a little time to heal." I stared into my cup, feeling the tears building inside me. I mumbled, "Like another four decades."

"You need to sleep," Margo said, taking the cup from me. "If you give me your room key, I'll go get your night things." She held out her hand like a booking officer demanding a prisoner's personal items on entering jail.

"I guess the key's in Mark's room."

"Then I need *your* key, Mark, to get *Brenna's*."

"Really, Margo," I said. "This isn't necessary. I can sleep in your robe. Nothing's going to bother me."

"Mind if I don't believe you? You're about to cry. The key, Mark."

Mark took the key from his pocket and slapped it into Margo's open palm.

"I'll be right back." She was out of the room before I could squeak another protest.

"That's that," Mark said. "How are you feeling…really?"

"Physically?"

"No. Emotionally."

"Do you really have to be told? 'Hell' is too soft a word."

"It wasn't a nice scene in my room."

Tears collected in my eyes. They quivered, about to spill down my cheeks. "I love Adam, Mark. This is all so absurdly idiotic. He can't believe I—" I swallowed, unable to say the word. "—that I'd be untrue to him. It's this silly wedding. It's got his parents, him and me all in a tizzy. All our emotions are shot to hell."

"Can I do anything?"

I sniffed, blotting my nose on the back of my hand. "But I don't know what. It's something I've got to straighten out with Adam."

The room door creaked open. Mark said, "In that case, start straightening."

Adam walked into the room. He glanced at Mark, then at me, but his gaze this time spoke of concern and love. "Bren? Are you all right?"

Mark stood up as Margo entered with my overnight bag. He took the bag, set it on the floor, and steered Margo to the door. "Let's get a cuppa, if the publican will let us." Calling to me, Mark said, "Apologize quickly. We'll be back in fifteen minutes." I hardly heard the door close as Adam gathered me into his arms.

"Adam." I lowered my head on his shoulder. "I'm so sorry. But it really wasn't what you thought."

He kissed me before he replied. "He told me."

"Mark told—"

"Minutes ago. He rang me on my mobile. I wasn't going to answer it when I saw that he was calling, but thank God I did." He kissed me again and hugged me to his chest. "Everything's explained. Everything, Bren. The two burglaries, the theory that you are being watched and followed, the, uh...overnight situation in Margo's room."

"Adam."

"I'm so sorry, Bren. I can't tell you how sorry. It's just this... this damned notion my parents have about the ceremony."

"I've got a solution. Well, I hope it will be a solution. A resolution we all will find acceptable."

"Salt explained that, too. My ceremony, the compromise with the reception, your honeymoon." His lips were against my hair and he whispered, "But I'm going along on your honeymoon. If you still want me."

I pushed myself away from his chest, staring at him. Humor and excitement shone in his eyes. "Does the sun rise in the east?"

"Actually, the sun is stationary. The rotation of the earth—"

The rest was lost in a kiss and us parting hastily when Margo came back. "She may not have told you, Adam, but we've got an early beginning to the day tomorrow. We need our beauty rest."

"Sweet dreams, then," he said as Margo shooed him from the room. "Ready to go to bed?" she asked me. She stood by the window, looking into the night.

"What's it doing? Raining again?"

Leaning her head against the windowpane, she cupped her hands around her eyes. "No. It's stopped." She turned to me, crossing her arms over her chest. "Typical. You get wet through and the minute you're inside, it stops raining."

"Do something for me, Margo?"

I must have looked pathetic or else I caught her in an unguarded moment, for she said, "Sure. What? More tea?" She started toward the electric kettle.

"No. Go outside and look for something."

"What? Lose something? Your mobile? It's probably in the grass by the pond, where you fell." Grabbing her torch from her kit, she said, "I'll get it. Unless it's in the pond. Even I'm not going to fish around with my hand in that stuff. Yuck."

"Not my mobile." I felt extremely foolish asking her to do this, but I had to know or I'd never sleep.

"God, not your engagement ring!"

I turned my hand so she could see its back. Wriggling my fingers, I said, "No. Still wearing it, luckily."

"Then what?"

"Dog prints."

"What? You're joking."

I shook my head. "Big dog prints. Like, maybe, a boxer or lab or Alsatian. Something on that order. In the mud or the wet gravel. They'd be clear enough to see in this wet soil. You won't have to get down on your hands and knees and hunt. Do you mind?" I screwed up my mouth, hardly daring she would agree.

As I said, I must have looked pitiful, for she nodded. "If it helps you sleep, fine. Where do I look?"

She didn't ask why I wanted her to look. She probably put it down to delirium from my ordeal. "Between the youth hostel and the pond."

"The youth hostel...the old school?"

"Yeah. Just along the grassy verge. The inner side of the road. You don't need to go any farther inland than a yard or so. The grass is heavy there and won't hold any prints. I-I know it's probably an impossible task, but—"

"Stay here. I'll be back before you know it."

She was right. I'd fallen asleep before she returned.

~

"I should be miffed at you for falling asleep," Margo said as we talked over breakfast in the pub Tuesday morning. "But you needed your rest more than you needed to hear about the dog prints." She took an infuriatingly slow sip of coffee before she recounted her adventure.

"I scouted the inner edge of the road from the pond past the old school on my way up the hill. By the way, did you know it's got a cornerstone that has a carving of—"

"Margo! Please just tell me about the paw prints."

"Oh, right. Sorry. I played the torch beam all over the ground, Bren. Right by the tarmac and about a yard inland, just like you said. The ground was quite soft by the roadside—if not bare mud, then gravel and mud. But that would still retain an impression. I know 'cause I pressed my thumb into a gravely area to make sure. It held." She looked at me, probably wanting either a slap on the back or to get encouragement.

I nodded. "So? See anything?" I didn't know why I expected physical evidence of the black dog. Ghosts don't leave signs of their passage, do they?

"I'm getting to that, Bren. Don't rush me."

I exhaled. Was she so precise on writing out police reports, too?

"I couldn't see anything. I went downhill, just to make sure. Not a thing. Then I climbed the hill again, but this time on the outer edge."

"The side the school and those few houses sit on."

"Yes. I worked my way uphill very slowly because I didn't want to let you down. Plus, I'd feel a right Burton if I discovered it later and had overlooked it. Anyway, I found a few paw prints farther up the hill than you suggested."

My fingers nearly strangled my coffee mug. "Where? What size?"

"More or less on the north side of the school. Kind of facing the church."

"How big were they?"

"I'm not a dog expert."

"You surely know a Chihuahua from a St. Bernard, Margo."

"Don't be insulting. Do you want to hear this or not?"

I apologized and swallowed my agitation.

"Like I was saying…I saw some paw prints. They were very large. Maybe a few inches across. Fresh, too, or else the rain would have softened the edges or obliterated them. I would've taken a photo of them, but I left my camera at home."

"In which direction were they headed?" I said, ignoring the comment.

"Oh. Downhill, toward the pond. That what you wanted to hear?"

Not necessarily, I thought, but said, "Yes. Thanks." I picked up the coffee mug, uncertain if I felt better or worse knowing that I hadn't imagined the dog pursuit. But what had happened to the dog after I blacked out?

~

The creation of the well dressing panels appeared to be going smoothly Tuesday morning, despite yesterday's disturbance in the village hall. The heavy, water-soaked frames had been filled with clay and now rested horizontally on sturdy saw horses. Boxes, sacks and buckets of natural items cover every tabletop in the hall. The designs had been pricked onto the sheets of waxy paper and they, in turn, covered the smooth clay. Like yellow tablecloths on picnic tables, I thought, gazing at the activity from the hall's doorway. Buckets overflowing with cut flowers stood at the front of the room. Blues, reds, yellows, oranges, purples, whites. Hydrangea, cornflower and iris, rose and phlox, coneflower and peony, marigold and coreopsis, wisteria, lilac and buddleia, daisy and anemone. A prism of color, their petals waiting to be plucked and plastered like roof shingles on the moist clay. And, like roof shingles or tiles, the entire design would be created from the bottom of the frame to the top. Rain would run down the upright decorated panels, shed like shingles and thus increase the panels' longevity.

I walked up the hill, wondering what Graham had lined up for today, smiling because Adam and I had overcome our difficulties.

The booths for the various events were taking shape. A few were being erected on the green near the pond and some were going up on the grass near the church. I could hear the men assembling the stage for the main entertainment, the sounds of hammering and sawing echoing up the hill. Camera in hand, Perry Bowcock followed an apron-clad worker as she walked around to the far side of the church to dispose of a wheelbarrow full of dead leaves and spent flowers. Three people were pulling weeds from around the metal lid covering the well opening near the south side of the church. I wondered where the other village wells were; since I'd been busy with the cases I hadn't had time to look. But from past experience, I assumed one would be at the old school and perhaps one by the market cross on the village green. Common enough places for village water supply four or five centuries ago. A panel would adorn each well, decorated in the flower petals, lambs wool, broken eggshells and other natural objects to depict the tableau that was part of the year's theme. It was a beautiful way to give thanks for the water supply, jerking us out of our complacency so we never took fresh water for granted.

I left the sounds of carpentry behind and walked into the incident room, but after pausing long enough to praise the gardeners on their cleanup effort.

Mark looked up from the book of news articles and called me over to the table. After asking if I still felt all right—and being assured that I did—he pulled out a chair for me. I sat and read the caption beneath a photo he pointed to.

"Miss Christine Stevenson, Queen of Cauldham's 2008 Well Dressing Fete, draws a winning name from the cake booth. Assisted by Fete director Reed Harper, Stevenson will carry out the duties of Festival Queen until next year's event. Stevenson said she is looking forward to judging the Harvest Home displays in September."

I looked at Mark. "What's this about?"

"You *must* have been conked on the head last night. You don't remember about Chris Stevenson?"

I nodded, a phrase coming back to me. "The teenager who left the village four months ago. She was pregnant."

"Right. She went to a bed-and-breakfast in Inverness. Her uncle, Perry Bowcock, told us about it."

"She had an affair with ladies' man Reed Harper."

"But she got pregnant just this past year."

"Oh, well, that certainly makes it all right," I said, my voice hardening.

"No, it doesn't. I mentioned that because the affair had started when she was sixteen—when she became the village's well dressing queen."

"Probably how they met, then." I pulled the book closer and read the other captions on the page. The photographs chronicled Chris' year as queen. They showed her presiding over the Harvest Home vegetable judging, the lighting of the Guy Fawkes Night bonfire, the ribbon cutting of a plaque dedication. I angled the book back toward Mark. "Nothing remarkable."

"No. But we know how Chris came to Reed's attention."

"Who's this in this other photo?" I asked, looking over Mark's shoulder at the book.

"Kevin Harper."

"I thought he looked familiar but I couldn't place him. What's he doing?"

"Handing Chris a bouquet. Her reign has ended, evidently. Some other girl's being crowned fete queen. In fact, it's a picture of the entire court."

I read the names aloud. "Clarise Millington, Queen; Ilsa Harper, Princess; Angela Lyth, Princess; Suzanne Hampton, Rose Bud." I stared at Mark. "This is 2009."

"So?"

"Three years ago Clarise Millington was nineteen. A bit old to be Queen."

"Ilsa wouldn't have been old enough. She'd be fourteen. Don't you have to be sixteen?"

I shrugged. "Maybe villages relax the age rule when there's no one running for the queen position."

Mark turned the page. "Why all the interest?"

"Just thinking about rivalries."

"No one from that happy group has turned up dead, Brenna."

"Guess you're right." We drifted over to the group of chairs and sat down.

Graham, I noted ecstatically, didn't ask about my misadventure of last night. Perhaps no one had told him, which made my day. I didn't want him chastising me again.

After wishing us all good morning, Graham began our discussion of Reed's murder by mentioning Marian's parting remark. "I mulled that over last night as I strolled through the village in the rain." He glanced at me, then returned to his topic. "I lost some sleep wondering if the cheating spouses comment could apply to cheating parents. After all, we have Harper Lyth fathering Vera out of wedlock. Could Harper's daughter Angela have found out about her half sister? Did she think Reed, being quite accomplished in the affair department, helped *her* dad dispose of Vera? Reed and Harper met frequently, talked privately. Did Angela think they were plotting Vera's demise? I considered it for half a second before throwing it out. It made no sense. Then I considered who else might have had reason to kill Reed.

"Maybe Jenny Millington, since she had attempted suicide over her love for him. But that didn't feel right either. The emotions are opposite, in my opinion. You either have remorse over the love that never blossomed, so you attempt suicide, or you're so bitter and filled with hate that you kill that person. You don't waffle back and forth between the two emotions. So I wondered about motive from another angle—not kill Reed over revenge for a lost love or anger over the village fete, but a personal revenge for a *victim*." He leaned against the edge of the table, letting the silence build and giving us time to think through all the players. "Clayton was involved with Vera, but there is no link between Vera and Reed, so who else might have had a desire to avenge a victim?"

The photograph flared up in my mind. A smiling, friendly teenager, so eager to make her way in the world, so desperate to achieve her goal. I said, "Chris Stevenson."

Graham nodded, his eyes on mine. "Why?"

"Chris knew Reed through her volunteer work with the well dressing event. She was queen several years ago. She probably spent a good deal of her reigning year doing things with Reed, since he was the director of the fete. Newspaper interviews, together at village events like Shrove Tuesday pancake races and mummers plays, and candle auctions. Whatever the village specifically has. I'm not blaming her. Reed Harper seems to have been a charming man. It would be hard for a young girl to withstand such charm and attention…and the promise of career help."

Mark snorted, recrossing his legs. "We've got the well dressing association, then, with Reed's burial."

Graham nodded slowly. "The clay and daisy petals plastered on his arm." He stood up abruptly and walked around the table. "That's a tempting sign post to Chris as the victim, but are there any others who might be associated with that? Either the flower specifically or well dressing?"

We considered the Harpers—Marian, Kevin, Ilsa and Edmund—but none of them had the link to the well dressing. And that appeared to be the link, for why else would the murderer take precious seconds to adorn Reed's body with that mute hint?

Ilsa had a bit stronger candidacy as Reed's killer, but she had been helping Uncle Kevin with the shop inventory that night.

Angela had no motive—she already had the coveted job as master of ceremonies. Neither did any of the others we considered. Lynn Warson seemed better to fit the role of Vera's murderer if we thought Lynn could be angry with Vera. But Clayton had married Lynn, hadn't even betrayed her with Vera, so where was the motive? If Lynn murdered anyone, it would be Clayton for keeping Vera's lock of hair all these years.

Seating himself on the table, Graham again asked us to consider the motive angle. I couldn't get past the daisy petals and clay on Reed's skin. I said so, and Graham asked whom I associated with those items. "You may also consider the body recovery site," he reminded me. "A site just doesn't occur. It has to mean something to the killer."

"Well, we know it's all tied together with the well dressing," I said. "Not the recovery site…the flower and clay. It means something to the killer."

"But that's at least half of the village," Mark said.

"Not when you take into account the victim—Reed—and the victims of *his* transgressions."

"Why link Reed with his own victims?"

"Because that's what the daisy and clay tell us, Mark. Reed was killed due to someone *he* victimized. Reed's killer wanted revenge for *Reed's* abuse of a woman."

"When you take all that into account," Graham said, "there really aren't that many." He listed the known victims on the board. "Also, when you link these names with a person who feels strongly enough to avenge a woman who Reed's tossed aside, you get…" He stood there, his gaze traveling across the group.

"Perry Bowcock," I said, the image of Reed's body and the words of Perry swirling in my mind. "Uncle Perry."

"Why?"

"Well, sir, for one thing—and it just now occurred to me because I saw him only minutes ago—he's the village photographer."

Graham looked amused and asked me to explain.

"The woman in the village hall spoke of Perry's photographs, he himself told us he was official photographer and, as such, went about the village. He could have come upon his niece and Reed, not necessarily doing anything physical, but maybe he overhead them talking."

"Reed smooth talking Christine, you mean."

"Yes, sir. And if Perry overheard this and knew Reed's history of telling a woman anything to get her in bed with him…" I looked at Graham, wondering if I were completely round the twist with this idea.

"If Perry did hear Reed promising the moon, Perry might certainly have become angry. He'd want to put an end to such piffle and rescue his niece from Reed's empty promises."

"Mark and I talked to Perry Saturday night. He didn't seem at all vindictive about his niece's death. Just a sad man calmly relating what had happened. His demeanor threw me, yes, but more than that I was misled by his words. Remember, Mark?"

"Yeah," Mark murmured. "He said he *would have taken* a great amount of pleasure in strangling Reed."

"Yes. That's what fooled me. I took it for a regret and nothing more. Like we all say 'I wish I would have known that before I accepted that lunch date,' or something like that. We all say things like that. So I just shoved it to the back of my mind. Until I remembered that Reed was knifed."

I hadn't time to consider Perry's verbal game, if it had been deliberate to throw Mark and me off the track. Setting us up to believe in his innocence and the pain of a still-grieving man. Maybe it was as I had stated: a way we all talked, nothing more than a fanciful wish. 'I would have.' So many things in my life were 'would have,' I thought, then I got up and went with Graham, Margo and Mark to arrest Perry.

We didn't surprise him this time. He appeared to be ready to talk, to accept that he had been found out. Mark and I sat again in his front room, but Graham led the questioning. He was all business, his voice unemotional and hard sounding as the pounding of a judge's gavel. Perry tried his verbal dance at the offset, but one look at Graham's stony expression convinced him to change tactics, and he confessed quickly.

"Ordinarily I harm no one or nothing," Perry said, clasping and reclasping his fingers. He sat in a low, upholstered chair, facing Graham. Mark, Margo and I bracketed Perry, alert and ready should he try to bolt. He spoke slowly, emotionally, a crack or threat of tears underlying his words. I would not be tricked this time, I told myself. I would listen to each word, consider the meaning and not let myself be fooled. I found myself sitting straighter, my back ramrod stiff, my jaw clenched. Perry would not assail me with pity.

"I live quietly and leave people to their own lives. But Reed Harper was a cancer in this village. Whatever he touched he contaminated and emotionally, if not physically, killed. He was a disease in my niece's life. He destroyed her happiness and spirit, sucked the joy from her life. He killed her as surely as if he had actually done it himself."

Perry sat back, the emotion of talking about Chris threatening to consume him. He took a drink of water before continuing. "You want to know why I killed Reed Harper."

Graham nodded, his eyes bright in the morning sunlight.

"Because he seduced her," Perry replied simply. "Because he didn't do a thing about it afterward, didn't even offer to support the child. And Chris was pregnant—there was no mistaking that. She'd gone to a clinic where they did a pregnancy test on her. She had the written report and showed it to him. He laughed." Perry pressed his lips together and stared out of the window, toward the Harpers' house. "Can you believe what kind of scum would do that? He laughed. Laughed to her face. Chris ran to me, crying, scared. She didn't know what to do." He turned slightly, looking at me. "I'd heard snatches of what he used to tell the others. Walking around the village, taking photos…well, you do see and overhear things. Not that I did it on purpose. But I knew what Reed would promise a woman in order to get what he wanted. I'd been around enough that I knew Reed would say the same sort of thing to Christine. I told you about that Saturday night, miss, when you asked about it."

"Yes," I said. It was all I could think of to say.

"I chose the wood to dump the body in," Perry said, looking back at Graham. Maybe it was easier to talk to Graham—another man, someone who might understand the male viewpoint. I might bring Chris too close to his mind. "I chose the wood," Perry explained, "that section of the wood 'cause Marian and I used to walk there as children. We played there. It had been a part of our family estate, you know, stretching back to the Plantagenets."

"You and Marian are cousins," I said, amazed that I had forgot.

"Yeah. That tract of land had been sold in the 1970s, but we still felt it was ours. We'd still take nature walks through it. We felt a special tie to the place not just because it used to be in the Good family but also because it housed the caretaker cottage—the one that Vera lived in. Anyway, I got Reed into my car on the pretext of talking about an idea I had for the fete. It was so easy—he was such a megalomaniac. I could tell he was already thinking of how he could turn it around to look like he'd thought of it…and he hadn't even heard my idea yet. Anyway, I drove him to the wood, got him out of the car on pretext of showing him my idea for a land development. He thought he knew the area, so he walked ahead of me, as though he were in charge. When we got to the spot, I stabbed him. Stabbed him in the back so he wouldn't see it coming, so he'd suffer like all the other women he's cheated on and lied to and tossed aside. I hid the weapon—it was a long-bladed letter opener. I drove up to the Howden Reservoir the next day and buried it in the forest. I-I could take you there, if you need me to. I'll never forget where it is. It's haunted me ever since." He took a breath, as though remembering his hike through the hilly wood. "Right before I buried him I smeared some of the well dressing clay on him and I pressed daisy petals into the clay. It was for Chris, you see," he said, standing up as Graham moved toward him. "'cause it's Chris' birth month flower. April…" He took a breath as he fought back a sob. "Ironic, that, the daisy. But it symbolized Chris—Innocence, Youth, Purity. And there's the other meaning for the daisy—goodbye." He looked at me, his eyes brilliant with unshed tears. "I crammed one into his mouth because…well, because daisies also don't tell."

Graham arrested Perry while Margo handcuffed him. They led Perry from the house, Mark and I following after. Mark ran ahead and opened the door of the police car and I locked up his house.

Edmund Worrall, Reed's half brother, was out walking Poe, his black lab. A lab…a large dog. A black dog. Edmund nodded at me, said something about hoping no one had complained last night about Poe getting loose and running about the village, and walked toward Cauldham Hall and the wood. I nearly ran after them, wanting to hug Poe in my great relief, but couldn't seem to budge. I leaned against the front door, watching until the man and dog had disappeared around the bend in the road, wondering if that was anything akin to how legends began.

But I'd keep that contemplation for my next day off. I wasn't able to think that hard. I pocketed the house key and walked to the edge of the porch, staring at nothing, yet seeing flashes of scenes from the past days.

Excited chatter drifted down the road to us. At the church, villagers were already assembling to work on the stage. One man squatted, fished about in the grass for a few seconds, and then removed the round, iron lid from the well opening. He leaned forward, his hands keeping him balanced, seeming to peer into the dark water below. In two or three days one of the well dressing panels would stand there, its two-by-four foot trestle keeping the huge picture postcard-vivid mosaic upright. A wooden box, probably painted green or blue, would rest on the ground in front of the panel. This box accepted monetary donations to offset supply costs. A small sign or plastic-encased sheet of paper would sit next to or be attached to the moneybox, explaining that panel in particular and the well theme in general. These items would remain on display for a week while the carnival rides, booths, tea tent and talent show went on. Not what the original pagan worshippers would have ever foreseen, true, but we still were grateful for water in our own way.

And all this activity would need a new photographer to chronicle it.

A loud glissando shook me awake and I blinked at the sudden blast of music. Two villagers, one carrying a clarinet and one practicing warm-up trills on his trombone, strolled through the church's lych gate. Hymn practice time for the parade, I thought. Friday evening the road beside the gate would be packed: robe-resplendent church choir, town band, clergy, retiring and current 'royal' retinue, visitors and villagers would follow the police car escort from well to well. The churchwarden would hold up the brass processional cross, the choir members would position their hymn sheets, and the brass band's first notes would soar into the twilight air. People would find their voices and forge another link with the generations who previously had given thanks for water. As another band member walked around the corner of the church, his tuba booming into the air, the image of the well dressing parade disintegrated before my eyes. I felt oddly alone and disappointed.

As Graham and Margo drove off with Perry, I fell apart. The work on the two cases, the fight with Adam, the emotional connection with a woman who died when I was just twelve years old, who had been about to marry her love and start a new life with him... Everything hit me at once and I leaned against a tree and cried. Mark came over, asking in his usual thoughtful way what was wrong. Again I accepted his handkerchief as I choked back the tears. I thought of Adam, of what we had come close to losing. I thought of Marian and the husband who had not taken his wedding vows as a sacred trust. I thought of Margo and Mark, of their concern and friendship. If it hadn't been for Mark's help, Adam and I might still be apart, might never resolve our differences. I glanced at Mark, at his calm face, and saw the strong resolve that lay within him. If Adam didn't ask Mark to be best man, I would ask him to stand up with me.

Thirty-Eight

Diary Entry, 11 February 1989

Little more than two months until I'll be eighteen. Doesn't seem so very old, but I feel old. No, that's a lie. I feel young and pretty and desirable. Clayton asked me to marry him today. Formally asked me, I mean. Before, we'd just been talking about 'what if' and 'when' and what it would be like years from now if we *would have taken* this huge step. His proposal has a vague sense of 'somewhere in the future.' Like something I've dreamt about even before I was born, floating about somewhere in the universe and waiting to come to earth. A dream that is so very precious that I can't say it out loud, not even to Gran or my best friend for fear it will shatter like frost in January and blow down wind to mix with the dirt and cobwebs of ordinary life. It's not like that, though, not for all my fears of losing his love and living the ensuing years by myself. He loves me, loves me deeply. I am astounded by the degree of my love for him, too. It's no fairy tale any more. He's formally asked me, given me a silver locket and a curl of his hair... Gol, it's *really going to actually happen*, isn't it? We're going to be married.

COMING NEXT!

FALSE STEP

by Jo A. Hiestand

Ninth in the Taylor & Graham Mystery Series

Each year the residents of Burton Abbey celebrate the village's founding in the time-honored way—with games, music, and performances by their sword dancers. But something new is added to the fancy footwork this year: in the middle of the dance a team member dies…murdered.

The CID Team from the Derbyshire Constabulary thinks they've caught a break in the investigation, for Detective-Sergeant Brenna Taylor was in the crowd, watching the dance. Surely she saw what happened.

The inquiry soon becomes as tightly interlocked as the five swords, or rappers, used in the dance, a series of complicated turns, jumps and clogging steps as intricate as Celtic knots. Group anger and jealousies explode during the investigation. Physical threats and implied extortion threaten to destroy the group and the dancers' lives. But this quickly takes a back seat for the CID Team when Brenna is attacked during a late night walk. Had she seen the murder during the dance but failed to realize it?

While recuperating from her near-fatal fall, Brenna has time to consider her future and makes a life-altering decision. But it is later, in the midnight-wrapped, rain-cloaked abbey, that a terrifying event changes her plan, and she is thrown together with the one person who's silently loved her all along.

Author Jo A. Hiestand

A true Anglophile, Jo wanted to create a mystery series that featured British customs as the backbone of each book's plot, while combining the information of an English police procedural and the intimacy of a cozy. The result is the Taylor & Graham mysteries, featuring a CID team of the Derbyshire Constabulary.

Jo's insistence for accuracy—from police methods and location layout to the general 'feel' of the area—has driven her innumerable times to Derbyshire, England. These explorations and conferences with police friends provide the detail used for the series.

In 1999 Jo returned to Webster University to major in English with an Emphasis in Writing as a Profession. She graduated in 2001 with a BA degree and departmental honors.

She has combined her love of writing, board games and music by co-inventing P.I.R.A.T.E.S., the mystery-solving game that uses maps, graphics, song lyrics, and other clues to lead the players to the lost treasure.

Jo founded the Greater St. Louis Chapter of Sisters in Crime, serving as its first president. She is also a member of Mystery Writers of America. When not writing, she likes to listen to early and bluegrass music, play guitar, take nature photographs, read, change ring and watch her backyard wildlife.

Her three cats—Chaucer, Dickens and Tennyson—share her St. Louis home.

For more information about Jo, please visit her on the web at www.johiestand.com

REVIEWS FOR JO'S OTHER BOOKS

Siren Song
"Siren Song is a mystery to sink your teeth into. Not only was the murder investigation top notch but also the peek into the life of the investigator added another layer to the mystery. This is my first Jo A. Hiestand book but it will not be my last."
—*Delane, Coffee Time Romance & More 4-Cups Review*

A Terrible Enemy
"Hiestand raises awareness of global issues, layered in the unfolding of this grisly whodunit. And the mystery continues, for once we know whodunit, we must follow through to the capture. This intriguing mystery is well worth the reader's time."
—*Mystery Lovers Corner Review*

Horns of a Dilemma
"Immaculate research, attention to detail and an elegant style are the hallmarks of Jo Hiestand's writing. An atmospheric novel."
—*Peter Lovesey, author of the Sergeant Cribb and Peter Diamond series*

"*Horns [of a Dilemma]* is a realistic look into the emotions and personal lives of officers. Instead of looking at police as superheroes, it looks at them as they are: real people with feelings and emotions who struggle with their own demons and lives while daily working cases."
—*Jon McIntosh, St. Louis-area police officer*

CPSIA information can be obtained at www.ICGtesting.com
Printed in the USA
BVOW012238181212

308622BV00009B/243/P